More Critical Praise for A Tall History of Sugar

- Winner of the Hurston/Wright Legacy Award for Fiction!

"*A Tall History of Sugar* is a gift for grown-up fans of fairy tales and for those who love fiction that metes out hard and surprising truths. Forbes's writing combines the gale-force imagination of Margaret Atwood with the lyrical pointillism of Toni Morrison."

—*New York Times Book Review,* Editors' Choice

"*A Tall History of Sugar* is captivating from the very first page. Mythic in dimension yet movingly human in its details, alive with atmospheric richness, it heralds a fascinating new voice in English-language fiction."

—Jennifer Egan, Pulitzer Prize–winning author of *Manhattan Beach*

"Forbes's ambitious, fantastic tale will appeal to fans of multigenerational sagas."   —*Publishers Weekly,* starred review

"A fascinating post-colonial blend of romance, social history, and myth."   —*Booklist,* starred review

"Haunting, intriguing, and absorbing . . . A memorable read."

—*New West Indian Guide*

"A powerful journey into the souls of two lovers, two countries, and people caught in the wakes of empires."

—*Kirkus Reviews,* starred review

"Forbes's skillful and instinctual use of local languages and dialects further taps into a rich Jamaican oral culture, in a story that dreams of being read aloud."   —*Irish Times*

"One of the season's most talked-about new releases . . . For readers interested in the history of Jamaica, the impact of colonialism, and the enduring power of relationships, this is a perfect book to pick up this fall."   —*Bookish,* one of Fall 2019's Must-Read Novels

"A Jamaican fairy tale set in 1958, *A Tall History of Sugar* is a love story between an odd, intriguing child, Moshe, and his soul mate Arrienne, whom he meets on the first day of school. Where Moshe is laconic and excels in the realm of the visual, Arrienne acts as both narrator and translator in a story that spans slavery, colonialism, and the aftermath of both." —*The Undefeated,* one of the Can't Miss Books of 2019

"[A]n epic tale of two soul mates: Moshe Fisher, born with mismatched eyes and pale skin that bruises easily, and Arrienne Christie, 'her skin even at birth the color of the wettest molasses, with a purple tinge under the surface.' Arrienne is his protector at school—and later his lover—but how they eventually wind up together is part of this unconventionally crafted story that spans decades, from the years before Jamaica's independence to the 2010s. Forbes's sentences are the stars here; it's a book that rewards slow, careful reading." —*BuzzFeed*

"Unbelievably unique and also crushing . . . It's a hard-hitting [book], but it's so incredible."

—*All The Books,* recommended by Liberty Hardy

"Curdella Forbes seamlessly weaves Jamaican English and the Queen's English in this captivating novel . . . Part love story and part historical fiction, *A Tall History of Sugar* is a refreshing take on race and colonialism that moves between Jamaica and England." —*Electric Literature*

Curdella Forbes was born in Jamaica and now lives in Takoma Park, Maryland. She teaches at Howard University.

A TALL HISTORY OF SUGAR

A TALL HISTORY OF SUGAR

BY

CURDELLA FORBES

BROOKLYN, NEW YORK

Published by Akashic Books
©2019, 2022 Curdella Forbes

Paperback ISBN: 978-1-61775-977-2
Library of Congress Control Number: 2019935261

Akashic Books
Brooklyn, New York
Instagram: @AkashicBooks
Twitter: @AkashicBooks
Facebook: AkashicBooks
E-mail: info@akashicbooks.com
Website: www.akashicbooks.com

In memory of my beloved niece Kettie (April 9, 1988–April 5, 2018)

and for my youngest, Kash and Koyo

PART I

before: the found child

CHAPTER I

i

Long ago, when teachers were sent from Britain to teach in the grammar schools of the West Indian colonies (it was Great Britain then, not Little England, as it is now, after Brexit and the fall of empire), there lived in Jamaica, near a town called Oracabessa-on-Sea, a poor fisherman and his wife, who was a farmer and a seamstress, and one morning they found a pale child in bushes in a basket made of reeds. The man's name was Noah Fisher, and his wife's name was Rachel.

They adopted the child and named him Moshe, which is to say, Moses, which in translation means "drawn out," and they named him in this way because Rachel was a Yahwehist, and because the bushes in which they found him were a tangle of sea grapes running low as a reed bed along the ground on cliffs above the sea, and when she found him (for it was she who first saw the child) the spray from below had made a pool around the basket so that in another few moments it would have sailed. Which is to say that in a manner of speaking, the little boy was indeed drawn out of water.

The grandmother, a longheaded woman of the countryside, tells me, "Yu nuh need fi go deh so," you do not need this long explanation of watery origins, since the ancestors of every Jamaican came over the sea, most of them in the ship's cakka, and moreover are we not an island, surrounded by water? So anyone born and found here is a child of water, and no more to be said.

But this child that was found did not look like anyone who came over in the holds of ships three hundred years ago, so it is important to give all the details of his name and how he was found.

The morning on which this happened was not unusual in the pattern of Noah's and Rachel's lives. It was a Friday, the day when they joined the long lines of sick and ailing from the town and its surrounding districts, who traveled to the parish's one hospital, mostly on foot, to get treatment for their ailments and wounds. The lines included women pregnant with their first, second, third, sometimes tenth, eleventh, or even twelfth child. It included men with machete chops all over their bodies from plantation disputes, children bent in the shape of safety pins from hookworm, young ones with yaws, whooping cough, measles, or mumps—the usual maladies of childhood in those times and in that place—and many young and old suffering from heart failure, blocked tube, hernia, unresponsive male organ, underresponsive female organ, testicular edema, old fresh cold, virulent fresh cold, consumption, out-of-control blood pressure, and various disorders from the surfeit or indigestion of sugar.

The extent and variety of ailments from saccharine indigestion on the island were both miraculous and unsurprising. In case this is unknown to you, Jamaica from its infancy had been a sugarcane plantation, where people perforce ate a lot of sugar or its byproducts and leftovers. Sugar in the boiling houses made the slaves drunk, the great vats of it with its liquorish smell when it was in the making, and when it was made, the shining crystals scooped into vast kegs for shipping to England, the mother country. The grains clung to their skins and got into their eyes and ears and even their secret parts— their vulvae and their scrotums—and that was the reason some could not have children, the grandmother said.

After the long cruel hours in the canepiece, being bitten by cane rat, sugar snake, overseer whip, hot sun, and cane leaf, when they went back to their slave cabins at night there was sometimes nothing to eat but sugar, but they could not eat it without becoming sick, or rather, more sick, since they were already sick in the beginning from too much consanguinity with its sweet stickiness. This is why it became a saying in Jamaica, *Is one of two tings going tek yu—if is not sugar, is heart failure.* (Which might boil down to the same thing, for heart failure comes from eating too much salt—salt for healing, for taste, even in your tea, salt for feeling balanced, salt for good luck, throw it behind you, salt for counteracting obeah and the ill effects of sugar. In Jamaica once upon a time and maybe still now, we ate salt like sugar. Against sugar. So it still goes back to King Sugar.)

Noah Fisher, a quiet man except when he was aggrieved, had his own views as to how this alchemy of sickness took root. "Foolish Galatians. Oonu don't know seh sugar be di one ting black people cyaan eat wid hinpunity," sugar is the one thing that black people cannot eat without a confrontation with destiny.

He would say this rudely in the clinic, from anger that he could not (it seemed) be rid of this history that was lodged in his flesh, and because he wanted to infuriate the nurses. These women, whom he hated for their demeanor of superiority, were among the few humans who could make Noah wax almost loquacious. In the clinic he cursed like a warner, telling strings of proverbs, but profanely—not in the holy-holy language that warners used. "Ole idiot tink dem better than people, just because dem carry out shitpan fi pay while poor people carry it out fi free. Monkey rise high, expose him raw backside. Ole ooman swear fi nyam callaloo, callaloo swear fi wuk him effing gut." A climbing monkey exposes the secrets of his behind. You have ingested your own destruction and thought it a gift. And how could it be otherwise? Can a person eat his own flesh? Not with impunity, not scots-free. You will see this in the annals of the sugar plantations, how it was that the bright brown crystals came about, how bone and blood got mixed in the métissage, tips of fingers, sometimes knuckles, and even whole arms bitten off by the great machines. The crystals at first wine-dark in blood, then soakaway to brown when the crushers smoothed them out.

This was not a history that Noah knew in its fine details, but his spirit apprehended it, and so his signature phrase of contempt, "Foolish Galatians, fool nuh jackass arse," was loaded with salient meaning. Their imaginations steeped in the hattaclaptic language of the King James version, even the illiterate people of those days understood that to be a Galatian was to suffer a lack of historical memory.

Noah was among the patients sick by sugar. He had on the inside of his right thigh a long-running diabetic sore that had to be hospital-dressed every Friday morning, though after many years of dressing it still had not healed. Rachel accompanied him on these trips to the hospital because he could not read or write, but she could, and sometimes there were papers that he was required to read and sign.

Some people depended on the hospital clerk to write on their behalf, *Donovan Bright, his mark,* or, *Mattie Longbridge, her mark,* or whatever their names were, their mark, and the hospital clerk would show them where to make an X on the line above this declaration. But some felt ashamed, even though many of them were in this category, illiterates who depended on others to write for them, and so, when they could, they brought their reading and writing relatives along, so that they would not have to depend on strangers to sign their names in good cursive on the correct line.

When the waiting lines were long and Rachel knew it would take some time for Noah to be attended to, or when he was misbehaving in the clinic, she went outside, around to the back of the building, to catch a breath of air. This particular morning she needed air more than ever, because she and Noah had quarreled, which meant it was one of those mornings when she hated him with a hatred that made her feel she was suffocating. Their quarrels were frequent, and grew more and more bitter as they discovered they could not have children, and Rachel felt in her heart that Noah did not renounce or protect her from the district's belief that if there was no child, it was the wife who was barren. Noah's rage, meeting her accusation, was simple: "Woman, yu tink me is God? If yu womb shet up, I can mek pickney out of the dust of the ground? Awright, mek one an call him Adam!"

She swear to God she going lef him this morning.

The hospital was perched above rocks rising three hundred feet above the sea. Boisterous waves leaped against the cliff face, scattering seaweed and stray fish. The fountains made a barking sound, like the cry of lost dogs, all along the coastline.

Rachel stood in the line of the spray and let it drench her from head to toe in a coldness that was a balm to her senses. She lifted her face and drew the raw air deep into her lungs. The taste on her tongue was the taste of the sea's travels in places she had discovered in her imagination, places as real as if she had landed on their beaches unhindered and planted a flag.

She unwrapped her tie-head, a striped cotton cloth, and casting it on the ground shook her plaits free, letting the wind and spray wash through them. Her dress was a thin, cheap chiffon; the spray wet it through quickly and exposed all her curves: her high thick breasts that were full from never having suckled a child; her rounded buttocks, the buttocks of an African woman though Rachel was part Indian; her belly which had the slight protrusion seen in women who had given birth or women who did a lot of manual labor on a diet of heavy starches, yam, breadfruit, and cassava. She was tall and beautiful, with muscled thighs and legs. She carried water in tin buckets on her head, long distances along shale hills to water her one-acre farm after the first plantings when there was no rain, and so her neck was long and always upraised and her back straight, like royalty.

From where she stood on the cliff she could see a straight line to the high school. The main building, flanked by several smaller ones, was a pile of sepia-toned brick, two-storied, raggedly torn between Georgian and neo-Gothic styles. To a fanciful viewer who knew the island's history, it would seem the architect had wavered between the construction plans given to him by the British colonial government and the desires of the French refugee who in 1776 had bequeathed his money to establish the school; a free school, he said, for the children of plantation owners in the colony that had shown him kindness so far away from home.

No such architectural struggle had taken place in actuality. The original building, housing the main classrooms, had been a barracks that served England during the colonial wars with Spain; the adjoining mess hall and armory had been converted into the school refectory and library. But the impression of architectural clash and uneasy cohabitation of styles was symbolic, in the way all colonial promiscuity is symbolic.

In the year 1958, when Rachel Fisher stood on the bluff, the school was 182 years old. Many things had changed, though more had remained the same. The population of backra children had given way to brown; increasingly, brown had become variegated with black, so that the majority of the students now were the children of the aspiring poor, the posterity of slaves. The old buildings were circled by a sprawl of new ones. The tallest was the science building, its concrete and steel a sharp contrast to the anomalous brick of the older structures. Its presence marked the turn of a different age and the oddity of the school, which was coeducational, unusual for high schools in those days, and liberal, with girls permitted to study the sciences and less academic boys sent to do typing. This was because no church was attached; the school had been a secular endowment, outside the control of missionaries.

Behind the school was the eighteenth-century fort named for the consort of a mad king, Fort Charlotte, its walls pitted with portholes and crenellations from which black-mouthed cannon gaped seaward, relics of wars fought over the island by people who were not the people who lived there now, over interests that had nothing to do with the interest of the people whose country it would officially become in another four years.

The fort was joined to the school by the undersea caves above which Rachel now stood. It was these caverns that gave the waves their barking sound as they beat up against the cliff. Adventurous children exploring the coastline had found ancient skeletons in some of them, and Rachel had heard rumors of wicked acts that still took place inside their entrances, where the water was only ankle deep at certain times of day and anyone, child, man, or ghost, could go a short way inside without having to swim, levitate, or drown. Because of the terrible things that were said to happen to girl schoolchildren there, Rachel's father had refused to send her to that school, though she was bright and the head teacher beseeched him not to abandon her schooling after she finished elementary.

Her father's adamant refusal broke her spirit. All her life she had wanted to go to high school and later become a nurse or teacher or civil servant. It was what you did if you were bright and black and poor and managed against all odds to get a postelementary education. In the end she apprenticed as a seamstress and married Noah, thinking that her children might go to this school in her stead. But that hope died too. Now, looking out toward the huddle of old and new buildings against the seascape, she remembered the stories she had heard.

A some terrible tings happen to people galpickni in dere. Dreadful tings di white man-dem do to people young girlchilds.

The echoes of such stories merged with her own bitterness.

"Sometime Ah wish di earth cooda open up an tek mi in," Rachel found herself murmuring, her voice low yet intense against the wind. "Sometime Ah feel Ah cooda lef dis man, lef dis dutty stinkin place, jus walk out inna di sea an never come back. If di wave tek mi, it tek mi. Woulda mercy. I dwell in di midst of a dogheart dutty set, jus a-wear mi down, wear mi down. Yahweh is my shepherd, I shall not want, yea though I walk through the valley of the shadow of death I shall not fear no evil. Only Yahweh keepeth me. But Ah nah lie yu, sometime Ah feel fi cuss a whole set a . . ." (An you know, she really cuss the badword, but she is the same one who wash out my mouth years later with soap and water for cussing blue, so even now I find it hard to put down on paper the words that come out of Rachel Fisher's mouth that day.)

Lost inside her quiet scream, it was a while before Rachel was able to discern the sound of the child's crying above the tumult. A high wail, and then an insistent shrieking in short sharp bursts, it broke through the surface of her mind and pushed her toward the clump of sea grape trees that lay tangled among the macca. Strange-looking trees. Instead of standing tall against the wind as sea grapes normally do, they lay low hugging the ground. They were several yards from the hospital building. The knotty trail they made among the macca was difficult to walk through. Nobody walked there. If a person wanted to urinate or make quick furtive love they stayed close against the side of the clinic, where the ground was smooth and baked. Only children hankering to eat the rich purple fruit that covered the branches in August ever went among the sea grapes.

But that was where the sound was coming from.

Rachel followed the cries until she caught sight of bright red cloth among the tangle. With sea spray in her eyes she thought at first there was a woman crouched on the ground. The woman, in a blue cambric dress, was shushing her baby as she struggled with one hand to release her breast to put in the baby's mouth, while with the other she hoisted up her skirt to piss.

Then Rachel's vision cleared and she saw that no woman except herself was there. She saw the basket with the baby's tiny legs kicking above the piece of scarlet cotton that had been tucked around him on both sides. She saw the milk-blue skin exposing the tracery of veins; the wisps of snow hair that later resolved itself into the famous two-toned bush, wild blond in front and jet black behind; the old man's wrinkled cheek that all newborns have, red with pain and rage as he screamed.

The left side of his face was hidden against the padding in the basket, which was in danger of stifling him. From his size and the timbre of his crying, Rachel, who had helped her mother raise eight children, could tell at once that the child was newborn. The basket had been padded with great care, it seemed in a pitiful effort to make him comfortable; it even had a bonnet-shaped canopy to shield him from the sun. But it had not shielded him from the line of black ants that were crawling over him and causing his cries.

Rachel ran the last few steps. Frantically she began brushing off the ants in the same motion with which she lifted the child out of the makeshift cradle. With savage instinct the baby snuffled against her breast, searching for the promise of comfort he was programmed to recognize before he even left the womb. He had been dressed in a small girl's bloomers and what looked like torn-off pieces of a red sheet, as though no preparation had been made for his birth. Swaddling cloths, Rachel thought, as the wide waistband of the panties shifted and she saw he was a boy.

The ants had begun to eat his foot, but even that pain had faded in the greater pain of his hunger as he snuffled for food. Not finding where to suckle, he began screaming again. Rachel rocked her body to and fro to quiet him, while turning the little face toward her, to see further what manner of child this could be.

What she saw of the rest of the face made her hide it in pity in her shawl.

There are moments in life when something, some object or vision or encounter, moves a person in the heart with such force that the future, that is to say one's way of looking at it, is changed forever. No course of action presents itself, and so, without condition, the heart surrenders; something irrevocable gives over. Such is the irresistible arrest. In the unique recognition of helplessness, the knowledge that there is nothing in the universe that could ever be done, no sphere of influence within which one has the power to act, we reach blindly for the familiar. For Rachel, the Yahwehist, when she saw the child's indescribable face, this was such a moment. (This she told me many years later, when she saw I finally understood that I had no power over him.)

And Rachel Fisher, a cursing woman in whom faith had the force of superstition, kneeled down on the ground there with the found child in her arms, and prayed.

The baby fell quiet. When she got up off her knees and looked at his face again, she smiled, a slow, astounded, beatific smile, and decided to say nothing to anyone about what had happened in that translucent moment when it became clear that she and the found child had been lifted, for an uncountable moment, out of time.

"Moses," she whispered. "Moshe." And again, "Moshe."

Then she added, as if in defiance of some objecting voice that only she heard, "Yu name Moshe, because I draw yu out of di water." As you can see, this account of how she found him was not accurate, but it was Rachel's account, the one that was told throughout Moshe's early life.

Rachel went back inside the hospital, entering from the front, an erect young woman with her hair demurely wrapped in a tie-head and her nylon dress that had got soaked through in the flying spray now chip-dry, floating softly around her hips. With the child cradled in the crook of her left arm, the basket in which she had found him hanging from the other, she was what she seemed: a decent woman, a real woman now, carrying her newborn child.

News of the find spread like wildfire and people came to look and marvel.

For a town like Ora (the short name for Oracabessa-on-Sea) and a district like Tumela Gut, where the Fishers lived, the baby's parentage was never in question.

No one doubted that he was the product of serial fornications between one or other of the nubile black girlchildren who attended the high school, and one or other of the white man-teachers from Britain, married or unmarried, who did the "bad things" (tek wife from the barely fill-out girlchilds) in the undersea caves and hotel rooms on school trips for which certain girls were selected. Nobody ever claimed the child, and no girl was discovered to have been recently pregnant, though police investigations were carried out. After a while rumor went underground, though people did not forget, and so Moshe Fisher might have grown up in a normal way if his lineage had been the only abnormality about him.

But it wasn't. For one thing, there was the fact that he didn't look like his adopted parents. Rachel was part Indian, and fair, while Noah was pure African and very black of skin. For another, even in a society bred in mixture and anomaly, the child was not any color or physiognomy that allowed anyone to say what he was.

Moreover, his mother was Rachel Fisher, who was a staunch Yahwehist, a true believer. There was no Yahweh church in Jamaica at the time and there probably isn't now, but Rachel got her religion the way many poor people at the time got their reading material (*Reader's Digest*) and overseas education (Durham College correspondence courses)—by cutting out coupons from the *Daily Gleaner* and mailing them to addresses in England or Scotland or America, receiving in return unconscionable masses of pamphlets and other small literature.

According to Rachel's understanding, an understanding which like all understandings of foreign goods in Jamaica was only a version of the original (the meaning change always began in the passage across the sea), the essence of Yahweh (the religion, not the god) was that the Christian Bible had distorted the truths of God by translation. The force of Yahweh consisted in returning to the Hebrew pronunciations of words.

As a retranslation, young Moshe was a virtual cache of symbols.

To begin with, Rachel and Noah's childlessness took after Noah's family, not Rachel's: the Fishers were known to be a mainly barren family who never produced in any of their branches more than two offspring, more often one, and sometimes none at all. In the district of Tumela Gut, this was the sign of a curse. So, quite apart from his prophetic name, his advent as a gift to the desperate couple who had no child of their own made Moshe not only the fulfillment of a hope and a dream, but a hope and dream that would break the curse of the father's line.

With characteristic superstition, his mother insisted on inscribing in his name the mark of fertility—the maternal line. He was Rachel's talisman of the future, a future in which her name would never be wiped out. So, above the objections of his father, she named him, in full, Moshe Gid'on Rachel-Fisher. "Gid'on" was the Hebrew spelling of Giddion, her family surname on her mother's side; the apostrophe was to be pronounced like a short *i* to produce the same sound as the family name. "Rachel," the first part of Moshe's hyphenated surname, was to be pronounced with a short *a* instead of the long *a* with which her own name was pronounced. That way it sounded less feminine. She did not want him to be teased at school. She had thought of including her father's last name, her maiden surname, Sharma, but could find no way of slotting it in without destroying the rhythm of the sentence which the name was becoming, unless she placed it before Gid'on, her mother's surname, which she was not prepared to do. In the end, her son's name was a whole sentence, of which the meaning was, *Drawn out of water, he was a small axe, ready to cut you down, but in the end he brought the comfort of fish for the hungry, 2 Kings 6: 5–6.*

This you must understand, if you are to understand how Moshe grew up, and how he died: a strong believer in signs, kabbalah, and cryptograms, forms of meaning that traditional Yahwehists regard with suspicion because such meanings begin in folk talk, not written holy words, Rachel was the kind of person who studied the license plates of vehicles to discern patterns of meanings in the arrangement of the numbers. A license plate with *AM 5439*, for example, to her mind was meant to show the sequential relationship among 3, 4, and 5, the fact that 9 is a multiple of 3, that 5 plus 4 equals 9, and that 5 plus 3 equals 8, which immediately precedes 9. In other words, although the creator of the license number thought he or she was choosing the numbers at random, there was always an occult logic at work that caused them to fall into predestined patterns, a logic beyond human control or comprehension, and it was this same logic of the universe (which Rachel called faith) that had caused her to find this child when she thought she would have no daughter or son, and at the precise moment when she had determined in her heart to leave her husband.

By this logic, Moshe was predestined to become a superstitious man, following in the footsteps of his mother. Moreover, he was destined to remain so, because he traveled and lived in many places all over the world.

(I cannot say what Rachel made of the fact that she found Moshe four years before Jamaica's independence. The number 4 was not significant in any system of signs that she espoused.)

In addition to carrying the weight of new translations on his birth certificate, Moshe carried in his body outlandish signs of illegitimacy, the peculiar transgressions from which rumor had it he was made. Please understand. In that country illegitimate did not mean what it means to you, not born out of wedlock, which most of the people were, but born from terrible occasions that placed their mark on you. If you were born out of wedlock you were simply a bastard. Nearly everyone there was a bastard. Illegitimate was something else altogether. A curse.

With his pale skin, one sky-blue and one dark-brown eye, his hair long, wavy, and bleached blond in front, and short, black, and pepper-grainy in back, the kind of pepper-grainy that people called "bad hair," or "nayga head," the child seemed to represent some kind of perverse alchemy that had taken place in the deep earth, between tectonic plates, where he was fashioned. People said the boy just looked like sin. Big sin at work when he was made.

For why else had the crossing come out in him not as a judicious mixture of yellow-gold skin, in-between hair ("pretty hair"), and a singular eye color either black or brown or the two blended for hazel ("puss eye"), or even sea-green blue, which sometimes happened even in children with black skin, as it did in the boy Brendan, the Wells's son from Tumela?

Furthermore, what a skin! The color of milk that had been watered, so pale and thin it gave off a sheen of translucent blue, like certain types of coral or small swimming fish, the kind we called gray angelfish, though they were not gray but grayish blue.

Only one of the male teachers from Britain who worked at the school had hair the color of Moshe's bleached blond. His was the name that call, meaning that people whispered the child was his. He was a married man and had brought his wife to Jamaica with him, but he fooled around with the black little girls in the school. The pepper-grain hair was more commonly distributed—it could have come from any one of many of the schoolgirls, except that the owners of that type of hair were not in the group that frolicked with the white man-teachers. The white man-teachers preferred brown girls with long hair and black women's bodies (breast, buttock, and hip), or very black girls who had hot-combed their hair to straight.

The mayor of Ora's daughter was black as sin but with beautiful long tresses, almost as if she had been high brown. At first her name call too, as the mother who was unable to throw away the belly before the baby came and had thrown away the baby instead. (Some babies are stubborn, resisting all boil-bush, guzzu, enema, heavy load, jump-up, exorbitant exercise, beat-belly-wid-bat, and other efforts to dislodge them from the womb.) But rumor stuttered somewhat on that score because of the mayor's daughter's hair, which had nothing pepper-grain about it, and then rumor zipped its mouth, *prrrrrrps!,* because the noise of it came to the mayor's ears just as he was about to give out Christmas work on the roads, and Christmas work came by favors. You didn't badmouth the mayor's daughter and hope to get on the list for Christmas work.

But as you can imagine, rumor didn't die, it only went underground for a while. Stumped momentarily by the problem of hair and the advent of Christmas, rumor would surface again in the coming years and go on its way, loquacious, malicious, and unrelenting, without any sense of trespass, and without any self-doubt at all. The clairvoyance of the poor regarding the secrets of their betters is fundamentally secure, and confident. But it (rumor) would start to kill Moshe, though it also started to set him free.

Skin. Hair. Eyes. Enigmas. Only in Moshe's infant face was there no equivocation. It was, uncompromisingly, a nigger face.

But what people did not know, even the most clairvoyant, was the face that Rachel saw the first time she picked up her son. This was something that she pondered in her heart, and kept secret, even from her own husband, until the day of her death.

It had not been a nigger face.

iii

There is only one other thing I need to tell you before the story begins.

The day Moshe was found was my first birthday. It isn't that I am superstitious. I am not; I am no Rachel Fisher, but experience teaches you to read itself, and somehow that coincidence, that we were born on the same day though one year apart, seemed a sign of everything that was to come, the way we belonged to each other and the way we kept missing and missing and missing each other, in one-step two-step, one step at a time. When he died, I was almost not even there, and we had been together all our lives.

I returned and found him slipping into sleep, the day after I lost my fear of him leaving me for America. Only it wasn't the sleep you wake up from, but the long one where you say goodbye.

iv

One last last thing. In parentheses.

You see that thing I tell you about how people say Moshe came to be born? I have to tell you that though what happened to Moshe touched me near and deep because I was his twin, not witness and bystander to his life, I cannot shake the feeling that the thing affect not just me or others like me who it touch that close and personal, but all of us—all of us get deeply affected. I mean to say I believe none of us who went to that school ever recovered from this practice of big man abusing little girl. None of us, even those who were only witness and bystander to that particular wickedness.

I feel it have a whole heap to do with how Mosh turn out in the end, meaning how it turn out in the end between him and me, why we never did anything that gave us children together. I feel that maybe if something in me never damage by it (even the rumor of it), I could have approached him more bold. But maybe deep down I have a shame or a terror that is more than the shame and the terror I absorb from him because of his mother—I mean not his mother Rachel but his birth mother. Maybe is the shame and terror of girlness in the face of that unspeakable initiation of the body, so premature and so soon. Maybe is this denuding that happen in a girl's body before its secrets reveal even to itself or its owner, that put what Rachel call my dutty willfulness at bay, and I just follow-backa that terror instead of pushing forward and taking the lead the way I used to do in everything else with him.

They say a parent or grandparent and maybe even a far ancestor can eat sour grape or wet sugar, and as a result, pickni who come long after, their teeth set on edge.

interval

One more last thing. (Forgive: I am losing brain cells, and moreover I am afflicted with the affliction of the people who come from where I was born, the habit of everlasting and divaricate endings, whether in bearing record or saying goodbye. It is the fear of departure, the final line. A fear that belongs only to people whose history began in death.)

So. This last last is about Tumela Gut, the district where Moshe was grown. To get there you traveled west five miles on foot from Ora-on-Sea, passing through another district named Jericho. Veering east at Fus Stick (First Stick—Elgin Town on the map, which was the first place where a freed slave planted his boundary line, sticking the center pole in the ground), and cutting through bushes at Mosquito Cove on the Montego Bay Road, you could shorten your journey by half. This was the route Tumela people took to catch the Morning Star bus or the Years of Jubilee bus to Montego Bay, or the Blue Danube to Kingston. (Yes, buses were named like that, for faraway places in the east of Europe, or Palestine, or even the heavens, though most of the people had never traveled beyond the circumference of their dreams, and those who had, had gone no farther than England or Panama or North America, not so very far away at all.)

Tumela, a place that was frightening to people in other districts far and near. Sometimes, especially at night, it was frightening to Moshe and me.

Tumela was then one of five districts that bordered each other. The others were Jericho that I told you of, Mount Peace, Georgia, and Cascade. To a stranger looking on from the outside, especially one who was not from our part of the world, the five districts were uniformly beautiful, the kinds of places that are called paradise. Lush hills stretched in every direction, and if you stood on any of them, you saw the deep blue sweep of the Caribbean Sea, which changed colors like a chameleon in certain lights and times of day.

A few people in these districts lived in wall houses (that is to say, houses built from concrete and steel). One or two had houses two stories high. Most, however, lived in small board houses (that is to say, houses of one or two or three or four rooms, and dressed or undressed wood) with fretwork eaves made by the skilled carpenters of Tumela and Mount Peace. Regardless of the size or modesty of the house, the eaves were always extravagant and beautiful.

Yet there were still some people, the desperate poor, who lived in houses made of bamboo wattles fortified with marl or papered inside with pages torn from magazines that had come in parcels of clothes from relatives in England or North America. Sometimes these houses had no floors. That kind of house has died out now, and it seems strange to imagine that such a house could have existed so long into the twentieth century, but that was the way it was, long ago, when we were growing up, Moshe and me. I suppose, in a way, such houses were beautiful, meaning picturesque.

If you, a stranger, were searching for a word to describe these five districts, picturesque would easily come to mind. All the districts were picturesque, like places drawn in a book to entice children to read; green, bright, and lush with their tiny hillside farms, sun-drenched valleys, and sugarcane fields. Paradise, you would think, arriving in these districts which were so bright and green that your eyes hurt, if you were a stranger coming fresh to these parts from somewhere that was not our part of the world. And your eyes, blinded by their brightness, would fool you into thinking that this beauty was all that there was and you wouldn't know that each district was, in its different way, a place of terrors, which you could escape or endure only if you knew its spells and counterspells for redemption or retaliate.

If an outside person threatened to fight or work obeah on a Tumela person, the counterspell was easy as pie. "You know where I come from? I come from Tumela Gut, where pot boil up without fire." That was enough to make the challenger run away, hurrying slow on his dignity until he was out of sight, then taking to his heels like the wind.

This is because it was true. There was a place in Tumela where pots boiled without any fire beneath. The longheaded grandmother, Mama Mai, described how many years ago a colony from the days of slavery had taken up residence near the center of the village, at the end of the long grassy slope below the elementary school, just behind the ceiba cotton tree above the red river. This river was called Raiding. (There was another river, Foster-Reach, where women went to wash clothes.) Was there a raiding that took place there? A hunt for runaway slaves? I do not know. I have wondered if that river was meant to be called Riding, perhaps Tumela Riding, after the West Riding and the East Riding in Yorkshire, England, since so many places were named after other places in England, until the people pronounced them in their own language, and then they became something else again—but I do not truly know.

The duppies were a known nuisance. They spent their days, but especially their nights, quarreling in thin voices and cooking insatiable meals in three-footed Dutch pots that roiled and bubbled on unseen fires, disturbing the peace. The meals, we knew, were meant to be seductive. The aromas they emitted were not so much inhaled as insidiously imbibed, through the mind and the pores of the skin, so that anyone who was unlucky enough to pass by while the colony was cooking was haunted by dreams of a feast in paradise, and bright red pustules rose on the surface of their skin and broke to release a liquid that ran down sometimes like boiling sugar and sometimes with a vague presentiment of crab soup.

As children, we (not just Moshe and me but the collective children of Tumela Gut) were afraid of this place, and if our mothers sent us to the shop in the twilight, we wept and begged not to go. Running past, we heard the wind in our clothes, sometimes the ghosts laughing or singing, but to us it was all one: we heard only the sound of terror.

I often wondered if they ever ate their own meals, or cooked only to entice us. It seemed to me that they were love-starved, and hungered for something more than memory—this kind of aggressive solicitation through food could only mean a desire for the attention of living hearts, above bare remembrance. But children avoided them like the plague. Though Moshe and I were twins, and identical, we had this difference, that I never reconciled to their dwelling among us, but Moshe had a natural affinity with ghosts. He thought they had a right to live, and if they chose to do it among us, right there, then why not?

The name Tumela Gut still disturbs my head. A lot of places in those days were surnamed Gut, and you will still find most of them on the map. Stony Gut in St. Thomas, where Paul Bogle rebelled against the British in 1865, Starve Gut Bay in St. Elizabeth, where people must have suffered unbelievable hunger, and Running Gut, another name for running belly, or diarrhea, that might have been caused from hunger, or from eating too much too fast after a period of starvation, or from eating food that was spoiled, or even, in babies, drinking, instead of milk, sugar water. This Running Gut was in the parish of St. James, Gut River was to be found in Manchester, which was said to have no rivers, and Tumela Gut in Hanover parish, near to Oracabessa-on-Sea.

Most of these are names of hardship, except for Gut River, which some foreigner on the Internet has written was a name given to the river by a German (was he a visiting German or a German from German Town, Westmoreland, which we pronounce *Jahman*?—he does not say; he probably does not know). According to this foreigner, who might himself be a German, "Gut" means "good" in German and the man who named the river gave it this name because he thought it was a good river, but I think that is not true, I think it is a place where people were gutted, impaled on iron, just as there are rivers all over the Caribbean named Massacre, because people were massacred in slavery there.

I guess at these names, how they came about, and I think my guess about most of them is probably the truth. But I still wonder what or who Tumela was. I suspect she was a woman of strong and secret powers. For years I tried to find out more, but could discover nothing in the archives in Kingston, and not even the longheaded grandmother remembers. Through many searches I came upon a book that mentioned a Tswana word, "Tumelo," meaning "faith," and I did wonder if Tumela was Tumelo and people had come to Jamaica from southern Africa—Botswana or Lesotho, not just West Africa after all, because Tswana is a language spoken in the south. I rather like the thought of a woman named Tumela. A dangerous, unfathomable woman, our very own Nanny of the Maroons, one who belonged altogether to us, we one. Miss Tumela Riding, in tall black boots and her skirts hitched up to ford a red river, her hair the same wild hemp as her riding crop. Skuy! Hiya! Di image seduce mi.

And Rachel had said no, the revenants' cooking is not a cry for love, not a sign of lack but a declaration that their God *Is*. The real God, 1 Kings 18:39, not the god of the ones who kill them with hot rod and old wuk, who done dead himself, can't see, speak, nor hear, nor stop from pursuing—check verse 10 plus 2 verses back, 10 fi perfection and 2 fi di two gods inna contest, si who win; the old duppy dem tallawah, that is all. And I was ready to believe her, even though she is the same one who would cuss them dutty raw and exorcize them rapid if they come into her house. Miss Tumela Riding, I decided early, was a woman whose God could see and speak and hear and stop Lucifer himself from pursuing, if she had a mind to it.

Tumela Gut was a different kind of place from Ora, which was a town and the parish capital. Ora had a cinema, a regatta, a country club, a hotel, a high school (where we went), a high church (meaning Church of England), bustling narrow streets, cars, blaring bus horns, the chakka-chakka noise of a thriving market town, a cache of white people (meaning people straight from England, not backra, not homegrown), and a tiny middle class with pretensions. Ora also had the sea, not as a distant shimmer but right there, beating low against the seawall that was almost level with the street along which we walked to school.

Yet some would say Ora wasn't all that different from Tumela, not that far from the canepiece or the bush, both running equally on rumor and gossip and a long history under the sway of King Sugar.

In one of his earliest drawings, when he was nine years old, just after we started going to the high school in Ora, Moshe drew the two of us standing with split faces, like moons on wane, half turned right, the other half left, at a signpost on a road saying *This way to*

Oracabessa-on-Sea on the right, *This way to Five Districts* on the left. We belonged to both places, as far as it was possible for either of us to belong anywhere (which was not very far), though he less than I.

Not until much later did it bother me that he had drawn our faces opposite to each other—where the right side of his face looked toward Ora, the left side of mine looked in the same direction; where the left side of his was toward the five districts, mine was toward Ora. Like images in a mirror, where you cannot get over to the other side where your reflection is.

But we were children of both places, Moshe and I, and like Ora and Tumela, completely opposite and yet like twins.

You can imagine it was hard growing up between this district and this town where every day he was mocked and admired for his skin— not so much skin but the absence of it (for his color was really because he was born before his skin was finished making); not so much admired if you are thinking of admired in the way that is meant by the twenty-two categories of words of approval that substitute for it in Mr. Roget's thesaurus, words like adore, appreciate, cherish, commemorate, delight in, distinguish, dote upon, honor, idolize, love, laud, venerate, worship, praise; not admired as in the four columns of ten synonyms under each of the twenty-two categories—but admired as in their antonyms: review, surveil, gaze, observe (keenly, as in pinning to the wall), eat up, size up, get down on, get high on, get off on, gaze, gawk, survey, put down as, price, put away. Assess, estimate, take the measure of, behold. Tag, typecast, inspect, peer at (but not see), wonder, look fixedly at in wonder.

Growing up under the crushing weight of this negative admiration, which sometimes became pity and even sometimes acclamation, almost like he was being hugged (as in "after all is said and done, him is one a wi"), he might have been able to bear all this—for cruelty and ambiguity were never an exception in our part of the world, but a rule—and even the daily surveyance, the intense look under the microscope, the two-faced giving of succor for the wounds so cruelly inflicted, he might have accepted as in their own way a kind of love.

But in the end, when he went away, it was not because of any of this but because of another trouble altogether, which made us inseparable and kept us apart. Yet I think the two things—his lack of skin and this other trouble—were one and the same, sides of the same basic coin. Judas silver.

It is only left to say that my part in all of this—to tell you what happened to us, in the way it happened—was always fated, though when we began, it was not only Moshe, but both of us, who could not speak.

It is totally fitting that we met and fell in love on our first day of school.

PART II

the district and the town

CHAPTER II

"Sit," she commanded without speaking, patting the bench beside her, her uniform skirt spread out around her like a queen's robe. The stiffly starched navy-blue pleats made him think of a peacock's feathers. Their preening matched her hair, which was done up in short, fat plaits and decorated excessively in the fashion of the time, with a fantastical array of ribbons and clips.

Many years later, when he was in art school, he saw a portrait of Queen Elizabeth the First in peacock costume, and he thought that he had been right about her even then, all those years ago. She did resemble a queen, in the way she carried herself. But he adored her more as a goddess than a queen. Yet the most thing was, she was his friend.

Obedient to her command, he sat, taking care to leave enough space between them so he wouldn't mash her pleats. He wriggled himself into a comfortable position, still sucking on his right thumb and without removing his left hand from under his shirt where it was kneading his navel, as it always did when he sucked his thumb, the perfect coordination of comfort that he had known in all of his six years. The two of them were suck-fingers.

She sucked her left index finger, her right hand feeling her navel under her skirt which was rucked up in the most unladylike manner in the midst of its queenly spread. The middle pleats would no longer be immaculate when she got up from the bench. She sucked the tip of her finger daintily, like an upper-class lady sucking on a pipe pretending it was only a pose. He, on the other hand, stuck his entire thumb in his mouth, and bunched his hand so that two fingers could fit up his nostrils. It was a sign of their two personalities: he wanted

everything immediately, viscerally; she ambushed and claimed everything in a more circuitous way. And yet he was timid and held his
wants in secret even from himself, and she was tallawah and fearless,
with horned hair and bold, flashing eyes.

They came here every recess to watch the chickens.

"Dah one-deh deh call egg," she announced, again without speaking, pointing to a large Dominican hen that had detached itself from
the clutch and was strutting around the coop, making the familiar
rhythmic noise in its throat, like coconut husk being rubbed on a
grater. It meant that the hen was about to lay. "That one is summoning eggs."

Arrested, the two children leaned forward, their eyes glued to the
disturbed hen. The other hens ignored her, sitting sleepy-eyed on
their own eggs or pecking desultorily at the feeding troughs in the
hope of dislodging some overlooked grain of corn or slice of coconut
from the morning's feeding. From his perch above the ground the
rooster flapped his wings, once and again, his eyes bright and expect-
ant as they followed the hen.

"Shi go lay," the girl said again, inside her head, and the boy heard
her as always. He heard her voice filled with triumphant satisfaction. She removed her right hand from its secret encounters with
her navel and pulled her uniform tunic in close, so that it no longer
described a distance between them. Then, as if this action initiated
a tacit code, they began inching across the log, he to the left, she to
the right, until they were touching at shoulder and thigh. Then her
hand went back in her navel and they settled again, absorbed, with
the deaf-ears concentration of which children are capable. Their
silence, secret and companionable, fell like a wrapped sheet around
them. The hen slowed down, looking for a place to sit.

Behind, the schoolyard was abrasive with noise, but they hardly
noticed: the din came to them like a rumor from a far country, vague
and distant. This was their secret place, this coop on the edge of the
school grounds pungent with the smell of chicken waste—pee, feces,
sometimes offal. The big boys, the ones who after years in school
still could not read or write, were charged with feeding the chickens morning and evening before and after school, but otherwise the

coop and its vicinity were out of bounds. Nobody except Moshe and Arrienne minded, because nobody else was interested in chickens, of which the district children saw plenty everywhere. Some had chickens of their own, specially assigned for them to take care of, pets that would later be ruthlessly butchered for the family pot.

Moshe and Arrienne routinely broke the rule, and were routinely punished. In the beginning he cried because she got beaten and he did not. She was a big, tall girl, larger than her seven years, with Maroon features. She was fierce and refused to cry, no matter how many and how hard the blows the headmaster, the man-teacher, inflicted. Moshe, on the other hand, could not be touched. At the slightest stroke of the cane his skin broke and gushed blood, which even in those days could bring a court case or the police, if your mother was Rachel Fisher, a cantankerous woman even by Tumela standards.

Then, for some reason, the man-teacher stopped beating her and the two of them began to receive the same punishment. And since this more often than not included staying in late to clean up the classroom (this was sometimes punishment for recalcitrants, more often duty for the whole class, when there were no recalcitrants to punish), they did not mind. Or rather, she did not mind since punishment of any kind meant little to her, and he had learned to welcome this punishment because it meant they would be set free after all the other children had gone. Then they could walk home alone, without fear of the ridicule that he dreaded. She wasn't bothered by the ridicule. She would simply fight to defend him from it. But she felt it was okay too, to walk home without fighting, if one didn't have to.

The hen had found a corner that suited her, and was sitting. The children grew tense with excitement, their heads stiff and close together. The rooster, who had spun around like a weather vane following the hen's every movement, turned around on his perch, flapping and squawking in her direction.

But the hen was taking a long time. She lay quiet and unmoving, her bottom cocked, her eyes closed, as if she were asleep.

The children were growing tired of the waiting, afraid that nothing would happen before the bell for end of recess rang. Without a word spoken and in exact coordination, they began kicking the space beneath the bench, to and fro, their upper bodies rocking in unison with the movement, the habitual choreography of twins who communicated in their own secret ways. Without speaking, they sped up the movement, never taking their eyes off the hen or their fingers from their sedate communication with their belly buttons.

They were trying to hypnotize the hen into doing their will.

Straining, he directed the force of his will toward the hen. Please. Please.

"Is Sylvia Pettigrew an Lionel Harper wen inna di grassroot yessideh. Dem did a-do badniss," the girl said, without apparent rhyme or reason.

She broke his concentration. This time she had spoken aloud, which she almost never did. His eyes opened wide; with fascination and fear, his imagination shifted to the other side of the land bordering the school grounds. This section was prohibited as well. At the border between the school and the red river was the dry-stone gateway over which a log was laid like a bridge. The gate led out into a bow-shaped clearing encircled by trees that gave it an intimate and eerie feeling.

The trees were the first thing that made it impossible to keep the children away from that place, despite prohibition. They were naseberry trees, which fruited in the summer just before school was out. The succulent brown fruit fell and broke on the ground with a splash and turned bees, flies, and children luminescent with desire. Beyond the shadow cast by the trees was the slope that the teachers feared and fought unsuccessfully by prohibitions to keep the children from haunting. There the sun blazed unhindered from an open sky and they could slide flailing on coconut branches down to the river, or play at hide-and-seek in the tufts of guinea grass that grew in abundance all the way down. The guinea grass was where the bad children like Lionel Harper and Sylvia Pettigrew misbehaved themselves, showing their cheelies and cocobreads and doing other things to which his imagination could not assign a concrete image.

"Sandra chat. Shi tell Man-Teacher dis mawnin. Man-Teacher go bus dem ass wid pepper-lick." She flashed her hand in the motion that meant a beating, clicking her thumb and index finger together.

They made a sound like a whip. She returned her hand to her na-vel and continued kicking, finger-sucking. Sandra welshed on them and now Man-Teacher is going to give them a serious beating, a bust-arse. The thought delivered an extraordinary satisfaction.

He shivered, shocked at the news and, as always, at the daring of her language. She was never afraid to swear out of the hearing of adults, whereas he censored even his dreams. He was so afraid to dream that he struggled every night not to fall asleep. He dreamed of a large gray mattress coming in the night, scooping him up and whirling him far away from his mother, while he stretched out his hands to her, crying, but his mother was in the other room and did not hear. He dreamed this dream often when his parents fought, and he thought his mother would be killed; he thought his father would kill her.

"Shhh. Look deh. Look deh." The gossip over, she had returned to speaking to him without words. He always heard the echo in his head, clear as his own voice.

The hen had raised its behind in the bed of straw and the round brown egg was protruding from its extended anus, which was push-ing it out with quick, pulsating movements. It fell out and the chil-dren thought "Plop!" in unison, their eyes shining with the unbear-able thrill that never waned no matter how often they watched this event which was to them a vast miracle.

"Shi go dweet again," the boy whispered in his head, breathing through his mouth, and sure enough the hen raised herself again, the process was repeated, and soon two bright speckled eggs lay like jewels in the straw. This had never happened before. The children heaved a mutual sigh of satisfaction, long drawn out, in tandem, first she, "Hah," and then he, "Hah." The hen started cackling, announc-ing the birth. The rooster, cockadoodledoing loudly, announced his accomplishment, beating his wings and springing down on top of another of the hens. The gaggle scattered, calling and protesting in outrage.

The children had seen this mating a hundred times before and were not at all as interested in it as they were in the miracle of the egg being born. Still, they liked to watch as the rooster tried to anchor the next hen's head in place with his beak, before wriggling on and then off her. This wriggling to them was stupid, unsatisfactory; they thought he looked ridiculous, and sometimes he did not catch the hen, but this time he did.

Recess was almost over. They could hear it in the receding quality of the schoolyard noise. Soon the bell would ring. Another silence descended, but not as secure. They were waiting for the bell, which they could hear before it rang, a jangling noise that made their bellies feel stiff and unwell. Slightly shocked, a little lost, they stood up and began to tidy themselves. She straightened her pleats with meticulous care and patted her braids to make sure they were staying down, which they were not, but pressing them down made her feel she had tidied away her and Moshe's secrets. It was like putting things away inside a secret drawer, where inquisitive people could not find them. Struggling to stuff his uniform shirt into his short pants, he was clumsier. She helped him as the bell rang, dusting him down with quick pats of her hands, removing imaginary fluff.

They dawdled behind the crowds pressing toward the schoolhouse doorway, a headlong rush that braked at the steps and slowed to a massed shuffling punctuated by quick, urgent whispers, shovings, angry hisses, and finally silence as the man-teacher appeared in the doorway to inspect the perfect lines and the hush into which the rowdy mass had resolved itself at the door.

He stood erect and tall—to the littler children, a colossus—a great high-brown man with a bullet head, flexing, with slow, deliberate movements, the cane that was the same color as himself, while his eyes, the color of fresh molasses at the bottom of a gourdie, surveyed the pack with a libidinous gleam, waiting to catch just one out of line. He caught two, shirt out of pants or imperfectly tucked, and the cane descended with gusto, raising a vague dust from the flour-bag drawers the boys wore beneath their short khaki pants.

One boy leaped from side to side, sticking his bottom out to deflect the force of the blows. He got a double portion for his pains.

The other boy, more savvy, merely roared for mercy, standing still except for the staccato jerking of his body each time the lash descended. "Mi mumma, mi mumma! Woie, Teacha, Man-Teacha, mi nah go dweet again. Mek mi put in mi shirt inna mi pants, Teacha, duu, Teacha, duu!"

Man-Teacher gave him a few more as well, for creating shame and disgrace on his school. "Boy! Anybody killing goat around here? You is goat? Anybody cutting your throat? This is a school, not a abattoir! Stop your cow-bawling!"

But the other, who was guilty of the greater crime of evading punishment, got a greater portion of licks.

A few girls giggled, amused by the triple entertainment: the boy leaping and calling "Sight!" while he stuck his bottom out so that he was contorted almost in the shape of a saddle; the other calling down God from the cross and bawling for his mother to convince the man-teacher that he was dropping dead from the licks. Above all, they were amused by the way the licks exposed the boys' poverty. With every fall of the cane, flour dust rose in the air. Only the very poor, which none would admit was most of them, wore flour-bag drawers, and who wore them was a secret poorly kept—exposed by the man-teacher's zealous cane, for no matter how well the mothers washed, some stubborn residue of flour remained, and flaked up in an aerial smoke when the cloth was beaten.

No one confessed to the crime of giggling, so the head teacher distributed a rain of licks on the heads, shoulders, and breasts of the girls standing in the general vicinity of the giggles. After this, Man-Teacher sweating in streams, the children were allowed to chant in unison, "Thank you, God, for work and play, and all the good things you give us every day," before proceeding inside in an orderly manner, dispersing into their various classrooms, which were separated from each other not by doors but by folding blackboards, so that the activities of all the classes, which included many chants of lessons learned by rote, resonated, with astonishingly musical cadence, throughout all the other classes and the doorways of the school.

Holding fast to Moshe's hand as they crouched without crouching at the back of the line (Man-Teacher beat for poor posture), Arrienne could feel him trembling beside her. She squeezed his hand in their secret signal, and as his fingers squeezed hers in return, the great wings unfurled and pushed them forward and they plunged, invisible, into the darkness of their classroom where, with instinct and without sight, they found their bench (three children to a bench fastened to one desk) and slid onto it without speaking to the third child, who was already sitting there. The wings that made them invisible also robbed them of sight for the small moment that the miraculous protection lasted.

Man-Teacher, counting the children streaming inside to make sure all were present, missed two, but his eyes were blinded from the sun and he thought he'd miscounted. Something brushed past his ear with a feeling of bats, as it often did, and it annoyed him, because he knew there would be a buzzing in his ears for the whole of the next week.

CHAPTER III

i

Rachel took her son to the big school when he was six years old. Until then, he had hardly appeared to the eyes of the world. She could have sent him to basic school, kindergarten, which was an option, when he was three or even two years old, but she did not. Quite a few children went; his friend Arrienne had gone; it was there she learned to read, and write her ABCs. In those days basic school was not compulsory the way the big school, elementary, was, and Rachel was not the only parent who chose not to send her child. Most preferred to save limited resources for when the children were old enough for the big school. (Almost every child was taught his or her ABCs and all were taught to spell their names at home, even by parents who could not read. Fear of disgrace was the fear of being unable to recognize one's own name on a bulla cake before swallowing it whole.)

Rachel was not among those who chose not to send their child early to school. She simply had a different vision from everybody else. Though the big school did not admit children until they reached the age of seven, she had gone and begged the head man-teacher to take Moshe the year before, and the year before that, until, a year before the officially required age, the co–head teacher, who was the head man-teacher's wife, saw that the child could read far above his years and could write his ABCs, so she relented. Rachel had taught him during the years at home, using the *Reader's Digest*s she got in the post and the Nola books she bought at the drugstore in Ora. And Moshe was a natural. He took to books like ducks to river water.

Rachel avoided the basic school for fear her son would be killed before he was old enough to defend himself. It was not that she feared the children at the big school less, but that she knew the children at that school feared the man-teacher and his wife more. The two, without any sense of irony, were known to beat without mercy for fighting and bullying in any shape or form. Moshe was delicate as stringing roses in April, and his transparent skin bruised at a touch, so that but for her obsessive care, he would have been a mass of scabs and wounds.

As it was, he was often bruised and wounded, since there were things from which she could not shield him—falling down when he ran; cutting his knees when he kneeled on the ground to watch snails or sow seedlings on his side of the kitchen garden; dreaming (this she did not know) of terrible flight and kidnapping by mattress when she and Noah fought in the front room (after such dreams he woke up black and blue); burning and peeling when he forgot to wear his sun hat (the wounds wept for days when the sun cut him like this, and she had to wrap him in white cloths loaded with cucumber and slices of aloe vera, and keep him confined to the back room, where he slept, in the dark).

For the first five years of his life he did not know any other children. His world was circumscribed by his mother's life, and his mother's friends, which were two. Rachel was a woman who kept to herself and seldom left her yard or the one-acre farm adjoining her yard. This was where she planted most of the provisions the family needed for their meals. She accompanied her husband to the hospital to tend the sore that never healed, and it was in the same place, Ora-on-Sea, that she shopped for necessities she could not plant— brown soap, mixed meal, kerosene oil, replacement lamp wicks, salt beef or salted cod—though she could as easily have shopped at Miss Caro's or Miss Lill's establishments in the district. But she shopped in Ora-on-Sea because she was a woman who liked to keep to herself and didn't like people knowing her business.

Miss Caro and Miss Lill sold groceries in extremely flexible amounts and combinations depending on what people could afford; the two shopkeepers also gave credit (trus), writing up what people owed on wrinkled strips of brown paper that they stuck on a wire spike attached to the wall behind the till. Giving trus was an act of kindness much valued by villagers who received their wages once a fortnight and had many mouths to feed, but trus was also in Rachel's view an invitation to open yourself to gossip. Rachel was a proud woman. She would rather do without than take trus, and she would rather avoid the local shops than be exposed to the knowledge of her neighbors' dependency.

She used to sew a little, earning a bit extra from the skill her father had forced her to acquire. But she gave it up at about the time Moshe was found, to shield him from inquisitive eyes and questions. People had no reason to come to her house if she wasn't sewing their clothes.

She had no relatives living nearby. Her two brothers and six sisters, who had not been as academically gifted as she was, had made opportunity for themselves and migrated to England. Her sisters moved to Canada when Canada opened up through the Domestic Workers Scheme. Her brothers, left lonely behind, went across to America. It was Rachel, the oldest, who stayed, because somebody had to look after her father after her mother died giving birth to Charlie, the youngest boy. Then, when she might have gone after her father died, there was Noah, and it was too late.

Every now and then she visited her one female friend, Miss Hildreth Porter, who lived two miles away. Otherwise Miss Hildreth visited her, and they spread themselves on mahoe-stump stools in each other's yards (that is to say, Miss Hildreth, a thick-girthed woman of great size, spread herself, while Rachel, more slender and dainty, placed her feet side by side and covered her knees with her spread skirt), and sitting in this way for an hour when Rachel visited Miss Hildreth, and three hours when Miss Hildreth visited Rachel, they discussed the foolishness of neighbors; the cruelty of some people to their children; the nastiness of people who gave their children bush-rat soup to cure whooping cough; the pedigrees of careless young men who sought to put themselves with the daughters of respectable families even though they well knew their own families were infected with yaws, consumption, madness, thievery, marley-gripe, fluxy-complaint, sugar, and other diseases; the indecency of girls who frequented the wharves in Ora when the ships came in from far countries, turning themselves into sailor-bait in exchange for English guineas and American greenbacks; the growing wildness of the young; the ungratefulness of those who had gone overseas and forsaken their relatives; the epidemic of divorce cases in the *Gleaner*, shameless men gleanering their wives—be it advised my wife Leonora has left the matrimonial home and I am no longer responsible for any debts she may incur—what a wukliss man, exposing his dirty linen in public like that; the coming of independence in 1962 (Moshe was four years old) and the memory of the first time they voted, dipping their hands in red ink; the goodness of Yahweh Elohim Most High.

Theirs was a strange kind of gossip because they almost never mentioned anybody's name (except Yahweh's), but spoke in generalities. If a name was mentioned, it was always a name from the past, someone they had heard of or who was long dead. They wove a history of districts without calling anyone's name who was living or who was not remotely dead, retailing stories without implicating anyone's reputation, as if history could be cut off from memory or kin that remained. But their gossip took this form because the two of them prided themselves on abhorring slander and backbiting, and this was why they were friends, and did not keep other women friends. (This was why Moshe so often drew people with vivid skeletons, and abstractions where their faces should be.)

Rachel had another reason for her friendship: Miss Hildreth lived alone, and Rachel's heart, despite her great pride, was compassionate.

Her other friend was Samuel. He came on Sunday afternoons, arriving in time for two o'clock dinner and leaving before sunset. He was Rachel's distant cousin from the remote district of Manyenni, fifteen miles south of Tumela. Their conversations were of a different kind from the ones Rachel had with Miss Hildreth.

Rachel and Samuel discussed the state of the world, the condition of apartheid in Rhodesia, the language of dreams, the lost codes in

the distorted scriptures, the existence of satanic verses, and the effi-
cacies of oils for healing the soul. Such oils were often stashed on the
back shelves of drugstores in Jamaica's capital towns. The trade in
these was brisk, a parallel economy on which the drugstores thrived
because there was always a large clientele of the rural folk and sometimes the upper social echelons who believed in these remedies. Oil
of Hold Him Tight. Oil of Do Wha Mi Seh Yu Fi Do. Oil of Tun Him
Back (Turn Back Evil). Oil of Win di Case (for winning court cases).
Oil of Tun Him Mouth Backa Him (for retributing insults).

One night, Samuel told her, it was revealed to him in a dream that
there was an oil, the Oil of Patmosphere, which was a wonder cure
for ancient ills, and he was astonished, when he went to investigate,
that it was sold in MacKenzie's Drugstore in Montego Bay, but at a
formidable price that would take him many years to save. "Man," the
drugstore owner told him, "this is rare oil, requiring special compo-
sition. In more than fifty years no one but you has come to inquire of
it. I cannot sell it for less."

Miss Hildreth and Samuel often saw Moshe, for he was allowed,
as children seldom were, to play nearby while the grownups talked,
though he was not a retarded child but overbright for his years and
forgot nothing that he heard. Miss Hildreth fell into the habit of
prophesying his future. "Him gwine have a hard time, Rachel. Dat
skin an dat hair gwine mek him way in dis world hard-hard. Hard
travail. Mi si it. Ehn-hn." This unresolved body in which history has
made ructions will make his pilgrimage difficult. This is what I have
seen.

And Rachel always answered her with a gentleness she showed
to no one else. Having decided to "keep friend" (she felt, sometimes,
against her better judgment), she had committed to accepting the
obligations, including soft speech, that came with friendship, "No,
him not gwine weary. It a-go sen him places, yu go si." (In her secret
thoughts, "yu go si" translated into "retro me, Hildreth," a counterspell.)

Moshe learned to distrust Miss Hildreth and would never go near
her. He found her unkind, and detested the things she said about
him. In her presence, which he endured because his mother made
him stay, he learned to close his ears, and if he allowed himself to

hear anything that she said, it was only so he could discover how to guard from her his palaces, rooms of escape where like all only children he had learned to make a home. Before the closed doors of such rooms, counterspell he pinned Miss Hildreth like the donkey's tail flat against the wall. The wicked witch of the west, knocking unavailingly at the door.

Samuel he loved. For Samuel did him the grace of ignoring him, most of the time. Not only that, Samuel was a man of dreams. Moshe beheld him rise like an issue of smoke from a labyrinth, and the child was enchanted so that later when he discovered his gift of drawing, he drew, over and over again, scenes of Samuel flying, streaming tails like a comet, while his hundred eyes gleamed among columns of hair.

Once in a while Samuel noticed him, but in the strangest way, as if the child were a strand woven in his outlandish skein of dreams. One day he said, "Why yu tink this boy is the color of milk and honey?" posing this as a philosophical question, to which he fully intended to give the answer. With Samuel, a question was ever a rhetorical ruse.

Arrested, Moshe paused the toing-and-froing of his homemade horse on the squeaky verandah floor. The horse was built from a water bottle fitted at its bigger end into two condensed milk tins mounted on wheels cut from discarded Michelin tires and attached to the tins by cord strung through holes in their tops. The tins had been roped together a second time by more cord strung through the bottoms. The narrow, protruding part of the bottle formed the horse's neck and head. The horse was flexible in the space where the two tins met, but with its wheels it could have been a truck except that Moshe made it a horse, shouting, "Giddy-ap, giddy-ap, skuy!" from inside his head as he galloped it across the breathless floor.

"Hush," he told the horse now from inside his head. "Hush, brrrrr," and held his breath, waiting for the answer to Samuel's riddle which had mentioned him in it.

"Is the Oil of Patmosphere. Is the same way. Same way. The answer is there."

"Wha di answer?" Rachel asked, smiling.

"You have to come at it in a special way. Can't come at it like how people think."

Rachel waited for the unraveling, still smiling.

"Is Revelations," was Samuel's final pronouncement. "The boy is the power of Revelations."

Moshe became oblivious to the good-natured quarrel that followed this cryptic comment, Rachel insisting that Revelations had nothing in it about milk and honey; that was in the Old Testament, quoting to prove it, I will bring them up into a land flowing with milk and honey, the land of the Canaanites, the Hittites, the Amorites, the Perizzites, the Hivites, and the Jebusites, and Samuel insisting that she had missed the principle, it was about the future when all that was different would be one. The lion would lie down with the lamb.

Revelations. The listening child shivered with satisfaction. He liked that. Revelations was the book in their Bible where everything was going to come to an end with a tremendous bang, and the world would be made new. It was horrible and exciting, all at once. On his knees on the verandah pitching marbles with himself or playing with his pitchy-patchy trucks and his horses of bottle and tin, he pretended not to hear the conversation, but he muttered and played with the word under his breath, seeing how many permutations it could bend into, like river eels. Revelation. Relevation. Evationreli. Revellelation, Revelelelelelelation, Reli. Vation. He giggled. The word astounded him with its beauty. The beauty of water playing on stones. He liked being associated with such loveliness.

"So how you use it though?" Rachel was asking. "The vision tell you that part?"

"Oh yes, oh yes," Samuel said in an exalted voice. "I receive everything clear-clear as day. I get up off my bed right there in the night-middle, and I write it down so that the vision would not escape from me. See it here." He showed crumpled brown paper torn from bags into which flour or sugar had been parceled. "Anoint your whole body and your hands with this oil, it must be on your palm when you shake another person hand. Say to the person, God be upon you and your hand will be like a grease, greasing the soul."

"Plenty people wipe all manner of thing upon they hand and shake other people hand with it and it kill who they shake hand with," Rachel observed. "Hidin murder in they hand. It good to extend a hand of fellowship."

"Oh God, oh God," Samuel said excitedly. "Das it exactly. Man, it sweeter than sugar."

The child frowned. It seemed on the one hand that it was not good to shake hands, but on the other, that shaking hands was good if it was done with the sacred oil. How would you know who had the right oil on their hand? Could you say, Mi nah shake yu hand cause mi nuh know wha yu put pon it? That would be rude to a grown person. He pondered that for a while and decided that it was the kind of question best left until one was grown up, since only bigpeople shook hands.

Twice Samuel brought him locusts to eat, a powdery brown fruit over a hard brown seed inside a hard brown shell shaped like a foot that you had to break with a stone. The fruit inside was delicious; it looked and tasted like cotton candy but had a foul smell like unwashed socks. Children called it stinking-toe. There were no stinking-toe trees in Tumela but only in Manayenni, the district beyond God's back where Samuel lived.

Apart from Samuel and Miss Hildreth, the only other persons who came to the house were the telegram boy who brought bad news on his bicycle, and was paid sixpence if the receiver of bad news had it to pay; and the Yahweh elder who journeyed from Ora once every hundred days to give Rachel scripture lessons, for in those days (and maybe even now) there was no Yahweh church in Tumela (Yahweh was not even recorded until many years later). The elder was a desiccated man who suffered from peptic ulcers and was uncomfortable around women. Because of this he muttered his teaching and left in a hurry. To supplement this desolate communion, Rachel received through the post office small books and pamphlets expounding the mysteries of Yahweh, and it was with these that she fed her strange beliefs and made her fragile peace with the life of poverty that she felt had dished her dirt.

So you understand, then. How growing up under the influence of these untoward ruminations and friendships and the isolations wrought by his mother's idiosyncrasies and his missing skin, Moshe became a mystic who soon lost the power of normal speech and could only be heard by someone who had also grown up in this way, or a way similar, like the boy in the story who, ostracized by his articulate siblings, falls back into nature and begins to ventriloquize the language of birds. When this happens, the boy is already in the forest, in the middle of his pilgrimage.

The only time Moshe saw other children up close before he went to school was during a short period in his life when his mother did her washing in the other river. Not the River Raiding, whose red water would stain the clothes and so was used only to fill cattle troughs, but Foster-Reach River to the southeast, the river which if you tracked it to its head led you to the next district, Jericho, the place where it sprang up from underground. The districts were joined to each other in many such ways.

Rachel did her washing on Sunday mornings (Saturday was Yahweh's holy Sabbath). Sometimes other women came, balancing their wash pans on cottas on their heads. They washed in the river while their children played. They looked at Moshe curiously, and spoke openly of his deformity. Deformity did not seem to them something to be sensitive about, since the district was full of such. People with feet turned backward, the result of being pulled from the womb the wrong way with forceps. Men with hernias weighing more pounds than they could balance in their hands. A child with a cleft palate. A grown man with the brain of a child, young men who fell down in trances at the sound of excitable words, such as preaching, and foamed at the mouth until their jaws were pried and kept open by a metal spoon. Others who sought physical love with animals. Yet others who acquired a deformity from being taken away by unseen forces while young, and afterward returned.

The women prescribed remedies.

"Yu ever rub him down wid castor oil a night an put him in di shady sun a mornin? Dat can mek di skin come harden, yu know. Him won't look like dead croaking lizard so much, an him won't bruise so quick so much."

Rachel, looking up in alarm once this well-meaning and insensitive conversation began, breathed a sigh of relief when she saw that Moshe was out of earshot, paddling by himself along the river in search of crayfish, while the other children watched him with curiosity and wonder. But the fact that he could not hear what was being said did not make her any less angry.

The women were in full flow, not noticing her anger as she bent, tight-lipped, over her wash pan of clothes, rubbing them with Guinea Gold brown soap after beating them on the river rocks to get out the worst of the dirt.

"Yes, castor oil good, but not too much. Yu want to harden di skin, not mek it too dark. Yu can si seh him a Red Ibo, him jus a dundus one. If yu can tone down di dundus, mek di Red Ibo come out clear, wi bi good."

"Dis a nuh dundus. Dis a dundus double. Furthermore, dundus usually have two pink eye, nuh one blue an one brown. Some curse is on di child from di way him born. Down in Ora dem seh is retribution. Dat is how dem talk bout it, but mi nuh know. Yu carry him out yet, Rachel? You need fi bruk di curse, enuh. Carry him to Madda Penny."

"Or Bredda John. Bredda John can help him too. Him a myal man."

"Di hair funny too, ehn? But it can easy tek care of, more dan di skin. Yu can dye it one color. Tek out di dundus color in di front, mek it all black. Den him wi look like Indian, like coolie royal."

"True, but wha yu go do wid di picky-picky back part? It nuh match up." The woman who said this made a face, and added comically, "No coolie royal hair nuh look like dat under di sun." You cannot fix the nigger half. It will always be mismatched.

The women laughed at this declaration. Up to this point the conversation had been intense, committed, serious, but now it exploded in laughter. And quickly became serious again, pushing back aganst the descent into charade.

"Shi can press it wid pressing comb, like how dem-girl do theirs. Bring di whole ting in one. If all-a it look straight it wi better."

"But look like yu nuh ha no sense. Yu waan bun-up di pickni head? Yu don't si di back part of di hair too short fi press? Pressin comb ooda fry him scalp."

"Yu carry him go a doctor, Rachel? Wha doctor seh?"

"Doctor seh mi pickni healthy, nutten nuh duu him, Suzie Q Francis."

The warning edge in Rachel's voice made some of the women back off, irritated others.

"Fi heaven sake, Rach, nuh go on so. Wi nah seh nutten, a jus try wi a-try help. Be reasonable, him nuh healthy. No doctor nuh tell yu seh him healthy. Him cyaan healthy an look so strange. A lie dat yu a-tell."

"Lef mi pickni alone, Clareese Bell." Rachel, trembling with fury, hauled up her wash pan, dumped her wet unrinsed clothes in it, and, heaving it on her head, walked away to another part of the river. "An all-a oonu, nuh mek mi haffi tell oonu sinting tiddeh." The real words she wanted to say revolted in her head; later she would kneel in shamefaced, bitter repentance before Yahweh. Yu bombo, Clareese Bell. Di whole-a oonu kiss mi arse. If oonu faas wid mi pickni again infronten mi, I chop up oonu rass. Oonu lef him. Lef him. Him nuh trouble oonu. How him look nuh none-a oonu damn business. A Yahweh mek him. I abjure oonu, contradiction of sinners. What God bless, no man curse.

The words she did not speak hung in the air like smoke everyone inhaled.

"But oonu si ya, sah. Mind a sinting yu a-hide. Mind a nuh yu have him wid di likkle white man fi true. Gi Noah bun an jacket down a Ora while him gone a-sea."

Driven to her limit at this unspeakable insult, Rachel was provoked to answer. "Yu mus know, fa di amount a waistcoat wheh heng up inna fi-yu man closet, no color nuh inna di rainbow fi describe dem, so yu mus know."

At this, Suzie Q let out a big malicious laugh, enjoying Rachel's riposte. Clareese was well-known as the chief burn-giver, jacket-and-waistcoat-maker; her husband, a ship's cook who came home once a year, was thought to be the father of none of her numerous offspring, whose births had followed each other a year apart, so that if they were lined up in order from the oldest to the youngest, they would form a neat stepladder.

✌

Avoiding her neighbors altogether was impossible, but after this bitter encounter, Rachel contrived to meet as few of them as she could by the simple expedient of arriving at the river while the dew was still on the ground. She waited only long enough for the mists to dissipate off the surface of the water before plunging in with her wash load. Most of the women came later, after morning service, or went on Saturday, after marketing.

This meant she now met very few, if any, neighbors at the washing. And if any arrived before she finished, their attitude took care of any potential reconciliation. Still enraged, the women decided to either ignore Rachel or resort to trowing wud. If their paths crossed with hers, they said howdy, or not, and Rachel said howdy, curtly, pleasantly, and concentrated on her washing. The others either then chose a spot far enough away from her to underscore her exclusion or plunked down in the same pool to show how much they were ignoring her. Which is to say, to provoke a confrontation via the undirected slinging of words.

Female malice in Tumela Gut was always religious. Rachel's adversaries lifted up their voices in song:

How great is our God!
How great is His name!
He the greatest one forever the same,
He roll back the water from the mighty Red Sea,
He said, I'll lead thee, put your trust in me!
Praise the Lord!
Hallelujah, praise His name!

"Clareese oh, yu sun di dawg yet?"

"Sun which dawg, Suzie Q? Mi dawg born white, is di color God give him, why yu tink sun gwine change dat?"

"Lef di ooman dawg alone, Suzie!"

"But wha yu si mi a-do, Pretty Teet'? Mi ongle a-suggest seh shi give di dawg a tan, so him can stan blackpeople climate!"

"Some people love dat deh color, a dem Jesus dat! Dem nah let it go!"

"Hol him, dawg, nuh let him go!"

"Hol him, dawg, nuh let him go!"

"Come, Rex. Come, Rex, whu, whu, whu!" And the long whistling call, summoning the imaginary dog, would be emitted through the lips pursed in the direction of the little boy, who hunted fish within hearing distance.

The truth was, they were not malicious women, except when rejected (and then they were vicious), and though they found the child strange, he was no stranger than most of what or whom they knew, except that his particular strangeness had no precedent. They wished Moshe no ill. And indeed they longed to lay down arms, but could not surrender in the face of Rachel's unyielding pride.

It did not take Moshe long to learn that it was he who was being talked about in this coded way. And he felt how his mother's contained rage, a bitter thing, roiled over him to withstand the neighbors' barbs. Rachel was determined not to answer or show in any way that their taunts affected her, but her anger and fear for her son were impossible to hide. In her effort to shield him, her disguised rage, the cloak of her protection, burned through her hands helping him undress for bed at night, and his skin broke out in great rashes that confined him to his bed once more.

Noah was at home irregularly. He went to sea in the night and sold his fish in the morning. He did this from Monday to Thursday, when he would return to Ora to sell the last of his catch and caulk the boat if it leaked. Then he would head for home and a long sleep. He sold his fish as he caught it, putting in to port at various places on the long route where he tracked his fishing pots. He laid the pots at evening and harvested them before dawn when the fish were still asleep in the cunningly fashioned cages of mesh. Working alone, Noah came in early before the sun's rays could fall on the catch and spoil it, putting out again before people had had their breakfast. His fish, with scales so fresh they were translucent, sold well, and the higgler women retailed them for good prices in the markets.

It was this habit of aloneness on the open sea that made Noah rough and impatient with standing in line, and distrustful of how to find his footing in polite company. (Rachel's aloneness was more a matter of choice, and pride, but she had great self-confidence.) Yet Noah, who, despite his social diffidence, was afraid of no one, was in awe of his adopted son, the delicate waif-child whose bleeding skin reminded him of his own long-running sore that would not heal even when Rachel took matters in her own hands and, ignoring the hospital's directives, dressed it with poultices made from bizzi mixed with oil and gave him molasses in his tea instead of sugar.

And yet the matter of sore and blood that bound father and son together was somewhat of a contradiction, for the surfeit of sugar that had given Noah his sore was the exact opposite of Moshe's affliction. The child was born allergic to sugar and could not eat it. Between the father's overconsumption and indigestion, and the child's abstention, the two were as different as two people could be could be who had grown up in the same place under the same sun under the same dominion of sugar.

It was Noah's awe that drew them together. He loved the child with an inarticulate tenderness that terrified him. Sometimes he felt the same tenderness toward Rachel, but he was unused to opening his inner life even to himself, so toward his wife he was undemonstrative except when they quarreled, and then his feeling came out in anger. The little boy's innocence made him soft, and as a result, nervous. He didn't want the child to grow up soft, though he feared it was already too late from the moment Moshe was born. Di mumma suffer, he said. Das why she trow him wheh. Trow wheh when him young, di heart weak. (Rachel, as you may expect by now, said no, and declared Exodus 2.)

When Noah was home on Sunday mornings, Rachel left Moshe in his care to go washing, but too often he was not there, and she took to fetching the river water, carrying it in buckets or kerosene tins on her head, and washing the clothes at home, but sometimes even this was not possible. Noah cursed her for a fool; why should a woman burn herself out to carry home a river, backbreaking labor the end of which could only be to hurt the child, by protecting him from what he needs must face, the tragedy of having been born? Such hard and terrible labor was the fate of everyone ever born, one way or another, Noah felt. The only difference was in the kind of tragedy that one's life became. He had no pity for himself.

In truth, having Moshe did not ease but actually increased the quarreling between them. Pania Machete, Noah nicknamed the boy, half with affection, half with philosophy, which is to say, mordant cynicism. Two-edged machete, which, facing backward or forward, would cut deep, for the child was placed like a sword between the husband and wife.

This nickname enraged Rachel. "Nuh call him so. Nuh call him so. Pickni grow inna dem name. Pania machete talk out of two side a dem mouth, an him nuh hypocrite. Nuh call him so."

Noah bared his large teeth in the humorless grin that with him passed for a laugh. "Pania machete cut sharp—cut yu, cut mi. Two a wi bleed. But machete can't work by itself, or rest by itself, enuh. Somebody haffi decide fi stop di war." Without even bothering to kiss her teeth, Rachel turned her back on him.

They were united in their love for the child and strove in their own ways to make his life good. (Good, not happy; for a people whose life began in death, happy was a child's fantasy, an immature dream.) Noah was the one who taught his ABCs and phonics. This was ironic, for, as I said, Noah could not read; he had gone to school just enough days to learn the rudiments (his ABCs; the speller's catechism r-a-t rat, c-a-t cat, m-a-t mat, look at that, look at that) before he dropped out in order to work so that his younger brother Cecil could go, their mother having died while they were young and without fathers. While Noah taught him these rudiments, Rachel taught him sight reading using her *Reader's Digest,* her kabbalistic brochures, and retranslated Pentateuch and psalms. There were no other books in their home, and this repertoire, beyond what he learned from eavesdropping on Samuel's luminous orations, is how Moshe came to live in the worlds of superstition, open sesame, and the cryptic arts of Byzantium.

He was a quick child, and read fluently from the age of two. He was wonderfully charming, and stole their hearts.

From Noah he learned the skill of making toys from scraps and waste, for Noah spent patient hours with him, showing him how to make trucks by fitting rubber strips onto the wooden wheels he carved from flotsam; how to strike a nail without bruising his hands, which Noah wrapped for him in cloth before he allowed him to hold the hammer underneath his own, guiding the small fingers; how to make and walk on stilts of cord and condensed milk tin (the stilts heaved him high in the air with his legs wide and his head up near the stars); how to make a calaban and arrange wiss-wiss to catch birds in the feeding tree.

But the child cried and would not trap the birds, and so the father abandoned this part of his teaching. The child's inability did not seem to Noah strange or unmanly, because he himself was not inclined to kill. From the day his wife brought Moshe home, he had not taken an angelfish. If they swam into his fish pots, he let them go. Their milk-blue edges reminded him too much of his son. He was exceedingly tender with the child, and if Rachel forgave him at any time for being rough and uncouth, it was whenever she saw the two of them, heads bent close together over a simple toy, Noah's bushy wild burr that to her fury he would not comb, and the toddler's strange blond bangs and tight pepper-grainy black kinks, the two heads of hair mingling as the father explained the toy's workings in low murmurs like a forest animal communing with its young.

It was from Noah that he learned the love of the sea. He listened with shining eyes as his father recounted his adventures: his vigils in the long night; the extended silences riding the waves at daylight while seabirds perched on the edge of his canoe and watched with him the great golden ball of the sun rise out of the depths; his encounters with sea trolls that he fought with a Christian cross and his lantern; the voice of the wind when he had to put up a sail; the eyes of fish gleaming in dark pools while they slept with their eyes open; the ghosts he surprised wrestling on the surface of the water, plantation people long dead fleeing their masters; his almost drowning once, in a storm, when the boat sprang a leak too wide for him to bail, and he was picked up by a passing cargo ship.

To the child hearing these tales, his father became a hero. He knew that one day he too would go to sea. He longed for it to be now.

"Dadda Noah, duu, mek mi come wid yu. Tomorrow?" Moshe begged, his widened eyes trained on his father while he sucked his thumb and comforted his navel under the hem of his vest.

"When yu big enough, yu can come wid mi."

"Mi big now." He stretched his arms out so his father could see how wide his span was, that it was like wings.

"Yu nuh so big. Wait likkle fus," Noah said, hiding a smile.

"When mi fi wait, Dadda?" Moshe's face screwed up, he was ready to cry.

"Till yu stop suck yu finger," his father said, not in a teasing voice, but gravely.

The boy came to see not sucking his finger as the mark of manhood. He knew he would not attain it for a long time to come. "Mi go stop suck mi finger," he consoled himself and his father. "An den yu go car' mi."

"Yes," his father promised, and Moshe believed him. It was enough. He waited for the day when he would no longer need his suck-finger. And though he did not know it then, it was in these communions, after tales of fishing, that the seeds were sown that later caused him to run away from home and the familiar sea.

He grew used to his father not being there all the time, though at first he cried each evening when Noah left. But it was all the life he knew, these bright Monday afternoons when his father said goodbye, these calm Thursday mornings when he came home again, bringing the sea with him; and moreover, he had his mother, with whom he spent every day of his life, and so he was not overdisturbed.

The child passionately loved his mother and father, and it grieved him that they quarreled and could not be at peace. And indeed, the story of how two people so tender-hearted married and lost each other and could not be reconciled, even with a fairy-child between them, is one of the great mysteries that can never be explained, though there was a history that might go some way toward an explanation, which later Moshe was told, and which he told me.

It was in keeping with Rachel's superstitious logic that the riverside attacks on Moshe ceased not as a result of her precautions, but as a result of events outside her control.

One evening, missing the river, and tired of being locked in the house (sunburn had kept him confined there for two days), the little boy slipped out through the back door while his mother was cooking in the outside kitchen, and headed down the path toward the river.

He was soon overjoyed. There were ripe naseberries on the path and his conversation with the birds was satisfying. He wondered if he would see the other children there. He hoped he would. He had begun to find friends among them, even though his mother always called him back in that sharp way that brooked no argument whenever any of them came near. One day, out of earshot around a bend in the river, one of them poked his hand into Moshe's skin and when the skin did not come off, he said, "Him skin don't splatter," his eyes round with wonder. The others, emboldened, took turns poking Moshe in various parts of his body to make sure this was true. Their questions came fast and curious.

"Why yu look so? Yu come from foreign?"

"A sick yu did sick? Why yu skin peel off?"

"A bleach him modda bleach him wid Ajax. Him a dundus."

"Look here, him blue-blue. A him a Boy Blue. Don't a-yu a Boy Blue?"

"Yu can ketch crayfish, likkle boy?"

They pulled his hair where it grew long in front, to see it if was real. They knew coolie hair, which was straight and black, but straight and yellow they had never seen, not being used to storybooks or having yet gone to Ora, where the white people from England were.

Happy to be in their company, he allowed himself to be poked and pulled, and explained that he had been born this way but his mother said it was all right, he was only different. The question of his admission to their play was settled when one of the boys said, "Mi si one boy like him inna book, inna mi big sister fairy-tales book," and Moshe put out his arm and shyly offered his fistful of crayfish to them all.

They were only three, four, five, and six years old. The littlest ones had never even noticed his appearance until the older ones said, Look.

But at that age, the wonders of the world do not last; that is to say, no wonder stands out above any others, since all the world is wonder. Moshe's appearance was no different. Once they became used to seeing him, he was just the blue boy; apart from this matter of skin, the same as any other boy.

They played together in the moments caught between their mothers' insistent shouts to come there, out of the way of trouble, which was something you could catch by keeping company or straying up the river to Big Water, the great pool where the intrepid drowned. Often they got slapped for pretending not to hear when they were called. Only Moshe was not slapped, for he was an obedient child, who would come when he was called and would play by himself within sight of his mother for the duration of time it took a small child to forget; only then would he go to his friends again. But Rachel could not spank him, even a little, for he would bleed, and when he bled, the flow could not be stanched.

It was a strange thing that among people deeply knit by kinship and ways of common care, children, not just the singular child Moshe, were discouraged from keeping company and were warned of the dangers of eating from people to the same degree that they were warned of the hazards of talking to strangers. Among these same people, food was always offered to the hungry, the traveler, and the aged in the community if they were indigent, and a stranger knocking at the gate could be assured of a seat in the shade and a drink of water. It was an even stranger thing that among people who lived so closely that everyone's business was everyone else's, a child could grow up living inside the circumference of his body alone, as Moshe did.

For it seemed that in the end, without having discussed this in so many words between themselves, Noah capitulated and both parents made a decision to protect their strange child by bringing him up in hiding, until the time came when they couldn't hide him any longer. People knew about him, of course, but the less he was seen, the more he became a matter of rumor and noise, more part of everyday legend than a living person. And in truth, because he was seldom seen, in the tales that were told it was not so much his appearance as his way of coming into the world that made him most strange. In Ora he was remembered as the Moses baby, the one found in a grung basket.

Now on the road to the river, the little boy hopscotched, chanting in rhythm as he hopped the names of children he remembered, "Maisie, Jonathan, OneSon, Sher . . . Maisie, Jonathan, OneSon, Boukman, Sher . . . Boukman, LikkleMan, OneSon, Sher," hoping he would see them when he reached the river.

He had had no idea before now what it meant to be alone. There was no one there. The winding coils of the river meandering between banks populated only by trees seemed to him vast, hostile, and uncharitable, and he shivered with premonition and turned to go back.

The rustling and panting in the trees and the two larger-than-life figures wrestling a dark object on the ground froze him in his tracks. He had never heard of the slave cooks of Tumela Gut, but his hair rising summoned an anticipation of terror beyond knowledge.

He began to run.

"Come back here, likkle boy." The voice was vaguely familiar, a duppy-relative of Miss Suzie Q, perhaps.

He ran faster. The footsteps thudding behind him were not louder than his heart. He fell on the soft ground, which was wet from rain the night before. Ghostly hands seized him, turned him over on his back. His eyes were squeezed tight with fear, and tears poured down his face.

"Open yu yeye, bwoy, look pon mi." The hands shook him vigorously, hurting him.

His tears scattered across his face and his eyes opened as if prized with a spanner.

"Wha yu a-duu duung ya, bwoy?"

"Mi nah do nutten, ma'am." He was weeping beyond himself.

The man's and the woman's eyes swiveled around the common, across the winding river, up the slope above the waterfall where the naseberry trees marked the boundary between the common land and the village houses. "Yu deh ya by yuself? Wheh yu modda deh?"

He shook his head, unable to speak. The question was repeated, roughly, urgently, and at last he said, "Shi up-a yard."

"So wha yu a-duu yah? Ehn? Yu modda know seh yu duung ya?"

He shook his head again.

Relief crept into the interrogating voice: "Ah-oh, so a-bad yu a-bad. A run wheh yu run wheh widout yu modda know."

Miserable, Moshe nodded his head in affirmation. It was the woman who was asking the questions and shaking him. The man held him by his knees, so that he could not get up or get away, but the man did not speak, only watched him and watched the terrain with a curious, worried intensity in his face.

"So wha yu si? Wha yu hear?"

"Mi nuh si nutten. Mi nuh hear nutten." His voice rose high with his crying.

"Yu sure?"

He shook his head again, his eyes closed tight upon his misery and pain.

"Yu sure? Yu sure? Look pon mi, bwoy, open yu yeye an look inna fi mi. Well, yu betta sure, yu hear mi? An yu betta don't seh nutten to nobody, yu hear me? Yu don't si nobody duung ya, yu understan? Yu understan? Yu don't seh nutten, an yu wi bi awright. Open yu mout, an Tumela duppy go come visit yu. Yu get dat? Awright, gwan home now. Run!"

As they let him go and he scrambled to his feet, the man duppy spoke for the first time: "Lawd God, Suzie Q, di bwoy a-bleed! Look how di bwoy a-bleed! Jesus Christ, yu ever si nutten like dat?"

He did not look behind him. Halfway along the path he met his mother searching for him, frantic, and he ran to her and was scooped up, mud, red-gushing knees, and all, and held so tight he could not breathe. His legs locked around her and she carried him home.

This was when his mother's already dwindling excursions to the river finally almost stopped because he no longer liked to go, though he would not tell her why. But on the few occasions that for one reason or another they had no choice but to go, Suzie Q no longer led a war against Rachel. Instead she said good morning with surly, downcast eyes, and from this time forward Moshe's appearance was not commented on by any of the women, and he was left alone. But he was afraid to look in the direction of Miss Suzie because he could feel her eyes on him, inimical and secret, willing him to silence. He understood that she was making an incredible exchange: his safety and his mother's freedom from harassment in return for his silence.

Rachel surmised that he had had an encounter with the colony of ghosts who had set up kitchen under the ceiba cotton tree and were famous for their wanderings and cantankerous interrogation of children walking alone as much as for their cooking. She anointed him with oil and put the psalm of protection, number 91, on his head for a period of three days and three nights until he slept without dreams.

This was his first encounter with fear, and the occasion on which he added an ability to keep secrets to the store of competencies he acquired from being alone. He had no idea what it was he was supposed to have seen, or who the man was who had held him down with Suzie Q or where he came from, or what the dark object they had pulled on the ground among the trees was, and after a while he forgot almost all of it except for the memory of the strong smell that remained in his nostrils, the odor of crab soup.

In the nights while the little boy slept, Rachel stood over him, searching his face for signs of the face she had seen that first day she hid him in her shawl. Driven by fear that it might come back, she scrolled him like a book, but the child's features remained the same as how they had appeared after she prayed, as if a veil, not made with hands, had been drawn over the former face and sent it deep within to hide behind his bones.

"We praise thee, O Yahweh of might and glory," Rachel murmured over her son, using the same voice that in the morning she would use to curse her husband like a slave.

CHAPTER IV

i

The summer before Moshe went to school, Rachel took Suzie Q's advice and tried to give him some color by anointing him with castor oil, mixing it for soft with aloe (castor oil was known for its harshness), and sitting him, not in the direct sun, but in the lee of it, on the half-shaded verandah. She thought of using molasses, but did not want to run the risk since molasses was a stage in the making of sugar, and she did not know how it would interact with his allergy.

Noah, on the other hand, swore by molasses, which he called the johncrow batty of sugar. "A fi wi part a di sugar dat," he quipped, "jus like how di johncrow batty a fi wi part-a di rum. It well strong, das why backra cyaan manage it. A Yahweh gif to poor people. Yu nuh si how it thick an black like sufferation? Rub di bwoy wid di molasses."

"Him a half backra, so mi cyaan put it pon him," Rachel retorted, measuring out the castor oil. She did not say, *Look how long mi a-gi yu molasses fi drink an yu nuh better.* In truth, he had not got worse either.

"All-a wi a half backra," Noah said, laughing his feral laugh. "Backra cloth, backra book, backra hospital." He pronounced it *aasspital*, mockingly drawing out the long *a*. "Wi kotch inna all-a dem. Even yu grung wha yu plant, look long enough, yu si wheh backra siddung in deh, chap him ten. Ongle ting, a nuh backra sea." We are all halflings, and all our halves belong to backra. We settle on the edge of our possessions. Even where you farm, look close, look softly, under the leaves, there he crouches, legs crossed in relaxation. But the wide sea escapes his conquest.

"Yu tink yu escape backra because yu a fisherman? Heh. Nuh bi so sure. A over sea him walk come tief."

"A under sea shark bite him."

"All dat palaver well an good, Noah Fisher, but it nuh put coco inna pot." Talk is easy, but it cannot solve a practical problem. "Di coconut oil nah work an mi nah gi him di molasses. Story done."

Noah counseled patience, and indeed by the end of the summer the boy's blue edges had given way to a more opaque texture of skin, like clotted cream. But his front hair acquired a reddish tinge, like carrots, and it worried her that this might be worse than blond, so she stopped the treatments.

On the first day of school, he saw again the children from the riverside, their hands gripped in their mothers' hands to prevent them darting away or getting lost, like mislaid parcels. They greeted him with exhilaration: "Koo blue boy! Blue boy, yu come-a school? Mi come-a school too. Look mi slate."

Shyly, overjoyed, he showed his own slate, and his new slate pencil, standing close against his mother.

Others, seeing him for the first time, stared. One boy, who had been removing his suck-finger intermittently from his mouth so he could weep at intervals in terror at this new experience called school, stopped crying and sucking his thumb, both, and opened his eyes wide.

Among the first-day crowds of mothers and children milling in the yard, hunting for classrooms, registration rooms, friends, pencils, exercise books lost, dropped, or snatched in the confusion, not half as many as might otherwise have done so noticed Rachel's son. Still, curious strangers gathered around him. These were older children who had come by themselves, or were escorting their younger siblings. Some of the new children walked with their faces turned backward like douen, staring in his direction as their mothers urged them on, hastening to get registered before the crowd of new applicants got too large and the best seats, in the front of the class, near the teacher, were taken.

For the second time in his life Moshe felt fear. He was overcome by the stares, the shy and bold questions directed to his mother about him—his lineage, his looks, why he had two different-colored eyes and two different hair, which fascinated them even more than his milky skin which was like no skin they had ever seen; why she had pressed the front of his hair but not the back, why his hair was pressed in the first place when he was not a girl, could he speak, what was his name, the origin of his strangeness, what class he was going to be in—and he struggled not to cry. But no one mocked him; it was not their habit to be rude in front of adults, and moreover, many were only curious, or puzzled.

His mother admonished them in a stern voice: "Him is jus an ordinary boy, him jus look different from the rest of you. I don't want any of you to tease him or trouble him, because if you trouble him I am going to the head teacher and your parents."

"Yes, miss."

"Yes, Miss Rachel, ma'am."

And some, thinking from her sternness and her deliberate use of (near) English that she was one of the teachers, said, "Yes, Teacher. Yes, Miss Teacher, ma'am."

To him, his mother said, "Don't come home widout mi. If school over an yu don't si mi, wait inna yu teacher Miss Yvette class. Yu hear mi? Shi know everyting bout yu an shi wi tek care-a yu till mi come. I talk to her aready. Yu stay wid her, because mi nuh want nobody trouble yu. Yu hear mi?"

"Yes, Mama."

Rachel crossed herself, Psalm 32:7, and departed.

Relief flooded him at last; he wasn't the only one who was strange. And now it was a good strange, a happy strange. The teacher made him read in the Nola book and he read it from beginning to end. She made him read another, and another, her brow puckering more and more each time he did. It was the same with the large girl in socks and shoes.

Most of the other children wore their bare feet or cheap sneakers; we called them puss boot, softly, softly, walk softly, nobody can hear you coming. These sneakers made a noise only when it rained and children wearing them gleefully plunged their feet in the culverts and temporary waterfalls. They could hear their feet go squish, squish, squiddish as the water worked its way out through the tops and sides of the sneakers. This was what Moshe wore, puss boot, but also socks, unlike most of the other puss boot wearers, who had no socks. The large girl, she was very large, wore real shoes and socks, and her uniform pleats seemed sharper than everyone else's, as if they had been cut out with a blade before being starched and ironed. He felt in a vague sort of way that she was rich, though he was not quite sure what rich was.

He read for the teacher, three different Nola books, each the reading book for a higher grade. The large girl did the same. Most of the other children knew their phonics and their ABCs, a few could read several words of the first book, or use their phonics to spell out some words, but only he and the large girl were able to read everything. She read like someone talking, so that the words in the books sounded real. "Stay, mother, stay. You cannot go. You must stay at home with Baby Bob." He had never heard anyone read like that before. He, on the other hand, read as if he were singing, because the words seemed to him like the sound of his mother chanting psalms. He nodded his head to the rhythm of his reading. "This is Nola. This is Mother. This is Father. This is Baby Bob. This is Baby Bob, Baby Bob, baby," improvising repetitions that were not in the book.

"You two are way ahead of A class," the beginners' class, the teacher said, and called Man-Teacher's wife, who was teaching across the room, behind the first partition. Man-Teacher's wife came and together she and the A class teacher listened to the rest of their reading, his and the large girl's. Man-Teacher's wife said something short, sharp, and brisk to their teacher, who made them get up from their benches and, taking them by their hands, one in each of hers, led them past the partition where Man-Teacher's wife taught the B class, the second graders, straight over to the second partition to where a slight, slender man with a small waist taught the First class, the third graders.

Their teacher spoke to the slender-waisted man-teacher, and he moved three children who were sitting at a desk in the front to a desk near the back, and made Moshe and the large girl sit there together instead. No third child was put beside them, although the benches were made for three.

He missed his teacher, even after so short a time. She was beautiful, like his mother, and though she was stern she was kind. He did not know how this man-teacher would be.

The man-teacher did not teach as well as Miss Yvette. He beat a lot more, when the children made noise. Miss Yvette did not beat at all. The man-teacher did not beat Moshe or the large girl. They both found the lessons easy, and finished all their work on time, and did not speak. Whenever he came around to inspect what the children were doing in their exercise books, he halted by their desk, Moshe and the large girl's, with a strange hesitancy, his beating strap hung up relaxed around his shoulder, and smiled and passed on without saying anything. He took away their slates, and gave them free issue exercise books and a lead pencil each, to write with. Only children in the A class wrote on slates. Children in the B class used exercise books with small lines. In the First class they graduated to regular exercise books with big lines. The exercise books the man-teacher gave Moshe and the large girl on their first day had small lines. In-between lines, Moshe thought to himself.

He found that he loved school, and was afraid of it. The vast concatenation into which the noise of children learning resolved itself, like a soup into which many ingredients had fallen, was to him like a rumor from another world. Sometimes it was the clamor of a great town awake in the morning and sleepless at midnight. But sometimes again it came like the chorus of an everlasting hymn that, spilling out across the open doorways and partitions and what seemed to him the endless schoolyard, melded the whole school together in one solid sheet of praise.

The singing sound of the school both estranged and hugged him close. He was afraid of its largeness and the big children who stared at him and whispered, yet everything felt so warm when he sat down to do his work or when he held a book in his hands, the reading book or the arithmetic book; it was like being in a good cave, nice like cotton and most lovely to the touch. He felt he was living in a place of adventure that he had always known. And becoming part of that mighty hum of children learning, in which he himself was silent, with the large girl sitting silently beside him, he felt that he would die of happiness.

When the bell rang for recess, all the children except he and the large girl seemed to know what to do. They filed out in an orderly fashion, the man-teacher keeping watch in case anyone decided to rush or straggle out of line. Once they hit the top step, the rush could not be contained and they poured into the yard, screaming, yelling, joyfully free for a whole half hour. Moshe and the large girl filed out too, lagging behind because they did not know what to do.

They stood on the top step.

"A lunchtime?" he asked her shyly.

The large girl shook her head. "No, a recess time. Yu suppose to go play."

"Oh." He digested this news, wondering who he was supposed to play with. Most of the children were playing in the yard; a few were sitting or standing, animated, in corners under shade trees.

"Yu want one paradise plum?" She pushed her hand in her pocket, pulled out two of the bright orange–and–red sweets, and offered him one.

"Mi cyaan eat paradise plum, because i' have in sugar an i' wi kill mi."

She accepted this without question, popped one of the sweets into her mouth, and put one back. "Mi have bubby plum too. Yu want one?"

He nodded, shy, happy, and at the same time relieved that he could accept something that she offered. He didn't want her to feel bad, or think that he was being proud, not eating from strangers. She was not a stranger. Her name was Arrienne. In his mind he called her Arrii, because she was his friend.

She gave him the bubby plums, a handful of the dark red–and–green fruit which he loved, and pulled out another handful for herself from the seeming cornucopia in her uniform pocket.

He did not know how they came to be walking down the steps together holding each other's hands. A boy shouted as they passed, "How dat deh bwoy look so funny? Hey, dundus boy!" and she said, "Don't answer him. Jus come on," and as she pulled him, her fingers urgent on his, they walked across the yard and found themselves, suddenly, abruptly, beside the chicken coop with the bench standing in front of it. They had come to the back of the premises and though it had taken them no more than three minutes as adults count, it seemed to them as if they had walked for a long time. To children, distances, like the passage of time, are different.

At lunchtime, those children whose parents could afford the daily or weekly payment ate at the school canteen; others went home where nobody knew if all they had was a bulla and cold water or a mug of brebidge—beverage, the drink made from sugar, water, and Seville orange or lime—with maybe a bright-red or yellow cashew fruit crushed into it for added flavor. A few who had hoarded their pennies and halfpence crossed the road to Miss Caro's shop and bought sweets and snacks: paradise plums, drops, grater cake, bulla or peg bread, jackass corn, bus' mi jaw, police button, cobbla, and the exquisite morsels of saltfish fritter dripping in coconut oil that they called achee, flittaz, or stamp-and-go. His mother brought him his lunch so he would not have to walk home in the sun, but also because she wanted to make sure he was not being teased. She found him waiting with the large girl in the canteen, where the large girl was getting stew beef and cornmeal dumplings made strong and tight, for her lunch.

"A mi fren dis, Mama," he said, introducing them shyly. "Shi name Arrii-Arrienne." He gave her his special friend name, Arrii, as well as her full name, her right name, just in case.

With enigmatic eyes, his mother surveyed the large girl. "Yu a Miss Dulsie daughter?"

The large girl nodded her head yes.

Rachel did not rebuke her for shaking her head at an adult. Instead she asked, "An Maas George Christie a yu fadda?"

The large girl nodded again yes.

His mother looked at the large girl for a long moment, and he could not read his mother's eyes. The expression in the large girl's eyes was not afraid as she looked back at his mother. It was frank and open and unwavering, and afterward, when he was old enough to understand the meaning of the word, he said it was without guile. His mother's look at the large girl was strange—it was a dawning look of wonder, and reserve, and an odd relief.

"Mi wi tek care-a him mek nobody nuh trouble him, Miss Rachel," Moshe said, when the introductions were over. He didn't know how he knew it was what his new friend was thinking, or how he came to say it in her voice, like a ventriloquist's double, or how he knew that she had sent him her words and given him permission to say them, but that was what he did, and the large girl seemed satisfied.

His mother did not say anything, but the look of wonder remained on her face when she told them goodbye and left.

Years later, he knew that this beginning of speaking each other's words was not the real beginning of their twinship. That began from the beginning, when they were able to read without error the same books on the first day of school.

In the evening he disobeyed his mother. He did this not intentionally, but because he didn't know what else to do. Miss Yvette had

removed him from her class and put him in the man-teacher's class—
the man-teacher's name was Mr. Brown—and he thought Miss Yvette
had forgotten him, and since she was no longer his teacher he was
ashamed to remind her that his mother had said he should stay with
her until his mother came to collect him. But school had dismissed
earlier than the time set, and he now had a friend, the large girl, his
friend Arrienne, to walk on the road with him, and so, after the bell
rang for dismissal and the whole school had stood up and sung the
evening hymn and chanted the prayers in unison, and another bell,
the final bell, was rung, Man-Teacher holding it high to make a small,
apologetic *ting* as the last echoes of prayer died away, as though
Man-Teacher were apologizing to God for making a secular sound at
such a holy moment—after all this had taken place, he put his hand in
the hand of his friend and together they walked out of the schoolyard
through the front gate.

That evening she fought the first of the fights she was to fight on
his behalf.

The memory of the scary morning came back in full force at the
sight of the big boy running in the road. He was throwing a foootball
to another boy and the two of them leaped to catch it, while other
children scattered out of its way.

And the boy shouted his question of the morning again, "How
dat-deh bwoy look so funny, like smaddy bwile him?" and his friend,
snickering, called out, "Bwile baby!" How strange he looks, as if he
has been boiled!

The friend was pleased with his own wit. Exhilarated, he cried,
shouting into the air as he leaped after the thrown ball, "An him look
like maggish too, enuh, bwile maggish!" And moreover he looks like
maggots, a nest of boiled maggots, communicable abominations.

The other screamed with laughter. "Maggish bwoy!" He bounced
the ball over to the two silent children walking hand in hand. The
other big boy followed. They planted themselves in the middle of the
road, blocking Moshe and the large girl. The two children's hands
tightened in each other. The large girl pulled Moshe aside and continued on, walking along the side of the road.

The first boy, the boy with the ball, pushed Moshe in his chest.

"Pickni, a wha do yu? A wheh yu come from? Mi know bout yu. A yu a di white man baby wha Miss Rachel find inna Ora bush."

"Tek yu hand offa him," Moshe said, in the large girl's voice.

"Yu want mi put it pon yu instead?" The boy chucked her in her chest. He thought Arrienne had spoken.

The large girl let go of Moshe's hand and dropped her books on the ground, the free issue exercise book and the reading book the teacher had loaned her for the day because her first teacher had put her in a different class. She took off her uniform belt and pushed Moshe behind her, and then she bent in the classic elementary school fighting pose, a crouching position like a wrestler, legs splayed wide, imaginary sleeves rolled up, arms cocked and fists at the ready, and she danced on her feet and brandished her fists like a boxer, and Moshe did not know what happened after that except that a sudden host of children appeared and began screaming, "Fight! Fight!" and jumping up and down and pushing and craning to see who would win, and the crowd quickly swelled and the screams changed to, "Murder! Two pon one a murder!" and then again to, "Woie, woie, di gal a-win! Di gal a-kill dem-bwoy wid licks, wid kicks, di girl a-karate di bwoy-dem, yu ever si gal karate, rahtid, a John Wayne, a Stewart Granger, bwoy oonu dead now, oonu bitch oonu dead now!" and several of them ran back down the road calling out for Man-Teacher, Man-Teacher, and suddenly Man-Teacher was there and so was Mr. Brown, and the two boys were being held by the seat of their pants by Man-Teacher and Mr. Brown, and Man-Teacher was demanding to know what had happened, and the crowd of excited children were chorusing to tell the story, but Moshe and Arrienne stood there not speaking, though Arrienne was panting hard as if she had run a very long race, and her uniform belt and one of her shoes were missing and dirt was on her face and one of her knuckles was bleeding, and one of the girls found her shoe and helped her put it back on her foot, and the two boys were all swollen in their faces and one of them was holding the front of his pants and crying, and Man-Teacher said Arrienne and Moshe could go home, and he and Mr. Brown made the two boys walk back toward the school with Man-Teacher and his cane and Mr. Brown in their wake, holding them by the backs of their pants so they could not run away, and it was over and the crowd of children were chattering with awe and excitement and wanting to know where the large girl learned karate like that, and someone said her father, Maas George, was a karate king, a black belt, from when he was in the Royal Air Force in England, and someone else said did you know di two of dem bright-bright, teacher skip dem today, put dem in First class, and another one said him a dundus but him bright-bright, and someone offered to walk them home, but Arrienne shook her head no and some of the children tried to walk them home, to spread the news and see what their mothers and fathers would do, but Arrienne-Moshe said, "Mi nuh want no tail backa mi," and the children who were offering stepped back, and Arrienne took Moshe's hand and walked with him home to his mother.

"Si mi car' him home, Miss Rachel," Arrienne said.

"Mi wi come fi him a mawnin," Moshe said in Arrii-Arrienne's voice, speaking Arrii-Arrienne's words. I will fetch him again in the morning. Always I will fetch him in the morning.

And she waved goodbye and left.

And the morning and the evening were the first day.

iii

She never asked him why he looked the way he did. She never asked him where he came from. And though she spoke, on average, more words than he, she hardly spoke any words at all, and those only to him, when they were alone, and mostly she placed the words in his head, so that they came out at his mouth, in her voice.

CHAPTER V

i

This is how princesses are born: Relatives gather, from far and near, and the princess is tested to see whether lying on a seed will make her black-and-blue. If she feels the seed's pressure under twenty skeins of new silk, over twenty mattresses piled on a box bed, you know she is a true princess.

Princess always born without skin.

When Arrienne was born, she went through many tests, though at the time it was not clear how many, since some tests were wrapped inside other tests and yet others inside those others. Some were immediate and apparent, and others belonged to the future, but their seed was inside the others, the way a fetus is inside its mother or future generations are inside those of the past.

The first test was when Arrienne's father pronounced a verdict: "Is not mine, is jacket."

His relatives came, led by his mother, but not to bring gifts. They came to inspect the baby for proof of false paternity, a posse of ten and every one a witch, eight female and two males. Some of them could not read a book but they could scroll a child like it was a book leaf, and there was no sign written in flesh, no fine vein-print, that they couldn't spell out with a moving finger: the way a baby turned its head, a certain cast in the eyes, the way the toes curled or the fingers made themselves into fists—anything, no matter how minute, they could look at and tell you if the newborn was one of theirs, and whose it was, if it was not. Never mind that the mother could have been forgiven if at the outset she failed to recognize her own offspring among a dozen others, since babies are almost always born nondescript. Fun and joke aside, how many babies have the same old man's wrinkled face, the same funny-looking head, misshapen from being haul-and-pulled-about by nature or forceps or midwife or doctor's hands, or by all of the above, on their hazardous journey to the outside? All of them!

But this Christie clan was a different breed of genealogical detective, massy mi massa, massy mi God. They brought to their private investigations a clairvoyance, a special faculty, that you might call self-righteous but Tumelans call frigging facetyness.

Still, in truth, the princess Arrienne was not a nondescript baby, which meant that she was singularly readable as a newborn. She was of an unusual largeness, weighing in at ten pounds nine ounces, almost killing her mother on her way down the birth canal, and for a long period she continued in this way, growing without let or permission of her aghast elders until she reached the age of eighteen, when she became six feet one inch tall and suddenly stopped growing. Because she was a female, this height appeared more than it really was, and it created a great disturbance because it meant she was unlikely to attract any man in a country of mainly small and average-sized men.

The princess Arrienne was moreover excessively pigmented, her skin even at birth the color of the wettest molasses, with a purple tinge under the surface. This purple had an elusive quality not unlike the blue that people sometimes glimpsed like a halo around the edges of Moshe Fisher's skin.

Later in life this contributed to her extraordinary good looks, as did her large bones and excessively thick hair, which was also very black with a rich purple tinge, and which, years after she stopped combing it, lay on her shoulders like hemp that had been twisted and then unmade and let loose. There was so much of it on the infant—not only was her head covered in the soft curly mass, but her arms and legs were brushed by a purplish down—that she could have been mistaken for a toddler of two-three years, a female King Richard with premature hair instead of teeth.

Nobody in George Christie's family had the skin color that was found on the little princess. The hair was worse, since all the Christies were dry-head. Nor were her bold Maroon face and unaccountably Arawak nose in any way Christie attributes: the Christies were Red Ibo—and I mean well red, ginger red, red-nigger red, with faces that seemed to have been painted on a flat surface, barely present and oddly receding, so one had the impression that the normal protrusions—nose, eyebrow, mouth-lip, eyelids—were disappearing by increments, as if the family had invented its own personal evolutionary process which was moving toward a physiognomy of a different kind.

Well then, the child's byzantine skin (purple-black!) and crude size were living proof, without investigating further, that there was not a Christie bone in her body. The relatives were outraged that the mother had had the effrontery to call George's name, and for a moment it seemed as though the case was going to end in disaster.

"Tell di gal fi go find her pickni rightful puppa and stop call George name."

"I know the mother well black, but no child who have Christie blood ever look like this. No matter what, if it was George child, the blood, the color would dilute."

One of the male seers, embarrassed by the knowledge of his own sexual proclivities, felt compelled to fairness: "It must be true him had dealings with her, for if him never go to school him name couldn't call," adding sheepishly so the others could barely hear him, "but it look to me like shi mistaken."

"Shut yu mouth, Ronald," a sister-witch commanded in righteous wrath. "You don't know nutten. Jus because yu run up an down di countryside widout boots so enny old fowl can call yu name with hinpunity don't mean everybody is di same."

But the grandmother, Mama Mai, was a better pedigree sleuth than all the rest of the family put together. With patient trawling over the baby's skin (that is to say, by dint of haul-an-pulling the woman's child), she discovered two indisputable marks of her son on the princess's immeasurably tender parts.

First, Arrienne all of a sudden began demonstrating a way of screwing her little mouth shut that gave her a very bloody-minded look, the exact mark of George's stubbornness, the scale of which his mother had found ineffable when he was a boy growing up. Mama Mai frequently said her son George was stubborn to stupidness. Now she let out a loud cackle. "Stiffnecked as mule batty, when mule decide fi siddung an don' move, no matter how yu bawl out, *Skuya! Skuya!*" Stubborn as a mule's arse, no matter how hard you shout or hit its backside. This one will devour her mother and father. Move over, Biswas.

Secondly, on the little naked bottom, so tiny that any eyes except a woman's trained in decades of finding fault with other women's daughters' offspring, would have missed it: the green-and-yellow-striped birthmark looking like a piece of sugarcane that had been cut off at the joint. It was the family mark. Every member of the Christie family had it, and at intervals, like a heraldic flag it flared up an angry tomato red and they could not sit on their buttocks. For this reason, the Christie homes were known for their beautiful embroidered cushions.

Mightily pleased with her own skillfulness, the grandmother emitted another gleeful cackle, rose up, and dusted off her hands, one, two, brisk, brisk. "See it dere! A George pickni. Jus like every one a oonu Christie, gal a-go fart fire when moon rise. Case close. Cetlyn, explain to di mumma seh shi haffi mek di baby sleep pon har belly when moon shine becausen shi cyaan lie down pon har back dem-deh time. Especially inna Augus, when cane crop." Cetlyn, tell the mother to lie her on her stomach when the moon rises, especially in the month of August, cane-crop month, the cruelest month, for twenty silk rolls will not alleviate the pain she will feel from that candy-striped pictogram that blooms on her royal ass. "Oonu come."

The princess was redeemed, the case happily closed, and the witches departed, leaving gifts of money, clothing, and a large plastic dolly baby with blond plastic hair and china-blue eyes. When Arrienne was old enough to play with the doll, she gouged out its eyes so that they hung downward on the string which had been hidden against its belly under its frilly pink crinoline. The string was attached to the eyes by some complicated inner contraption and, when pulled, caused the doll to cry out, "I love you, I love you, I love you," in a high squeaking voice. After the eyes were gouged, the doll never spoke again.

It was the first and the last doll that Arrienne was ever given.

This was because, from her earliest years, her father set out to make her into a boy.

Having proven by relative that the baby was his in spirit and buttock, George sought to reward Arrienne's mother (her name was Dulsie Sweet) with his hand in marriage, but Dulsie was fiercely in love with her freedom and mortally enraged that George had not only accused her, but permitted his relatives to invade her home on their ridiculous errand of discovery. She could not forget how they had searched her daughter's private parts as if they were surveyors and her child a parcel of land that they were mapping. So, with some choice bumbocloths that made Rachel's language look holy, she turned him down. George married another woman, Purity Malcolm (who was superblack like Dulsie, but docile), and contented himself with playing such a major role in his last-born daughter's life that, as her mother said, she might as well have grown up in his house, since she spent more time there than at Dulsie's, where she supposedly lived. That was before the pull of Rachel's house, because of Moshe. That princess had no allegiances except to her own obsessions. In that, she acknowledges now, she was a true princess.

So everything about Arrienne was different: her size, her color as a member of the Christie clan, her unusual black beauty, the hair on her body, her upbringing like a boy, her unusual intellect (which was all the more outstanding in a family that was famously dunce). But the thing about her that the Christies considered most different was the thing that made her most fit into the clan: the pea-sized cane-striped birthmark that would hurt her in August even with cushions under her.

The next thing I have to explain is very important in the history of this sugar, so listen well, and I am speaking slowly. This is the essential difference between Moshe Fisher and Arrienne Christie, who was later to become his twin: that Rachel and Noah brought up their son to cope with his difference by never speaking to him about it, so that he never knew it existed, or, if he knew, was not aware that it was bad until people outside told him so; whereas Arrienne was taught from the time that she could walk that her Christie difference was important and that it would both harm and save her, for it would make her tough as hell. Between the two of them, I would say she had the best of it, but in later life she came to believe that her differences caused her great harm, since because of their differentness Moshe continued to take her for his twin, when she had come to think of him as a lover.

George Christie was, by the standards of those days, a man of the world. He was over forty years old, much older than Arrienne's mother, who was nineteen when Arrienne was born. He had fought for the British in World War II as a paratrooper, and this alone made him, if not a celebrity, at least a set-apart figure in Tumela. He returned from the war with a peg leg and a story of his adventures that sounded like an invention from the fantastical town of Ora-on-Sea.

ii

The narrative of Flight Lieutenant George Horatio Hannibal St. Aloysius Christie, being the father of the princess Arrienne, in which he was captured by the Japanese when his plane crash-landed at a place called Changi, near the sea at Singapore.

There, in Changi, George was tortured and starved until he and two comrades, both white men, doctors, were able to escape by bribing one of the Japanese guards with fake pills to cure gonorrhea, but the pills were only aspirin rolled in rice paste. At some point in their long trek through the countryside he got separated from his comrades, whom he never saw or heard from again. A woman of the villages took him in and hid him for three hundred days, during which she fed and nursed him back to health. And to pass the time in the long, dark winter evenings alone on a moor where the house they lived in was the only one for miles around, in a place of perpetual twilight where the sky, grass, earth, and stones were shades of Prussian blue, she taught him this martial art, tae kwon do, which Tumela people had never heard of, so they called it karate, one of the martial arts names they were familiar with from Hollywood films shown on reel-to-reel discs in the district piazzas on celebration nights—Independence Eve, Christmas Eve, or any day the traveling cinema passed through.

This woman, according to George's story, had been taught this form of self-defense by her father, a widower from Korea. He had taught her this in a country where it was forbidden to teach women such things, but he was afraid that one day when he was not there soldiers would break in, and this was the only way she could defend herself. One day the woman's father mysteriously disappeared from their village, leaving her alone to fend for herself. It was thought that the soldiers took him. This tae kwon do that George learned from the woman who had been taught by her father was what he began teaching his daughter from the time she was three years old.

Arrienne's father also told another story of how he was rescued, almost by accident, when the woman—he called her Chanioon—went into the village to buy supplies and heard that the war was over. She saw prisoners of war being evacuated, and came and told him. She was crying bitterly, because she did not want him to leave, but he kissed and calmed her by promising to return, though he knew he would not.

When he got to the village he found everything as she had said. He gave himself up to the British officers who had come to release the POWs and take them to England, where, he said, he could have stayed, but he was not treated all that much better there than he had been treated in Japan, only in England it was because of his color, not his enemy status, that he was not treated well, and this was something he could not wrap his mind around, after he had fought for the mother country in the war and been taken prisoner in her service, so he chose to come home, but only after he had stayed enough years in London to accumulate a tidy enough sum of money to take more disgrace out of his eye than his mere war medals could. To return home without money was self-incriminating—it proved beyond a shadow of doubt that you had not really been to the war but had hidden out somewhere for the whole duration and come back trying to lampse people you hoped were naive enough to believe that you had fought and won medals.

The story in the district was that George's veteran's pension was sent to him on a regular basis, and it was this that kept the Christies a cut above their neighbors, who did much of their buying and selling by barter, for in those days, the 1940s (which was when George came home, not when his princess daughter was born—that came much later), money was a scarce-scarce commodity among the rural folk. The Christies were only the least poor among the poor, but they were considered rich because of this so-called pension, which came in pounds, not shillings or pence, and the family was happy to keep up the image and to make sure that no illegitimate (person of wrongful paternity, jacket-child) was able to slip crabways into their ranks.

In truth, the much-vaunted pension promised by the British War Office was a pipe dream for George as it was for the majority of his black comrades. Most of them who survived were given twenty-eight pounds for the voyage home. If they opted to stay in England, as George did for a while, they didn't receive anything except bus fare, and not even that if they could foot it to their destination. But George's skills acquired in the Air Force and his demobilization rank as a flight pilot opened postwar job opportunities for him in the great project of rebuilding the cities of the mother country that even then was devolving into Little England for its sins—though England did not know it, Rachel said, predicting how England would become a small island in a book of that name—and then of course it became Little London after the Brexit vote.

The pay he got was fairly decent, though it was less than two-thirds of the earnings of a white engineer with the same qualifications and workload. Careful husbandry and shrewd investment earned him enough to retire in four years and, once back in Jamaica, purchase cane-land and tractors, as well as a fleet of market trucks (two at the outset, but he soon acquired more) in which he or his foreman transported market women on Fridays and Saturdays for a satisfactory fee.

This was all the "pension" he ever had, but George could not convince the district otherwise, even if he had tried, which he didn't. The mother country stood by its own; this was what Tumela people learned in school; it was written in the books, and since the books never lied, George was getting an RAF pension and was quite filthily rich, but blasted mean.

It did not take long for the obvious question to occur to Princess Arrienne: the question of what other dance, besides the martial dance of tae kwon do, her father had danced with the woman of the East, for she knew him to be a great womanizer, and growing up in a place where dogs did that sort of thing in the streets, she was not unaware of the happenings between women and men. Her father was very forthcoming; it was a matter of pride to him, though also of regret, that he had left behind in the womb proof of his strong manhood, which the woman Chanioon had welcomed though she knew it would cause her further isolation on the abandoned moor.

Arrienne often thought with wonder of this brother or sister whom she did not know, who seemed a figure of dream but was also real. She wondered if this sibling of hers had lived, or was alive. The thought that he might be dead rendered him more real than the thought that he might be alive: it seemed to her, even at a young age, that the one human emotion that could put a face on a stranger was sorrow, and as soon as she thought that her sibling was dead she was able to give him a face, and a gender, because the thought of his death made her cry, and then she knew he must be a brother, not a sister, for she had no brothers and she felt that if this sibling in the East had been a sister, Moshe would have come as a girl. For once she heard her father's story, she was convinced Moshe had come as a replacement for the one she had lost.

It never occurred to her that she might have some siblings in England, given her father's reputation for womanizing. He never spoke about any women he met in the years he spent there. But listening to his story of how he was treated and why he chose to come back home so she could be born, she determined that this was where she would stay—she would never go to a place where her father was treated as though he was not a person, though if she did end up in such a place, she would fight.

Like Moshe, she was brought up alone, for her mother had no other children, and though her father had a reputed bevy of daughters, they were all much older than she was, grown women with their own households, all of them by different mothers, none by his wife Purity, who was past childbearing age when they married. Arrienne was the attaclaps, the unexpected arrival long after malicious rumor decided that diabetes had put paid to George's powers and his ability to roam among Tumela's young maidens.

Her father taught her the martial art because he too mourned the son that he imagined, and because he thought of Arrienne as his surrogate son, but especially because he looked at her great size and thought that she would go through life encountering grief for having the body size of a man. He felt that in giving her the skills that went with her kind of bones, he was giving her the most sensible gift a father could give: the ability to defend herself from advantage-tekkers. This decision might have seemed to an onlooker quite contrary, for he took equal pains to bring her up a lady, paying particular attention to her deportment, which he fostered by making her walk around rooms with books balanced on her head, as the upper classes made their girlchildren do, her hands straight at her sides, her back and wide shoulders upright, and her rather rounded stomach pulled in (for she was a chubby as well as a tall child), and in this way she attained the posture of a queen, and great unself-consciousness about her height. (Other Tumela girls, like Rachel, acquired this same posture by carrying kerosene tins, wash pans, provision baskets, and buckets of water on their heads, but Arrienne, being a princess, never carried any of those.)

Her father saw early that she was unusually gifted, and he thought that this too would put her at a disadvantage with men, not in Tumela (for among the poor, intellect was admired regardless of the sex of the body it was housed in) but in the more privileged world outside with which he was well acquainted and where he intended his daughter to make her mark. He planned for her to have access to the world of learning to the uttermost degree. She was to have a career, and with it, total independence, so if no man married her she would be quite fine, and if any man married her he would know not to mess with a woman who knew how to earn her bread and butter. And like Moshe, he called her Arrii; this sounded more like a man's name than Arrienne. Arrii was a name almost like Harry, especially if you pronounced words the Tumela way, without haitches.

So her father encouraged her in her voracious love of reading, driving her in his haulage truck to the branch library in Jericho, where they borrowed books for her in his name as well as hers so that she could have extra ones to read. In this way she seldom ran short of food for what was becoming, without his realizing it, a morbid appetite. And when on her seventh birthday he took her on a trip to Ora-on-Sea and she spied a great big illustrated book in a drugstore window, *The Crackerjack Girls' Own Book*, which she made him buy with the last shillings in his pocket, he began the practice, unusual among the book-loving-but-insolvent poor, of buying books for his daughter to keep.

In his own house, up to this point, George had had a total of three books: a paperback copy of the Jamaican constitution (our country had gained independence in the year Moshe and Arrienne were four and five years old); a water-stained volume of *Das Capital* which someone had given him on board the ship on which he sailed from England; and a strange volume that he allowed no one to touch, though Arrienne was allowed to look at it where it occupied pride of place on a shelf in the glass-fronted cabinet where chinaware was kept.

It was a large clothbound book, handwritten, it seemed, in Chinese calligraphy (but it was in fact Korean), on the finest silk cloth, each page luminous and glutted with embroidered scenes from the stories that were told in the writing nobody in Tumela could read. The colors of the embroidery and the ink drew the child like a spell: she could often be found kneeling in front of the cabinet, her nose pressed up against the glass, her open mouth breathing mist that clouded the glass but could not diminish the glow of colors that bled into each other on the exquisite page. Every morning, at her beseeching, her father unlocked the cabinet and turned the book to a new page so that she could see a different set of embroidered drawings, and in this way, deciphering the pictures, she made up the stories she thought lay like secret treasure in the book. She called it *The Book of Things.*

The contents of her father's library were unusual for this one thing: he did not possess a copy of the Bible, the one book that every household in Tumela had a copy of. It was used in all matters of the spirit, or necromancy or magic, though only in the case of the spirit was it thought necessary to read its actual words. After three years of experience with war, George did not believe there was any such thing as a god, so he kept no religious book in his house.

On the days when her father was too busy to take her to Jericho, and her cache of books ran low, Arrienne wrestled with these three books that she did not understand (the words of two and the embroideries of the other), without any inkling of the role they would later play in her separation from Moshe and indeed her entire personal fate. What she read in them tied her to the place where she and Moshe were born as surely as his dreams of elsewhere pushed Moshe inside the hold of the cargo ship on which he would sail away to the other side of paradise.

There was one other kind of reading that Arrienne was exposed to before she was six, and this was an experience that Moshe also had: the Sunday newspaper, which the telegram boy brought on his bicycle, at erratic times between dawn and duskfall. Arrienne appointed herself the job of waylaying him at her father's gate, the sixpence (later the five cents) that was to pay him clutched tight in her hand. Her heart pumped first with fear that she might turn her head in the wrong direction for a split-second and he would pass by unnoticed, and then with excruciating joy when the bicycle appeared around the corner, the telegram boy riding at top speed on the rutted road with both hands off the handlebars, singing out, *"Glean-er! Glean-er!"* the name of the newspaper, to announce his passing.

Rachel too bought the Sunday paper. Whosoever could read or

had children old enough to read for them bought the Sunday paper. Only the well-off (by Tumela standards) bought on the other days. Men, and indecent women who could not read or buy, assembled in the shoemaker's shop during the week to have the paper read to them. Women who were too decent to congregate in shops with the leggo beasts but were just as poor or illiterate depended on the bush-telegraph and the radio, theirs or their neighbors', for news of the outside world.

In one trembling motion, the princess would seize the paper and thrust the sixpence into the telegram boy's hand. Then she would flee to her room to devour as many of the fat pages as she could before her father called his turn with the paper, your time is up, princess. Her favorite parts were the horoscopes, the brightly colored comics, the horse racing reports (gaming and betting) made musical with the names of horses, and the transcripts of divorce cases spread over several columns. From the vast tracts of such rubbish that cluttered her mind from early, she developed the ability to think in balloons, distinguish between decrees nisi and decrees absolute, guess the results of horse racing, and foretell the significance of dreams.

At first her father was not bothered by the fact that she was an unusually silent child. For him it was enough satisfaction that she was a more-than-apt pupil, but as her words increasingly dried up and finally ceased altogether unless she was made to read aloud, he came to blame himself for his indulgence and lack of supervision that had nourished the indiscriminacy of her reading, which he now sought, when it was too late, to quell. He did not know how it came about. All he knew was that seven months before she went to the big school, she stopped speaking, as if her ferocious absorption of the words of others had driven her own underground, like a river that hides its head on its way down to the next district or the sea. He grieved that he had added to his daughter's handicaps a worse desolation, the remission of speech.

Tumela wisdom, the wisdom of far districts, counseled a visit to Madda Penny or Bredda John. "Is enchantment, Baba! Smaddy put guzzum pon di child! Carry her out before it too late!"

Even poor Miss Purity came in for suspicion. "Fi all me know, might be di wicked stepmodda. Jealousy. Dem stepmodda type can be wicked, yu know."

"A true. Snake under cool shady!"

But the one thing George and Dulsie had in common, apart from their daughter and an insatiable appetite for sex, was their scorn of superstition. They chose doctors instead. The doctors saw that something was wrong, though it was nothing physiological. They could propose no solution. George was a man devoid of superstition, a genuine atheist, but after the various doctors failed to get Arrienne to talk, in desperation he allowed himself to try the skills of Bredda John, who told him his daughter was reading too much.

Arrienne could have told her father, though she had no idea how she knew this, that the real culprit was not her entire reading repertoire, but the great book of embroidered secrets in the glass cabinet. *The Book of Things*. It had stolen her words and become an enchantment she could not cast off until she was able to translate its mysteries or find some other way to release herself from the spell that pulled her to kneel, helpless, every evening now, before the cabinet.

"Gimmi back mi talkin," she admonished the book, fiercely, angrily, inside her head.

The book laughed, a cackling, malicious laugh like Mama Mai's, not the graceful gurgling she thought would have emerged from among its lyrical illustrations.

And it spoke, "이 멍청아, 이 세 가지 수수께끼를 먼저 풀어야만 해!"[1]

Of course, the princess had no idea what the book was saying. This made her more angry, but still, every day, she found herself kneeling before the cabinet as if in prayer, helpless, pulled.

She was afraid to tell her father what she knew.

Being only a child, she could not have known that her words dried up because she was aware, by pure instinct, in some still-inaccessible part of herself, that to understand anything that was worth understanding about her own life, she would have to discover a vaster language than was at that time available to her. Neither could she have known that such a language, even the search for it, was possible

---

1 Much later, Arrienne's daughter Betina, traveling through the book, which she inherited, and finding a Korean friend, had this translated: "You little fool! You have to guess me the three riddles first!"

only at great cost—the cost of suffering. She could not know that her encounter with impotence in front of this book was because of this instinctive knowing and the lack of words-which-are-enough.

(Years later, she received a low mark from a teacher of English for writing a fanciful story instead of a real one: *The little mermaid bled on her feet so she could love enough, and become human, and be able to speak. Because she loved the prince.* She also lost a mark for a full stop after a sentence fragment. Then further, she lost the remaining marks for a story that was stolen, for as you can see, the story was written by someone else, in another language and country, but she was trying to find through it a way to save her soul. It would not be the first nor last time Arrienne became a word thief, in desperation.

Yet this loss in front of her father's book was the beginning of a mercy, for it was the beginning of her quest, as yet hidden from her, to search out the words for a counterspell, which in the end made legitimate her life and Moshe's.

And because she was always inhabited in this way by the words of others, she liked to imagine that she could hear the silent thoughts of others, not in the way she heard Moshe's—his true-true voice an echo in her mind—but an intimation that she stitched together from gesture and image and circumstance, and above all from words written or spoken, as if gesture and image and word were seams that could be mined for hidden treasure, treasure that flashed in sudden gleams along the shelf, and then the seam closed up with a lucent surface that she had made. This was to her a form of revenge against the hermetic book, and it is the way she came to tell stories, such as the story in this book, her own story. Moreover, sometimes it seemed to her that she overheard the inner lives of passersby who troubled Moshe, as if a line had passed from them through him to her, warning her of dangers by which he was surrounded. Of course, she often imagined such dangers from pure jealousy, when other people who desired him were near him and she was not.)

When, before the big school opened that September, Rachel Fisher went to the head teachers and Miss Yvette to explain her son's case for special protection, George Christie did the same, to seek protection and understanding for his daughter.

Arrienne's affliction became a grace for Moshe. One of the first lessons he learned from the princess was that he did not have to talk at all. This was a source of unspeakable relief.

In the Tumela elementary school of that time, learning entailed the acquisition of a number of survival skills. Among these was the ability to shout with strategy. Smart children learned to avoid the cane or leather strap by bawling out answers, at the top of their voices, before cane or strap descended on their shoulders. This was especially necessary in exercises such as mentals, a form of arithmetic in which they were called upon to work out complex relations in their heads at top speed without benefit of page, pencil, or pen.

Moshe and Arrienne became the first-known pupils allowed to stand at the blackboard and write their answers, because apart from reading when forced, they did not speak. If they had been of average or slow intellect, Man-Teacher would have ignored their parents' plea of a disability (which in Arrienne's case came with a doctor's certificate) and whapped the hell out of them for wasting teachers' time with a foolish pretense. As it was, they learned, without knowing it, speed writing. Through this skill they also always won at the game of spell-an-tek-down.

Moshe's part in this speechlessness, which was not pretense but a transmitted affliction, like a disease of sugar passed from kith to kin, did not happen overnight. At first, as you saw already, he became Arrienne's go-between, collecting her thoughts from her head and speaking her words for her. But by the end of that first school year he had come to know and crave the absence of sound, which was only an extension of the aloneness in which he had lived his life up until then. He was a child who had always lived inside his own head, as his mother did not "keep company" and his father, except when angry, was a taciturn man. This absence of noise that was so opposite to the great hum of schooling in a single divided room, was in some strange way complementary to it. He discovered that there was no need of his words in order for him to get by, and moreover he loved Arrienne, and wanted to do whatever she did. So it was natural that he stopped speaking as she did. At exactly the same time, even their ability to read aloud atrophied and died, as though a mirasmi had seized their tongues, and they went through the rest of the big school in a silence as spectacular as their extraordinary intellectual capabilities. They invented a form of sign language that their shell-shocked parents learned to read if not reproduce, but no one else that I know of ever understood that speech. This pleased them, that people could not understand when they signed.

CHAPTER VI

i

The first time his Arrii brought home the frail boy with mis-matched eyes and hair and clotted-cream skin like some-thing out of sci-fi, George, a man who had lived in a blue twilight for close on a year with a four-foot woman who could kill a behemoth with one flick of her wrist, was not unduly startled but glad that his daughter had found a friend. In later years, however, when they entered puberty and both became strikingly beautiful, George began to watch them closely, as all men who have been promiscuous watch their teenage daughters and their teenage daughters' friends who will become men.

For Moshe and Arrienne, the years passed as years do in the lives of children. They survived in the kinship they forged to protect each other. With the passage of time they became uninteresting to their peers. Children have short attention spans, and where novelty is concerned they are very apt to forget the quality that had fascinated them in the first place. Moshe's and Arrienne's scholastic brilliance, which was exceptional even in a place where unusual intellects often burst into ken like comets (and, like comets, often petered out again, in the absence of sheer money to push them into the future), went a long way toward easing their life in the community. Indeed, the district began to speak of them with pride, as if they were Tumela's own accomplishment, the mark of its genius in producing strangeness.

The two children fell into their place in the orders of strangeness for which the districts were known.

It had been years since Stanford Wills the idiot, a grown man with the carriage of a pope and the understanding of a child, had fallen into his place as handyman for Miss Lilla, Tumela's chief shopkeeper.

As Dadoub the scarecrow mansion builder also fell into his place. With the fury of a zealot he kept on adding new rooms and floors to his house of scrap and wattle, until it stretched from one end of the public square to the other, and began to list against the sky. This was the first person I knew who attempted to build a skyscraper. His mansion of ruins eventually reached four stories, which in those days was an astonishment, a fairy castle among the reticent bungalows of Tumela.

Alvin Thomas the drunkard fell into his place, coating his tongue with Vaseline so that he could pour tumblers of johncrow batty down his gullet neat, without harming his intestines. The rum resurfaced in the permanent glow that lit his face, and in his sweat, which flowed with the consistency of paraffin.

Katie Vamouze, who chronicled every death in the five districts by beating her tambourine and following the hearse with a mourning cloth tied around her waist, could trace her ancestry back to Dahomey and was always going home. Along with Tumela's dogs, she took the role of a prophet. Her funeral cloth was the same with which she banded her belly as she went about the district weeping before a death occurred. She foretold each death in competition with the dogs, who howled in unison night and day until it was accomplished. Katie had named her two daughters Shirley-Goodness and Mercy, based on her comprehension of the final verses of Psalm 23. These verses she understood to be a declaration of the names of angels who walked behind the righteous, and because she believed that the transference of names was also a transference of qualities, nothing could convince her that her daughters, both whores, were not denizened among the heavenly host.

The nicknames the children bestowed on Moshe and Arrienne marked their place in this insane order. An odd gesture of belonging. Man Sally and Lady Boy, because she was mannish-boned and he delicate. And because she could fight and he couldn't, Bonnie and Clyde-duppy.

Two of their nicknames, Machine Brain One and Machine Brain Two, switched back and forth between them, depending on which of them topped the class in a particular year, beating the other by half a point. If they tied for first place, as they often did, they became, together, Double Deuce Two.

Blue Boy and Mauve Gal, because of their skin. These last showed the children's awareness of the fluidity of color, and how they saw, when Moshe and Arrienne stood together in a certain light, daybreak or the edge of duskfall. Then the twins appeared to be caught in the stream of a single glow, made up of their two undertones, blue and purple together.

They skipped two more grade levels so that when he was eight and she nine, Man-Teacher and his wife and co–head teacher, Miss

Lynnette, entered them for the Common Entrance examination that determined whether a child would go to high school or not, even though the exam was supposed to be for students aged eleven and older. Outside of that, a child's only hope was to pass a special entrance test set locally by the high school, and if he or she passed, be sure to have money, like counterspell, to pay fees.

Most children who were thought to have the potential were sent up for the examination at age eleven. Those who were not, or whose parents balked at the prohibitive cost of a high school education, stayed at the big school until they were sixteen, their education ending when they reached the last grade, grade 9. (This was why elementary was also called "all-age," and indeed it was all-age in quite another sense, since a child could stay in grade 1 until he became sixteen if he was dunce enough, or reach grade 9 by the age of nine if he was bright enough, which Moshe did, and was.) After sixteen or grade 9, a child went for a laborer or a trade or was selected for training as a pupil teacher by Man-Teacher and Miss Lynnette. After pupil teacher, if you were lucky in the British overseas exams, first, second, and third year, you could go to Teachers College. In those days they called this the "poor man's university," even though there were women there, and there were teachers' colleges for women alone, as well as some for men alone. (No one ever said "poor woman university," only "poor man" or "poor people," as if women were either never poor or they never existed on their own the way a man could. Even the princess's father, who thought she could do anything a man could, thought of her in that way since he thought of her as his son, the one he had left behind. Yet women where we came from accomplished a great deal, and made men look foolish much of the time.)

At any rate, all this is to say Moshe and Arrienne were among a few children who people said were the fortunate ones.

At high school, the same school near where Rachel had stood on the bluff behind the hospital at Ora-on-Sea and heard Moshe cry, the two children learned for the first time the true hostility of color. Blackey and Whitey. White-Like-Duppy and Black-As-Sin.

The other names came later. Batty Bwoy and Butch. Those were names they learned in Kingston, the big city.

interval one

The cane is burning. Soot from fires twenty miles away floats through windows and doorways, soiling chenille bedspreads and the pristine white of lace doilies artfully strewn on tables. (Doilies are always made in white, even during cane-crop time.)

To the children, the soot flies like charred paper planes, or rat bats, birds of ill omen. Tumela women cover the beds with rags and remove the doilies, hiding the precious delicate things in cupboards until the cane is fully reaped. They put newspaper over the dressing tables. The newspaper will soil the tables black, but you won't see the stain unless you wipe the table with a clean cloth or put something clean on the surface.

Sometimes people close their windows, but the soot seeps between the jambs and slats. And it is hard to be so confined, in a place where nobody locks a door, even at night, except in fear of things that are not human.

But it is crop time on the two estates near Tumela: George Christie's and Busha Parkinson's. Busha Parkinson's property at Point, three miles east of Ora, extends twenty-five miles toward Montego Bay, the last rump of what had been a great plantation in the days of King Sugar. George's, a much more modest outfit of forty-nine acres, but bigger than everyone else's in the five districts, rises from the summit of Baptist Hill in Tumela and slopes all the way down to the Georgia depression at Jericho. The smoke of the two plantations meets and congeals over the districts from two opposite directions.

The burning will not stop until every field is cleared of trash and underbrush and the cane stands clear for harvesting.

Cane rats, snakes, and mongoose scuttle to safety or are burned

with the trash. The men kick the skeletons, whatever has not dis-
solved into ashes, with the toes of their water boots. Then they go
through the cane swiftly with machetes, the long stalks falling behind them like hurdles in a race. The lines of women come behind,
bent in a row like a great land animal with many humps on its back,
sweeping the stalks into bundles that they tie with trash to be lifted
onto the waiting trucks and taken to the boiling houses at Frome.
Before the burning, the cane fields are awash with wind, rippling
in every direction like a green sea, or an enormous woman's skirt
spread on water. After the burning, the fields are black and skeletal,
but indomitable, like ancient pillars left upright after a cataclysm, or
the remains of a city that has been bombed.

In every Christie household groanings can be heard. You groan
low like that when you are respectable and don't want to spread
abroad the sound of your disgrace. Cushions bloom like jewels, an
arc of color looping one Christie house to the next to the next. Maas
George's canepiece is large. But now he cannot oversee the opera-
tions on his own property, and has to delegate. He cannot ride a mule
or drive a tractor because the fire in his behind is excruciating. His
foreman, a coal-black man with the improbable name of Thomas Jef-
ferson, handles the overseering with gusto, setting everything up so
that half of the profits will come to himself. They call him T.J. for his
name, but also for Tief Jukutuu, because he walks with a staccato
limp and tief no rass, the kind of man who steals milk out of coffee.
Maas George knows T.J. is robbing him blind but is in too much agony
to pursue his knowledge.

And just like spite, his wife, Miss Purity, is down with flu, so it is
Arrienne who ministers to her father's household, cooking inedible
meals in the outside kitchen (her father and stepmother are afraid
she will burn the house down if she is allowed to use the stove in
the inside kitchen); fetching boiled rags and hot water; changing her
father's soiled cushions (the wound leaks pus); and emptying the
chamber pot which starts overflowing with the effects of her culi-
nary efforts on Miss Purity's digestion.

It isn't her father's physical pain that is terrifying. What frightens
her and makes her stand in the dark closet trembling, her eyelids

shocked and open, as if someone has prized and kept them apart with pins, are the bouts of delirium when he writhes in remembered smoke; shrapnel and cockpits falling through air. When he cries out the names of the dying and dead. When he wakes from these nightmares, red-eyed as Alvin the drunkard, he has forgotten what he dream-remembered, but he calls for and drinks tumbler upon tumbler of hot rum flavored with molasses. Arrienne is bent with terror because she has never heard a man howl before. And this is her father.

She forgets. She makes herself forget as she has made herself forget to speak, after finding the book of strange writing in the glass cabinet.

All she remembers now is his physical, manageable pain that she tends with rags and hot water. It is her first encounter with the family mark. The mark lay dormant for seven years, and has returned with vengeance, like a cancer after remission. George has hallucinated in the past, but never so badly as now. Will she be delirious like that when her time for bleeding comes?

She does not know that today, the start of the cane-reaping season, is the anniversary of July 9, 1944, when her father's plane was shot down over Korea.

She tries to forget too the "Talk" Dulsie has given her about being a big girl about to go to high school, "and now that yu bubbies comin out, boys go look at yu rude."

She stares at her mother wild-eyed and flees back to her father's wounded house. She will never return to her mother's house without kicking and screaming. She thinks that she has scrubbed her mind clean of the memory, but the Talk is scored into her mind like writing, and from it she has learned to look at people sidewise, like an enemy.

The child is moved with sympathy for her father although she does not yet know the agony of a backside set on fire by forces that cannot be controlled. She is not supposed to tell anyone about the family's secret affliction, but she tells Moshe, how can she not, he is her twin.

The children mull over the mystery, sitting side by side on the bamboo bench by the never-die tree in Rachel's yard.

"How you don't get it, Arrienne?" Moshe asks, wrinkling his face in curiosity.

"Don't know. All my cousins have the bleeding. All the baby-one. But mi have the mark."

He squints at her. "Yeah?"

"Yeah. Maybe it won't bleed until I get big."

"How big?"

"Big-woman big." She moves away from him, looking at him now out of the corner of her eyes, like an enemy. She has heard Mama Mai say so. She doesn't know what it means, nor does he. But they are uncomfortable. They have never been uncomfortable with each other before. She almost offers to show him, but along with the thought there comes to her mind the picture of Sylvia Pettigrew and Lionel Harper hiding in the long grass, doing bad things Man-Teacher would bus' arse for, and superimposed upon this picture is her mother's mouth, disembodied, opening and shutting fast with unhearable words, and she feels tainted and ashamed, and does not speak.

interval two

Moshe has discovered art. This luminous Friday morning their teacher brings out pots of loose paint powder, blank drawing books, and paintbrushes, and, putting the children out in the sunshine, gives them their head, carte blanche. Moshe's pot is full of a bright-yellow gold like the sun, and he borrows the colors of smoke from Arrienne's pot. He paints Samuel Farradeh, his mother's cousin, many times over, with trees, smoke, fire, and a great sun rising over Samuel's head.

Arrienne draws a house with tied-back curtains in the windows the way she has seen it in the Enid Blyton books she is devouring. She adds a picket fence and a cat snoozing on the front step. Her father has just given her a kitten and she has named him Miggle, after a Blyton elf; she cannot now think of a house without a kitten, any more than she can imagine a place without Moshe.

She draws Moshe and Arrienne and a baby in a perambulator which Arrienne is pushing while she and Moshe walk side by side. She paints her picture in bright yellow, blue, and green, concocting the green from the mixture of yellow and blue. She shields her picture by hunching her shoulders over it and curving her left arm around it in the shape of a C with a very long middle. Moshe is confused. Why will she not show him her drawing? They have never hidden anything from each other before.

She shrugs and stuffs her picture into her uniform pocket. "It nuh good. Not like yours," she lies. Then, "Come on, let's go see the chickens," and rises abruptly to her feet.

His eyes become more puzzled. It has been ages since they've gone to watch the chickens. He thinks they have outgrown that spectacle, and he wants to paint.

"I can finish my drawing first?" he asks her timidly, afraid of her anger.

She kisses her teeth. "Draw what you want, idiot boy," she responds cruelly, walking away.

He screws up his face to stem the tears, watching her go. The tears fall anyway.

He returns to his drawing. The eyewater splashing on it turns Samuel's halo into an indeterminate blob. He tries to fix it by shaping it into another comet with streamers, but the tears come thick and fast and he is forced to abandon the drawing until all the wet in him has run dry. He turns to the side of the schoolhouse building and stands with clenched fists rigid at his side while he weeps, waiting for the tempest to subside. Arrii, he whimpers, Arrii. No one notices. The children are enraptured in the miracle of paint, the universe of color and its magic in a jar.

iii

They will start high school in September. But, like a premonition of adolescence, today, the day he discovers paint, the first time they quarrel and the first time he does not follow after her, marks the beginning of their separation. The children are nine and ten years old.

CHAPTER VII

i

"I think there's no help for it," Arrienne said. "We just have to find the old woman and confront her. Radical." She cut her hands across in a sharp gesture, showing radical, bam, kaput.

"But how you know she even exist? Suppose she just a figment of mi imagination?" Moshe objected, as he watched her rummaging in the outside pocket of his schoolbag where he had stuffed his lunch to avoid grease leaking onto his books. Rachel couldn't afford a new lunch box yet. Arrienne had a large fancy one with a pink cat face on the front panel, a cat's tail and a cat's behind on the back.

They were practicing speaking aloud. With few words of their own (though they were top of their class in languages), they drew on the slang and cult phrases their classmates made up from the speech of the boys and girls in the English books they read—*ah, radical! what figments of imagination, don't you know! oh goody, it seems you have lost your marbles, quit whining, full of baloney, oh jeez.* Foolish phrases like that, used half in mockery, half to show off their smarts as alpha, the top stream in the school.

At first Moshe and Arrienne had had a hard time with this inhabitance of other people's words. Moshe especially. His mouth bled with the struggle of learning to speak again, until Rachel found that slipping cucumber slices between his back teeth and jaw helped him to enunciate without biting his tongue or the soft inside tissue of his cheeks. Arrienne suffered because he suffered. But she spoke earlier.

At last, like a skin, the alien words saved them from exposure. And now, the artificiality of the words—*radical! figment!*—was saving them once more, helping to push away the slow feeling of horror that had begun to engulf them ever since Moshe first told his dream.

This school was hard. It was not nearly as forgiving of difference as Tumela's elementary school had been. And so they had learned to reserve their secret language for things they needed to protect and couldn't protect any other way. Things like fear, communion with insects, each other's stillness, the creeping shames of puberty. But at school they were forced to speak, in good English, aloud; it was a public language, and the school made it a law. In moments of stress, like now, their speech became a jumble between English and the everyday speech of the districts and the town. It was a compromise that hinted at the separations they would soon face, which neither of them apprehended but both felt as a curious shiver each time Moshe had the dream. The old woman was walking between them, though as yet she had no form or substance.

"Ah goody. Seeitya!" Arrii emerged from her rummaging, waving a wadded paper bag.

Rachel had packed a large hunk of cornmeal pudding in Moshe's lunch bag because she knew Arrienne would look for it.

"This is mine. You tek dis." She pushed her cucumber-and-cheese sandwich over at him with one hand, holding with the other the piece of pudding, sticky with hallelujah on the top, while she peeled the pudding from its wrapping with her teeth. The sandwich skittered the short distance that separated them across the stone ledge and rested against his side pocket. He picked it up, peeled back the aluminum foil, and began to eat in slow, half-hearted bites.

They went silent. Arrienne consumed her pudding avidly between gulps of cola champagne mixed with syrup and condensed milk from the flask Dulsie had filled for her. He could drink only cow's milk or water. Sugary drinks made him swell, his lips blown up into thick rubber balls, his tongue a dead weight, so that he could not eat. Today there was no milk, just coconut water that had gone rancid in the hot schoolbag. They poured it for the ants below the porthole. They ate his fried dumplings and with reluctance threw away Rachel's last egg, which had also gone bad in the heat.

Except for the two of them and the Goat Girl, the fort was de-
serted, though the ban on going there was lifted at lunchtime. They
sat hunched side by side in their usual porthole facing the harbor,
legs dangling into the tangle of sea grape bushes that ran down the
slope toward the blue water.

They were in the third form but they still took lunch to school like
first-formers. Arrienne was George Christie's daughter; she could buy
her meals at the school tuck shop or the Chiney shop downtown and
still have money left over for snacks on the way home. She brought
lunch to keep Moshe company while he ate what Rachel could afford.
She didn't mind; Rachel always put something homemade-sweet in the
paper bag for her.

Now she swallowed the last of the hallelujah and sucked on her
fingers, collecting the remains of the sticky sweetness. "Well, one
way to find out," she admonished, picking up the dropped thread of
their conversation. "Follow the trail from your dream, go see."

His face struggled with the effort to bring out more words. Speaking tired him easily, and he had already said more than the few words
he could without stammering. "If is jus a dream, is jus either something bad I eating or my unconscious. And if is something bad I eat, I
jus have to stop. And if is jus my unconscious, there's nothing to find.
Except maybe something I fraid for deep down and don't know."
The old people said if you ate heavy food too late before bed you had
bad dreams, but the biology teacher had started them on Freud that
week.

"Nobody don't eat something bad and get the same dream every
night." She reverted again to the everyday speech, giving force to her
objection. "Yu ongle get colic. Maybe random dream pon top-a it, but
mostly colic."

His thin shoulders lifted in a shrug, half-lost, half-pleading. "So
don't I tell you? Maybe is something I fraid then and don't know I
fraid. Defense mechanism and ting."

"But maybe is not. People see vision all the time. Yu modda see
vision. Samuel see vision. Dat a nuh nutten. Yu can see vision too."

"Well, according to . . . her, I don't . . . have anything for them." I
haven't inherited any trait from them.

She looked derisive. "Who yu calling *them*? Yu mean yu modda an yu fadda?"

He flushed. The blood flowed up under his skin like groundwater from a well. His thin features filled out, the blue edges wiped away by the spreading crimson stain. He was thirteen; he blushed a lot these days, to her intense fascination.

"See what I mean? Yu already believing what she say."

His tone was defensive: "Mi mother and mi father never tell me any lie. I know they not my real parents." She heard the slight hesitation before he said "real" but decided not to argue. She wanted to hear the rest of what he was going to say.

Rachel and Noah had in truth never told him any lie. In fact, they had told him nothing at all until his first high school year, when his classmates would not stop hounding him about the difference in his parents' looks and his. And he in turn could not rest until his parents told him the truth. He still did not like to remember the terror and un-surprise of that day.

It was funny; in Tumela, vicious people used to call him bastard-parcel and bush-baby, but he thought it was just because he looked different. High school was a rite of passage that completely upended his mind because, armed with their new biology textbooks, his classmates insisted, "It is not genetically possible." He knew they didn't mean just the relation to his parents. They were also saying, "*You* are not genetically possible."

"But is the other thing that she say that just weird," he went on, pushing this memory aside. Again his features twisted with the struggle to express his thought, or his fear. The color had receded with the swiftness of a sea wave, leaving his face bluish and more transparent. The taste of rubble filled his mouth; he had said too many words and the effort was taking its toll. He reached for his schoolbag, pulled the drawing pad and pencil from the inside flap, scribbled jerkily and fast while she peered over his shoulder, following the outline of the letters as he wrote. *She said I have to go over water. Soon.* Whenever either of them wrote, they wrote in strict English.

Arrienne frowned. "Yu mean like oversea? Foreign?"

She felt his silent yes. The pencil hesitated, then, *It was scary. Be-*

cause didn't feel strange. Just like it was there lay-waiting all the time. It jumps out of the bush, but you're expecting. His letters were huge, loose, and sprawling.

Recognizing the extent of the strain he was under from words, she reverted to unspeaking:

She say something that you know though you never know that you know.

Yes.

But the silent language was leaving them, becoming more and more difficult to hold onto as they grew older; soon they would not be able to speak it anymore.

"Right," she said decisively. "We going this evening. If is just dream, we will know."

She had rummaged and found the last Otaheiti apple in his paper bag while they were talking. She munched it thoughtfully, her eyes brooding on the blue water below. She had an enormous appetite and was long and limber as a colt, her future stunning beauty already apparent in the smooth matte of her skin and thick rich hair that had grown thicker and longer with adolescence. The Miriam Makeba Afro cut from America was hugely popular but it wasn't allowed in the school; black girls could not wear their hair loose unless it was permed straight. Girls with natural hair went for sleek ponytail twists secured with bubbles or rubber bands threaded onto metal fasteners. But Arrienne had managed to find a thin wedge between conformity and rebellion. She wore her abundant tresses half-corralled, pulled back from her face with a plain decorative comb, but loose and high at the back. The style revealed the round warm lines of her face and gave her a subtly wild aura. She had long slanted eyes and her lips were beginning to pucker and thicken with the lushness of puberty.

The white women teachers from England and Wales had hardly noticed, but the two local female teachers, one very black and the other very light-skinned, had taken her in hand and commanded her to restrain her back hair. In the end the blacker of the two brought her up before the white English headmaster because either she wouldn't do as they commanded or her efforts to obey were insufficient. I cannot tell you which was which.

The teacher had hair straightened with a hot comb and pockmarks from healed acne on her face. The headmaster, embarrassed by the girl's subtle hint of sexual blossoming and the discomfort of being called upon to arbitrate female decorum (his own daughter, a prefect in the fifth form, wore her horse-brown hair straight down her back to her thighs), admonished her, without meeting her eyes, to pat the hair in a little.

"You don't have to flash your hair in the teachers' faces, you know, Miss Christie. Even if it is beautiful hair," he tried to soften the blow.

Arrienne patted in the hair in his presence, making exaggerated gestures, so that he said, his voice dry, "That'll do. No need to overdo it." The hair was still standing up wild, without noticeable change, but he still said, "That'll do. You may go, Miss Christie. Don't let me have to see you about this again."

The teacher cringed. She felt this last admonition as an admonition against her, not the girl.

After that, the teacher left Arrienne alone. At least concerning her hair. But the teacher was mortified in a way from which she never recovered. Arrienne had no idea then that she had become the cause of a lasting feeling of humiliation and the catalyst of a push to oust the headmaster; this would come to a head a mere two years later.

The teacher began a number of small persecutions that she allotted to Moshe as well, knowing that whatever hurt him would hurt Arrienne more. But these attempts stopped after, in the midst of a rain drizzle, she sent them outside for talking to each other during the math lesson, and Moshe caught a hacking cold like whooping cough. In truth, they hadn't minded being outside; they liked the wet, and neglected to tell the teacher what she could not see from inside the classroom, that it was raining. Rachel descended on the school in her madwoman self and according to rumor kicked up such a ruckus in the headmaster's office that it took the headmaster and his deputy together to calm her down.

The news spread through the school like wildfire, and though no one besides Rachel, the headmaster, the deputy headmaster, and the math teacher knew what happened behind the office doors, the pupils declared that the teacher had been forced to apologize to the mad countrywoman in her tie-head and puss boots and would never recover face from that encounter. If this description of Rachel added to Moshe's daily humiliations, the rumor of her own defeat took its toll on the teacher and she eventually left, but not before she lived to see the headmaster's ouster. Long after, in her mature years, Arrienne thought that an institution marked with such deep colonial imprints was bound to be a place of strange and petty revolutions. Who could have thought a coup could be all about hair?

But Arrienne was beautiful, like an irritatingly flawless jewel. The skin complaints of adolescence had passed her by. Moshe, on the other hand, was tormented by its eruptions, his face in constant pain from pimples that itched so much he felt compelled to scratch, and when he scratched they turned into boils that rose like hillocks on the flat plain of his face.

In the last year he too had shot up tall, taller than she, but he was conscious of his height and walked a little bowed, as if to draw himself into a folding piece that could be put away. His face was very long; she thought he looked like a portrait of King Henry V of England that she had seen in books they raided from the old armory-turned-library that was left unattended because the school librarian had migrated overseas and had not been replaced.

She found him very pretty. She didn't think of him as handsome, though he was a boy. Handsome (like aquiline, hidalgo, arrogant) was how men in the romances the girls in class read in secret were described. She thought men like that stupid. Moshe was not like that. He was delicate, and beautifully drawn. The bones of his face were defined, pushed up under the blue-white seal of his skin. He was all bone and sharp angles. He seemed to her as if someone had made him with a very skillful and lovely knife.

Why she so sure is my father and not my mother who come from foreign? he wrote on the writing pad, abandoning English.

I don't know, she replied, again seeking out the last vestiges of their silent language. I tell you aready, is only one way to know. Quit whining. Mek wi do wha wi haffi do.

She tossed crumbs and an apple core with an angry gesture toward the water. They fell in the sea grape bushes and were quickly overtaken by the ants. The boy and girl stopped talking, pondering the old woman whom they had never met but who had so destabilized the tenor of their lives. Moshe kept on dreaming her; he hadn't had a straight night's sleep in days. And because he hadn't, neither had Arrienne.

Their eyes followed the Goat Girl. "She don't eat any lunch again today," he said, distracting himself from the maddening riddle of his thoughts.

The Goat Girl was walking to and fro in the open part of the fort, her arms wrapped across her midriff the way one wraps a person whom one loves. Arrienne, brooding, drew skeins of imagining around the Goat Girl. The Goat Girl always threw her lunch into the bushes on her way to school, because it was poor. The kind of lunch poor people ate if they put forward their best. The Goat Girl's lunch was wrapped in a brown paper bag—sometimes half a brown paper bag torn off so that the other half could be saved to wrap the lunch for the next day. Sometimes it was fried dumpling with sardines or cooked-up saltfish that had a high and embarrassing odor, which would make their classmates laugh, because though everyone ate this kind of food at home, you were supposed to pretend you didn't. Worst of all, the Goat Girl's lunch drink was brebidge, lemonade made with brown sugar and Seville orange or lime. Like bush tea, it was the kind of drink you pretended you had never drunk in your entire life, the drink of the desperate poor.

The Goat Girl's mother got up at dawn each morning to prepare this lunch and the Goat Girl's breakfast. The Goat Girl never ate the breakfast because her mother's early rising was never early enough; the girl was always late catching the one bus to school if she took the time to eat, and so she simply stopped, turning deaf ears to her mother's aggrieved curses. Yu a-tun topanaris now since yu deh-go a high school, too good to eat what mi provide, I call upon God Almighty to witness, I bare my bress before God, pray for yu, retribution tek yu, the mother would cry, suiting action to word as she pushed the bodice of her dress down to her waist and exposed her breast that had suckled the ungrateful child, and raising her eyes to heaven, she called upon God to vindicate her by striking her daughter with deadly remorse.

The Goat Girl ran from her mother and threw away the shameful lunch that after pronouncing these curses her mother had nevertheless wrapped with care and stowed into the girl's book bag, where more often than not it leaked and soiled the books, leaving behind the high odor that the Goat Girl feared.

Throwing the lunch into the bushes did not make the Goat Girl accepted or stop her from being teased and bullied. She felt it was the price she paid for dishonoring her mother, toward whom she felt no allegiance, only hate. But the knowledge tormented her and wrenched her face into morbid expressions that made the other pupils laugh and mock. She was nicknamed and called the Goat because she held her head down and glowered with a bucking gesture when she was mocked. The fort was where she took refuge; at lunchtime, the three of them were often the only ones there.

They offered her lunch once, and the Goat Girl was offended. Now they only said hi, and the Goat Girl said hi back, or not, depending on the nature of her thoughts.

Boats began to appear on the long sweep of the harbor, preparing for the great harbor race. First one, then two, high white sails like giant scalene triangles, then a whole fleet launching into the water from the jetty below the Barclays Bank. The sailors looked like little stick men from this distance. The boy and girl could see their arms waving, their mouths opening and closing with shouts that got lost on the wind.

The harbor was huge, wide and curved like half of a great calabash; it had made the town both an irresistible lure for the seventeenth-century English invaders who captured the island from the Spanish, and a perfect place to build a fort, a lookout point from which to intercept and demolish the enemy. Now it served as the venue for the annual Cross-the-Harbour regatta and a quick scenic attraction for tourist groups passing by in JUTA buses on their way to Negril or Montego Bay, where the real tourism happened.

Below the fort, crabs scuttled backward and forward, confused between hunkering down in the beached piles of seaweed and following the enticing flow of the wave, buoyant as a swing, that surged up to the cave mouth, yawning black under the rock ledge on which the fort's entrance was built. The class had been taken to the cave once, on a field trip, by the biology teacher, a man Arrienne feared because he touched her twice when she was running in the corridor toward their classroom.

He had touched her only on her arm, where she held it across her chest as she ran, afraid of being late for class, and then on her waist, lightly, saying in a fatherly kind of way, the way her father might have touched her, and the way her father might have said, "Whoa there, young lady, careful, you don't want to fall."

She didn't know why she felt uneasy, why she felt he touched her like her father but not like her father, why she felt he did not need to touch her at all; it wasn't as if she was skidding. Maybe she was afraid of him because of what it was said he did with a girl in the fourth form, a vivacious brown girl with wide hips and a swinging walk; she had become a prefect in fourth form even though that never happened, not until the fifth form did one become a prefect, but this girl had become a prefect very early and was famous because of her vibrant personality and confidence; everyone said she would become an important person in later life.

On the field trip Arrienne stayed close to Moshe, avoiding the teacher and shaking her head when he said, "Come, Arrienne, can you tell us what species this mollusk is?" gesturing her to his side as he held the shellfish in his palm. His palm was pink and wet and the wet gray shell winked inside it.

They were at the cave mouth; some of the pupils had wandered farther in but the teacher called them back, teasing, "Haven't you heard there are dead men's bones and ghosts deep inside?"

"Is that true, sir?" one of the girls asked, unbelieving. She stepped back, but all the while laughing as if he had said something exceedingly funny.

"Of course not," the teacher said, gleaming at her. "Just pulling your leg. If you're going to be a biologist, you can't be afraid to explore—caves or anything else."

The girl shivered delicately, theatrically. "I am not going to be a biologist, though, sir," she said, laughing again her bright laugh.

Several of the other girls and two of the boys joined in, as if her laughter were a cue or a contagion that no one could resist. Their high-pitched giggles jostled to outdo each other. They laughed as though the girl had said something hugely funny, or as though what she was going to become was hugely funny and everyone knew the secret of what that was, even though no one did. They laughed without being able to help themselves, the way teenagers do, the effect of rampaging hormones, which made them feel like strangers in their own bodies, to which they apologized with laughter. Some teachers, annoyed, gave detentions for giggling, but this affliction was hard to overcome. The two girlish boys and the girls especially could not stop.

One of the two girlish boys joked to make the laughter feel less uncontrollable. "Beverley Smith, wha mek yu laugh like hyena so?" he accused the first girl who had laughed, himself sniggering.

"Cause Ina is her middle name," one of the others cried, eliciting a fresh burst of amusement, even from the girl who was Ina-hyena.

Embarrassed and glad to be in company, everyone laughing so no one could be thought silly for laughing, they drew around the teacher, gazing at the caught sea creature in his hand. He was a tallish man with a slight potbelly, an unsettled mouth, and brown hair that fell like fashion over his eyes, which were blue. He was in his early thirties and wore the clothes of a twenty-year-old, silky brown Elvis shirt and broad leather belt around bell-bottomed polyester trousers that hugged his hips well below his waistline. He smelled of cologne and a vaguer, more elusive smell, plucked chicken feathers or something from the sea. He was the only one of the foreign teachers who had brought along a wife who did not also teach. But she soon got a job as the mayor's secretary, running the harbor race.

Arrienne hung back, Moshe's hand secret in hers. They were too old for hand-holding. She was determined never to become old enough for giggling; how she hated it, the silly vulnerability of it. Even in the most hilarious episodes in class, she kept her teeth locked against the snickers bubbling up in her throat. She practiced holding laughter in, the way she held her pee in when the school bus took forever to reach Jericho Square and she had to walk another half mile before she could find bushes thick enough to crouch in while Moshe kept watch for passersby, standing in front of her with his back turned.

The biology teacher glanced across at them. A secret, mocking smile flickered in his eyes, as if he could tell they were holding hands behind their backs, like children. "Come, Arrienne, can you tell us what species this mollusk is?"

"No sir, Mr. Archer, I'm sorry, sir." Arrienne gazed back at him, her large eyes bold and insolent, knowing he could not accuse her just because of a look in her eyes. How she hated that man; she had never hated anyone like that.

She had always wanted to explore the cave, by themselves, but Moshe was afraid. Of caves, of being underground.

"Bathophobia," she said. "That's what they call it. Fear of depths and sea. But how come yu not fraid-a sea?"

"Mi fraid plenty-plenty. Mi woulda fraid more if mi did haffi swim inna it. When mi think bout swim inna sea, mi fraid, like mi go drown."

"But yu go to sea with Papa Noah."

"Mi father a fisherman. Mi haffi go."

"How?"

He shrugged. "Just—mi haffi go. Him is mi father."

She understood this as his deep need to belong to Noah. To belong.

"Fraid of water, and they find you by water?" Another girl might have said this teasingly; she said it broodingly, like something to be mulled over and studied.

"Das why. Maybe why," he said. "I find I save from something."

"You go travel by water," she said with conviction. "Das how it always happen. Ennyting yu fraid of, happen to you. Is not jus old people say that." The image of the biology teacher discussing Freud flashed upon her vision, his unsettled mouth drawn in a smile, gleaming at the class from his place at the blackboard.

Disturbed, she struggled to her feet, gestured her thoughts. Mek wi go, Mosh. I have to go pee-pee before the bell rings. She felt angry and strained, her body hot and prickly all of a sudden, and, feeling the tension in her that wasn't the tension of his predicament, he cuffed her waist gently as they walked past the Goat Girl, herself now hurrying in her ponderous way toward the fort gate.

ii

The path veered sharply to the left off the main road and wove between thick bushes that sheltered their climb toward the rounded hillocks that rose high before them. When they looked up, the steepness seemed insurmountable, but the climb was easier than it appeared, because the hill-mounds had pathways circling between and around them, like the bands between cultivated terraces.

But these pathways were not made by hands; they had been forged by centuries of feet passing to and fro, perhaps slaves when it was cane instead of grass that covered these hills, and before them, perhaps Taino people planting and reaping corn, carrying the harvest in baskets on their heads. Only ghosts now. The hillocks were curiously shaped, like middens, and scattered far apart. Moshe thought to himself that they looked like boils erupting on a face. Arrienne had a vague memory, the Cockpit Country on the map of Jamaica, only more weird. *Lord of the Rings,* Tolkein's Shire . . . a place of grave dangers, smiling on its face. Picturesque. She shivered a little, thinking of graves. It didn't help that it was late November and shadows had fallen like tongues on the hills, though it was not yet four o'clock. They saw how their own shadows walked, silent companions beside them.

Above the last mound they could see the sprawling pile of a white three-story house with colonnades and on each level verandahs that seemed to run its entire circumference. It had the look of an old great house, and if they had asked people who traveled from Ora or Tumela to Montego Bay, those people might have told them, We know it well, a Frenchman owns it, a Count Something-or-other, but he is hardly ever there; some black servants run it while he's away.

But to the boy and girl climbing, the house seemed like something out of a witch story they had read, and they could not imagine that an old woman who was like any old woman they knew could live in such a place. The thought came to them that if the old woman existed, she must be an obeah woman, a serious kind like Annie Palmer, the white witch of Rose Hall whose house could still be seen on the outskirts of Montego Bay and had been written about in a lurid book by a man called H.G. de Lisser. De Lisser was also the name of the people who once owned the big plantation at Point, which they had passed along the way, a mile farther down. Rumor had held once that they were Moshe's people, he a throwaway because of their upper-class shame. But the de Lissers were red people, they were not angelfish white, or gray, or blue.

The thought that they might be going to see an obeah woman began to frighten them a little, far more than any thought of punishment from their parents when they had to explain why they were so late getting home from school. They had already decided on the story they would tell; or at least Arrienne had, and Moshe had fallen in step, as usual. "Jus tell them wi go-a library go do research fi wi geography project."

It was that simple. Rachel would believe Moshe, who was a good child, one who never lied (a great deal of his unease on this journey stemmed from the shame of planning to lie to his parents). Any explanation from Arrienne, whose lies were serial and inventive, would be taken at face value by her father, and if her mother, wiser and less starstruck, voiced any suspicions, the girl had long ago learned to bring her father in on her side, slipping quietly away once the two adults lost themselves in quarreling with each other. (She had seen men slip away like this from the field of battle when rival women for their attentions fought each other in the streets.) Her mother and father never agreed on her upbringing. As for her stepmother, Purity had grown less inclined to exert herself as she had grown more plump, and paid no more attention to Arrienne's comings and goings in her house than if the girl had been a nice-ish but unobtrusive puppy; anyway, she preferred to leave George's daughter's upbringing up to George.

No, as yet they had no reason to fear their parents' wrath. It was the sight of the white house that began to unnerve them. Seeing it for real brought sharply home the possibility that the old woman might exist after all. They hadn't been afraid most of the way, in part as they hadn't quite believed that the journey would lead to anything or anywhere, and they had walked with the unspoken consent that they would turn back soon because they were bound to come to a dead end, which would lay the dream to rest once and for all.

She felt the tremor that went through him when the house came in sight and she asked one question, "Is there you dream see?" and when he nodded they both stood still and could not go on. The acknowledgment that yes, he was tracing with unerring accuracy a journey he had never taken before and for which he had no maps but the trajectory of a dream, horrified them beyond description. They stared upward in silence, mouths slightly open so that their breathing was loud.

After a while he said, "People there. Is okay, people there," pointing to where they could now see workmen moving busily about the house, unloading crates from a lorry that they hadn't noticed before. Parked on a gravel driveway to the left, it must have driven in from an upper road that ran behind the house and was not visible from below. Hearts beating, hands still locked, they resumed their climb. Before, they had been equal; now it was Arrienne who seemed to lead the way, though they still walked side by side. The boy moved with the steady yet faltering steps of a person who has been blindfolded and brought on his journey by an escort of seeing guides.

❧

They had got off the school bus at Kew Bridge, two and a half miles outside of Ora, instead of riding it all the way to Jericho and then walking the mile and a half home. They took the left-hand turn into Elgin Town, toward Montego Bay, and after a trek of a good two miles veered left again at Mosquito Cove, where the road led from a different direction into Jericho and where Tumela people ran down the shortcut to catch the Morning Star or Jubilee or Blue Danube bus toward Montego Bay twenty miles ahead, or Kingston more than a hundred and seventy miles to the east. The path they had taken now was yet another left turn off the Jericho path. In all, three left turns into what they felt must be another world, a fate whose end they could not predict. Left, left, and left again, Moshe thought. What would his mother Rachel, interpreter of signs, have made of it? No second to the right and straight on till morning this, no halcyon route to a happy ending despite Captain Hook, just a left-hand road that he felt in his bones would lead to something terrible.

The first part of the journey on foot had been comfortingly if ironically familiar. People in roadside yards turned to stare, sometimes throwing comments over their shoulders at other people in the houses or the yards behind them, either because Moshe and Arrienne had never been seen passing this way before, who were they, strangers; or because the dundus boy and the night-dark girl made an odd-looking, even laughable pair; or because a boy and a girl, both nubile, had no business walking alone in their school uniforms along what was usually a bus route, not a walking path, where would they be going without companions or an adult chaperone, these many hours after everyone in Ora knew that school was out?

At the Mosquito Cove turnoff, they passed a Rastaman hawking sugarcane and water-coconut to passing tourist buses from a roadside shack surrounded by a startling garden of African violets, periwinkle, and sinkle bible inside a border of conch shells. He yelled at them, "Hey yout, wheh di I-dem a-go pon dat-deh lonely road? I and I hope di I-dem nuh inten any wrondoings inna Jah-Jah face!" His matted beard and dreadlocks had seemed like an omen on the road, though Moshe and Arrienne could not have said an omen of what. This was 1971; a Rastaman was always a cause for superstition. They turned away without answering.

Now they toiled on uphill for another half an hour, until they were standing in front of the verandah where the men were stowing the last of the crates underneath the house, which was not like the underneath of any house they knew but more like a large airy room, with a stone floor and latticed mahogany surrounds instead of closed walls. In the districts, if a house had an underneath it was usually bare ground, above which the house rose on concrete columns or wooden posts. It was called the cellar and it was both the place where at nights people herded the family goats, and the biggest adventure land where children played the kinds of games that required secrecy. Underneath Maas George's spacious cellar, Moshe and Arrienne hunted dust-turtles, soldier crabs, sand lice, Anancy with his bags of eggs, or stray hens hiding to lay, and looked in secret in each other's underwear.

The men had seen them coming before they arrived; one gestured briefly toward them with a jerk of his chin, then he and his fellows turned away without interest and continued their unloading. The ordinariness of the acknowledgment reassured the children. They crested the summit more quickly, in total silence now, and, trying to look as neutral as possible, by mutual consent they let go of each other's hands as soon as it became apparent that they were seen.

"Wha oonu want?" one of the workmen paused in his work to ask. He seemed annoyed at the interruption, but Moshe and Arrienne knew this was his way of warning them they were in the presence of adults and had better behave respectfully. "Who oonu come to?"

Arrienne looked at Moshe.

"Miss Mattie," he said in a half whisper, half croak.

"Anybody here name Miss Mattie?" the man shouted toward his two companions who were ramming a long cardboard-encased package into the cellar.

One of them answered in a muffled grunt.

"Can't hear yu, man," the first man rejoined. "Di two pickni seh dem come to Miss Mattie. Wheh shi?"

There was no answer while the men finished hauling the heavy package in various directions until it fit to their satisfaction. They straightened up and the man who had answered turned and looked keenly at the children. "Nobody nuh deh-ya name so. Oonu sure oonu know wheh oonu a-go, who oonu want?"

Moshe found the sudden courage of shame. "Yes sar, mi sure," he said strongly. "Good evening, sar. She short an ben' down and she love wear black tie-head."

"Good evening," Arrienne also said, careful of her manners.

"Oh, yu mean Miss Myrtle." He pronounced it *Myrkle*. "Mi nuh know har as no Mattie." He lifted up his voice in a big shout: "Myrkle! Two pickni out ya come to yu! Roun a front!" There was no answer and he shouted again, this time so loudly that Arrienne jumped.

A faint voice came from the back of the house.

The man seemed satisfied. "Go roun di back and yu wi si a outside kitchen. A-deh so shi deh."

The men's eyes followed them as they went. They could feel the comments that were made in a low murmur and knew they were not nice comments, speculative maybe, but not nice. Arrienne felt her skin crawl in the way that told her men were looking at her in a certain way. A way that felt like hands, the biology teacher's hands. Moshe felt her shrinking and caught her hand, squeezing it hard before letting go.

The outside kitchen was attached to the house by a long, covered walkway, the stone floor under the board roof red and shining with polish. The kitchen itself was a square concrete structure with smoke-blackened windows placed high up near the ceiling. Through the open doorway they could see creng-creng hanging from the ceiling loaded with onions and garlic, and a wood fire on top of a high brick hearth. The creng-creng, like the windows, was thick with soot, clumps upon clumps like black stalactites. Breadfruits were roasting on the fire and an old woman was turning them with a long iron hook. She put down the hook and moved to the doorway as the children came round the yard. Banks—no, seas of bougainvillea and croton—flowed behind the house right down to the kitchen. The color was riotous. They seemed one with the flames that crackled on the hearth. To the children's overwrought imaginations, the contrast between the colors and the darkness in the interior of the kitchen was weird.

The woman was indeed small, and ben'-down-low, like somebody had pressed a hand into her back and squashed her until she became an upside-down U. She wore a dark tie-head with two wings like a bat's, with a pencil stuck in the fold at the left side. Her dress too was of some dark material, almost the same color as her face, which was all wizened; she seemed to issue out of the dark space of the kitchen like its spirit. Her dress was down to the ground and wide-skirted, like the dress of slave people from long ago. Over it she wore a plaid apron with wide pockets, and in one of the pockets a huge pair of scissors stood up straight with the cutting part upward.

She rocked on bare feet out into the light and peered up at the children from under her eyebrows. Her look was slow, as if raising her eyes cost her an effort. "Good evening, Miss Ma'am," Arrienne said, and Moshe echoed the greeting.

The old woman went on looking at them without speaking. At last she made a grunting noise deep in her throat, in her nostrils, a sort of "Hu-hum" grunt that when Rachel made it, spoke of warning and confirmation and prophecy and sometimes derision. Her eyes, sharp and small and shiny as a bird's, were trained on Moshe. She toddled farther out into the yard and pointed without words to a big rock near the back-verandah step.

They both made to sit down but she grabbed hold of Arrienne's arm with a clawlike hand and said, "No, not you. Him. You stand back." The voice was surprisingly strong for such a tiny old woman. It sounded like the voice of a big-man preacher, deep and soaring.

Moshe sat. Arrienne stood back. Now that they were here, and the old woman was real, and there were men in the yard who smelled of flesh and blood and sweat, they were no longer afraid, only mesmerized, as if they were positioned at the bottom of a mystery that would soon be revealed. They felt as though they were swallowing deep breaths, like gulps of water.

The old woman crouched in front of Moshe. "So yu come. Never sure yu woulda ha di balls"—she pronounced it *bawse*. "But yu come. Gi debbil him due."

Moshe's voice came out aggressive: "Wha yu sen call mi fa? Mi know yu? Who yu?" He stopped, shocked and stunned at his own rudeness and temerity. The words didn't seem to be his.

The old woman cackled. "*Mi* know *yu*," she said, putting emphasis on both pronouns. "Nobody nuh tell yu seh yu have a cousin name Myrtle?"

Moshe didn't answer that; he felt she already knew that the answer was no. (But in his dream she had been Mattie, not Myrtle.) "How yu come inna mi dream?" he heard himself asking instead, the unfamiliar feeling of aggression still rising in him. He didn't know where it came from; it frightened him because it was so alien to his nature.

Arrii. Of course. He glanced across at her and she smiled slightly.

Thank you for helping. He sent her words.

You're welcome. She was laughing, he could hear her inside his head.

"Yu ever hear bout converter, young boy?" the old woman rejoined, picking up his challenge for what it was. "Well, mi is converter. Mi can call yu if mi want, if mi get di vision, and command fi sen di message."

The depth of her voice unnerved him. "Who gi yu message fi gi mi, an how yu come to be mi cousin?"

She regarded him as if feeling his fear and being amused by it. At last she countered, "What yu parents tell yu?" and when he didn't answer that either, she said, "Yu a thirteen-year-old, yu a-tun big man now, time yu know di trut'." She added, eyeing him shrewdly so that he blushed as if he thought she could see into his soul, "Yu nuh tell nobody but it a-haunt yu. Is time."

And then she began to speak as if to some invisible person or persons, as if Moshe and Arrienne weren't there: "Ah tell har, yu know, Ah tell har, bes' yu trow wheh di belly. Mi try, mi counsel har, mi seh, Yu cyaan manage dis, it gwine blight yu prospec. Better yu sen it back to the Almighty bosom, Him know how fi welcome it. Stubborn? Wouldn't lissen. Seeit dere now, pickni born, half born. An now shi fraid. An don't Ah tell yu, yu can't burn yu bridges an afterward turn back? Don't Ah tell yu once it born not to dash wheh di child or give it away? Dat yu haffi choose fi live wid yu choice? But no, yu pop 'tick put inna yu ears, seh yu shame an yu life done. Yu tink I never si when yu go round di back a di hospital and lef di likkle boy dere? Yes, Ah si, Ah si, Ah seeit!"

Her eyes closed, she was rotating softly on her bare heels, and a wind off the slope picked at the hem of her skirt so they could see her feet and why she walked like a toddler; her feet were turned backward, like Dadoub the mansion maker's, and they were also short; they were not like feet but like the image of feet held under water.

Her eyes opened, trained on the riveted, horrified children. Then on Moshe. "Shi ded, yu know. Soon after shi trow yu wheh, shi ded. But nuh look so frighten, a nuh retribution. Shi did young an confuse. Baby fever tek har, fly up inna har head, an shi pass. Dat kinda ting happen often-often."

"Wha shi name? Wheh shi come from? An wheh har people?" he said, his voice rough and angry, though that wasn't the way he felt.

"Dat is information Ah cyaan give yu, young bwoy."

"Why? Why yu cyaan give me?" There were tears in the boy's voice now.

"Parraps because Ah don't get dat vision."

He felt she was hiding something, and he felt Arrienne feel it too.

"Yet yu say yu is him cousin. Then how come yu don't know?" Arrienne interrupted now; enough was enough.

"Ah don't seh Ah don't know, Miss Sharp-Mout' Ma'am. Ah seh Ah don't get di vision to tell yu everyting yet." The last part of her words she addressed to Moshe, but from the beginning her back was turned to the girl.

The boy became frantic. "Yu a four-eye. Yu suppose to know."

"Converter, four-eye. Four-eye nuh know everyting. Is what Ah get in di message Ah can tell yu."

This old woman was speaking in riddles. "Who mi father?"

"Fi find out dat, yu go haffi cross water." She repeated the exact words she had spoken in his dream.

The boy felt cold fingers run down his spine. "Which water? Canada or Murca or Englan?"

Instead of answering, she turned at last to Arrienne. The girl was standing apart but with her bottom cocked at an angle ready for action, whether flight or hitting down the old woman to protect Moshe. "Yu right bout dat teacher-man. Is a tradition wid dose people. From before yu parents time it begin. Don't mek dat man put him hand pon yu. Already yu worryin yuself an di worry gwine harm yu in yu relations wid man. An yet him nuh touch yu." She gave a sudden jerk, as if someone had stabbed her in the back. Her back jerked forward and upward, so that she levitated a little off her feet. "Oooh yes! O yes!" At the same time her hand shot, open-palmed, up into the air by the left-side bat wing of her tie-head. "Ah seh don't let him touch yu!"

Arrienne stared at her, enraged. Her eyes locked with those of the old woman, daring the woman to try to pull any further information out of her head. She locked her mind, clamping down hard on her secrets. She threw up her will like a rampart, a solid wall the other could not breach. But the old woman shrugged and looked away, losing interest in her.

Arrienne hid her relief. "So a Englan yu father come from then," she informed Moshe in a dry, sardonic voice. "Jus like Missa Archer." It stood to reason. In all their three years at the high school they had had one Canadian teacher, a woman, and one from America, also a woman. (The students had laughed at the American woman-teacher because she gave away marks like stupid; students who never got above a 60 percent average were scoring 90 in her class. Nobody had explained that in America the grading system was different; they thought she had no sense.) Everyone else was from England or Scotland or Ireland or Wales.

"Wha him name? Wha mi mother name?" Moshe couldn't be held back now.

The converter woman looked at him and it was her turn to be sardonic. "Yu modda name Rachel Fisher. Yu fadda name is Noah. Anybody else yu lookin for is someting else, different relation, different reason. Don't waste yu energy pon ting yu cyaan fix. I is yu modda cousin Myrtle Kellier. Ah see you in mi vision an Ah call you, long before yu reach up here."

"So what yu call him fa, ma'am, if yu not going tell him anything?" Arrienne fumed, keeping her voice as polite as she could. She was mindful of not getting anywhere because of being rude. She knew she had already crossed a line with her aggressive interrogations, and the old woman might decide not to say anything more at all.

"How yu know all-a dis, lady? An how come my mother and my father never talk bout yu?"

"Don't waste yu energy pon ting yu cyaan fix," the old woman repeated, again ignoring the girl. "Ah si yu in mi vision an Ah call yu, long before yu reach here. All Ah want yu to know is dat yu come from good people. Yu birth modda never trow yu wheh so. Shi did want somebody good fi find yu. Das how shi pray. An somebody did find yu, seeit dere." She turned abruptly on her heel and toddled back into the dark interior of her kitchen, where the only light was the red flames of the breadfruit fire on the high hearth.

At the doorway she turned. "Time oonu go back home now, fore it dark. Di shortcut safe. Di spirits walkin ahead-a oonu." Then she disappeared inside.

"I don't know no Myrtle Kellier," Rachel insisted, growing irate. "I have no cousin of any such name. Noah, yu have any such?"

Noah didn't. Neither did he as far as he knew have any relations by the name of Kellier.

"Where yu meet dis woman?" Rachel persisted, wanting to get to the bottom of this mystery that her son was telling her, of an old woman who had told him his father was an Englishman and his mother a young girl who had thrown him away and then died. She vex no bull, not at her son but at this unknown woman who had taken it upon herself to faas in her life without invitation. She couldn't wrap her mind around the thought of an adult being so cruel, so irresponsible toward a child.

"I meet her on the road, Mama," Moshe said, flushing deep red. In a way it was no lie: he had met her on a long road, a journey of months pursuing him through dreams. Still, he blushed for the implied lie, the things he could not tell her, and the literal untruth that he wanted her to believe, that he had been walking on a road and the old woman spoke to him. And if she ever found out he had been to a guzzum woman, that might be the one and only thing in the world that would cause Rachel to kill, flay, and nyam him raw. (Yu si how Rachel contrary? More superstitious than she yu can't find, yet is only her brand of superstition she accept, her one idea of her God.)

"Which road? School bus pick yu up, drop yu in Jericho Square. No old converter woman don't live in Tumela or Jericho, so you couldn't meet her on Jericho-to-Tumela road. So which road?"

"Mama, yu feget that we walk to the public library from school an if we go downtown to Agu shop go buy tuck, is walk we walk?"

"So which one? Library road or Agu shop road?"

"Library road, Mama," Moshe said, not looking at his mother. Library road it had to be, after the first lie he had already told, that he had come home late that Friday because he had gone with Arrienne to the library to do research for their geography project.

Rachel opened her mouth to request again in minute detail a description of the old woman, and then closed it. She was not in the habit of harassing her son and she fully intended to do her own investigations concerning this old woman (she never doubted that the woman in fact existed or that Moshe had told her the truth). But the question from her son had thrown her off balance so that she was acting out of character.

And she could imagine how Moshe had been rocked on his feet that he would even come to her and say what he had said: "Mama, I meet a old woman Friday who tell me she know my birth mother and that my father is a white man from England and my mother dead after she throw me behind the hospital, and she know you and Dadda and she is your first cousin, her name is Myrtle Kellier. She say she is a converter and she see vision, she see me in a vision." Her son had never spoken so many words to her in one go in his entire life. And now he had spoken a single lilting sentence of so many clauses, stringing his words together on a rapid chain of "ands," as if terrified he would lose them if he didn't push them quickly out of his mouth. Yeshua, keep me near the cross.

"Come eat yu food, son," she said now, handing him his plate of bean stew, callaloo, and white rice. But his mouth was tender from speaking so many words, and he had difficulty chewing the food. Noah, as the man of the house, had been served first, his dinner not handed to him in his hands but placed on the plastic-covered table in the little front room. Rachel served him brown-stewed chicken in a round bowl and ground provisions—yam, boiled breadfruit, and dasheen—on a broad plate. Rachel always served his food like this, the meat or fish-kind separate from the starches. Moshe would not eat meat. Noah hated vegetables so there were none in his plate. Rachel herself ate in her own time, whenever she felt like, but usually after Noah and

Moshe had finished. This evening she was so disturbed she wasn't eating at all.

Noah ate his food in silence, adding no more to the conversation than Rachel had demanded when she asked him the one question, "Yu have any Myrtle Kellier or any Kellier at all in yu family line?" As was often the case, you could not tell what he was thinking. Growing older had made him more taciturn, except on the few occasions when he drank rum, or the many when he felt abused by people in power—the latter was why he still quarreled with the clinic attendants when he went to get his leg dressed on Fridays.

But over the late years he and his wife had attained a measure of peace together, so the marriage that Rachel had thought would never last had survived. And its survival was thanks to this son whose presence had twice threatened a greater upheaval—once when that busybody Suzie Q Francis had taken it upon herself to announce to the child that Rachel and Noah were not his real parents, and now with this converter woman appearing out of nowhere to declare the identity of these parents which neither Rachel nor Noah knew and which the district mouthamassies had not been able to bring forth in thirteen years.

Their mutual obsession with the boy had at last left the couple little room for quarreling; further, caring for a child who could not or would not speak had brought out in Rachel a profound capacity for listening that spilled over into her relationship with Noah, who thrived in that ambience. So much so that though he would never be a Yahwehist, he became almost willing to listen to Rachel's "teachments" on the subject of Yahweh and even managed not to fume, but quietly let be if he was at home when the Yahweh elder came to give Rachel her lesson every hundred days.

If Rachel's patience with her husband was of the proxy kind, a spillover from the patience she had to exercise in learning to translate her son, she found that in the end it did not matter, for though she did not love her husband as at the first, she no longer felt judged by him for not having a child, and so she could sleep in the same bed with him without anger. Sometimes, when pushed by his need or her own, she could even open her legs to him in peace.

Peace comes from many directions. Despite her investigations, prayers, incantations, and searching of the scriptures, it was many years before Rachel came in contact with the old woman who had terrorized her son, and by then none of it mattered any at all.

But during this time Arrienne felt that Myrtle Kellier had affected their lives for the worse.

None of the other intimations we have seen of a coming separation between her and Moshe registered in her mind, but passed over her head like smoke. Except Miss Myrtle. Arrienne marked the rift between her and Moshe from the November afternoon when Myrtle Kellier told them this tale of Moshe's parentage and warned Arrienne herself about Mr. Archer, cloaking her words in half parables. She came to feel that the old woman was poison.

Immediately after the encounter at the house on the hill, Moshe became withdrawn and silent. He was growing up. He spoke more words, and his mouth did not hurt as often and healed more quickly now when he did speak. But he seemed to have drawn a cover around himself that he allowed no one to penetrate; for the first time, not Arrienne, not his mother.

Rachel, though hurt, understood this as a combination of the effects of puberty and the boy's need to deal alone with the strange revelation, if revelation it was, that the old woman had landed him with.

Arrienne went wild with grief and she cursed him fiercely, "Yu mek dat stupid old woman turn yu into idiot, how yu so fool, she just a stupid obeah woman"—forgetting her own insistence in the beginning that if the old woman turned out to exist beyond his dreams, they would have to accept her revelations as truth. "She could easy have heard the longtime speculation about yu parents and jus use it against yu," she added, trying to justify her own sense of contradiction. "Yu heard what Mama Rachel said—that when she found yu, people were saying yu father was some Englishman teacher who trouble a second-former and get her pregnant." The sound of her own words frightened her and she stopped abruptly, shutting her eyes against the image of Mr. Archer with the pink-shelled clam on his pink palm by the seaside while the girls in the class milled about him, laughing.

In her anger against the old woman, she forgot her own conviction that he would go over water, just as Myrtle Kellier had predicted. Now she heaped scorn on that prophecy: "Dat a nuh nutten. Plenty people go a foreign. People go a foreign every day."

"So how yu explain dreaming her?"

And there was no answer to that.

She fought with all her might to bring him back.

He shut her out of his room, which was his studio, and painted and carved in there all the time with the door closed, as if the art had become his new only friend. And yet perhaps in a way, everything that had happened since they went to high school had prepared them for this struggle that each struggled against the other. There, they had never become known by the old monikers Machine Brain One and Machine Brain Two. In the district they were stars. At the school in Ora they were not any particular kind of star but just two among the thirty in the alpha stream, the elite group that had won full or government scholarships in the Common Entrance examinations. In this setting, where outstanding achievement was normal, pupils were marked by their particular gifts, none by any outright ascendancy over the others. In almost every subject except history there were students who never wavered in taking the top spot. Arrienne wrote better than anyone else in their class; everyone accepted that the prizes for literature and English language were going to be hers, long before the end-of-year examinations.

History bored almost everyone, with its recitation of dates, its long lists of heroes of European wars and navigators of straits—Magellan, Cabot, Cook, Pizzaro, Drake, Hawkins—so there were no takers for that crown. In the second form it had been worse, endless pages of a soulless book on slavery, read to them in a monotone by a disinterested teacher who made them spend a great deal of time memorizing, drawing, and labeling the stages and machinery of sugar and rum production on slave plantations. The teacher was sleepy all the time and moved heavily, mostly not at all. She was a minister's wife and very pregnant. Arrienne was fascinated by the way she caressed her swollen belly with slow, loving hands, her eyes soft and distant all the while that she read them the boring book, as if in her mind she was in another place, not there.

Despite their democratic acceptance of the distribution of talents, the children vied for first, second, and third place in the class; nobody wanted to come last. From the beginning, overall first place went to the one girl who always managed to do well in history. No one else had the discipline to memorize consistently the bald, soul-destroying agglomeration of facts, and because of this, no one begrudged her her overall win. They thought her a hero.

(In elementary it had been different. There they heard stories of young warriors and revolutionary heroes, names tripping off their tongues like poems, Nanny, Tacky, Cudjoe of the Maroons, Juan de Bolas, Simón the Bolivar, Three Fingered Jack; legends of a wild woman and wild men that had set their imaginations on fire during lessons held outside under shade trees in the afternoon. But that was in elementary school, a lifetime ago.)

But Moshe's gift was in his fingers. He drew nimbly, spectacularly, green fields in which powerful spirits lurked; you could see them only from the hint of wings lit at their tips with fire. The fields were scenes he had seen in books, but the spirits were Tumela's, and his own. The rough cedar walls of his room were plastered with these drawings that pulsed with strange fire, and on a shelf that he and Noah had raised on one wall were assembled with loving care the dolls he carved out of various soft woods: pimento, never-die, and dogwood. These were woods you could afford to waste because they were not valuable, like mahogany or cedar or lignum vitae.

Arrienne lay on her stomach on his bed, one leg cocked up against the window wall, half reading a Hardy Boys mystery and half watching him draw or carve or paint, keeping very still so as not to disturb him with her watching. They were a harmony then, her presence a low hum somewhere at the center of who and where he was, that gave energy to his hands, a contentment he had never tried to explain. Sooner or later the silence broke down; she was jealous of his painting.

He was making a likeness of her from carved dogwood. The carving was mostly hair, Medusa locks that sprouted into tree branches. She liked this image of her hair. "Samson can't show me nutten. Nazirite, me." (They had religious knowledge at school, and Rachel's Bible readings at his home.)

Then, "Hoi, a nuh so mi nose long," she complained. "Fix it."

"Yu haffi have likkle patience, yu know. If yu wait it wi come right."

She felt extreme pleasure as the silence broke in which he had been encased.

The nose grew longer.

"Heh, what yu doin?"

Moshe grinned. "Mekking yu nose, what else? Is not literal, art not literal. Is yu Pinocchio spirit comin outa di wood. Is not my fault. A dat di wood seh. Pinocchio." Sorry, it's not my fault if the wood unveils your penchant for lies. The wood has spoken: Jack mandora, mi nuh choose none. As I received it, I have carved it.

She put down her book and grabbed him by the two sides of his shirt collar. They rolled over, wrestling and laughing.

Rachel, listening, put her head around the door and called them out for their lunch.

It was the last summer. Later they would go walking, tree-climbing, and Arrienne would have naseberries and mangoes for dinner (almost nobody ate a cooked evening meal at the height of the mango season); Moshe, grown allergic to almost all sugars, even the sweet in fruit, would eat steamed vegetables from Rachel's kitchen garden.

Now, toward the new summer, the summer after Myrtle Kellier, in late May or early June, he shut his room door, he wanted to paint alone.

"Give him space," Rachel advised the furious, crying girl. "The two of oonu growing up, it nuh so healthy to be in each other's pockets so close. Girl things happening to yu, boy things happening to him, it tek a likkle time. Both of oonu have private things to sort out an then come together again. Trus mi, oonu too much good fren fi lose oonu one-anedda. It not going to happen, nuh fear. Him fadda an mi haffi let him go too, you know. So him can come back to wi. Yu get what mi sayin?"

Getting it was different from accepting it. Rachel had turned out to be just like other adults in the end, a disappointment, devoid of understanding. Arrienne went away more furious than before.

She felt in her heart, as profoundly as Moshe had felt the hum of her companionship as he carved or painted his wild representations, that none of what Rachel said was true, that it might have been true for other people, this parting and coming together again, but not for people such as she and Moshe were. If they parted it would be for keeps. For them, such a tearing could not be mended.

That was the summer he made a new friend, who turned up on Rachel's doorstep one morning in July.

"Good morning, Miss Fisher, I come to visit Mosh."

The boy's name was Alva. Alva Lawrence. He was in their class at school, a very dunce boy who by money had slipped into the alpha class, who sat at the desk on Moshe's left, the opposite side from Arrienne. This boy Moshe used to help with his homework, hastily under the desk in the short minutes before the first teacher arrived in their room. Arrienne could not believe her eyes when she went to Rachel's house and found him there.

CHAPTER VIII

i

ut it was also the summer when Arrienne had her own changes, and was reminded that she had been born a princess, with a certain destiny assigned.

It is a week before the cane burning, and the princess is approaching her fifteenth year. She is frightened. The flow of blood had come first in itinerant blotches on her underwear, then an avalanche. Dulsie had stanched the flow, hitching her to the Safex pad with a belt like a harness around her waist.

For the women in the house, it is a momentous occasion, a time to prophesy; to issue warnings about keeping boys at bay, about stopping running, about sitting and walking with decorum.

Dulsie's efficiency has put the blood out of sight. But still the girl is frightened. She fears her mother is not in her right mind.

"Oonu tell mi wha fi do!" Dulsie is screaming, terror turning into fury. "A fi oonu legacy deh pon di pickni, oonu mus know wha fi do!" You Christies have bequeathed this foolishness to my child, solve this riddle, now!

"Castor oil and a soft cushion, but mek shi lie down on har belly," advises one of the female clairvoyants. There are two of them in the house, from the same posse that had invaded the house to check out the princess's paternity all those years ago. This time they are there by invitation, because Dulsie, having reached her wits' end and seeing that they both live nearby, has sent to call them in the hope that they know of some treatment not known to her or Arrienne who has nursed her own father through more than one bout of the Christie malady.

"It depend on the amount of delicateness shi born with. If one cushion don't work, try several," advises the other clairvoyant.

"Yu nuh tink mi try dat aready? Oonu tink mi a idyat or what?" Dulsie fumes, disbelieving their stupidity and self-importance.

"But I never see it like this, is not cane-crop time yet. So someting more might be needed," the first clairvoyant says, murmuring to her sister in a voice of consultation, as if to shut Dulsie out.

"Yes, it seem like someting more than we used to," the other replies in the same kind of voice. "But then again, though is not exactly cane-crop time yet, it right round the corner. Maybe the conjoining of the season and the child coming into womanhood, seeing her nature for the first time, is what cause it."

"Full moon last night," the other murmurs. "Wi might haffi call family council. Big meeting."

"Call Mama Mai if anyting. She wi have an answer."

Dulsie kisses her teeth in a long-drawn-out cheuups. "Set a idyat," she says loudly.

The first cushion had made the pain worse. Even though she was put on her stomach, the girl screamed so loudly that the neighbors came running. Dulsie told them that her daughter had a boil and she had lanced it, so the child, prone to histrionics, was bawling cow-bawling.

Advice came from all directions.

"Yu shouldn't did lance it, dat too painful, shi bound fi bawl. Next time, quail a bird-pepper leaf in di wood fire an tie it on wid likkle kerosene oil from di lamp. Mek sure is oil dat use, di one from di lamp, not new oil. Di boil wi break by itself after dat, den yu can squeeze it out."

"Mek mi si it, mek mi help."

"Is awright, Miss Suzie Q, shi resting now," Dulsie lied. "But thank yu fi yu offer, mi appreciate it," she added, telling another lie to sweet up this woman whose nosiness knew no bounds in Tumela.

When they were gone she shut the door tight and sat on the edge of the bed, rocking the suffering girl in her lap, placing her on her stomach because any other position resulted in excruciating pain. As she rocked her child, Dulsie sent out mind-telegram to the rest of the Christie clan to whom she had already sent messages hotfoot by the telegram boy. "Some curse mus deh pon oonu. Oonu dutty bitch, oonu always faas wid decent people, think oonu better dan dem because oonu skin tun, an look now pon di nastiness oonu pass on to mi pickni, inna har blood. Oonu dutty bitch oonu, oonu better know wha fi do now." Light-skinned trash, condemning other people's pedigree because you have wishy-washy skin, what have you done to my child, what horror runs in the blood you have bequeathed her?

She knew from experience that no doctor's prescription could help this Christie horror that had finally come upon her daughter. George's two cousins, both sisters, had arrived in answer to the summons Dulsie paid the telegram boy to deliver in Black Shop on the south side of Tumela. By the time they arrived it had already become clear that the cushion-and-hot-water-castor-oil remedy was not going to work.

Enraged and frightened by the sisters' incompetence, Dulsie curses them and expels them from her house.

Mama Mai feels the scorch of Dulsie's rage across three districts and comes to see for herself. Nobody has to call her.

She looks at Dulsie's cushions and kisses her teeth. "Damn ass. Yu call dem-ya sinting cushion? No wonder di pickni ass ketch a-fire even more. Look inna di bag over dere an pass mi wha yu si."

Di bag over dere is a big crocus bag tied at the mouth with string, which Mama Mai has brought along with her on her donkey's back that she rode across the three districts, from Mount Peace to Tumela, to get to Dulsie's this early Saturday morning. Trembling, Dulsie unties it and finds within another bag, a plastic one, tied also at the mouth. In the end, she unties six bags of the same kind, tied in the same way, before a riot of cushions tumbles out on the floor, small, squeezed up, and flat as they come out, and rising to magnificent sizes as they hit the free air, as if someone has injected them with a great amount of yeast.

"I put them in di seven bag to keep out di air," Mama Mai explains.

"Dem is Christie female cushion. Yu cyaan help dis kind-a ting wid ordinary cushion. Not when di two influences conjoin."

"What two influences yu talking bout, Mama Mai?" asks Dulsie, showing the old lady more respect than she has accorded to the sisters. It isn't just Mama Mai's age, it is her authoritatively filthy mouth and assurance that command respect.

"Woman ting an fambly inheritance," Mama Mai says serenely. "She start see har blood same time as crop time comin near, an is di firs time she getting di fambly swellin."

Di damn blasted old woman declarin dis fartness as if is some sort-a blessin or riches, Dulsie exclaims to herself in disbelief. The whole set of these Christies mad as shad.

A Christie female has not started her period on the cusp of crop time in over forty-four years. It is an occasion. Arrienne is bound to suffer more than a normal share.

There are twenty-one cushions in Mama Mai's plastic bags in all. No exaggeration, I tell you the gospel truth. The old woman piles them one on top of the other on the bed. When she is finished, the mound almost touches the ceiling. She lifts the moaning girl in her arms with a strength and tenderness completely belied by her age and her foul language that rivals the grieving mother's, and lays her on top of the great mountain of embroidered fluff as if she is the most precious gift in the world. Arrienne lies on her stomach and is still.

Her grandmother nurses her for the next three days and nights, anointing her bottom with a cocoa butter and sinkle bible mixture while she lies in a coma on the jeweled mountain made of colors and patterns so gorgeous that tears of happiness seep out of the corners of her eyes in that deep sleep from which she does not wake for three whole days.

The room, barely bigger than a closet, is lit up by a play of colors from the cushions like the sea at daybreak, so that Dulsie does not have to light the lamp at night the entire time Arrienne is sick. Mama Mai is singing in a droning quaver and intoning all sorts of prayers to multiple gods, as if she is mixing the sound of her untuneful voice in the mixture with the sinkle bible and the butter, catching after whichever deity might on the off chance hear.

When on the morning of the third day the young girl's eyes open wide as if her lids have fallen apart without volition or have been jerked by a string, and she sits up abruptly in the bed, Mama Mai looks deep into her face and nods, as if to confirm a truth. "Hand put on har," she says, and refuses to explain to anyone what she means. "Divine hand put on har, and har life set." And she commands Dulsie to feed the girl a teacup of cane juice or, if there is none in the house, a tablespoon of brown sugar. "Hair of di dog dat goin bite yu," she adds by way of explanation, which leaves everyone still in the dark.

The girl vomits the sugar and has to receive several spoonfuls mixed in water before one spoonful stays down.

That was the first time Arrienne met her grandmother, up close.

She had been sick for two weeks—the last week of school, and the week after that, which was the first week of the summer holidays—while her bottom healed. What was strange—if anything regarding either Moshe or Arrienne could be called strange—was that the Christie curse, which came to her so late, seemed to leave her altogether after that first summer. She had irregular periods, in the normal way of teenage girls, sometimes with pain or discomfort, sometimes not. The birthmark on her bottom faded and became almost invisible after Mama Mai's applications of cocoa butter mixed with sinkle bible and castor oil. She stopped putting sugar in her tea, and drank water with her lunch, like Moshe. She could not say the order in which these things happened, whether what came first was that she stopped eating sugar or if it was the cessation of the crop-time blood. All she remembered was that she grew to hate the taste of the crystal grains on her tongue, and was glad to share something else, even an intolerance, with Moshe. She felt that why she was healed and the other Christies were not was because, unlike them, she never cherished a lurking vestige of family pride in the curious mark, that the sheer virulence of her will against it held the affliction at bay. (It was not long after, not many years, before she learned, from the frail boy to whom she thought she had lent her strength, that even her indomitable will had its limitations.)

The most powerful effect of that moment, however, was the

change in her attitude to Moshe. She realized with fright that she had become a little afraid of him. Something had happened to her, the woman thing, that put a wedge between them. She did not know if she could tell him about it. At the same time, she could not think how she would not tell him, when they had always shared everything. The uncertainty between telling and not telling him made her afraid.

The first morning Moshe woke up from a wet dream, he told her. There wasn't anybody else he could tell. At least, he didn't tell her what he dreamed or if he dreamed anything at all, but he told her about the wet in his briefs in the morning. He was terrified of the whitish stuff coming out of his cheelie; he thought he had contracted a terrible disease.

But she, more precocious than he, at eight years old had read about these things in a set of booklets the big girls in the upper forms of elementary school read, hiding them in their desks. At first the big girls drove her away, Shoo, you are too young for this, but she followed them about like a slave, refusing to let up until one of the bigger girls relented, feeling it was only fair since the child was in their class (having skipped the lower forms). So they let her in on the secret. She had giggled in derision, unbelieving, until it happened to Moshe and she had to explain everything to him.

When his cheelie acquired a life of its own, a habit of leaping up straight-straight in the air without reason or provocation, she teased him with laughter until, ashamed, it shrank away and went back down. Watching it deflate itself like a pricked balloon (she almost expected to hear it make the same sucking sound a balloon makes as it ejects the last gasp of air) was a source of astonishment to them both.

"It used to jump up like that before, from I was little, but only in the morning when I wake," Moshe said. "Sometimes it hurt and wouldn't go down and my mother put it in warm water, then it okay."

"But now it jumping all over the place," Arrienne said, eyes shining with intrigue.

"All over the place."

It felt strange that something had happened to him when he was little that she hadn't known about. The thought gave her a queasiness in her stomach.

They looked to see if his pee made froth when he went to the bathroom, the way it was said a boy's pee made froth when he was becoming a man. (Women cursed their back-answering teenage sons in this way, "Yu tink because yu piss making froth yu is man? Boy, I wi kill yu!") But there was no difference that they could see. His pee increased in quantity ("That's just because your cheelie is getting bigger," she said), but that was all. His voice changed the same way his cheelie changed, suddenly and without warning. It didn't go deep sometimes and squeak upward at other times the way the voices of the two girlie boys in the class did. Instead it went low and deep, with a faint hint of a stringed instrument played far away.

They both got bushes of hair in their armpits and between their legs, above their "things," at more or less the same time.

So there was no reason she should not tell him about her own rite of passage. The moment she had realized that the thing they said happened to boys was true, it had become plain to her that the thing they said happened to girls would also happen to her. They both expected it. "*You* going bleed like yu get cut," Moshe had breathed, wide-eyed in astonishment, putting the emphasis on the "you" to distinguish what had happened to him and what would happen to her.

She could not understand her own shyness, which popped up out of the blue like Moshe's stiffened cheelie. It occurred to her, remembering Freud, that maybe she felt shame from her mother's and cousins' admonishments. "Yu can't play with boy now, yu know, yu can't climb tree an run around like yu used to," all interlaced with vague yet unmistakable warnings about pregnancy. It was the "Talk" that Dulsie had given her when she was almost ten, but in more detail, and in such a way that she could not escape its meaning or bury it in forgetting as she had done when she was almost ten.

The warnings humiliated her. What boy were they talking about? She wasn't quabs with any boy, she didn't know any boy, she spent time only with Moshe. The first time the big girls let her read the booklet on the facts of life, she had thought the baby, if it was a good baby, would come out through a woman's navel, the bad ones through her bottom. But first a man would have to do badness to her. The idea of doing badness was at first unimaginable, in the most basic sense, and then disgusting. Even now, at near fifteen, she did not associate it with herself and Moshe. It was the sort of thing men like Mr. Archer did to nasty girls. (Until Mr. Archer's biology class, she was not even sure where she was supposed to bleed from. Some girls in the class had used a mirror to look between their legs. Arrienne never had. It was true of these two children that they were unusually innocent, and came to sexual awareness late.)

Dulsie was walking up and down in exasperation. "Why yu have to go up there now? Let Moshe come an look for yu, yu not well enough to be movin up an down."

"Nutten nuh duu mi," Arrienne said crossly. "An mi nuh trus yu, Mama. Mi know him wi come look fi mi an yu run him wheh."

This was uncomfortably near the truth, so Dulsie flared up in a rage fueled half by guilt, half by relief that her daughter was recovered enough to be as facety (impertinent-stink) as ever. "If yu lef outa dis house tonight, don't come back, stay by yu fadda."

Twice she had turned Moshe away at the gate: "Shi nuh waan si yu, shi sick." And the boy, distraught and believing, since Arrienne had done almost nothing but quarrel with him since they came back from their journey up the mountain, had gone back home to his room and brooded and painted in silence. At school her empty seat was a devastation.

"Okay, no problem. I will stay wid mi father. You ever notice staying wid him give me any headache?"

Dulsie's jester pot came flying. Arrienne ducked, "Sight!" and fled up the hill to Rachel's house.

"Me'll walk with you," Alva said, falling into step with Moshe as the two boys headed toward the school gate.

The school bus to Hopewell, the one that would drop Moshe and Arrienne off at Jericho from where they walked the mile and a half to Tumela, had broken down, and Moshe was on his way downtown to catch the public bus instead. Alva lived in town, at Haughton Court, so he walked to and from school.

"What happen to yu fren Black Beauty?" In the beginning of high

school they had been Whitey and Blacky. Arrienne's stunning transformation the summer after second form had modified her nickname. Moshe's remained the same.

"Shi sick."

"Oh. Sorry fi hear. I thought she was just sculling since this week
is break-up week, nothing much happening after exam except class
party. But you guys don't usually come to class party. You guys don't
usually come to anything."

Moshe gave no response.

Alva was apologetic: "I not criticizing though, man. I just saying."

Moshe hoisted his schoolbag on his other shoulder.

"Good thing she was able to do her exams before she get sick." Alva
seemed unable to stop himself talking. At least he didn't ask what was
wrong with her. Lawrence was a dunce boy but he wasn't insensitive.
"Thanks for the help with the maths again this morning. Boy, I tell you,
I really couldn't have managed another dust-up with the Bing."

"Bingham not so bad. He not a ogre. Just overzealous."

Arrienne imagine how glad the dunce boy must be now to hear
Moshe answer him; him heart mus kin puppalick, turn a somersault,
in gratitude to unknown powers, Lord have mercy, Fisher actually
speak a dozen words, as if one answer make up for the three he didn't
give. Outside of explaining homework, Fisher just never spoke. Except to his Black Beauty sidekick—sidekick, the word some of the
classmates called her all the time though she was the one who led.
Droves of schoolchildren were walking into town now, chattering
and observant, and tomorrow the class would be buzzing with speculation as to how Lawrence had got Fisher, Whitey, to walk with
him, and what Whitey's Black Beauty twin would say when she came
back to school and heard all about it.

"Yeah, awright, if you say so." In his joy the dunce boy growing
loquacious, words heaping upon words as if they going out of style.
"Mi nuh quarrel pon dat. You coming to the political meeting in town
tonight? Is a big thing, you know. Joshua really talking something
different. Youth service an ting. An black people rights."

"Can't get bus that time of night. But is okay. He having a rally in
Jericho next."

"You going?"

"Huh-huh."

"The man cool, man, even though him a brown man. Him grounds with the people." Breaking off abruptly, the dunce boy began to sing, "*Young, gifted, and black! And that's a fact*! Nina Simone, man. You dig her?"

"I dig her."

"Who else you dig?"

Moshe sang softly, under his breath: "*On a cold and gray Chicago mornin, a poor little baby child is born, in the ghetto!*"

Startled, Alva joined in, his voice a light, high tenor over Moshe's husky lower tones: "*And his mama cries, cause if there's one thing that she don't need, it's another little hungry mouth to feed, in the ghetto!*"

The two of them are singing now, Moshe barely audible, as if he has gone shy at his temerity in speaking: "*And then one night in desperation, the young man breaks away! He buys a gun, steals a car, but he don't get far, in the ghetto!*"

They began to syncopate, turning back to the missing stanzas and singing the song through to the end, Alva singing one stanza and Moshe coming in on the refrain, "*In the ghetto!*" then reversing roles, Moshe singing one stanza and Alva coming in on the refrain, until they got to the last stanza and with unspoken consent sang it through together, harmonizing on the next refrain. They didn't even know what a ghetto was, nor did they know anyone, except policemen, who had guns.

Alva was laughing in astonishment. "I dig Elvis, man! I really dig Elvis. You have singles or LPs?"

Moshe had neither. He and Arrienne listened to the music on the radio in his mother's house and LPs on her father's turntable. He didn't tell Alva this, he simply lifted his shoulders in a silent shrug.

They were almost in town now; they passed by Miss Tillerton's shop, across from the mayor's house—the mayor whose daughter, it was said, threw away the child behind the hospital. Alva wanted to go into the shop to buy chocolate fudge. Moshe shook his head at the other boy's inquiry, waited outside with his face turned away while

Alva went inside, coming out a moment later with four fudge squares in a paper bag.

"Here, take one."

Moshe shook his head no.

Shrugging, Alva bit off half a fudge and chewed it noisily.

Alva dawdled again, forcing Moshe to walk slowly, but soon they reached the center of town. "You want to see where mi live, man? Is not far."

"Next time, thanks," Moshe said, already turning away. "See my bus coming."

Alva watched him board the bus and find a seat. Only then did he move off. He was a short boy, but he took up space; he had a lot of bulk; a broad-shouldered boy, he looked like a wrestler. For a boy who was dunce, he had remarkably bright, large eyes, the eyes of someone who was very intelligent and aware. He was the class clown, always making jokes and playing pranks on their classmates. But he had made no jokes on this walk into town. It was as if he had put on another persona, trying to be as serious as possible in the hope of winning over this boy whom he had tried to court for so long.

Moshe was thinking in surprise how he hadn't known Lawrence could sing. But then, Lawrence had not known that about him either. Only Arrienne. The thought of Arrienne brought a slight unease, as if he had done something he shouldn't, though he had not.

Passengers on the Morning Star were laughing and mimicking the way the driver pumped the horn, "A pretty-gal-mi-want-a pretty-gal-mi-want-a-pretty-gal-mi-waaant!" The Blue Danube bus roared behind in competition, tooting its rival horn. "Some-a-dem-a-hoppin-dick-some-a-dem-a-gaulin-a-chichibud-oh!" The driver stepped on the gas. The Morning Star driver grinned in exultation and pressed more gas. The passengers roared.

ii

Seeing her in Moshe's house, Alva could not call her Black Beauty to her face. "Hi, Arrienne," he said, looking sheepish. The flame that surrounded her, as if she had bathed in some fiery liquid, unnerved him and he found himself tongue-tied.

"Hi." She strode past them through the house to where Rachel was shelling peas on the back doorstep. She could have gone around the house, she didn't have to come through the small verandah where they scrunched over the table playing cards. Alva had brought the cards with him. She stomped through the house as if she were trampling on something.

Rachel gave her a wise look but said nothing, simply held out the basin of unshelled peas for her to finish and went to the outside kitchen to blow up the fire.

That night they went to Jericho Square to hear the man who called himself Joshua speak. They each went with their parents but he found her in the crowd.

"Wheh yu wrestler friend?" she mocked.

"Him never come to stay. Was just the one day." He didn't tell her he hadn't invited Alva. The other boy had simply decided that he wanted to come and see where Whitey lived and Moshe, in his quiescent way, had not said no. But he was ashamed of his two-room house and would not have invited anyone from school to come. Especially Lawrence, whose family had money. But Lawrence had been easy and natural, fitting in without awkwardness, and Rachel had liked him. Not hard for her to do, when he went crazy over her cornmeal pone, Arrienne had thought, her mouth sour.

She gave him a scornful look and he put his hand down by his side, searching for hers. He found it and held it tight. She pushed him away fiercely.

The crowd that night was massive. People poured out of the five districts into the small square, swelling to several thousand strong. Some had even come up from Ora, riding on lorries that were so crowded that various parts of their bodies hung over the sides in every direction. In the square and on the lorries was a sea of orange flags that people were waving and chanting, "*Yu wrong fi trouble Joshua, yu wrong! Wi come fi bury JLP, wi come!*"

And there was actually a coffin, draped in green cloth, the color of the rival political party, that was paraded in the middle of the crowd, with the effigy of two johncrows, bald-headed vultures, squatting on top.

Joshua had galvanized the people, nothing like this would be seen again for a long time. The crowd was dizzy with his words, which found a deep echo in their experience. "Nearly ten years of independence and what do we have to show for it?"

"Nothing!" the crowd roared.

"A dat mi always seh!" Noah shouted, feeling vindicated in his weekly quarrels with the clinic staff at the Ora-on-Sea hospital.

"White people and brown people, people like me, still have everything and poor people a still sufferer! Das what wi have to show for it!" Joshua waved the big rod, giving his own answer.

"Sufferer!" the crowd threw back with one voice.

"We don't want to take away anything from anybody, the way they spreading rumor and lie about what I plan to do, we just going to have a more equal distribution in this country, a more socially just society, a democratic socialism in this country!"

"Hail the chief! Speak it, Joshua! Equal rights and justice for all!"

Someone broke into song, "*All for one, and one for all!*" and the rest of the crowd joined in, drowning out even Joshua's booming baritones. When he was finally able to make himself heard again, he rode on their refrain: "People, oonu get it right! *Out of many, one,* should not mean that one set get everything and the many get nothing! All for one and one for all!"

He spoke about women's labor; women's rights; rights in the workplace; the right to protest. (People remembered that he had once lain down in the street in the path of oncoming soldier tanks, daring them to roll over him and eradicate his right to protest, and the tanks had stopped within an inch of his head and could not proceed.) He spoke to them about a living wage, minimum wage; maternity leave with pay; fair treatment for tenants and domestic workers; about getting locally trained teachers, not imports from the former colonial power, so-called Mother England; about rescuing our bauxite from foreign hands, into which it had been ceded in perpetuity for a shilling a ton by the first premier of the opposing party, which was now in power; about universal free education for poor people's children up to university level; about a government that talked to the people in language they could understand, so ordinary people could follow the budget debate in Parliament; about national youth service, community organization, and many more.

It was a lot of promises, but even sober-sided villagers such as George Christie and skeptics such as Rachel and her friend Samuel, who would later dissect every word and wonder if this Joshua could or would do any of the things he promised, were not immune to the combination of fiery words, flaming lignum vitae rod carved at one end like a fist, which Joshua held up and shook toward the night sky to punctuate his passion, and flaming silver hair like a beacon around the gleaming face flushed with his own words and the people's response.

(But even he did not hold them in his hands. Long after, and beginning even then, in the way of a people accustomed to resisting stories that traversed a singular path, which to them was death, they would take his speeches and ring them in another voice, branch them into myriad other forking paths, some destructive, some resistant, some full of other dreams and visions, translations that suited them in their circumstance and place.)

Arrienne listened open-mouthed, tears pouring down her face. Her pores felt completely saturated. She felt as if in that one summer every major turning that would decide her life from now on had come upon her and this was the final and redeeming grace. Her period had come and made the turn into womanhood a most horrible thing. Then the unthinkable happened: Moshe had abandoned her for that dunce boy Alva Lawrence with his head shaped like a sawyer-man dumpling. These two had driven her to despair, but Joshua's speech was different. Like many another young person there that night, she felt that she was irrevocably changed; from now on she wasn't going to live for herself anymore, she was going to serve community and country, a higher ideal, freedom, like Nanny, Tacky, and Bolivar! Fidel and Che! (You have to remember this was a girl who had read *Das Capital* and the Jamaican constitution before she was eight—though she had not understood a word of either and had only absorbed their ink through her pores—and, more than that, had imagined the impossible through the mysteries in a book in a language she could not read. A speech like Joshua's, and a night like this, were bound to unhinge some vital part of her mind. So this carrying away by exaltation was not unexpected, nor would it last short for her.)

The surfeit of this emotion coming after everything else, or indeed happening because of everything else, felt like too much; her body felt exhausted beyond capacity, and longed for Moshe to lean on. He himself listened unmoving, with a grave, locked face, the way he did when he was arrested or had retreated behind his walls.

Like them, many were silent with the weight of annunciation. But the crowd was wild throughout the long night. Teenagers and children screamed along with their elders, people climbed back up on the trucks and bonnets of cars to wave and chant. In the staged intervals the crowd rocked to Ernie Smith, shooting clenched fists into the air: *"Hail the man, that's your brother in the street! Hail the man, every time we meet! Hail your brother, equal man, hail your sister, shake a hand, it's a brand-new day, and we can say it anyway! Hail the man!"*

The meeting broke up in the small hours of the morning, but even then the music wasn't stopping, people were moving off to the tune of Bob Marley and the Wailers: *"One love, one heart! Let's get together and feel all right!"*

Some people held hands, even though, Rachel cynically remarked, the next morning they would be ceitfulling and tiefing their neighbor same as before, never mind the lovey-doveying excitement. In fact, they going to read this equal-rights-for-all as license to help themself to what don't belong to them. "Is the way they been livin all they life, all they goin do is fit what di man seh into dem tiefery, watch an si how dem a-go mek up big lie-and-story outa all what him seh."

But Arrienne was galvanized. Her ears were not catching any cynicism that night.

People flowed, then straggled out of the square, still waving and singing, though the voices were now hoarse and subdued with exhaustion. Rachel and Noah turned to go as well, moving with the Tumela-bound part of the crowd.

Looking around for Arrienne because he was a creature of emotional habit and had not digested the reality of her rage as any true separation, Moshe felt when her hand brushed against his, held it, and convulsed. They walked home, fiercely clenched like this, in their parents' wake. Their hands unlocked only at Maas George's front gate when Arrienne's father said, "Good night, boy," his voice thick with the displeasure he had not been able to conceal about their closeness since they first started growing tall and Moshe's voice broke.

Sometimes after they had been holding hands for a while, it took several minutes before they could let go. This was a purely physiological event; their fingers spasmed and had to be allowed time to unlock. Arrienne was surprised now; she didn't think it would happen when they had quarreled.

Their parents, used to the strange phenomenon and knowing of nothing truly amiss between the two (George Christie wished he did), waited patiently while the process completed itself. When it was over, Moshe rubbed his hand inside his pocket to ease the familiar pain. But the pain lingered and became unbearable. He turned away, walking ahead of his parents so they wouldn't see it showing in his face.

They had arrived home and Noah had lifted the latch from the front door before Moshe's hand relaxed enough for him to grasp the night bucket and fill it with water from the rain drum. It was water to take inside for drinking in case anyone needed it in the night.

The sky was already lightening beneath its weight of stars. Dawn seeped through the banana trees that Rachel had planted around the house. Seeing this, their red rooster started crowing from its perch in the yard.

Over by Maas George's house Arrienne fell into bed and into a deep dreamless sleep. Moshe's sleep, coming later, was restless. He dreamed himself wrestling with Alva Lawrence, then with Joshua, glimpses of Arrienne's sardonic face flitting in and out somewhere above their heads. In the morning his sheet was wet, his clothes soaked through to the skin. He was disturbed by the thought of Alva Lawrence in his dreams, and Arrienne mocking at the fight.

Hearing her voice at the gate greeting Rachel as his mother was going out to her grung, he smiled and went out on the verandah to meet her.

PART III

cities

London bridge is falling down, falling down, falling down, my fair lady!
—Children's nursery rhyme

My heart is down, my head is turning around, I had to leave a little girl, in Kingston town.
—Lord Burgess, "Jamaica Farewell"

CHAPTER IX

i

"It's rising."

Startled, he looked round, but there was no one. The voice seemed to come from inside the oleander bush two graves to the left. It seemed that the bush was speaking.

"The wind. It rises suddenly, like this." A brisk, run-on kind of voice, the kind that ushers people indoors for hot tea and cakes. In its wake came a plump, bustling figure in a bright blue mackintosh, green brogues, and a red woolen scarf piled around her neck, in folds that resembled coils of rubber tubing set atop each other. She emerged from behind the oleander bush, holding a bunch of new jonquils aloft like a torch in her hand. The yellow flowers clashed with her outfit in the sunlight.

"Those togs are not for weather like this, young man. You'll catch your death of cold." Shrewd blue eyes surveyed him up and down, as if he were a parcel she had been given to inspect. In a flash she had measured the long, thin body clad in short-sleeved cotton jersey, Levi's, and open-toed sandals; the two-toned hair and racially ambiguous features. "You're not from here, are you?"

Like a Fauvist painting, Moshe thought, looking away, half-amused. Was "here" this village, Ramsgate—or all of Kent, or England?

"Cat got your tongue, dear? Or don't you speak English?" the Voice continued on. (He found himself thinking of her as the Voice, because the burble of it seemed to have a life independent of its owner.

It had an odd pru-pruing accent, like barble doves calling; he thought she might be Celtic or from the north of England, though her words were not.) "Hungarian, is it? There was one of yours down here the other day, sitting in this same churchyard. Just over there, he was, gave me quite a turn, he did. Thought he was a ghost. Thin as a rail too, undernourished. But that one was Polish, I think. A lot of your kind in these parts lately. Dearie me, I hope it is not an epidemic. No offense meant, dearie, I'm just saying. There are no jobs down here, if that's what you're looking for. If you can't find any in London, not hardly likely in Kent. These are hard times for everybody, and with those black people from Africa or wherever they come from always rioting in London whenever they have a mind to, it is bound to get worse. Bound to affect the public purse. Now then, look at you, shivering! I told you you're not dressed for this weather. It comes off the Stour, you know. Flows into the sea down at Pegwell. Chilly winds way up until summer. Dearie me, you haven't understood a word of what I've said, have you? And how will he be managing then?" The running stream finally paused; she said the last sentence to herself but she was looking at him as if nevertheless demanding an answer from him.

"Not Hungarian. Just foreign." His voice was low, as it always was, but he was trying to conceal the urge to laugh.

"You *are* one of those Eastern Europeans, though, is that right, dearie?"

"Yes, ma'am," he agreed, deciding debate wasn't worth it. He had grown tired of English people's questions, after three years defending himself from their curiosity about what kind of foreigner he was. Most of the time they ignored him, except surreptitiously, but when they asked questions they could be intolerable. And he told himself he wasn't responsible for this woman's suspicion or impatience. England was where he had learned, in self-defense, to lie without blushing.

She did not trust his answer. Her gaze narrowed and he could feel her assessing him in a different way now. "Hrmph," the Voice snorted, a summing-up kind of snort. He wondered what conclusion she had come to, and about what. His appearance was a conundrum that left people aggravated and unsatisfied, even with their own conclusions, which, once made, kept slipping away, with the slipperiness of water.

But she had darted off on another tack, the Voice still accusing: "You're sitting on our-Sheldon's grave, dear. In the way of my flowers."

"Oh, I am sorry." He jumped up and began moving away, but she was lowering herself to her knees on the marble slab and he hesitated, hand half stretched out in instinctive protection, for she was heavy and might have fallen or hurt herself on the stone. But she was already kneeling. She grunted as she did so, as if the effort gave her pain. He withdrew his hand. She rested her forehead against the column above the plinth. He could see her lips moving and he looked away, feeling ashamed, not because she might think he was eavesdropping on her private prayers but because as she kneeled, pushing her coat ends under her knees to cushion herself on the stone, her legs were exposed, and the bottoms of her shoes. Her shoe soles were worn, uneven, more on the left than the right.

That means she leans on her left side when she walks; the right gives her pain.

She wasn't wearing stockings. That was odd. Her legs looked hurt; he could see the thick traceries of varicose veins, the broken capillaries bunched in webs. Something about the sight of them moved him, and in a flash all he saw were these broken symbols of her mortality, a vulnerability so stark that he found himself deeply sorry and at the same time wanting to paint her like this, the hurt legs and the depleted shoes, and it was this intrusion on her privacy, this reduction of her to an idea of her shoes and her legs on canvas, which he could not help, that made him turn away in shame. (He did not doubt that he would paint her anyway, and in just that way, the way she had been exposed in that moment, kneeling.)

"Wait!" she was calling after him, and as he hesitated on his heel, "Wait!" again.

He turned, reluctant.

"Sit." She waved an arm across the whole expanse of the cemetery, an oddly prodigal gesture, take your pick of it all. "I wasn't meaning to send ye away, dearie. Sit, let me just finish talking to our-Sheldon here."

He might have felt annoyed or cynical that she thought to command him to come and go, or stand or sit, or wait, a foreigner she was free to interrogate as she pleased, but a more familiar feeling, the brutal ache that was making his chest break open and bleed again, after so many years, when he had thought he had grown strong and healed, assailed him and he sat, on the next-nearest lichen-covered slab, his back to her, his hand on his chest to stem the beating of his heart and the faint flow of blood.

Arrienne hadn't answered any of his letters. Not even the one hastily scrawled and mailed straight after he staggered off the ship letting her know, *Don't fret, I arrived safely at Southampton Dock, seventh of July 1976, and I wasn't discovered. Nadie me descubrió.* He added that part, *Nadie me descubrió*, misquoting Columbus, only to make her laugh and not be anxious, knowing she would appreciate the allusion.

"Sit," she used to say when they were young and she was in command. He seemed to himself to have been always at the command of women who thought they were queens. *When they were young.* Yesterday he had turned twenty-one, a birthday spent by the riverside at Stour watching the seals. Lumbering and Neanderthal, they made him feel old beyond his years.

He was incapable of thinking that she would hate him, so at first he worried that something terrible had happened to her and she could not write. He imagined her covered up under a white sheet. "No," Alva said, his voice grainy over the pay phone making static in Victoria Station. "She's fine. I saw her making hell in PNP election campaign. She's a major activist now, you know. She supposed to be at university studying but all she doing is kicking up hell in political arena."

He didn't know whether to believe Alva or not. He was angry, he and Alva were both angry that he had to turn to Alva for news of her, when they both knew that when he left he had had no intention of contacting Alva again, and he was ashamed that Alva knew something so private about him, that he and Arrienne were estranged. He felt that Alva would lie to him, to make him feel that she didn't care, and so he could not trust what the other told him.

He felt that she would not be able to survive if she separated herself from him. He thought her sense of self-preservation was too strong to allow her to do that. So he imagined dire explanations.

Perhaps she hadn't got his letters. England was a far way away. Stuff got lost in transit.

Twenty-one packages is a lot to get lost.

He had written her in his journal every day, cutting the pages out meticulously with scissors and mailing them in batches. One batch for each of the years he had been alive, seven per year from the day he arrived curled in the cramped engine room, July 7, 1976, until today, the last day, October 31, nineteen hundred and seventy-nine. He had to say it like that to himself, nineteen hundred and seventy-nine, not in numbers but in words, to anchor for himself how important those letters had been, an anchor more necessary than a ship's cable, and to instruct himself that he had come to the end of a period in his life.

The date of his arrival in England threw Rachel's way of doing prophetic calculations out by one: it should have been the seventh of the seventh seventy-seven, Yahweh's perfect number, seven times three. People at home had talked a great deal about Garvey's prophecy, the year of apocalypse he had predicted, when two sevens would clash. As far as he knew, nothing of major unusualness happened back home a year after his arrival, July 1977. Unless you counted the fact that a lot of people barricaded themselves in their houses on July 7, calling in sick to work, in anticipation of a major catastrophe in the streets. Some lost their jobs as a result, which was not an unusual result for sculling work, though it could count as a personal catastrophe.

Nothing that he could remember happened either on that two sevens–and-a-half day, July 7, 1976, except that he had stowed away in the belly of a container boat carrying a cargo of bananas, and by coincidence arrived at Southampton port on that day.

The riots came later, in August.

He was a child of coincidence who had been born and brought up in a place where coincidence (the exquisite or appalling concatenation of circumstances) was the route taken by history, and so nothing was surprising to him and everything was a route to an expectation.

His mother had chosen June 30, 1958, as his birthday, because that was the day she found him among the macca. There was no coincidence in this choice, only common sense, since he had to have a birthday, and this was the first day of his existence that she knew. So, according to his mother's calculation, yesterday, June 30, 1979, he turned twenty-one years old. One day before he meets a woman burbling like a bird of omen among graves.

By the end of the first six months, of course, he had known she was alive and well, just as Alva had reported, and going about her business indeed kicking up ruckus on political circuits the way she had kicked it up in fights throwing tae kwon do punches on his behalf on the Tumela school road and later at high school, telling their classmates to f-the-f-off when they called him White-Like-Duppy or her Black-As-Sin, the same classmates who sang "To Be Young, Gifted and Black" with the force of a gale and marched against the white teacher of Spanish for calling them black monkeys. They refused to go back to that teacher's class, and were fierce and proud, and alert and bitter toward any aspersions against their skin. Yet they didn't hesitate to use these names, White-Like-Duppy and Black-As-Sin.

Once, on a very bad day, someone had gone even further than the Duppy nickname and called Moshe Backra Bwoy! Offspring of white overseer, plantation owner, slave maker! He didn't like to think about how Arrienne went on then. She was suspended from school for a week.

But he smiled a little, remembering the time Rachel caught her by her abundant hair and washed her mouth out with carbolic soap to cure her of badwordcussing. A habit she had acquired in secret until the day it jumped out of her mouth in front of Rachel. "Pick up yu arse, boy, yu a f-ing fool?" she had screamed in terror at a child too terrified to move, a little boy of five years old, who had fallen on the ground running away from an irate bull in Foster-Reach cow pasture.

In the end she had run at the bull, flinging wild stones until the bull diverted, snorting, and the child got to his feet and ran.

That act of heroism did not stop Rachel from washing out her mouth with the soap.

Suddenly he laughed.

It had never worked.

Rachel wrote in her run-on cursive without commas or stops:

Sorry I take so long to write son but I so glad to hear you Yahweh be praised for He is good and His mercy endureth forever your father sends love and Samuel too ascording to him you are destined for great things there in mother country he dreamed a dream of you standing before the house of parliament in Westminster Square and when he look you have a paper in your hand it was a petition to the queen and you are going to win the case you know Samuel everything to him is occasion for vision and parable but I know long time without doubt or need for prophecy you bound to go far my son how is the weather up there I think about you there in the winter and I am not happy wrap up warm wear a little flannel on your chest and don't forget the asafetida I give you for fresh cold it stop flu and bronchitis I know it don't smell too good but wear it at night wash off yourself in the morning but use warm water don't bathe in cold water in the cold up there better you don't bathe but wash possibles instead until spring if you was here I would boil fresh jackanna and jubawarrin but the asafetida tea is best when you don't have the fresh bush Suzie Q dead bury yesterday doctor say is heart failure people ceitfulling saying is Brown Man you remember Brown Man her sweetman poison her for robbing him of the ganja money you remember them how they use to plant ganja plantation by the riverside and nearly kill you off one evening when you surprise them you was little. Arrii is well.

One full stop followed by the sentence she knew from some deep well of instinct that he craved more than anything else. *Arrii is well,* using his nickname for her. And in every letter after that she always had a small observation like that, sometimes at the end but more often any-which-where in the run-on paragraph, woven casually among the strands of news with which she regaled him about people he knew.

Rachel had found her second métier (her first was motherhood) in this thing of letter writing that Moshe's departure had pushed her into, but the ready-made air-letter sheets, though invented to cut the cost of airmailing, were expensive for her, and after she had filled the page and then turned the thin blue leaf so she could write crosswise on the four edges before sealing it to post, there was no more space left to write, and so perforce the letters which she had come so much to enjoy writing were short.

She made up for that by writing often, his letter in reply to her previous one often crossing another of hers on the way. Sometimes she wrote half of one letter on one airmail sheet and followed it with the rest of the same letter in another airmail sheet, whenever she could find the money. So sometimes he got a letter from her that halted in midsentence and he had to wait for the next air-letter to finish the sentence.

And he was grateful to her for making up for Arrienne's silence and for the kernel of news that Arrienne was well, said in a thousand different ways in the belly of the letter that gave him a picture of Arrienne's life whenever his mother could glean anything of it, Arrii in Kingston making ruckus, hear her on radio last night, and people see her on TV where they watching the news in Pa Brown shop, people proud of her, fighting for poor people rights, they say she going be prime minister, Arrii run down to Tumela last week come look for her old people, I glad to make hallelujah the old way for somebody who appreciate it still.

And when she could not glean information directly with her own eyes, she would write, *Maas George say Arrii doing well he don't like how she big up in the PNP politics business especially now when we country gone killing and murderings like I never see or hear of before but she lead a charmed life.* Later she told him with palpable relief, *So*

Arrii graduate now and it look like she settle down with a little more
steadiness she get job with UNICEF she fighting for the children now
so she don't have so much time for the party politics though she don't
stop she still carrying on fiery for the fighting in her bone.

In twenty-one batches, he had written Arrienne more than three
hundred pages of letters, crafted in his room above the shop in Brixton on Coldharbour Lane. Some of his letters were not in words but
drawings, sketches in which he told her of his life and the ferment
that was Brixton and Ladbrook Grove in the wake of the Notting Hill
riot, the wake of Linton Kwesi Johnson's *Dread Beat and Blood* and
the '76 Race Relations Act. He didn't write her to make her feel guilty
or to force her to write back. He wrote because the cable of trust that
had bound them together from infancy remained unyielding, at least
for him, though she would have said what an irony that he should
think such a thing, when he himself had broken trust. She was still
the only person he could trust with his thoughts. It no more occurred
to him that she could have thrown away any of those letters than it
occurred to him that he could have chosen not to write them.

"It's always nicer to come by myself. Sit a bit quiet with our-Shell."

His companion had got up off the tomb by herself, and it took a toll. She sat heavily on the next grave across from him, and began rocking herself to and fro while she got her wind back. He could hear her breathing asthmatically, as if she had just finished running.

"Are you all right, Mummy?" He was half-turned toward her, his left hand still pressed over his shirt front so she couldn't see the blood.

"What's that?"

"Sorry. It's a title of respect in my country."

"And which country is that? You don't fool me, dearie. I know you were just playing with me when you said Hungarian."

Hungarian was your idea, Mummy.

"Not Polish either," she complained, but seeming caught up in the riddle she had set herself to solve. "Nobody in those countries says Mummy."

I was only translating. Mummy. Mutter. Madre. Mater. Mammy. Miss Mama. Mam. Mama in a thousand languages. Rachel.

"Don't take me for a fool, dearie."

"I would never do that, Mother. Are you sure you're all right?"

The Voice had regained its balance. The wheezing quieted. "Yes, yes. Just a twinge from the kneeling down and getting up sudden. Happen sometimes, I come over queer. But I try to be careful. I don't know what poor Brampton would do if anything happened to me. Now that it's just the two of us."

"Is Brampton your husband?" he asked politely. And because he felt that the question was too personal and he ought to offer something of himself in return: "I come from Jamaica. In the West Indies."

Her gaze on him went sharp. Confusion was on her face, taking in the clotted-cream hue of his skin, the mismatched colors of his eyes, and the shiny straw bangs so at odds with the uncompromisingly black features that those features were rendered ambiguous. "You don't look like any of those that I've seen," an odd expression crept into the Voice, "and I've seen some. You're not a black?" This last was half a statement, half a question.

"I suppose so. In truth, I do not know." He added, gently, "I am sorry I teased you. About being Hungarian. Where I come from not everybody is black or looks black." *No, but not everybody is mixed up in such a way that the pieces don't come together in any way that makes sense or form.* He suffered the feeling of his own fraudulence in using a truth to sustain a lie, defending himself against the charge of homelessness that dogs the nightmares of those who are not at home at home.

"Is that so now? How is it?" The Voice held genuine interest.

"Jamaica used to be a slave plantation owned by the British. A lot of consanguinity went on between the slave masters and the slaves." *Some of us came out red, scarlet as sin, and some even more pale.* The memory from Arrienne broke into his mind, one of the many recalcitrant outbursts she had inserted in her history essays, triumphantly earning a zero for being, again, out-of-order and rude.

She flushed brick-red, the color of her multitubular scarf. It made her look like the Red Queen. He knew he had offended her beyond anything; even if she did not know the meaning of the five-syllable word, she understood its intention.

"I know Jamaica used to be the pearl of the Empire. Rum, sugar, bananas, we imported. I remember. There was a poem—how does it go now?" She fished about in her memory, brought it up at last triumphant, like a sweet rescued from the bottom of a large handbag, "Yes, I have it. *Thou also O land abounding in thy native nectar* (that's the rum and sugar); something something something, *join in with gladness due; no more shall I complain you lie in the farthest reaches of the kingdom, no more will you be the last point of Anna's rule; gaze now upon an English South—I see you in the middle of the world and the British Empire.*[2] That was from a poem we learned at school. I've mostly misplaced it now, never was good at remembering recitation, but our-Sheldon knew it by heart. He had a prodigious memory, our-Shell, held on to anything he learned like a hawk. I don't suppose it's something you'd be familiar with?"

"No, I don't suppose it is. They didn't teach that kind of way where I went to school, not really," he said, marveling at the level of ignorance and folly that was as familiar to him now as bread after three years of hearing the white English people talk about black people. Familiar, yet it never failed to make him speechless with astonishment and something approaching pity. (Years later, rereading his letters, Arrienne found the right words for his astonishment elsewhere, in one of the many books of others she had ravaged for words: *How does a person get to be that way?*)

The woman understood his statement as an admission of deficiency in his education. He could see the triumph in her eyes that showed she felt vindicated; her pride had been salvaged from the blow dealt it by his quip about slaves and slave masters, which had not been a quip at all but the truth.

"You were going to tell me about Brampton," he said, to deflect the moment, both because he felt bad for her and because he was curious, giving himself more time to sketch her in his mind. He could afford the time—after a whole morning exploring the village, he had nothing in particular left to do and nowhere in particular to go.

"You don't look familiar that way at all, though." She had shifted gears again, still caught up in the mystery of his appearance. "And I've seen some."

No. I don't look like anyone. I know.

The face his mother had seen on him, the day she rescued him from the ants and macca bush, had not been a black face. This was the last thing she had given him except her tears, the day he went to tell her he was going to London.

"I pray and yu face disappear," she had said. "And yu get a new

2 "The South Sea Trade" (Commercium ad Mare Australe) by John Alleyn (1695–1730), referring to the Alleyns in Barbados. Translated from the Latin by John Gilmore.

face, not like the one I find yu with. I think if yu had that face, yu couldn't live among wi."

"What face?" he cried. "Mama, tell me!"

But nothing he could say would make her reveal more. "I think it going come back, and then yu will know. That is what my spirit say to me to tell yu. Be patient, son. Everyting come in its time."

"But Mama, suppose it help me to find somebody in England?"

"Hmm. If yu to find him, yu wi find him, don't worry. Yahweh go wid yu, mi son."

Had he been found deformed? Would he return to his deformation?

All his life he had been surrounded by mad people. His mother the worst of all. But it was no use. He would have to wait for the day when he would look in a mirror and see that like Gregor Samsa he had turned into a cockroach. Then he would know, once and for all.

Pure mad people. And now here was another one. In a graveyard in Ramsgate, Kent, England, north of the river Stour. Talking to a duppy in his grave. And they say only black people fool.

"Was our-Shell your son?"

At last she responded to the gentleness of his voice, as people did when they heard him, his voice that was gentle not because of any feeling inside him but because of the trouble of speech, which he had learned to modulate by speaking softly, the words barely touch-ing the sides of his mouth. And yet his spirit was gentle and retiring, though it had nothing to do with his voice.

"No, he's my brother," she said, speaking in the present tense, as if our-Sheldon was still alive to her. "He died young, you know. I took care of him when he was little. Our-Mam got sickly after he was born. Never came back to herself. So I took care of him, being the oldest and a girl. That was how it was in those days. If you were the oldest girl, you looked after the others. He grew up in my hand, so to speak."

Our-Mam. One more to add to the store of words for mother.

Grew up in my hand, so to speak. I didn't know people talked like that here too. That's how we say it in my country. Grew up in my hand. I grew up in Rachel's hand. More than in Noah's.

He didn't have to ask what our-Sheldon had died of. He had read the inscription:

In loving memory of Prvt. Sheldon Atkinstall, sunrise Septem-
ber 4, 1932, sunset April 11, 1954. He died of dysentery serving
his country against the enemies of the Empire in the Guiana
territory, West Indies. Taken from us too soon, but always
alive in our hearts. Father, Brampton. Mother, Mavis. Brother,
Brampton Junior. Sister, Mavisette. Rest in peace.

It had seemed natural to choose this particular grave as his seat, in response to the leaping if ironic sense of recognition that this soldier had died in a place that was his, Moshe's, own—not Jamaica, but still West Indies, and of course in England one became West Indian, here everyone from all the former colonies became a person from the West Indies, not Jamaica or Guyana or Barbados or Antigua or Trinidad, but West Indies, West Indian, as soon as one's feet touched English soil. The irony of the fact that the soldier had died fighting a war of oppression against the Guyanese people simply made Moshe's recognition of the dead man keener.

The soldier had been very young, barely twenty-one years old, Moshe's own age, when he died. Moshe had imagined him, eager-eyed, bold and afraid, with all the world before him, bright in his new soldier's red uniform and black helmet with plumes, his English redcoat uniform, maybe he had a girl, maybe not, but surely he thought of himself as a hero going to faraway to serve his country, and then he died, so fanfarelessly, so without trumpets and without honor, emptying his bowels on soiled sheets in a tent without a single shot being fired either at or by him in that distant place that he had known nothing about, at least not anything he would have thought worth knowing, and whose people he knew nothing about, at least not anything about the kind of people they were.

The sympathy he felt for this soldier, who had not known him and would not have cared if he had, seemed to skip over all the history that made them enemies, his heart pulled to this strange feeling of kinship with a youth he imagined bold, eager-eyed, and afraid, maybe having a girl, maybe not, dying with ignominy in a soiled tent in an unknown place, in a cause he probably had no idea about at all.

And how strange a coincidence it should be, that he had chosen to rest his feet on the one grave that belonged to this woman whose eyes filled with nostalgia for the days of the Empire, who demanded a declaration of origin from strangers and brought bright jonquils for her brother's ghost. Yet England had greeted him with nothing but coincidences from the time he arrived, so much so that he had never ceased to feel that whatever he did here was destiny.

Her eyes followed his in the direction of the inscription. "Yes, our-Shell was the youngest. Our mother and father passed, Mum a year ago, our-Dad in 1973. Now it's only me and Bram. Bram's disabled, so I look after him." She added, as if in answer to a question he hadn't asked but which she thought he should, or would, "Mum and Dad are buried in Exeter. That's where we live now. It didn't seem much sense at the time to bring them all the way to bury here, when we haven't lived in Kent for so long, and me having to leave Bram all by his lonesome to put the flowers on the graves and exchange a thought or two with our-them."

There it was again. Exchange a thought or two with them. His mother would have said "change thought with them." But it was such a similar way of speaking.

"It's a bit lonely out here for Shell, so I come to see him a bit more often than just the anniversaries. Can't make it every end of the month, of course, the way I do for Mum and Dad, but I do what I can, three times a year, sometimes two, if Bram is having a turn. You're shivering, young man. I told you, you cannot dress like this for this weather. This is not the tropics, dearie."

The wind had freshened considerably since she sat down. It was rising on the ground, making scurries in the oleander bush and little circular eddies in the grass between the gravestones. His shirt blew in against his torso and she could see the thin musculature. A woman with a voice that ushered people indoors to tea and hotcakes. The streaks of blood had congealed on his skin so she did not see them through his shirt, except as a thin shadow she might have taken for body hair.

"I know it is not the tropics, Miss Mavisette." He schooled his voice to express patience, not irritation. Arrienne would have told the woman two choice badwords by now. The thought of Arrienne cussing made him smile again, conscious of a feeling of warmth belied by the cold seeping inside his skin from the wind.

Miss Mavisette was studying him now with very shrewd eyes; he had the feeling she was treating him a bit like a wild animal treats a place it has found to forage in, digging little by little, picking up a bit here, a bit there, advancing and retreating, staying a little longer each time, until it owns or thinks it owns the terrain.

So she had thought everybody from that place was dark-skinned. And of course she had never seen pallor quite like his, like bean curds, almost. Hhn. Remembering the last cruelty that made him run away from home, Arrienne, reading, grew aggressive, wondering what else the fauve woman thought she saw and what she thought as she saw. Was she judging the soft gesture of his hands, his delicate beauty and the way he crossed his legs as he leaned against her-Shell's grave plinth? Did she think he looked like some kind of familyless waif or that if he had people who loved him they wouldn't include a girl-friend? Did she think he was the sort of man who in his old age would have not a woman but only a sister to look after him, the way her own brother Brampton did? Arrienne's protectiveness and her jealousy are fierce because she does not like this woman and because she, Arrienne, has sworn to malice him, which makes her perversely hold him closer still. But her own imaginings betray her, for as she thinks Brampton may be the kind of man who might have been attacked on a men's hall for being not-man-enough, for being the unspeakable name, she draws back very fast for she does not want to imagine this woman's brother with fellow-feeling or sympathy or pain.

"What are you doing in a graveyard, all this way in Kent, dear? Do you have somebody buried here?"

He smiled, a touch of whimsy. "I don't know. It is possible. I have sometimes thought that my father might be underneath one of the head-stones I come across in churchyards, but I have no way of knowing."

"Why do you say that? If you come from Jamaica, why would your father be buried in a grave here?"

The concupiscence of slave masters and slaves.

A young girl denuded of virtue in a canepiece. Or a cave.

Do you know my mother hanged herself in a cave? Because I was born? That is what another madwoman, Myrtle Kellier, told me one of the last times I went to see her, without Arrii. Long after Arrii became too angry to know I was still visiting Myrtle Kellier. I couldn't tell her. Not then.

Did she hang herself for the misfortune of giving birth to a child without a father, or for the blight of her life, or for the horror of his unspeakable face? He would never know. Just as he might never know what his birth face had looked like.

He knew it was a mad question, but the time and the place were mad, and here was a slightly mad woman who might just have an answer—his life had been serendipitous that way for too long to allow him to despise madness. So he asked the question: "Do you know anybody buried here by the name of Newland?"

She cocked her head inquisitively, what? and he flushed, but persevered: "I figure you know this cemetery very well. Did you know the families too?"

"Humph. Most of them. I know the names, studied this graveyard by heart the years I come up here to see our-Shell. Funny you ask. I found I knew the families most of the names belong to, even some of them going way back to Magna Carta. Grew up with them, right here, or with their grandchildren and great-grands. Nobody named Newland. Newbolt, Newby, Nesfield, Newport, no Newland. But there was a family named Newland where we used to live in Bristol. We moved around a lot, you know, after the war. Dad had to find work where he could get it, and in those days Bristol had the mines. Next door to us they were, though we never played much with them. Lot of raggedy little children. The husband went away and it seemed to do something to the mother. Kept inside after that, kept the children inside. Funny you should ask. Look, dearie, there's a pub a little ways down the road where we can go in and keep warm until the tide turns. Give the breeze time to die down. Everything in life needs time, I always say. You don't look like you have anything to do in particular, and I'm in no hurry to get home yet—well, I am, for poor Bram's sake, as he'll be fretting after me if I stay away too long, but can't be helped, the next train is not until five o'clock, I have all that time to kill. I brought me a couple of sandwiches. We can have them with a pint. They'll let us eat our own food so long as we buy something. Come, let's get out of it, you look like the wind will take you away any minute."

And because it was true that he had nowhere in particular to go and she was content to talk and not wait for real answers, Moshe shrugged okay and went with the fauve woman he had met by chance for a pint-of at the Horse and Crown Inn, Ramsgate. But most of all he went because she had known a family called Newland, whose husband went away once, and the thought of finding out more about such a family gave him an irrational feeling of hope.

CHAPTER X

i

Arrienne

She was speechless, but she had plenty of words under her skin. Not to mention grief, the underside of rage, which threatened to eat her up, in a moment. In a moment she would burst, plouf! like the wet slap of a gobbet of smoke after somebody throws water on the conflagration.

. . . And so, after a year and a day, the fresh prince to London town came. Well, not exactly a year and a day, though that is the time it usually takes to climb from underworld to glass mountain and down the other side and come back to crossroads where you find sword rusted with blood, omen telling you that somebody who wasn't supposed to die in your absence died and you have to find a way to bring them back from the grave.

Speaking exactly, it took him three weeks. Even if it felt like fifty-two, plus one day, a leap year. How else could it feel, battling heat and bilge water every day under ship cakka hole, not knowing if you are going make it through? Especially when yu a smaddy who nuh like underneath because underneath remind yu of cave? Have mercy, the frigging boy mek mi nearly dead from terror.

It took another year and a day (exactly six months), before she could bring herself to read anything he wrote or drew to her. She broke her promise to herself to rip up and dash 'way everything he sent. But every day a letter came she hugged it up fiercely against her bosom like how you hug-up a baby, and tears squeezed out of her eye-corner so hot and salt they left long white marks that take a week to wash away. She starts to look variegated. She bawls, beating her bed with her fists in a tempest, till her body buckles over and makes a cage over the letter-baby. The sound of her crying runs deep, like a harshly plucked bass instrument. In between her sobs she flings like stones the most words she has ever uttered in one go. They come out tattered and broken but it is still a long skein of claats that she sells him, a rosary of badwords longer than a journey. She feels when exactly in the night they reach their target. His body jerks in his bed as he hears her, and he screams her name, "Arriiiiii!" and sit up in the bed and start to bleed. She smile, Yu raas yu, Moshe Fisher. Yu raas. She say it again like a noun that is his name. Yu-Raas-Yu.

London, he said, was hard, but not as hard as he might have expected. The British Museum was the worst, it nearly killed him. While he is writing he is doing his best not to remember that part. He doesn't tell her about it for a long, long time.

When he thought London, he didn't think Brixton, which was where he lived, even though Brixton was supposed to be within the Greater London. London was the part that they called the City, a different place altogether. London was a world apart.

Half of what made it hard and not so hard was the way it turned out that he had always known this city.

In the beginning, the first few days, he couldn't stay still, couldn't stop walking, just walking, his head in a fever, sometimes panicking if he had to go inside a building where a door would close behind him, as if after the long weeks scrunched in the ship's belly he needed to feel his feet on solid ground, needed to feel that his legs his hands his being his body could move, that the open air was still accessible to him and he was still a candidate for grace.

Throughout all of this he walked in places that looked so I've-been-here-before that he found himself saying to Arrienne over and over again, It strange, don't? though he didn't know if she could hear him from across the seas, from so far away. (After a while he knew that she could, if she wanted, because twice in the night he heard her weeping, in that angry, tempestuous way she had, and another time he heard her laugh with malice aforethought.)

Charing Cross Piccadilly Circus Kings Cross Regency Street Big Ben Bayswater St. Pauls Westminster Parliament Square 221B Baker Street Hyde Park still with the soapbox "the-city-does-be-hearts" corner where his namesake Moses in the first West Indian novel he ever read used to jive in the summer. Buckingham Palace (they used to call it "Bucknam Pellis" at school, laughing, after they read *Pygmalion* and took turns imitating Eliza Doolittle)—Buckingham Palace was the one surprise, he hadn't expected it to be so ugly or so bland, though the changing of the guard was nice, so quick and seamless and robotic, as if men could truly be in charge of their own bodies and make them into machines. Covent Garden Mayfair Shepherds Bush Notting Hill Tyburn Tree Victoria Station Waterloo Trafalgar Square the River Thames. Everywhere was strange yet nowhere was strange, because he had seen it all before, in the books he had read at school, almost all of them from England, and then at last a few that were still from England but written by people from the place where he was from and these had opened like a light to him that first year he and Arrienne went to university, before the year of bitter discovery (that first year before he ran away and left Arrienne to go it all alone), and it was because it dawned on him that the map of this city was etched on his mind through words he had read that he felt accustomed yet apprehensive and cheated.

Sometimes he had the strange sensation that he was leaking, not body fluids but ink, printer's ink, that had made his skin porous over many years of exposure; he was poisoned in his bloodstream by other people's words written down, and he couldn't tell what the outcome would be, except that because of such words a foreign place had become more familiar to him than any place should be that he had never been.

Still, one night thinking about it he wrote, *No. Not just books. England was all around us, all the time. Right next door. Not just any door but a glass door you could push and go straight through to the other side.*

The sight of so many of his own words written down unnerved

him, so he rubbed them out and drew the glass door, with Big Ben and a pale garden and a soldier on a pale horse on the other side of it. Then he drew the door again, this time with a mess of images on the other side: Fort Charlotte with its ode to the mad king's wife in olde worlde calligraphy on a brass panel; the jumble of drystone walls at Tumela that people said had been built by slaves in the English fashion, only they had added molasses to suture one stone to another; clumps of women floating like style above Foster-Reach River balancing wash pans on their cottas, and in the wash pans stacks of embroidered white doilies with which his mother and Tumela and Ora women garnished their center tables, the way the English did. Like the English, so they thought, they hung lace curtains in their windows and displayed Christmas cards showing pictures of snow in the glass fronts of their best-chinaware cabinets.

Jammed up against these he drew people walking through the doorway of a strict church, no jewelry, no wild song, the kind of church that only fancy people in Ora attended, Church of England church, and then he drew a jester-pot full of a haze that ascended above all the rest, like soup smell rising from the root of silk cotton trees while the district slept. The clash and turmoil of the drawing gave the impression of a street that had collapsed in on itself or a town in which everything had fallen through everything else at the end of an earthquake.

It was the first picture in the letter packs that Arrienne framed.

Soon a hunger for Tumela and Ora hit him like an ache. He missed the old people's voices giving good morning, good evening, offering warnings like benediction, tikya wheh yu walk, nuh buck yu toe, tikya wheh yu talk, bush got ears. He missed the sound of sea waves at night, sometimes when he fell asleep on the boat with Noah, missed the sun's heat that brought the oil in skin to the surface (though his pale skin did better in London's watery light than in Tumela's harsh glare), missed most of all Samuel and his mother on Sunday evenings making smoke with mystical thoughts of another life that had driven him to brush and paint almost as soon as he was old enough to know that this was the one fluent language he would ever speak. In the same way that he was driven to paint, he thought, some people were driven to drink by irresistible forces. He went through life in London in a drunken haze.

It was mainly thanks to Joseph that his life was saved. Joseph found him a room, an upstairs in a rooming house in Brixton. The kitchen, toilet, and bath were shared between him and two roommates, a Nigerian of indeterminate age who with a straight face introduced himself as a prince, and an English youth with acne, a student at North London Polytechnic. To Moshe's great relief they went out early and came in late, so he hardly ever saw them or had to be around them in the communal parts of the house.

His room, at least, was his own.

It was a tiny room, he could barely turn from one wall to another without bumping into something, his bed or the washstand or the radiator, which were his only furniture until he bought a secondhand table, cheap but strong and sturdy, good pine, where he could spread his brushes, drawing paper, pens, and journal. He learned to move sideways between things, without breaking up his motion, so that if he wanted to get from the table to the bed, he made getting up from the table and walking to the bed a single, seamless shuffle, like a crab. That way he did not bump his elbow or his hip and bleed.

The wallpaper was torn in places, showing the ugliness of the wall beneath. He papered the holes and then the entire walls with his drawings, so that the dingy slate-pink interior soon became a blaze of hallucinogenic light. When the landlady discovered this just before he gave up the room, she tried to fine him and then to have him arrested for defacement of property, but he left before she could follow through, not because he was crooked but because he had to go. He hoped the paintings would compensate. He would have given her the money if he could, but he had none, he was paying half his earnings in rent, and sending the rest home to his mother every month and to Alva to repay his student loan. He economized on food so he could spend anything left over on painting supplies. That wasn't hard. He had never been a big eater.

Years later, when he became famous, and especially when he died, the landlady missed out on an opportunity to become very rich, for she did not keep the incredible gallery of painted light that he left behind him but instead tore it down to put in wallpaper that was real and that gave her a reason, which she did not need, to raise the rent on the next tenant. It was perhaps just as well that she never learned about his fame.

He was glad the toilet was not in the bathroom with the tub but in an alcove off the bathroom, with its own door. It was a great relief not having to wait to use it if someone was taking a bath and he was desperate to "go," a great relief not to worry that one of his roommates would burst in and use it while he was the one taking a bath, or, worse still, if one of them burst in to take a bath in a hurry while he was taking a piss or a big one; a great relief not to be privy to the embarrassing odors and noises of other people's personal intimacies or have them be privy to his. He felt he could never have relieved himself again, had everything been all in one and the toilet not had a door.

The bathtub was awkward for him who had always bathed in rivers or dipped water from rain drums outside and poured it over himself with a calabash, except when he went to university in Kingston. Standing upright under the spray in the shower stalls had not been much different from pouring the water over himself with the calabash. Now he substituted for his calabash a dish like a scoop to pour the water after he soaped himself, but he still had to decide between kneeling in the tub to wash all of himself at once, or sitting on the tub's edge with his back to the floor to wash his front, then turning the other way to wash his back, or pouring the water standing up so that it splashed on the floor and the whole bathroom was soaked. If he had the time to mop up, he washed himself standing. Otherwise he sat on the edge of the bath with his back to the floor to wash his front, then turned the other way to wash his back. After a few days he improvised a shower, attaching a hose to the faucet and a nozzle to the end of the hose.

At university he used to rise at dawn so he could take a shower before anybody else was likely to be awake (except at exam time, when no one slept, and getting to the showers alone was pot-luck). At school he never used the urinal in front of the other boys, instead learning to hold his pee with the tenacity of a girl. The boys were merciless whenever, unable to hold out, he finally went to the urinal, turning his body away from the others. Whitey don't want to show his wood because is no wood, is a half-size termite grub. In the house in Brixton he waited until his roommates had left for the day before washing himself, but he soon found that he needn't have bothered since they didn't use the bath except, at most, once a week.

This was the first strange thing he found about people in England, that they were not so fussy about attaching their bodies to water and soap as his people were. Tumela people were obsessive about clean: clean food clean yard clean body, especially underarm and crotch, clean underwear. They were obsessive about such things as only people can be who toil under the hot sun and once upon a time were told they smelled bad, like beasts (though no time was given to them to wash themselves, when the sugarcane fields and Massa's dinner, Massa's baby, Massa's bath were waiting, and though most beasts did not smell bad then, any more than they do now).

So this is why the houses don't have showers, he thought. People don't wash themselves all the time. Baths were fine if you were going to have them only once a week. You didn't have the time for more if you had to go out to earn your living. *Maybe only retired people here bathe every day*, he joked to Arrienne, wanting her to laugh and answer his letter.

Arrienne reading his letter thought, Those English people are so damn nasty. As she had always thought, from the time one of their teachers told them she went in the sea at Ora and called it bathing. But he didn't think about this English strangeness in the way Arrienne did, though at first he was a little shocked, hearing in his head his mother Rachel's voice raised sharply at him if he ever went to his bed without first "washing up," or "washing yu possibles," and Samuel's voice recounting true stories of what happened to people who went on the road unwashed and fell ill, and were taken to a hospital where nurses and doctors pulled up their clothes while they were unconscious, revealing the shame of their dirty underwear and unwashed skin. It seemed to him that in London perhaps it was all right to be not so fussy, because the sun did not shine to make you sweat (in the winter it would not shine at all), and moreover you never had to walk far distances. And he wondered at how hard his people worked at staying clean in a place that often had drought and where they had to go to the river and carry the water in buckets on their heads. Shame, he thought, was as irresistible a force of history as painting or drink, and could burrow just as easily under one's skin.

He made it a point to shower as if Rachel were spot-checking him several times a day.

He paid two months' rent in advance, most of the money he had brought with him. Money he had hoarded from his earnings selling fish after he started going to sea with his father and Noah let him keep the proceeds from whatever he caught.

"Is a reasonable rent," Joseph said. "Yu not going get it any cheaper, unless is a cockroach nest or a rat hole. And it don't mek no sense paying in advance for more than two months. Even that I think is too much. Suppose the place turn out to be a rat hole in truth? But yu ears hard, yu wi learn. Don't seh mi never warn yu."

But he wanted to pay so that he would have a roof over his head for a good while in case he didn't get any work. "Dat nuh possible," Joseph said, "yu wi get work," but such was his fear of homelessness that he wouldn't listen.

Joseph found him a job and accompanied him on his first trip to the art school, a place where a man like Joseph, a rough sea hand, ship's oiler, would never have gone in the normal course of his own life.

"But nutten bout you nuh normal, bredda," Joseph said, shaking his head in that half-wondering, half-exasperated way he had in talking to Moshe. "Yu is a case an a half. But school yu come fi go, school mi a-carry yu. If yu risk yu life stowing away pon ship fi di privilege of daubing paint pon paper, who is mi to tell yu no? As I seh, yu wi learn."

But after the letter came in the mail, signed by the director of the art school, saying they had reviewed Moshe's portfolio and were impressed enough to offer him a scholarship covering tuition, book grant, and a small stipend toward board and lodging, starting in the autumn term, October, Joseph had eyed him with new respect. "Well, bwoy, yu knock mi fi six. Maybe there is someting in it after all. Of course yu know yu color help yu. Even though mi nuh know wha kind-a white man yu be. Never see a black white man before." He laughed his sudden barking laugh, showing all his teeth. "I don't think di art school people ever see one either!" He gave another shout of laughter, enjoying the memory of the look of confusion on the receptionist's face when they walked in.

Joseph had been wearing his best suit and had shaved his beard, so he looked quite distinguished, though he was built like a football player and rolled a little on his feet and when he stood still he spread his legs a little apart as if he were feeling the ship's roll in high tide underneath him. It wasn't just his looks that were transformed though. Moshe listened in astonishment while Joseph addressed the receptionist in the Queen's English with an impeccable English accent, the kind of accent his high school teachers had told their students was acquired by speaking with a large plum in your mouth in the course of lessons in elocution.

It was rare for a black person to turn up in these halls, but it wasn't Joseph who was causing the receptionist's confusion. She kept staring at Moshe, but without saying anything. Back in the street Joseph muttered, "Bitch. I bet if we turn back now we'd catch her searching through your application form to see what you wrote for 'race.'" He was having trouble shifting back to Jamaican. "By the way, what did you write?"

Moshe blushed the color of dark blood. "I ticked 'other,'" he said, adding defensively, "I didn't know what to write."

"Who quarreling with you, man?" Joseph said. "But don't worry. One thing for sure, shi don't decide yu black. At least not yet. I told you they wouldn't. Yu either white, or dem confuse. Dem going decide yu is Eastern European or some such inferior white species. Watch me and see." And he laughed again, so much that Moshe found himself laughing too, his heart unaccountably lifted.

He didn't tell Joseph that, confused, and feeling that the application form was some kind of hidden test, he had also checked three other categories—"white," "African or Caribbean black," and "Indian"—

the latter for good measure, just in case, because he didn't know, but there had been rumors that he might be part Indian. His entire life, growing up under Rachel's stringent Yahwehist tutelage, he had been scrupulous about telling the truth. He was so afraid of appearing to lie that he was often driven to confess to possibilities which he wrongfully accused himself of, doubting his own motivations. So he checked all these things on the application paper in case he might be found to be transparent and they would think he lied.

But in the end he lost his nerve; even he found these answers too doubtful, and remembering Joseph's injunction, he crossed out everything except "white" and "other." He asked for another application form but the receptionist said, her voice sounding so polite that he read in it her scorn, "It is all right. You may cross out any errors."

When he didn't hear back from the school he thought in despair that it was over. But then they called him in for an interview, in an oak-paneled room where the director, an ascetic man with an ironic face, asked him a lot of questions and it finally dawned on him that this was because he had written "other" on his application and they didn't think anybody named "other" or "white and other" could produce the kind of work they had seen in his portfolio.

It wasn't hard to convince them that he'd done the work himself because they made him draw in a sit-down exam where, his hand shaking so that he had to start over again several times, he tried to draw Arrienne and found he couldn't; she kept receding behind a veil of smoke, so he drew his father on the boat at dawn, the sun coming up like a huge cockerel's comb on his shoulder, his burned-logwood legs all rope and sinew except for the white strip where his thigh was bandaged so his perpetual wound would not leak.

He didn't think the drawings were very good, because he was so nervous and he felt like he was looking at his family through the glass door he had imagined led through to England, only now they were on the other side. He couldn't see his way clear to draw them in the way he wanted. The director looked at the drawings for a long time, lingering especially on the spoiled one of Arrii that he had crumpled in his fist to throw away, but the director said, No, you can't take anything out with you, not even rough work, let me have that please.

The director didn't speak while he looked at the drawings. He made a sound between his nose and his throat, a bit like the way someone might sound if they said, "Hmmph," distributing the sound equally between their nose and their throat.

At last, "Thank you, you may go. You will hear from us, Mr. Fisher," he said.

But before all of this happened the director had said, "What is 'other,' Mr. Fisher?" asking the question casually, too casually, Moshe thought. Though he had never heard the word used in that way, to refer to what a person could be, and had never before been given it as an option by which to name himself, he was alert to its implications for he had lived them a thousand different ways, from the day he was born to this moment facing a white man with an ironic smile across a mahogany table in a paneled room hung with paintings from around the world, some that he recognized, only none from his part of the world.

Other. He had seized on the word with relief for it gave him a way to gather his contradictions together in one place. And now the word, he sensed, had become a danger.

"What is 'other,' Mr. Fisher?"

"I don't know," Moshe said, truthfully.

But in his heart he said, It's your word, it was on the application, why do you ask me?

"But you ticked it on your application." The irony in the director's face intensified. "Are you both white *and* other?"

"I wrote it because I don't come from here."

"I see." The director contemplated him for a long minute, his fountain pen held loosely in the fingers that he was flipping slowly up and down, like someone steadily opening and closing a shutter.

Moshe felt himself change color several times under the steady gaze. His face went hot and cold and hot again, and he could only surmise, with humiliation, through the memory of Arrienne's words of awed fascination whenever he went from red to white to blue and back again, like a symphony in flags, what he looked like to this Englishman.

"So is white not white if you come from elsewhere? From the colonies?"

I don't come from a colony. My country became independent in 1962. He would have said this aloud, correcting the man, but he felt the words jostling the insides of his cheeks and the cavity between his tongue and the roof of his mouth, and knew he had to keep speaking to a minimum, or all his words would run to rubble and bleed. Lately, since Arrienne had not written, this had begun to happen to his speech again.

"I don't know. What people think here." He said this in two sentences, not one, to make a pania-machete meaning that would elude the Englishman.

In his heart he upbraided himself for following Joseph's advice, "Say 'white.'" Why had he allowed himself to write that foolishness?

The director made the noise between his throat and his nose again. "Is that why you also ticked 'Indian' and 'black'?" The ironic smile that seemed to be a perpetual expression stretched the corners of his lips across more of his face. His lips were a long narrow line, like a knife slash in canvas.

I crossed those out.

He had always been told no one was supposed to score the rough work. That it was an unforgiving act.

"I probably have some mixture of that. I don't know."

He wanted to say, "The truth is, I am a black man," but this was not something he could claim, in the face of laughter down the years, "Whitey!" Voices behind him and Arrienne, tightly holding each other's hands, "White-Like-Duppy, Black-As-Sin! Mauve Gal! Blue Boy!" Voices in the boys' urinal, "Whitey nuh got no wood, it short and swizzle like termite grub!"

I think you could say I'm blue.

Immediately he hated himself for trying to sound facetious and sounding precious instead. Even if only he heard himself.

He was angry and offended, and though he knew his face was running the gamut of color from crimson to angelfish, he met the director's gaze unflinchingly and it was the Englishman whose eyes finally fell.

"You have an unusual talent, Mr. Fisher," the man said, backing off abruptly as if the subject he had been pursuing had suddenly grown dangerous teeth. "Very—energetic."

What does that mean? That I paint like a barbarian?

He was angry in a way that was radical, like Arrienne, almost the way he had been angry once with Alva.

But the director didn't say anything more. Just put him in the room to prove that the drawings were his.

That time he had gone to the school by himself. He didn't tell Joseph what happened, because he was ashamed. It didn't occur to him that for the director to interview an applicant was unusual, that the strange encounter might not have been all about his ethnicity but perhaps also about the unusualness of his work.

Three days after this interview, the letter saying he was admitted with a scholarship came.

In between, the British Museum happened. But he didn't tell Arrienne about that for a long time.

CHAPTER XI

Before all of this, of course, there was Joseph.
(Whom he had accepted simply as providence, fate. He was, after all, Rachel Fisher's son. Superstition ruled his thought.)

Everything was Joseph. Joseph who had realized before anyone else in the crew that the dark color on Moshe's skin had been carefully painted on but was in danger of coming off in the heat of the engine room where he scurried back to hide whenever the whistle call, "Captain ahoy!" went out from the group that had banded together to hide him after he was discovered. Joseph who had pulled the Rasta tam off his head and exposed the straight straw bangs and pepper-grain nigger-mix he kept concealed throughout the voyage. The paint and tam had been his camouflage, to protect himself from puzzled stares if he was discovered, and it had worked, until Joseph blew his cover.

Joseph had come down to the engine room to fiddle again with the temperature gauges so he wouldn't roast in there.

"Hey boss, is bleed your skin bleeding off you?" Joseph was no fool. He didn't just know every crevice, corner, and device of the ship's lower levels, he had eyes like a hawk and a nose for fishiness and had been watching the stowaway for days without a word.

Frightened, Moshe went so red and then so pale that all of it showed through his disguise. "Jesus Christ," Joseph exclaimed, "is a white man stow 'way!" and that was when he pulled off the tam and rubbed his hand against Moshe's neck (mercifully, not his face, he had run out of dark paint, he could not replenish his color again) and the smear came off on his hand.

Joseph leaned up against the girders and crossed his legs at the ankles and his arms at his chest like someone settling down for a long chat that was going to be amusing, but his eyes were wary and distrustful as a snake's, and this time he was speaking in raw Creole: "Awright, boss. Start from di beginning. And don't try to tell mi no fuckery because if yu do dat, it worse fi yu. Where yu come from, how yu really get on dis ship, an how yu come fi learn how fi play Jumaican black man, even down to di language?"

The captain must have been asleep because they were down in that engine room for a long time. Joseph gave him a scarf to wear against his neck, which was a godsend because this far out on the Atlantic the breezes were often cold. The first day he had tried hiding among the containers on deck, slipping between the cells that held two rows of the monumental cylinders together, but he had almost frozen to death and wriggled himself under cover of night down the stairwell to the engine room. And there too he might have died if Joseph, moving about on his rounds oiling the controls, hadn't found him before the chief engineer went down to do his inspections.

"Yu don't know how lucky yu be. Yu see ships like dese? Stowaway get trow overboard," Joseph said.

Moshe thought he was joking.

Joseph shot him a dry look. "It happen before, bredda." More than that he would not say.

"I would never have guessed. Yu really skill wid yu hand," Joseph said, surveying his painted face. But he made him wash everything off as soon as they came to shore. "Trus me, dat color of yours, strange as it be, go help yu here far more dan any blackness go hurt yu. Dem not goin work out quite what yu be but dem not goin tink yu black. Jus one ting, try get di English accent an don't talk no patwa, even to me. Dat way yu won't slip up. Is so yu get job. Yu bring school certificate?"

He had. Eight straight ones on his O Levels and three As on his A Levels. But he hadn't wanted what Joseph called a proper job. A white man's job. He wanted to stay in Brixton, among people who were more like people he knew, and he wanted to work where he felt mostly safe. Which, Arrienne thought, was quite ridiculous because he hadn't been all that safe among the people he grew up among in Tumela. Unless he meant where people wouldn't exactly beat or kill him. What he meant was not "safe," but "familiar."

Yu was readin too much foolishniss, Arrienne told him later. Yu get mix up. Is America dem kill black people. English people wi oppress yu like hell, but dem nuh so quick fi kill yu. Dem nuh ha' nuh gun. But she knew about SUS laws, and warned him in her mind.

Joseph found him a job working evenings and weekends at a pub on Coldharbour Lane, two streets down from where he had found his room. The pub was called the Green Man, which he thought was not a bad name for someone who had been called Blue Boy most of his life and loved the colors of paint. Indeed, in his superstitious way he received it as a good sign. *There's no sea here, why it should be called Coldharbour Lane?* he wrote to Arrienne. *But it's nice. It made me think about Fort Charlotte and the evenings when we walked all the way home, the sea always on one side, always either jumping up or calm and still, and blue till it hurt your eye.*

In the end Joseph gave up on teaching him the accent. He couldn't produce words for long enough at a time to get it right. "Yu mus be di firs Jumaican in history who can't mimic accent," Joseph shook his head in amused exasperation. "Dem is monkey people, man. Maybe yu is white man fi true. How yu manage fi grow up mongst monkey people an can't do wha monkey do?" And he broke into derisive song, *"If yu shake a leg, monkey shake it too! I don't know what to say the monkey won't do!"*

The pub owner was a red-faced man with a walrus mustache who made him think of the policemen standing to attention at Westminster. He put Moshe to work washing pots and tableware and scrubbing the stovetop, for one pound and twenty-five pence an hour.

A heavyset Jamaican woman named Elsie Wauchope cleaned the toilet and public areas of the restaurant. Her face was set in a perpetual scowl, except when she was talking to white people, especially the boss, and then she smiled and smiled without stopping. Moshe could imagine her making up for her ingratiating smiles by saying the nastiest things about them behind their backs. Moshe she regarded with special frowns. One day he heard her muttering under her breath when he passed her, "Hmmph. Nebbasicomesi. Monkey climb tree, soon expose him ass. Red Ibo people tink dem better dan black," and he knew she said it in patwa for him to hear. Normally she spoke English with an in-between accent, like a cover-up, cockney thinly spread over broad Jamaican. She thought he was snobbish because he did not speak or acknowledge her in any way. But he held his head down out of inveterate acute shyness, especially in the presence of large, strong women. And he was timid in the face of her capacity for pretend smiles; he knew how dangerous she could be, like crab soup boiling without fire.

The kitchen staff consisted of Moshe and three others: the head cook, the assistant cook, and a morose brother from Poland with so much foliage on his face that the pub owner made him wear it in a net to avoid hair from it escaping into the food. The others complained that they had a hard time understanding anything he said because his words got lost in his beard and mustache. But to Moshe, who had lived his life deciphering the vibrations of words rather than their sound, Piotr's voice was clear as a bell and the two of them got on just fine.

Piotr did inventory and the floors but was expected to chip in at the stove whenever rush hour brought a larger crowd than usual. When Moshe arrived, the crew looked at him with curiosity but nobody said much. One of the cooks handed him an apron and plastic cap. With his head covered, the kitchen dim with haze from the stove's heat and everybody concentrated on dealing with the orders shouted through the hatch, nobody noticed his double hair, and his whiteness, if sickly looking, appeared normal.

The work was rough but not difficult once he learned how to operate the dishwasher. He wouldn't have minded it except for the constant fear of cutting or bruising himself, a knife slipping, a glass accidentally dropped, the rough scrubber that he had to use on the big pans making contact with his palms through a tear in the rubber gloves he was given to wear. The fear that then he would bleed in front of everyone and that would be the end of his job.

None of the things he feared happened—no knife, no glass dropped, no tear in the rubber gloves—but the unaccustomed labor took a toll on his hands and they bled, once almost filling the gloves with blood so that he had to dash to the toilet where mercifully no one but himself came in until he had washed all the blood away and wadded his hands thick with paper towel over wax paper he took from the kitchen.

At night he bandaged his hands in cloth and taped the cloth down with Sellotape, but the bleeding began again almost immediately and this time the other kitchen hand, the boy from Poland whose name was Piotr Pulaski, and the chef's assistant whose name was David Schweppes, though he was no relation to the Schweppes of Schweppes Bitter Lemon, saw what had happened and whispered in the ears of the head chef. Moshe trembled in panic because the head chef was an irascible man who barely spoke except to snap orders. His name was Albert Beat. He looked across at Moshe for a moment before barking something around the matchstick which was always in his mouth.

Moshe was taken off washing up and stovetop and given Piotr's job instead, except for the cooking. "Can't have you bleedin all over the grub, mate," David Schweppes said, explaining the head chef's decision. "Bloody not on."

He lost the job anyway. The rough broom handles were no kinder on his hands than the steel-wool scrubber had been. His improvised bandages gouged deep and would not come off without taking skin with them. The nurse assistant at the hospital bandaged his hands and told him to stay away from water for a week.

"Jesus Christ, man, what yu be? A man or a mouse?" Joseph shouted in frustration. "Yu mumma an yu puppa never mek yu do no work at all?"

"Not really. Not this kind," he admitted sheepishly. He used to reel in a fishing line. But always with his father's help. Noah's hands over his, taking most of the weight when the fish pulled.

"Cho rass." Joseph sucked his teeth. "I don't know what di rass dis I tek upon myself. Chinese proverb true fi true. Save a man life, yu end up owning him. Awright, come. But listen to me good, yu hear me? Yu tekking di job dat available for yu to do, not di one you tink yu shoulda get. Which mean dat yu mighta haffi go lef Brixton. Yu just haffi learn fi relate to all kinds of people, is all. Dat is someting yu haffi learn wherever yu go. Is yu run wheh come-a foreign, nobody never sen fi yu. So yu better survive. Dis is di ongly job I know bout right now, and I leavin tomorrow, ship ready fi di next sail, I don't have no more time."

The announcement of Joseph's leaving was not unexpected but it made him feel empty and more than a little desolate. He had been in London only a few weeks. He did not know that Arrienne would never answer his letters, or that the feeling of loss that knotted in his stomach was to become so familiar, with the familiarity of a close friend. He went with Joseph to the docks.

"Take care of yourself," Joseph said, suddenly formal in English. "And don't do anything too foolish."

"I won't," Moshe said.

They shook hands.

He put his hands in his pockets and watched the big man walk up the gangway, the Atlantic wind blowing his battle jacket into a half balloon. At the top of the gangway Joseph turned and waved again, shouting something that got lost on the wind.

"Yu tek care, man," Moshe whispered, turning away.

CHAPTER XII

Despite Joseph's threat, the new job was also in Brixton. So he didn't have to travel far. It was a most unlikely job, looking after an old white man who needed someone to cook and shop for him in the daytime. At night his daughter came home from her job as a nurse's assistant at King's College Hospital on Denmark Hill. A nurse, not his daughter, came in twice a week to check his blood pressure and vital signs.

Moshe's job also included small intimate things like helping the old man get to the toilet, changing his diapers when he pissed in them, and helping him count his money, which he did incessantly, obsessively, pouring the bills and coins onto the table from the metal strongbox he kept under the bed, refusing his daughter's attempts to get him to open a bank account.

He really irascible, Moshe wrote to Arrienne that September. *Miserable as johncrow batty. Take up this. Put down that. Sit down up. Walk up straight. The food too hot. The food too cold. Mi hot, take off my sweater. Mi cold, put on back my sweater. Yu rass, I tell him in my mind. First I ever cuss so. Maybe I miss you. Please write.*

Sometimes irascibility shaded into downright spite. This happened when the pain in the old man's extremities became too much to bear. He would spit out the food, all over his front, so that Moshe would have to clean and change him. At other times he threw the food against the wall, aiming with surprising strength for someone so scrawny. Moshe was sure he couldn't weigh more than a hundred pounds.

You never know ill will could make a man so strong, he wrote in his journal to Arrienne. *And he almost hurt my feelings. You know cooking is the one thing I can do when it come to housework. Mama really teach*

*me that before we went to Kingston, so I wouldn't starve on campus
or have to eat badfood. So when this little maaga Englishman finding
fault with my cooking I am not amused.*

But funny enough, he wrote, *I don't mind the work. I so used to tun-
ing people out, you know, that easy. He cuss all day but I just go somewhere in my head. I think I find him a bit of a relief. He's the only one
I've met who has decided what he thinks I am and stuck to his guns
on that. Don't ask me no question, make up him mind all by himself. It
bring a certain amount of equilibrium.*

"Dirty little Chink!" the old man would crow in his most devastated
moments. "You think I don't know you, but I know you! Chinky! Why
don't you go back to Hong Kong?" And then, as if he had lost something incredibly precious among the piles of trashed newspapers
and magazines that he tore up when he had nothing better to do, he
would skitter his hands through the piles and ask, weeping, "What is
my name? Do you know my name, Chinky?"

"Your name is Mr. Durham, Mr. Durham," he'd say, showing the
old man his name on the lid of the lead strongbox.

Once he saw the box, the old man became mollified, and would
start counting his money again. "Percival Durham. Percy." Saying his
own name interrupted his counting, so he would lose track of the
money and have to start all over again. Soon afterward, he would fall
asleep. Moshe would sit in the living room beside him and draw.

The house stank of urine and no amount of cleaning, not even with
Jeyes Fluid, seemed to get rid of the smell. It was a nasty house, un-
cleaned for weeks after the previous caregiver had walked out, fed
up with the old man's rudeness, and the nurse-daughter had been
too tired to do anything about it herself. Moshe tried his best, doing
all the meticulous cleaning things he had seen his mother do, to little
avail. That dirt and its accompanying smell had been ingrained in the
pores of the house over centuries. It was an old house, and a lot of
people had left their deposits there; it wasn't just the old man's fault.

He knew he ought to curse Joseph for landing him in this crazy
mess, but the hole in his spirit, what Arrienne called his antic bone of
compassion, but what he thought might be more an inherent sense of
despair, kept him going and he soon found that the job suited him be-

cause he did not have to talk, only do his duties quietly. In some odd way his silence seemed to soothe the old man, or at least quiet him. His eyes, pale blue behind a milky layer of cataracts, would follow Moshe with a look of speculative cunning, and he would grow quiet and shrink into himself as if something in the young man made him feel both wary and cold.

One day in September, Moshe brought him outside, because for the first time in more than forty days, there was sun warmer than a force-ripe orange, and though there was no front yard, only the street, there was a space by the front step into which he could push the wheelchair and it would be safe. He wasn't supposed to do this. He had been given strict instructions not to take his patient out of the house. The daughter had found it easy to believe him that he would obey this injunction, for though he was muscled and wiry, this did not show. He was fine-drawn and so pale that it was easy to think he hadn't the strength to lift the old man out of his chair. But Mr. Durham was exceedingly light. It was easier to carry him, cradling him like a large baby, than it was to roll the chair through the front door and half lift, half push it to the bottom of the steps.

Mr. Durham's eyes lit with excitement when he realized what Moshe was doing. He was trembling when Moshe lifted him, clinging tight around the young man's neck like a child being carried to claim a long-awaited gift.

They sat in the sun below the steps, a rug covering Mr. Durham's legs. Moshe in jeans and a thin white T-shirt that almost blended into his skin that would not burn, but neither would he tan, even if they stayed there until evening. But by then he would have regained his sheen like the color of clotted cream in sunlight, with a slight tint of blush in his face. These shifts in his color would disappear by morning. I start look like a croaking lizard, he thought to himself, hearing the jeers in his mind, "Crokkn lizzad!" as if he were back in Ora.

Wild with excitement, Mr. Durham was calling and waving to everyone he saw passing. He even waved to the group of young black men standing at the corner of the record shop across the street. "Hey, geezer! And how be you this fine summer morning? Bloody geezer. A Paki used to live in that house, has the Paki gone home? Called it

quits, huh?" The old man cackled with glee. "Our strong British culture too much for him. Bloody nerve. Buying house. Bloody nerve."
The young men waved back. "And a fine good day to you too, ma'am,"
bowing and tipping an imaginary hat.

Moshe smiled wryly to himself. The Durham house was a stone's
throw from the headquarters of Race Today, a hotbed of activism
that the old man cursed when he heard about it on the radio. The
race riots in Notting Hill had taken place just weeks before, and Mr.
Durham had only heard of them over the radio, but enough to make
him lean from his chair through his window in Brixton and scream
at the dirty bloody heathen kaffirs, attacking decent British police,
why don't you go back where you come from, monkeys! Pigs! (He
had learned "kaffir" from some relative in South Africa.)

For all the irascible old man knew, the young men congregated on
the neighborhood steps were not the Good for Nothing Jobless as he
liked to call people of other races, but planners of racial revolution.
Still, today was Jubilee, everyone within sight was a friend, as if each
had personally conspired to gift him with this freedom outside in
the sun. How small are the things that make people happy, Moshe
thought. A drop of water falling off a green leaf after rain. Its shape a
perfect pear. The yellow sac swelling with life under a lizard's throat.
To be an old man with no hair, and then to have a morning in the sun,
its rays falling warm on one's scalp so bereft. To receive a hand wave
from a stranger who in other circumstances you might have hated
and who is too far away on the street corner to see your face, or care.
The inexpressible gift of a seaman's feral smile saying, No, I won't
out you to the captain. Not so much the not-outing as the smile, its
sheer fullness of humanity. Holding hands with Arrii. Understanding without speech. All of these are precious things. (Sometimes he
thought he would like to cleanse the world of speech.)

The sudden taste of freedom in the sun had made Mr. Durham
a prisoner of joy; he could not help waving again to the young men
on the street corner until one or two returned the wave once more,
cursorily, their curiosity fleeting and distant. Then they returned to
their earnest colloquium; a few others joined them and they disappeared inside the record shop.

Moshe knew that shop. It was one of the first places that drew him because it was like somebody had lifted up a piece of Jamaica and placed it right there on Atlantic Road.

It was all in the sound. A sliver of Gregory Isaacs's voice, flowing cool, hot, gritty and smooth all at the same time over funky rock-steady reggae, washed into the street when the door opened, and receded as if it had never been, when the door closed. The sign on the shop front said, *Desmond Hip City, London's Top West Indian and Soul Shops,* and over a picture of three LPs, *Clubs and Discotheques Served.* He had wondered why it said *Shops* when it was only the one shop, its address given, *35, Atlantic Road, Brixton SW9,* but maybe *Shops* was a dream of the future that could be.

Moshe bent over the sketch pad on his knees, his bangs falling forward over his eyes. People passing eyed them with curiosity and amusement, the raucous old man and the silent, girlishly and strangely beautiful youth absorbed in his drawing. Some passersby answered the old man's greetings; a few stopped to exchange pleasantries. This sent him into a knee-slapping paroxysm of delight.

This youth doesn't know what the hell he doing, Arrienne thought, receiving this news. Mama Rachel talking true when she say Yahweh protects the innocent, and sometimes the foolish. The police surveillance intensify in black neighborhoods after the riots. This boy had better understand what it is all about. He arrive so green, the chaos in North London streets barely begin his education, and it don't look like he learn it yet. Suppose somebody had reported him to the police or the social worker come on the scene unexpectedly and put his pale ass in jail, where would he be then?

The social worker never comes unexpectedly, and I don't think I could have borne another day without sun. It was, after all, only for a few minutes. And I wrapped him up warm. I promise.

Mr. Durham ate his fish and chips right there outside, spewing chewed food in every direction while he hastened to continue greeting everyone he could as if this were his last chance on earth and he could not bear to lose a single moment before the trumpet called. "Was like he wanted to let the indifferent universe know once and for all he was here," Moshe told Arrii, drawing a lean sailor in rags in a tattered boat at the edge of the world.

Was like you wanted the SUS police to know you was there, Arrienne said, her heart-shaking fear unassuaged.

The old man stared at the sketch of himself and cried. Moshe had drawn him as he was in his chair, his face unwrinkling as he called out to neighbors he did not know. He cried so hard Moshe was terrified he'd get a stroke. He tried to take away the picture but Mr. Durham held it tight in his fist and wouldn't let go. He fell asleep with it clutched in his bony fingers clasped upon his chest. He murmured a name, "Muriel," in his sleep.

"My mother," the nurse-daughter explained, shrugging. "He remembers her sometimes. Then he gets maudlin. But he didn't treat her well." She looked tired, slow bags under her eyes. Soon she too would go to bed.

The bus wouldn't arrive for another half hour. Moshe walked home in the dusk, needing the fresh air against his face. *Arrienne. Arrii.*

The offices of Race Today were closed, but there was a light shining in a front window. He had wanted to go in many times when he'd passed it open, but he'd been afraid of being seen as white, and coming under suspicion, so he'd resisted the urge. He couldn't take it if they told him he was not black enough for whatever was being done inside.

Alva had called again the day before, and Moshe had struggled with whether he should say, Please don't call, but he needed a voice from home, and somebody to tell him if Arrienne was all right again.

CHAPTER XIII

The funny thing was, a part of him loved London. He was grateful to the city for giving him the anonymity he craved. He was rarely noticed in the rush and grind of moving crowds, and if he was, the curious glances were fleeting, turned quickly away in politeness. *English people are very polite.* This, he found, was not just a stereotype; it was true, though several of the English people who had taught him at school in Ora had been rude. (There was that teacher of Spanish who had called his first form class black monkeys when they made noise and could not be made to sit down to be taught on a rainy day.)

He found that politeness too could be rude.

Even in Brixton, where so many black people lived, he was not stared at unless he went into a shop that was black and asked to buy West Indian food, or a reggae single, or loitered pretending to be buying an LP when all he wanted to do was drink in the sounds of ska or rocksteady or reggae blasting from the amplifiers. But even then people would think he was a white man fixated on black things, until he opened his mouth and, hearing his accent, they also finally saw his face.

Apart from those occasions, the times when someone would stare were usually when he was in some place where people were sitting or standing still, like on the train, and had the time to notice. While most would glance away when they saw him looking back, their gaze targeting a point above his head or across the room, one or two were bold and asked him a question.

Sometimes, hearing he came from Jamaica, some grew bolder still and asked him such foolish questions and said such foolish things

that he changed his mind and wished they would be silent altogether. There were the ones, like the fauve woman, who commis-
erated him on the end of the Empire: how would his poor country get
on now? Or the ones, like the man on the steps of St. Mary's Church
in Cambridge, who said he had just returned from exactly that part
of the world, Cape Town, South Africa, where he was surprised to
find that his shadow there was always shorter. "It's because of the
sun, you understand. The tropics. Shorter in the tropics." And what
says the twilight? Moshe thought, not answering, only whimsically
hearing Arrienne's voice countermanding, "So there's for you, Derek
Walcott."

Once he was mistaken for an Eastern European and once for someone from the far Nordic isles, a Greenlander perhaps, who was particularly pale because he lived where the sun did not rise for months
on end.

But by and large there was no reason to look at him. People were
busy getting to and from work, on and off buses, up and down trains
and the Underground. His looks may have been pure confusion, yes,
a white black man or a black white man was not a sight one saw every
day, but the city was full of strange-looking people, Tibetan monks
in saffron dresses, hosts of Chinese with cameras click-click-click-
clicking away at everything within sight, West Indians in hallelujah
garb gone out of their minds and prophesying in the streets, transves-
tites tottering on high heels, strangers smelling of exotic foods, mum-
mers panhandling for their daily bread, and the amorphous tourist
hordes that spilled into London from every place in the world. There
was no time to stare or pay attention to anyone unless they looked
suspicious, a thief perhaps, or a pop-lit version of a Russian spy.

When he was homesick, what he missed was not people (the relief of not being stared at!) but landscape and sun and warm water,
cooking fires and voices raised, the taste of a place on his tongue as
he breathed.

A part of him would have been happy if he could have accepted
this new and marvelous freedom that enticed him to believe that he
would never again have to adjust to stares like a new rite of passage,
the way he'd had to when his mother first let him venture out of her

house to the riverside and then to the big school, or later when he left Tumela for school in Ora-on-Sea, or later again when he left both for university in the city. Questions he could opt not to answer, but stares were harder to escape.

(Kingston had been altogether different too, in a way he came to dread. Nobody had ever told him before that there could be something about the way a man's body moved when he walked, and the gesture of his hands, that should be taken account of, like a warning.)

Yet he himself gazed at people, his glance surreptitious but keen under lowered eyelids. From the beginning, he was searching for a pale man who might have something of his own looks. (But the four-eye woman had said no, the man who had spoiled his mother was not pale at all; he was a man with a very red neck, like a turkey, a florid, handsome man who on weekends wore an earring in one ear. "And he never look like you at all–at all." But afterward she changed her mind, she did not know what his father looked like, she said.)

And he was Rachel Fisher's son, and ambivalent to the core. Surreptitious looks at his face, sparse as they were, made him uneasy. So side by side with his relief, he almost wished people would be as outright and rude, staring, as strangers would have done at home, where the loud amused remarks—some addressed to him as though it was a perfectly natural thing for him to be involved in speculation about his own aberrant or missing skin—would end in a verdict: "Lef di yout alone, a nuh fi him fault why God mek him a dundus." And the inevitable mock-aside delivered in a voice an octave higher, so everyone could hear: "Though in truth him don't look like any dundus I ever see." The verdict would clear the air and release him. But after Kingston, and more particularly Kingston and Alva, he could never be sure that what strangers would remark on would be only his strange coloration and the unresolvable nature of his facial phenotype. Still, at times (he was a little crazy) he thought he might prefer people saying things out loud, in the way he was accustomed.

Then one day, taking the short train to Stratford, he found himself in the midst of a group of American tourists and one of them cried, "Look, a nigger in whiteface!" and pointed. That was the first time, pointed at, that he ran. Not stood frozen like a nocturnal animal in a headlight's glare, not raced into the shadows like the animal released when the light shut off—just turned his back and walked away as straight and careful and unhurried as he could down a side alley, then almost running to the opposite trains. That was when he knew the merciful reprieve of English people's polite silence, and their busy, deliberate blindness.

He took the train back to Brixton without seeing Stratford.

interval

Slink. Verb intransitive. To slink. To walk furtively away. Not glide or crouch with royal slyness, like a fox hiding in heather to catch pheasants, but slide secretly sideways with shame, then run in the opposite direction to where one was going.

Slink. Verb transitive, as in "to walk shame."

To discover shame in one's skin is to discover a new word.

Brixton. The borough had a thousand faces.

An oasis of familiar energy with its reggae shops, its sense of wild surprise, its pulse of a different beat that caught his breath the minute the train roared in from Westminster, leaving the swift, anonymous rhythm of Guildhall behind like a dream. Its rhythms came in colors, as rich and hot and deep as home. In the huge market row that spilled over four streets he could buy Jamaican ground provisions as fresh as if they had just come off a farmer's truck in Ora or Denbigh or Coronation, and his pick of fresh parrot, kingfish, snapper, or bonito, their scales still gleaming with seawater. But the borough was amorphous. There you could buy everything else too, from African snails to samosas to saris.

Walking through the labyrinth of streets that slipped into each other without warning, he learned that there were entire blocks where the houses were owned by West Indians, most of them Jamaicans. He learned to recognize the council houses by their green doors. He felt a ridiculous pride in his people, the way they had set themselves up against all odds and carved out homes for themselves. He wondered if Elsie Wauchope owned a house. She looked like the type who would.

They run away from the sugar plantation in the country-bush and poverty in the town and come like a Columbus to this dark place that savage to them and they mark the place with their presence like how dog mark tree and ground with piss.

But he knew this was not altogether the truth. The other truth was that many had seen themselves coming not to a dark and savage place, but to the mother country that was going to receive them with her arms wide open. The shock they received must have been great. Almost as bad as Columbus shock when he realize the people on the beach not welcoming him but wondering how him so sickly and so mad or so lost or so fool, planting stick with cloth on it in the ground and shouting out gibberish to him absent gods. (That was Arrienne's take on the Columbus issue.)

He himself had come here looking not for a mother but a father. Without maps or directions but blind with the faith in providence he had inherited from Rachel.

The part of Brixton he wasn't prepared for was the part that reminded him of Dungle, the Kingston slums which he used to catch a glimpse of from a distance on the train going home from university in the summer, or returning. The train rode on the backside of the city, giving him this glimpse of Dungle from afar. But he had been told you could get the best view if you stood outside any house on the westward side of Beverley Hills on a clear day and looked straight out.

While he hadn't exactly believed like Dick Whittington that London streets were made of gold (*nuff a it mek wid sugar*—Arrienne interrupting again), he wasn't prepared for the parts of the borough beyond Frontline, with their rows of ramshackle houses, their facades disfigured with sheets of corrugated metal, their windows smashed in, some papered over with black paper and tape, others with the holes—both window space and brickwork—still yawning. Dungle was an astonishment of cardboard and rusted zinc, much worse than all this, and yet not worse, because of the place it was in.

You expected that kind of place in a poor country. He hadn't thought England was poor. (Years later, Arrienne rereading, scribbled notes in this part of his letter: *Somebody now call it Small Island.*)

Curses, shouts, laughter, and music of every kind leaked from the pockmarked enclave of Brixton's Dungle. The music was something else again. It redeemed a multitude of sins, his mother would have said, if it had been music she approved of. He thought it was the best place to come for a free concert. He heard more Jamaican music there than he had heard in Jamaica. Toots, Sugar Minott, Tinga Stewart, Dennis Brown, and Bob Marley and the Wailers blasted through the bric-a-brac from huge amplifiers. But it was inter-mingled with many other sounds: the Mighty Sparrow, Lord Kitchener, Elvis, the Beatles, Mahalia, Count Basie, Roberta, Aretha, and others he did not know. Later he learned the names of some of the foreign kinds: Ghanaian highlife, Congolese rumba. That was something else he learned by asking questions in the record shops. Arrii, did you know that our rumba box come from Africa? I actually heard what theirs sounds like.

Yes, Mr. Discoverer, I hear you.

The row, they nicknamed it Squatters Garden, was supposed to be abandoned but it was full of squatters of all races and walks of life; poverty and misfortune had spared none.

Some were there on purpose, in protest against discriminatory housing practices and not because they had nowhere to live.

"Some of our people involved in that slackness as well," Joseph had said disapprovingly. "That's a ridiculous way to try and bring about change."

"But what you think they should do?" Moshe argued. "You have to get radical to get heard." He thought of Arrienne back home, chaining herself to the clock tower in Half Way Tree on behalf of the poor against the IMF. This, Rachel had reported in one of her letters.

"Cheuups." Joseph kissed his teeth. But he didn't answer the question. "All they do is give our people bad name."

Joseph had grown up in Nain, St. Elizabeth, where the sun hot no hell and people depended on rainwater tanks or dug wells because of drought. He still had a home there, in addition to his flat on Electric Lane. His woman and two children lived in Nain, surviving on the land and Joseph's remittances. His impatience with protesters stemmed from his belief in hard work as the remedy for all injustice.

"Stay away from there," he admonished before he left. "It's not just pretty protesters living there. That's a den of drug pushers and criminals. Just remember that you are a foreigner, yeah? An yu can't even tek hot sun, much less police lick."

"Sugar," Moshe had murmured, turning away so Joseph didn't see his smile. He didn't want Joseph to think he was laughing at him, though he was, a little. But only a little. Joseph was still awesome to him.

"Eh?"

"Sugar. Is sugar I can't tek, not sun."

Joseph bared his teeth. "Well, whatever yu poison is. Tek advice, young boy."

"You or I could be living in Squatters."

"Who me? No, bredda. I work too damn hard. And as for you, count yourself lucky that your parents work hard and send you to school so you would have more sense than that. I see that you grow up in a hothouse. Cockroach and bedbug and rat and winter without central heat, none of those things plant peas at your boundary line. You couldn't be living in no Squatters. So hol' yu corners an cool yu foot, young boy."

Moshe thought about Rachel and Noah, how hard they worked, and how poor they were, through no fault of their own, but because of this history of sugar that had directly or indirectly brought all the black people, even Joseph, here, and set him, Moshe, adrift in England looking for a father who the four-eye woman had confirmed, not once, but twice, had traveled to Ora and then gone back to England again.

But he understood the contradiction of Joseph. Joseph was the kindest people he had ever known, but for sheer survival he had cut himself off by finding refuge in his doctrine of hard work. He wouldn't let his children come to be with him in England until they were grown. "I don't want no schoolteacher to tell them the best they can be is bus driver or hairdresser, not even ship's oiler like they daddy," he declared, and in saying this he saw only his own common sense, no contradiction of his mantra that hard work and determination could get you anywhere you wanted, in any place that you happened to be.

Squatters Garden was the first place he saw people scurrying from police—their possessions, or their loot, on their heads. It was an eviction raid, not a drug raid. One of those running was a bearded youth in his shirt and women's underwear. Two were children about six and ten years old. He was glad the police, like blue-seam constables back home, did not carry guns, only batons.

When she read that, Arrienne fumed. None of those police with baton don't sus him yet because when he walk fast with him black backside under coat and they can't see him niggerface, they think he white. You 'member Notting Hill Carnival riot? '76? Three thousand police turn up sussing black people who breaking no law, just having they annual fun. Say they come to arrest pickpocket. She's so angry, so running scared for him, that she's complaining about the ways his afterward don't suit her neither: my boy in for a shock because he go to carnival the next year, and the police force with baton grow so big since the year of the riots, he couldn't believe it. From what he tell me, it was growing fast toward the 11,000 it become by the time they elect Donald Trump in America and Brexit bruk out in that same London. That was when he learn that carnival not costume and pretty nor peacetime and theme, but blood and fire and race war and he better watch him back.

She's an old woman replaying it now, near sixty, and losing memory but not consciousness. She still trembles to think how he cried that next year waking to the fact that when is more than 10,000 police, baton don't look so harmless, even if they not using them. Even in the squatter eviction he saw where baton draw blood. The instruments of the state always draw blood. If you think is joke, ask di duppy-dem on di slave plantations who work under overseer whip. Blood use to all drip inna di sugar when di cane crusher chop off hand and sometimes even foot.

Still (Arrienne still downloading), I love my people, wherever you find them, for they don't take baton nor nothing else lying down. He tell me he meet for the first time Lord Tokyo 1976 commemorative riot calypso. It blast through the bruk-up windows behind Frontline and he don't hear the words so good but he hear enough to make me laugh:

Carnival in Ladbroke Grove last time end up in disaster
I wasn't up there to see but I got the news after
Riot begin in [something another] Street, whole place on fire!
Police getting bruise for so, they all run for shelter!

I remember that part from reading about it—how the black people send the police that attack them with baton running for shelter behind garbage can.

Nowadays they have gun. And the young people have to find another way to fight.

But Mosh, he fraid. He fraid to talk to black people in case they think he white, and he fraid to talk to white people in case they see his black face and arrest him on suspicion. I see how he bleed, watching revolution from afar. He can't claim any of that as his own. But his heart soft, and he bleed.

Meanwhile, he walking through this city trying to learn everything through his eyes and ears and anything the tip of his fingers can touch, his fingers moving blind like how they move when he feeling the contours of a sculpture he just make, without having to talk to anyone. Even when he go to the carnival he go as spectator. He stand on the fringe looking for thing to paint, not getting involve, for he know that thing don't happen in real life the way it happen in book. He know if he was to go in his own face like costume, people might stop noticing him for they would think it was real masquerade. But he said, "What's the point? When it over, I still me. Futhermore, this is my face that either I born with or God give me, according to Rachel my mother."

CHAPTER XIV

Hematidrosis, also called blood sweat.

A very rare condition in which a human sweats blood.

From the Greek aima, meaning blood; and hidrōs, meaning sweat.

In which a human sweats blood. How strange. Had it been a cat, or a goat, or a zebra, or even an unidentifiable entity with wings, would such a disorder still be called hematidrosis?

In which. A Human.

Yet only the dead or the nearly dead sweat blood. When the ghosts of Tumela cook, the aroma inhaled makes the skin of those they have captivated leak red. Of such captives, people have it to say, "Wi nuh know if dem a still smaddy." There is no guarantee they are still persons, no certainty they have remained human.

Ghosts, idiots, and the lost are always so greedy for life, they never let go of it, though it lets them go.

Hematidrosis. A disease of nearly ghosts. Of the nearly dead hydrating. The skeleton beneath expanding, swelling, becoming succulent with water. Finally levitating. Then they bleed red water.

He always said he should not have lived; he came out of the womb half-made, so he nicknamed himself a not-yet. That's why he accepted everything that came his way, as if everything in life is some sort of a gift. Once he said to me he wanted to feel everything, all of love, he would never hide himself from love, even if it killed him. He was that obsessed, as if his difference, the way people thought of him as a kind of dead, made him crave to be more human than it was possible to be. Yet that is a big irony too, for when he said this, it was at the height when we knew our love was the one thing that could never be, no matter the force of obsession.

Listening in the night for the sound of him on the wind, I think of the maps that rose on the surface of his skin each time his veins erupted. Blood-sweat. A disease of the nearly dead, of supersensitive people who live too near the skin.

?◆

But do not pity him. Take care of my son, Miss Arrii, Rachel said. But it is I who am in need of succor. You see how even my words are taken over? If you think is joke, answer me this riddle: whose story I telling? Not mine.

Sweating blood, he levitates in the water of my words.

While I thirst.

I say this last part but I know it is not true. I know that without his life I have no words; this story I am telling is a ventriloquist's caul (storytellers and people who make translations of others are said in Tumela to be born with a caul, even if they are not); I know that in the end it is my story, not just his; and I know I levitate in the water of his openness and his love.

CHAPTER XV

"You're good. I mean really good," the girl said again, peering over his shoulder at his drawing.

Moshe blushed.

It was his first nude.

He could feel her chin there, near his shoulder. It was like being butted by a sheep. Her face had that sheepy kind of look, blind, elongated.

"I'm no good with charcoal," the pink-and-red girl persisted. "It gets so smudgy." Everyone had been required to sketch in charcoal. "I don't know what it is with me," she added, as if accusing the charcoal, or herself, of something. Her voice was like a sheep's too, plaintive and persistent. A performance. She was always performing.

Her name was Ada. As if someone meant it for a joke or emphasis—Ada Pink. She had red hair and unusually pink skin. Her eyes were large, almond-shaped, and green, the most outstanding feature in her curiously flat face. They were framed by rings of black kohl and impossibly sooty lashes that she fluttered at Moshe, laughing behind her hands in mock imitation of a geisha playing with her fan. Their classmates gave knowing smiles or looked politely away. She was a demonstrative girl, very vocal, prone to hugging and touching in a let's-be-friends way, speaking her feelings out loud in a voice that hovered between aggrieved and self-deriding.

An odd kind of girl, hawking her oddity like a price to be paid in order to belong. Or, Rachel would have said, as if the cry in the dark could be stifled by beating a tambourine. This was Rachel's way of mocking the Pentecostal church sisters who in bright clothes on Sunday mornings raised incredible ululations at their altars, their grief-stricken praise so reckless that the noise of it disturbed the peace for many miles distant.

In truth, Ada Pink was often extremely funny, making him want to laugh, but his heart withstood him. He did not laugh easily. An image he might imagine made him laugh, for sheer joy at its perfection that art could hint at. But not much else.

"Yu married to mourning," said Arrienne, whose sense of humor was spare and always sardonic. They had both changed, their personalities shifting course but only in the direction they had been meant to go. Her silence had increasingly become a matter of choice, whereas for him, speechlessness, the fear of communication, remained visceral, and words never stopped causing him physical harm.

His class was small, and everyone fell by natural selection or consensus into what seemed to him like slots that had been prearranged. Ada Pink's role as class clown was one such slot. Yet she felt that they despised her. She was too loud, too wide open, too lacking in self-regulate. She embarrassed herself, and therefore everyone else. Moshe she envied, and soon coveted, because he was the only one without a slot. He was solitary, he never spoke, it made them afraid to ask him questions, and it was impossible to decide what to make of his appearance, his paleness that was so pale, not the kind of pale of someone who has been locked up in a house or a prison, outside of sunlight, for many years, but this pale that resembled the look of sunlight falling on curds, with a hint of translucence like a hard egg peeled. They didn't know either what to make of his uncompromisingly negroid features or his colonial accent and so, apart from one or two desultory assays of curiosity and even friendliness when he first arrived, they let him alone.

She couldn't let him alone. His wordlessness irritated something inside her, the way a parasite irritates the inside of a shell, provoking a birth of some kind. Nacre, perhaps. Hopefully pearls, that would eventually drop from his mouth. She never stopped talking, it seemed. During lectures she peppered the lecturers' delivery with sotto voce witticisms from where she sat, by design, directly behind or across from the silent Moshe.

She had a ventriloquist's quick gift; she threw her voice at and beyond him so that the room heard, and people laughed. The art history lecturer paused once more to remark in a dry voice on the unknown intruder Mr. Nobody, who was disrupting the class again without showing himself. He waited for the ripple to subside before beginning again.

But it was toward Moshe that she directed her real attention.

Arrienne was irate. *Girl fool. She don't have a clue. But mek she go on try. Fall flat on her face like Columbus in chains.* Ever self-aware (having lived all her life inside her and Moshe's head, she knew her own contradictions), she admitted without shame that this mocking outburst was fueled by jealousy. She could feel the slow burn of anger in the pit of her stomach.

The pink-and-red girl had a great contempt for boundaries. Yet she kept her distance at the edge of Moshe's force field of solitude that he wore like a cloak. She put out her hand toward him once, and drew it back all-in-a-sudden, as if burned. Her eyes narrowed, then widened, as if awaking confused from sleep. After this she became nervous around him, and didn't try again to touch him. But she couldn't help herself. She could not stop testing his limits, even from a distance.

He never judged her or found her slight or ridiculous, and this no doubt added to his attraction for her. This was the way he was. She liked him immensely. She could see that he was discomforted in her presence. But at last, once, after many months of trying, a faint smile tugged at his lips at something she said. She smiled and nodded to herself, like someone who has found a precious clue, the answer to a riddle. Now she felt encouraged, and she pursued him with her large eyes, dropping looks in his way like one might toss flowers, carelessly, nonchalantly over one's shoulder, knowing someone who loved flowers was walking behind. Arrienne read her like a book, extrapolating: underneath her wild exterior the pink-and-red girl was patient, determined in pursuit of anything she wanted, and very much in love with anything that gave her a fight.

Sometimes the glances she gave him were puzzled. Arrienne imagines her puzzlement; why does he seem so innocent and why isn't he shagging anyone, a whole year in this class and he hasn't noticed a single girl, or boy for that matter, this is 1977 for gee's sake, everybody is shagging everybody. *He doesn't even seem aware of his own beauty*. (Why are the British so phony? Shag is such a feeble word for this hot desperation and marauding.) And she imagines the pink-and-red girl imagining herself pushing up against Moshe in a dark corner and committing rape.

But up until now the pink-and-red girl had allowed him his distance. Which she breached at last when she craned to look at his nude, the point of her chin like an inquisitive sheep's air-brushing his shoulder.

Sketching the nude had undone almost everyone's inhibitions. The mood in the class lightened, everyone jockeying for laughs. The pink-and-red girl lost her assigned place as clown-in-chief.

"Such a surfeit of flesh—bound to be inebriating!" someone, not the pink-and-red girl, said to chuckles, explaining the class's descent into levity. His name was Clement, pronounced the French way.

They had studied nudes in every imaginable pose and, it seemed, from every known artist's point of view. The visceral gaze of Klimt, whom Moshe loved, and Matisse's light-filled serpentines. Michelangelo's cool dispassion, painting the young David with love. (Such an objective love, he thought, a love moved not by passion or exaltation but the mere and marvelous assemblage of bone and musculature. He himself couldn't love like that.)

Their after-class discussions were always serious, eager, competitive, bright. It seemed to him that the seriousness was not always real but the expression of a hidden disquiet, the fear that they weren't good enough, would never be good enough, and would always have to strive to prove themselves wrong. And though their fear was also his own, their effort exhausted him, and he shrank more into himself. Yet he was excited and drawn by their conversations, which opened his art to him so that sometimes in the midst of their voices he stood trembling, like someone arrived on the summit of a bluff watching the contours of a whole new world swim into ken.

If he liked anything about Ada Pink it was that she never took any of it too seriously. She never seemed as though she thought one might die from not having the right thought or feeling the right excitement, from not deserving one's place in the line.

But the nudes set something free. Some taboo against levity in the serious rooms gave way, as if in shock or protest at what the pink-and-red girl said was "all this mortality and sex jostling each other side by side."

"You've got it the wrong way," another girl protested. She wore round tortoiseshell glasses and carried a tote with *All Men Are Equal* painted on the front. "This is not about sex. It's about the—" She shaped her hands as if carving two halves of a circular bowl in midair, a pained gesture as she struggled for words to express the profundity of her thought. "The—the incredible *astonishment*"—she said the word just like that, in italics—"of what the human body is capable of, what it can reveal?" Her assertion ended on a question, as if begging someone to see the light and agree.

"Oh yeah?" the rejoinder was derisive. "So why are we having this conversation?"

"She studied her lecture notes well!"

"And put them into poetry too!"

"Admittedly, poetry of a rather inferior sort," mocked the boy called Clement the French way. "Diction more purple than Rubens's fornicating gods!" And flinging his arms wide in a mock embrace, imitating the tortoiseshell girl's voice, "O Gawd, what's wrong with you people? So much sex!" Then, "It's enough to put you off shagging altogether," he added, winking at Moshe. They were in the cafeteria line. The joke raised a fresh ripple of laughter, a few frowns of disapproval or disgust.

"I agree," Ada said. "You might drop dead at just the eureka moment!"

"Eureeekaaa!" Clement screeched, simulating a convulsion.

Disgusted, two of the girls pushed him out of the way.

"Well, it is called the little death, you know," someone else pointed out, rather unnecessarily, and another, with a snort of laughter, "Now you put it like that, way to go!"

"Would you be able to get it up at all?"

They went on laughing and joking until a plaintive girl said, raising her voice above the rest, "But why do they have to make you think of death all the time?" and at her whining tone a silence fell and everyone looked at her queerly.

But Ada was contrary—insisting that the nudes were all about mortality. Not death, but mortality, which was not quite the same thing, regardless of what anyone might say; death was never funny but mortality often was, and some of the nudes were hilarious—her exclamation started another round of talk, fierce and passionate; the female students were set against the men, a vehement quarrel ensued, some of the women saying the male gaze was insulting looking at women (let's be honest now, not the female body but women, a certain view of women—the "nude" body is just the occasion), and always narcissistic looking at itself. Eunice Golden was hilarious and exciting, they loved the way she answered back; yes, some of the men agreed—"because she left our penises alone, she didn't try to cut them off!"—but the men were unanimously against Sylvia Sleigh—"*She* is the insulting one, and ridiculous!"—and that quarrel too was full of laughter, and liberating, as if light had rushed in through an open door (though there was nothing special about it; generations of art students before and after them had had and would have the same quarrel, but still it was liberating). But not all was laughter—some of the men never forgave the women who called them stupid, nor the women the men who called Sylvia Sleigh ridiculous. Clement pronounced the French way had his ring given back to him by his girlfriend for the cruel things he said about Sleigh.

In spite of herself, Arrienne found herself almost liking Ada Pink. But, she thought, "the pink-and-red girl" suits her as well as does her name, or better.

The lecturer wanted them to do self-portraits at the end of the module. Clement, jostling the pink-and-red girl for center stage, had drawn a mock-portrait of himself clutching his erect penis like Egon Schiele, and, captioning it in bright red *Head Start: Response to Surfeit of Naked Flesh,* passed it around in the middle of the ascetic lecturer's monologue on Lucien Freud's *Boy on a Bed.* Somebody snickered and the lecturer stopped and waited wearily once more for them to calm down. He was used to the yearly foolishness of beginners. Moshe turned the color of arterial blood, bending over so his blush wouldn't show.

"Gross," Ada said, her breath fanning the back of his hair. "Isn't he gross?"

Their model, a heavy-boned young man with a shaven chest, had been posed reclining on a yellow couch. The couch was angled toward a curtain in an alcove but the model's body was fully visible and unobscured. The lecturer had instructed them to do the body first, without the face. Let the body do its own speaking, he said, line by line, color by color. With charcoal. "You don't need paint to suggest color," he said.

"First chance I get to outshine and pay back bloody Rodin," Ada fumed, "and I mug it. Just because of bloody charcoal." She hated on Rodin: "Peeping Tom hunkering down between women's legs as if he lost something in there, the eff-er. All puns intended."

"I'm sure your drawing is fine," Moshe said lamely, feeling helpless to comfort her.

She wouldn't let him see what she had done. He saw that she wasn't just funning this time. She was perfectly miserable about her drawing.

"I'm sorry," he said, absorbing her misery through his skin. "I'm sorry."

"If you want to help, come and have a drink with me. Right now I need some sustenance," she said, jumping up in that impulsive way she had and hauling her satchel over her shoulder. "C'mon."

And he went because he was sorry.

"Holy pub, here I come!" Ada announced as they entered the crowded doorway of the Hind and Swan. "I'm going to get as drunk as a nun in a bunghole!"

He laughed, surprising them both. Ada stared. His laugh was fleeting, a short, sudden sound made of breath, but it made a sensuous curve of his mouth, and both his brown eye and the blue one darkened. Arrienne knows how arousing that can be—his eyes always darken behind a screen of light when he laughs. You could eat him for breakfast, I know. And then. Lord God help me, and then.

He couldn't imagine any nun he had ever seen getting drunk, but a picture of Sister Marie-Sainte, the cowled headmistress of the Catholic girls school in Half Way Tree, with her head stuck in a wine cask, her super-ample bottom and tiny, spaghetti-thin heels wriggling in desperation behind her, had flashed before his eyes and made him laugh.

The Friday-afternoon crowd was overflow so they had to wait to be seated. They stood crunched up against each other in a clutch of waiting customers inside the door. Her hair smelled of aniseed. Its strands tickled his nose. She leaned against him slightly, feeling his chest through the thinness of his cotton jersey. This was London in 1978, still prim and proper (and the height of the Cold War, Arrienne thought, mocking). Nobody stood close enough to anyone to touch if they could avoid it. Ada pretended she couldn't avoid it. The waiting space was small and the gaggle of standees thick and growing. His body felt warmer and more solid than he looked. She wanted badly to touch him.

At last they managed to get seats side by side on a banquette in the far corner. She had to raise her voice over the din that seemed louder in the smoke-wreathed half dark than it had when they were standing outside. "So, when I get plastered, will you walk me to my room?" Her eyes giggled at him through the smoke.

They had both ordered beer. She lifted her foaming glass in a silent gesture of "Cheers" and drank, watching him over the top, wincing as the polite half smile touched the corner of his mouth and withdrew, tentative as a butterfly's wing.

"Relax," she said, her voice quiet. "It's okay, it was just a joke. I won't rape you. I promise."

He reddened, feeling her shame in the unaccustomed quiet of her voice. But he was also annoyed at the insult in her words. "I'm sorry," he said. "I'm not—" he struggled for words that would not give offense, "—used to talking a lot."

"Or to people who talk a lot. Like me," she said drily.

His face felt like a flame tree in August. "I didn't mean—"

"To give offense," she interrupted. "No, I know. Don't worry, I'm used to it anyway." She answered the puzzled frown on his face: "Being told I talk too much. No," she held up a hand as she saw his start of protest, "don't. You don't have to. I know it's true, I do talk too much. Of course, the irony is—" She waved her hand searching for words, then shrugged as if giving up. She saw the question in his face and laughed. "The irony is of course."

He drank his beer, finding nothing to say. She was a complex person, complex in a way neither he nor Arrii was.

He didn't really like beer. He thought that if he could ever bring himself to taste horse piss, that was the way it would taste, like beer.

"Aren't you going to ask me what of course means?"

How self-absorbed she was, how in need of affirmation!

"Of course you talk a lot because you're scared of not talking?" He hoped he didn't sound bored.

"Something like that." She swallowed another large mouthful of beer, laughed in self-mockery. "How'd you guess?"

"It keeps people from staring. Seeing. If you can talk like that, people notice your words, not you. Nobody stares." It was a long speech for him. His face was burning, lest he had shamed her. But also lest he had revealed too much of himself.

She stared. "Wow. Some psychiatrist, aren't we? I didn't even know you had five words inside of you." She threw up her hands, "Okay, okay, so I did ask."

He felt her perpetual hurt and was sorry. He wanted to say, Don't try so hard. If you don't try so hard, it'll come better. But he was tongue-tied.

She bent her head, fiddling with her mug. The beer was icy cold and made beads of condensation on the sides. She stroked them off with the tips of her fingers. Her nails were long and beautifully shaped. She had painted them in scarlet and blue and oversprayed the colors with gold glitter, like a Christmas tree. She seemed to be contemplating something, her eyelashes, darkened with mascara, making crescents on her flat cheeks.

She moved slightly, as if coming to a sudden decision, but didn't lift her eyes as she spoke. "Fisher, you know I like you, right? I've made no bones about it, right from the start." He could see the bones of her hands stretched and tight around the glass mug. Her hair half hid her face but now she was looking at him, through her hair, like a nude model playing a game of hide-and-seek. "And you know why."

"No," he said, stunned. No one had ever said such direct things to him before. Except . . . He tore his mind away. Arrii knew him better than anyone. She had never had to say words to him. Or he to her.

Ada chuckled. "Aw, come on, guy. You've got to know you're sexy." Her voice came out rough and relieved, as if she had heaved something off her chest that had traveled from a far way down, the base of her feet to her throat, for example. She was throwing every damn egg into one basket; she might never get another chance.

She wasn't joking.

He went very pale, and if she hadn't seen it happen before, she might have thought he was ill.

"I think you're the sexiest guy I've ever seen in my life."

He wondered what she saw when she looked at him. She was an odd person; odd people had strange tastes, like red and blue nail polish oversprayed with glitter.

The memory her words stirred was a dark path down which he didn't want to go. He wanted to leave, put an end to the conversation.

"Are you English-born?" he asked stupidly, saying the first thing that came into his mind.

She laughed again. "Too forthright to be English, right? That's pure stereotype." It wasn't what he had meant, but as a distraction, it served. "Yes, I am, Kensington born and bred. This pommy accent isn't fake, it's blue in the blood. Half Welsh though. My mother came from Llanddewi Velfrey."

"Came?"

"She died," Ada said shortly. "It was a long time ago. Let's not talk about it, okay?"

"Okay," he said. She barely heard him.

She had said his nude was beautiful, but in truth it had to have shocked her. It was stunning and violent, in a way that was both angry and erotic. Sure, she wanted to ask him about his work, what gave rise to that mixture of earthiness and mystery, distance, as if he struggled to wrestle something ethereal down to the demoniac earth.

"I'm adopted," he said, wanting to give her something in return for the vulnerability she had risked. "I never knew my mother or my father."

Then he was sorry, thinking that the personal confession disrespected her request not to talk about her mother. Stammering, he stopped. She waited for him to continue if he wished. With her untimely confession she had burned all her bridges. Anything that would happen between then now, including conversation, would be on his initiative. She wanted to hear more, she wanted to hear everything about him, but she waited, not prompting or discouraging. For her, it must have taken a great effort of self-control.

But the moment had gone, lost by his fear of offending. They sat there for a while longer, not speaking, just drinking their beer, watching the pub crowd and being sheepish, each waiting for the right moment to say, "Shall we go, then?"

Every now and then they smiled at each other, pretending to be companionable. Then she said with characteristic candor, the minute she finished her beer, as if only the obligation to drain every last drop had delayed her, "Look, this sucks, doesn't it? Let's get out of here."

Afterward he walked her back to her dorm. It was evening and stars were coming out in the bleached sky. The night wouldn't fall until much later, maybe seven, eight o'clock. They walked side by side; he touched her elbow lightly once when she would have stumbled, and he said, his voice anxious, "Are you all right?"

"Yes," she said, but apart from this they did not speak.

They said good night at the porter's lodge.

"Are you—do you have somebody back home?" she asked, as if impelled, now that he was going and she might not have another chance.

They stood for a moment frozen. His face flooded and then paled.

And it was as if something fey came over him because, not knowing he was going to do this until he did, he bent and kissed her cheek. "You're beautiful," he said. "Thank you."

She watched him walk away, her hand touching the cheek where his lips had touched. His mouth had felt soft and firm all at once. He walked like a dancer, on the balls of his feet, his limbs loose and limber and his head held straight above his shoulders which were thin but not narrow. She didn't mind his paleness, his odd look of clotted cream which the sun seemed to have touched ever so slightly, in a fraction of time, or the way you couldn't tell from his coloring or his textures or the shape of his features where he came from or where he belonged. Only his voice gave him away. People from his country had that kind of accent.

No doubt she was furious with herself that she had not grabbed him and kissed him until he screamed for mercy or lost his breath.

Like me, Arrienne said, speaking to the silence she had made between herself and Moshe, *she can only think of him as lovely. But he is lost to both of us and that's the way he will always be. She doesn't know that yet. She will. I've always known.*

He made himself a quick salami on toast for dinner, washed it down with cold water, and grabbed the bus instead of walking, because it was late, to Mr. Durham's place. He gave Mr. Durham his supper and then his bath. Afterward, the old man smelling of talcum powder in new pajamas his daughter had bought for him at Debenhams as a special treat for his birthday, they played dominoes on the dining room table scarred from the slap-slap of dice and the old man's temper tantrums, the times he harried the wood with his pen knife.

The game came to its usual end when Maas Percy, as Moshe had started to call him in his mind, fell abruptly asleep in the middle of cheating. Nothing gave him a buzz more than winning by fraud. "Gotcha, damnit!" he'd crow each time his machinations paid off, while he stomped his feet on the floor. And sleep came to him in this sudden way afterward, sliding him sideways in his chair so that he deposited a swift blop of drool on the table's edge.

Moshe wheeled him to his room and helped him to bed. The old man grabbed his hand and would not let go. "Stay," he mumbled in his sleep. "Chinky, stay."

Moshe waited until the insistent grip grew slack with sleep and fell away. Then he sat at the dining table reading and sketching until ten o'clock when the nurse-daughter came home. He sketched the old man's body underneath his clothes as if he saw him through the lid of a sarcophagus. The body he drew was still clothed but gave the impression of being separated from the clothes, so that everything was visible: the depleted musculature, the brittle bones and slack skin, the shrunken half fistful of the genitals eerily rising beneath the draped cotton of the pajamas. It was a brutal and cruel drawing.

Struggling in his sleep in the night, Moshe dreamed that the pink-and-red girl came down to the wharves to clear a shipload of sugar she was expecting from Madagascar. She offered him a cupful of the purified grains, bleached white as salt. He shook his head no, is not salt, is sugar, and the scene shifted; he found himself fleeing through a rain forest before a river of molten sugar in hot pursuit. The river came within an inch of his heel and as he opened his mouth to cry out, Joseph lifted him onto the deck of the ship and smiled. "I shot the sheriff," Joseph said, and turned into Alva with cocked fists and an angry face. He heard Rachel's voice saying, "Yu eat too late, man. Man eat too late bound to have bad dream," and woke out of his sleep.

CHAPTER XVI

"Man, you look good," Alva said, the afternoon of their bitter fight.

Moshe was so angry that day, he had never been angry like that before.

Why say a thing like that? There was no reason. Not when he, Moshe, looked like nothing anybody except his parents and Arrii had ever seen. I mean, really seen.

If you really see somebody, down to the skeleton, you love them. He was not lovable, except to those who had seen him, bone and all. Even his skeleton was distorted.

⋙●

His nude self-portrait brought him the attention that was later to become fame. They compared him to Michelangelo. There was an irony in that, to be compared to the master he could not love—how do you love the monumental? But they said he was like Michelangelo in the way his self-painting conveyed the mortality beneath the skin, not the touch of death but the conundrum of being alive, the messy imperfection that made a question of everything. He never admired that comparison for he thought it became a way of saying he didn't fit, that after five hundred years of art moving and changing, he was frozen in the past and irrelevant to a future. Moreover, he could not understand why greatness must always be measured by comparison with someone from this part of the world, the northern part, why it was never said that he was a reminder of any painter from the part of the world that he was from, or any part of the world that was like the part that he was from, although there were such, including some who had become famous.

> *"His painting of the translucent body with the faint impression of blood flowing through intricate pipes under the skin is a profound and masterly apprehension of the life that dies." —*The Spectator

Reading this review in the newspaper, he laughed a little, thinking half-whimsically, half with a touch of irony, how unbelievable was the reality of his life, that people thought it was just art, not anything that could literally be. *A crucial lack of conventional means to render our lives believable. This, my friends, is the crux of our solitude—*Arrienne, responding to his thought, could not resist quoting Gabriel García Márquez, borrowing words for counterspell.

Moshe remembered the first time the eruptions appeared. Arrii had touched his belly in awe and longing. "They pretty, Mosh," she had whispered, watching fascinated the imprint of the web of arteries, veins, and capillaries which though faint as a whisper were nevertheless clearly visible, like the face on the Shroud of Turin. "They pretty bad. I wish mine would rise up like yours."

But he had wept frantically in his father's arms. "Mi go dead, Dadda? A dead mi a-dead?" and the mother and father, torn apart by his bereft wailing, had answered no, praying they were right, broken with relief when the doctor said no, he was as healthy as he had ever been, except that he had to be careful not to fall and bruise his torso or his abdomen; he might bleed more heavily than he had bled from scrapes and falls in the past, the vessels being now so near to the surface of the skin. Much later, he did bleed from his heart, not when he fell but under extreme stress, which he encountered only in England, when Arrii did not write or call.

This uprising of blood vessels had happened in early puberty, as if with the stretching of his limbs in rapid growth spurts, either the skin had been too small to contain all that he was becoming and had stretched and thinned impossibly to reveal the fountains of his life, or the vessels had stretched themselves upward with the strain of his growing and come to rest just under the skin, like the bones of Noah's ark under the last of the waters on Ararat.

The parts of him that showed, his head, face, arms, and legs, were not affected. These, in contrast to the increasing near-transparency of his hidden parts, became more uniform in their color and more solid, acquiring the color almost of clotted cream placed in half sunlight, a delicate gold, but this was a slow and erratic process and his blue edges had a way of surging back in certain kinds of light.

Alva, lifting his shirt to reveal his hidden deformity to a stranger for the first time in his life, said, "Man, you look good," and the voice in which Alva added, "You're beautiful," was husky and hurt as he kissed Moshe between his shoulder blades and turned him around, dropping to his knees to kiss his belly.

Paralyzed at first, his bones and muscles frozen, and then violently, hotly surging where the other cupped and then rubbed him between his two hands, so that his sperm leaped and spurted in Alva's face and hair, he fought to pull away, from the sensation of pleasure and horror, and saw Arrii standing frozen, her hands clasped at her mouth as if praying, her eyes widened in shock and disbelief.

"Please, please," Alva was saying (he said it in the Creole way, "Duu, man, duu, Ah beg yu duu"), but Moshe pushed him so that he fell and then he kicked him, again and again, screaming, sobbing, "Stay away from me, you dirty dog," and Alva didn't retaliate, just shielded his face with his hands and absorbed the blows, though he was much bigger and stronger than Moshe and could have defended himself and made the blue youth bleed.

She was still crying, facedown on her bed, when he burst into her room. (The front door was open, as doors usually were in Tumela, and only she was at home.) He dropped on his knees beside her, his hands hesitated toward the bed, wanting to touch her but feeling unclean.

She pushed him away with a part of the sheet that she bunched in her hands, and turned her face to the wall. "Don't come near me, Mosh. I can't bear it." Her voice rose on a thread of sound.

"How can I not—I didn't do anything, Arrii."

"How can you say that?" She turned round and sat up in a flash, her eyes blazing. "I saw you, remember?"

"I didn't do anything," he insisted. "I just—I didn't know he was going to do that. I didn't invite him."

"Didn't you? Who called him here for cookout? You don't call that invitation?"

"Invitation to what, Arrri? What you think I invite him to?" He didn't think to defend himself by explaining that even the cookout, or Alva's coming to his house in the first place, had as usual been at Alva's self-invitation; he had had no idea the other had planned to visit until he turned up in the yard that morning. He had begged her to come with them but she wouldn't, she never did, she never stuck around when Alva came to visit. Her aversion to the other young man was very strong.

"You tell me. I know what my eyes see. Oh God, I can't bear to look at you." She covered her eyes with her hands, turning her back, and when he moved as if he would touch her, she pushed him with her elbows hard, tae kwon do. "Get away from me."

He lost his balance and they fell together to the floor, she landing on top of him on her back. She rolled off quick as an eel and they wrestled, silent and fierce, until at last she gave in and lay still, her head across his belly. She could have done him serious harm with the one blow, but even in her anger she held back, afraid of how easily he could bleed, or, she imagined, die.

They fought to get their breath back. He couldn't wait. He wanted to sit up to speak but was afraid she'd move away. "We were in the river," he said between heaving gasps. The water had been soft and warm, sliding off their bodies like silk. "We finished cooking and everything. Then we went in the water. Afterward . . . afterward," he swallowed hard, "he wanted me to take off my T-shirt." Why you can't swim in your skin, Fisher? Is not like I don't know what you look like. Cho, man, mi know aready you white as sea froth. Alva himself swam in his skin, strong and proud as an ad for Duluth Trading.

"I told him I don't swim in my skin, back off, but he wouldn't. He just kept horsing around, trying to pull my shirt off in the water. I got angry and came out. I was walking and he—"

She watched him swallow again hard, knowing what he was going to say but determined to hear him say it.

"He pulled away my shorts. Truth to tell, I think—thought—he was just trying to grab me to . . . make me stop. And then—" He closed his eyes tight. He kissed him, there, on his back, and turned him around and then—that happened. "I didn't want it. I didn't encourage it." His body had clenched in pleasure when the other kissed him in the valley of his back, in the dent just below his waist.

"I know. That you didn't *encourage* it," she said, the pause between her words and the emphasis on "encourage" carrying a meaning he understood, and he cried out in protest, "I didn't want it!" and again, "No!" at the look in her eyes.

"I came to look for you because I felt you upset," she said. "I thought you were hurt."

"I was annoyed, and then I was angry. Because he wouldn't let up trying to take off my shirt."

She rolled away with her back to him and he turned on his side toward her. But their bodies didn't touch; she had left a space of inches between them and in shame he couldn't move to close it. She was making a statement and it was the space of his shame and he felt stained, unable to touch her and unable to move away.

They lay there a long time like that, hearing their breathing and the sound of themselves quietly crying. Then she said in a small voice, "Do you think this means that you're gay?"

He would be everlasting grateful to her for that phrase "do you think," giving him the freedom to doubt, to be unsure, to escape.

He answered her like a man given an intricate equation to solve in a last chance of life or death. Rehearsing answers in the hope of arriving at the one that is safe. Buying time to save his life. To bring himself to an understanding of the question of himself. "I don't know. I don't know why you say that. I have never thought of him that way. I've never longed for a man to touch me. Maybe it was just a neurological reaction. I do not know."

"How yu goin know?"

"I don't know," he said again, and then, spreading his hands in frustration. "How can I know?"

It was a tacit undertaking not to see Alva again, and she read it as such, but still she said, as if to make her question clear, "You know of course he's gay. And he's been after you for ages."

"Actually, I didn't know—either of those things."

"You're blind as Bartimaeus," she said angrily. "Why yu tink Mama Rachel don't like him? Yu never notice she never give him food to take away when him come, not after the first time? Yu ever know any visitor Mama Rachel don't send away with food?"

"I'm sorry," he said unhappily, recognizing that all of this was true, now that it was said. Though he wanted to say stupidly in self-defense, Mama hardly have visitors.

She shook her head, half-exasperated, half-remorseful. And after another long time she said, her voice quiet and sad, "You were never like that with me."

"*You* were never like that with me," he responded.

"Maybe I was and you didn't know." Her voice issued a challenge he didn't understand.

He rose up on his knees, reached out, and, turning her face toward him, looked into her wide-open eyes. They were red-rimmed from her recent crying but she still managed to look like the most beautiful creature on the face of God's earth, he thought. "What yu mean, Arrii?"

She had seen him without his clothes all her life. He had seen her. When they were younger, on the threshold of their teens, she had held in her hands his cheelie which was no longer a cheelie but a budding cylinder of hot flesh somewhere between that and a man's organ, and she'd laughed at him because it wouldn't stay still in her hands or stop stretching. By unspoken consent, as if the taboo was instinctive, they'd stopped touching in this way when she had her period, the year the Christie curse insurrected in her body before it began to seem to pass her by because she willed it to do so.

"When?" he insisted to her silence. "When, Arrii?"

He had never known anyone so unpredictable, except himself. She was smiling, her face malicious and inscrutable. "Maybe in your sleep."

His own face was sober and clenched as he looked down at her. "Do you want us to?"

She stared into his eyes as if trying to find her way to the back of who he was. Her heart beat a little, she felt her mouth grow dry. "You mean do I want us to make love?"

He nodded yes.

"Say it." She said it the way she used to say "Sit," uncompromising. "Yes."

She didn't stop looking at him. Her gaze was as frank as he had known it, and he felt that somehow she held him in her hands and no matter what had happened, they were still fused to each other and he was safe.

"No. Maybe. Yes. I don't know," Arrii said. And she cried out again, her voice tormented, confused, now squeezing her eyes shut, "I don't know!" She sounded like him answering her question, "Do you think this means that you're gay?"

"It might answer the question," he said.

"Do you? Want us to?"

"Yes," he said fiercely, and again, "yes."

Her lips parted a little, showing the white edge of her teeth. Her mouth was wide and generous and perfectly curved; when you looked at their mouths you could think they were twins, the same full, carved lips, only hers a little bit crushed in the middle, like an indentation in the fold of a rose.

"Yes."

Not here, of course, not now. He didn't know how long it would take to scrub away the taste of Alva on his body. He wanted to give her roses and wine.

They heard her father calling from the front doorway, "Arrii, yu home? Arrii! Ah hope is not gone she gone an lef the front door open," and Moshe got instantly to his feet, offering her his hand and pulling her up beside him.

They fixed their clothes hurriedly, making their jeans neat at their waists and their tees firm over their rib cages, before going out into the hall, Arrii answering, "Yes, Papa?" A mercy that the front door was open. Otherwise Maas George would never believe they, or rather

Moshe closeted with his daughter, was up to any good in the inner room; even with the door open he would be suspicious. Moshe knew he would say hurtful things to Arrii after he, Moshe, had gone.

Afterward, when she wept again, it was because of his wound, where his big toe had broken with the force of his attack on Alva as he tried to kick the other youth to death. (It was hours later that he realized he had wounded himself. Before, in the heat of emotion, he had felt no pain.)

She had cried once like this before, years ago, when she tried to fix his hair. Tried to straighten the pepper-grain back of it with the hot comb, "make it all-in-one so people won't stare at you so much anymore," tried to fix the variegated boy with his white and black unblended in him so he was no familiar kind of mongrel, his black so black it looked crazy attached to his whiteness, his white so white he was no proper kind of dundus, you couldn't even call him dundus because his skin had no blotches of brown, his eyes no pink in the rim. And nobody would have laughed or gawked if this was how he looked, like a dundus, for he would have been as ordinary as the sun shining while the rain fell, odd but without surprise.

After the straightening they were going to bleach his hair to a uniform blond; people would think he was white, identifiable as one thing and not another, once and for all. She knew how to obtain the right kind of bleach in McKenzie's Drugstore, from the shelves where they stocked things for hair. Black was an easier color to get than blond, but black hair would make him look like a death's head, with his skin so angelfish white.

How, when all this was done, were they were going to account for his nigger face?

They were very young and did not even know they were to address the question.

The hot comb heated on her mother's new oil stove burned his scalp and did not change his hair. His head leaked for days, swathed under white calico packed with slices of cucumber and aloe vera that his mother used for healing and keeping the scalp cool. Arrienne cried until her eyes caked with salt, and then she went on crying dry-eyed for days until he was well again. And because she could not crawl inside his skin to share his pain, she tried to brand it into her own body.

Sniffing the odor of burned flesh in his kitchen, her father rushed to investigate, thinking meat on the stove was burning, and found his daughter branding her own head with the pressing comb heated so hot that the edges glowed blue and red. The damage was minimal; she had had trouble finding the tender scalp under the abundant clouds of her hair.

When her father wrested the comb from her locked hands, she was like a person demented.

She would never forgive herself for trying to do to Moshe what she would never have done to herself. Change a part of him.

That was a long time ago.

They were going to give each other roses and wine.

In the end, nothing happened. Because the day before they left again for Kingston and the start of the new university year, their second year, Rachel took Arrienne aside in her kitchen and said, "Look after my son, Miss Arrii," using Moshe's nickname for her.

Arrienne's temper flared. "Why? Because him is man and me is woman? Why is always woman job fi look after?"

"No," Rachel said, her voice quiet and sober. "Not because him is man and you is woman. Because you is the strong one."

Tears came to the girl's eyes. "Mama Rachel, I been looking after him all our lives."

"I know." Rachel said. "But now is different." Her eyes were distant, looking out at some place toward the river, as if seeing but not seeing. "Now he go need you more than ever." She reached out and wiped the girl's cheek gently with her work-roughened fingers. "God bless you, my child."

With that one request Mama Rachel awaken a guilt so ancient, she make it impossible for me to trouble her, Miss Fisher's, son.

CHAPTER XVII

They rode the train back to Kingston, one or the other sometimes falling asleep and in sleep loosening the clasp where they held each other's hands. Watching her sleep, her head resting on his shoulder, he thought how it was many months since their hands stopped growing onto each other and needing time to unclasp without bleeding, and he wondered with terror if it was an omen in the way the river was omen. That time with Alva had been the first time he went back to Foster-Reach River since the dreadful afternoon when he was little and the man and woman with the crocus bag of ganja accosted him and sought to jail his silence with threats.

He had insisted on that river as the cookout spot instead of the Raiding, because it was the one place he had not walked with Arrii. He didn't know if this was because he feared her anger or because their shared places were set apart in his mind.

He was already upset because Alva had come visiting again, without invitation, and it was the first day of the first summer he and Arrii had come home, the end of their first year away. He thought it was his fault, for telling Alva they were coming home. He had kept in touch, by letter or phone, at first mostly by Alva's effort and then by his, reciprocating because of his feelings of guilt about taking and not giving. The same sense of guilt, two years later, made him kiss the pink-and-red girl goodbye at the porter's lodge instead of just saying good night and walking away.

But he had hoped Alva would have been more sensitive, not come up the first day they would have together with their people. (Alva had, as expected, not made the grade for university, nor had he wanted to, but had gone to work in his family's business, the string of stores they owned in Ora and Montego Bay. He was managing the Ora store, and doing well.)

Arrii hadn't quarreled the way she used to, that way she had of not speaking but pushing out her bottom lip and letting the glitter in her eyes curse him. She shook her head no, her eyes still and meditative with that newfound quiet that had come over her in the past year of sudden and rapid change from girl to woman.

She had changed in ways that both unnerved and impelled him. Even her physical beauty was different—it had matured and grown more defined, as if keeping pace with an inner maturity that produced in her an other self, introspective, secret, and somehow withdrawn.

It wasn't that she pushed him away. On the contrary, she seemed to need his company with a different desire that he did not understand any more than he understood this other person that she had grown and stowed away under her skin. At times he caught glimpses of this person looking profoundly at him. Like a wild creature peering outside a burrow to survey the terrain in secret. Darting quickly below once it sensed it was being seen.

"Arrii unfathomable sometimes," he said to his mother, and then was sorry, because the words wounded him like a betrayal. They never spoke about each other to anyone.

"She jus turning woman, son," Rachel said, her voice gentle. "That part of a woman that turn away, don't be afraid of it, it just mean she needing other woman company now. What she learn from them teach her how to be with a man."

He wondering what his mother mean by, "What she learn from them teach her how to be with a man." What man? After Arrii never tell Rachel she looking for any man—of that he was sure. But it gave him a vague disquiet, which crystallized into annoyance with his mother.

Yet indeed, since their return she had spent a great deal of time not with her own mother or stepmother, but with his mother, Rachel. Any time he in his room painting or gone to sea with his father, she either in the kitchen or on the patch of farm with Rachel, the two of them cooking food or sowing the winter-crop seed, or harvesting yam, digging deep with the fork or machete and then with they bare hands so they could enjoy the feel of brushing the warm dirt from they fingers. Nobody know what they talk about.

"You need to spend some time with your mother," Rachel insisted. "It don't look good, an I don't want to get in trouble with Dulsie, mek she start pass mi yard and not speak."

Arrienne shrugged and smiled. "You don't want me here, then, Mama Rachel?"

"You know that nutten don't go so," Rachel replied briefly, turning back to her fire to roll the breadfruit over on the other side so it could roast even.

"Well then," Arrienne said.

"You stubborn. Stubborn-stubborn bad."

"Yes." She kissed Rachel on the top of her head and turned away, back to her task of peeling and slicing the other breadfruit that had already been roasted and laying the slices out on plates. It was a Friday and Noah was home, sitting out in the yard mending his fishing net and listening to the conversation. Moshe in his room painting. The whole place quiet, except for one or two bird squeaking in the naseberry tree that lean over the house. We all so taciturn, Arrienne thought, contented. We belong together. We is family.

Over on the other side of the district, her father groaning in pain because the sugar crop start this morning and he just come home from briefing his workers and starting them on they job. The welts begin to burn and Miss Purity bringing out the cushions. But Arrienne not there. She busy learning Rachel. And feeling fierce and holy because Mosh in a parallel room doing what he love best, and she love him.

She never know what attaclaps a-come.

interval

There are too many spelling and grammatical errors in A Tall History of Sugar *to make automatic corrections. Use the "Review Spelling and Grammar" tab to insert corrections manually.* That is what the computer just write in the pop-up. Or words to that effect. Oh Lord, what is the one correct and singular language to carry this freight, this translation of griefs?

CHAPTER XVIII

Later he was to think of that year, their first in the city, as their living year. Nine months like a gestation that test their being-together in a way that make them reflect on it for the first time instead of taking it for granted the way they used to, the way you take for granted that the bed I sleep in for seventeen years is mine, the room I do my schoolwork in over two thousand five hundred twenty and one nights is mine, the parents in my house is mine, they will always be mine, even after they die.

Now for the first time the two of them know in all the ways that matter that he is one, and she be another, she is one, and he be other. The separations that draw them into this double knowledge is what finally reach a point where it mek him get in a ship belly and run wheh, sailing as far as he could, northeast of paradise. Yet he never forget that year how it special, because they never had another like it, and it was the last year of their perfection. After that, as you already see, trouble start and never stop starting, for that is how you know you turn man and woman at last, when crisis come in battalions.

But I running ahead of myself telling you how it happen, going backward instead of forward, following the way pain loop through a body, like seesaw or pattern that unravel, instead of explaining to you how it happen straight down the line. This first time that I am telling you about happen the first time they live away from home, from one October to the following June, nine months on the year-calendar but a full year of university schooling. The melodramatic thing to say is that something give birth. And after that, this other thing with Maas Alva in the middle, that rake up a whole set of question without any answer and send Rachel halfway out of her mind. (For don't mek duppy fool yu, Rachel may not have known exactly what happen that day by the river but she have a pretty shrewd idea, is why she speak to Arrienne and frighten the girl clean out of her wits and her seduction plan. Noah, he be man and therefore slightly blind, especially with him eyes always seaward. He don't know what o'clock did a-strike.)

So now they return to the city with this shadow between them.

Their change had been so gradual, they could almost not have seen it coming. At first, despite the change he saw in her, the strain of self-seclusion that now ran in her spirit like a narrow ribbon of water through vegetation, she was spending more time in his room in the all-men's dorm than she did in hers. At nights they studied there together, dragging his armchair and the extra one his roommate wasn't using onto the balcony outside the room and sliding their beating boards across the armrests for makeshift desks. Later, as the year wore down toward exams, they stayed up all night, catching a few minutes' shut-eye on the mattress of his single bed that they also hauled outside when needed, squeezing it in the tiny space between the armchairs. They fell asleep sealed like Siamese twins back to back, but when he woke to the sound of the clock alarm, more often than not he found that they'd turned toward each other in the night and slept spooned, their arms clasped around the belly of whoever was in front.

It was easier for them to be together like this in the men's dorm than in the women's. For him, it was a kind of shield in the super-macho culture of the all-men's hall. He had a girl, and therefore nothing to prove and no need of a performance to prove it with. For her part, spending time with him in his room instead of his spending time in hers meant she avoided ruckus with the hall rep for bringing a man to sleep on the women's hall, where it was not permitted.

Everyone knew her as one of the shameless girls who slept openly with her boyfriend in his room. Neither Moshe nor Arrienne cared.

They didn't have much money, so the meal chits they used to purchase food at the cafeteria were never enough and they had to find creative ways of feeding themselves. They shared a hot plate, kept in his room, on which they improvised meals, mostly packets of chicken noodle soup that they emptied into too much boiling water, adding large flour dumplings because flour was cheap and filling. Moshe had a gift for finding odds and ends to add for flavor and sometimes nutrition. Arrienne, thoroughly spoiled by her father who had wanted her to be a boy, could not cook, but he could. Rachel had made him learn; it was something she felt everyone should learn to do for themselves, men especially. "Cooking is not a woman's place just because man have things hanging," she explained in her trenchant way. But her real concern had been that he should be able to look after himself when she was not there to do it for him.

The reason they had to scrimp on food was not because of any serious money shortage. This was 1975, halfway through the Joshua years. They had been given a generous boarding grant that covered a surprising number of expenses. Moshe had obtained a student loan to cover what was left over. Even with the extra that he got from the student loan, Arrienne had more than he did: her father, determined that she would not begin her working career saddled with debt, was financing from his own pocket whatever her grant did not cover. But even the monthly allowance he sent her had to be carefully husbanded since his resources, above adequate for living in a small country village, were stretched by the costs of higher education in the city. Still, with their pooled resources, they could have managed in reasonable comfort. But they spent most of their food allowance on books, paint supplies for Moshe, and escape.

"Escape" meant sudden, unplanned excursions out of the city. (Hungry for green fields, small districts, and open land, they had traveled through the countryside of the fourteen parishes before they finished.) It also meant the plays that came to the city theaters, a change from the on-campus student productions that were cheap with their student IDs and often excellent but minus the sense of freedom that came with going outside, to the professional theater, by themselves together. Sometimes they strayed downtown to the harbor, to watch the ships unlade. At other times they took the ferry to Port Royal, and came back late, when the pelicans sat folded on the buoys and the lights of Kingston made columns in the water.

Port Royal became a frequent pilgrimage. The sunken half city with its low stone houses, black beach, and sailors' mixed-color children diving for Spanish coin in the blue water filled him with strange longings. Seeing the concupiscences of history so dramatically placed side by side, he could not but think of his birth father and mother. He wondered if the sailors' children ever saw their fathers. Port Royal was surrounded by marinas, the harbor filled with boats from far countries in North America and Europe, even Australia. Were any of the fathers the owners of these boats? Did they sometimes come to see their black-and-white children, or did they just come for fun and move on?

It didn't occur to Arrienne and Moshe to think that they were dating each other. But dressing up to go off campus to a play or art exhibition brought a sense of new adventure and the knowledge that they were standing on the threshold of a different door. (It was only the door of adulthood, but Moshe did not even consider its implications.)

Like most people who live inside their heads and are solitary, they were seduced by spectacle and shape-shifting, and the theater was their haunt in the same way that the hens' coop and the drama of the egg-laying had been when they were small.

Moshe wore his brand-new bush jacket and flared pants. Arrienne was gleaming in blue polyester, a halter top gown that outlined her curves without clinging. Her abundant hair, in dreadlocks long before dreadlocks were respectable, flowed down her shoulders like a ribbed shawl.

She spun around him, admiring. "You look grand!"

"And you! Like Nefertiti!"

In high heels, she was as tall as he, their faces on a level when they kissed on the lips, as when they were children. She turned her face away, the light in her eyes darkening as though a shutter had come down.

"What's wrong?" he asked anxiously, still attuned to her every change of mood but now afraid of the new dark streak in her.

"Nothing. Silly, don't look like that. You just ruined my lipstick, is all."

He watched her remove the trace of his kiss, outlining a chocolate curve on her mouth with expert hands.

You two are just like an old married couple, some of their friends said.

For, oddly, they had friends, in a manner of speaking. Torn between the habit of their twosome silence (in which speech had increasingly become for her a choice) and her hunger to be of use, she had joined the Union of Democratic Students, a radical socialist group that took their inspiration from the writings of Che, Fidel, and Martí. This she did not long into their sojourn on the campus. It did not surprise Moshe. He had known there was no turning back for her from the time she caught fire from Joshua's incendiary rallies calling the youth to love of country and revolution. Arrienne was one among thousands of young people who had responded with a fierce patriotism and the conviction that they could change the country's future forever. She'd wanted to sign up for the two years of National Youth Service after they finished school, and he would have gone with her, but Rachel had said bluntly, We can't afford it, it is either one or the other—either you find paying work, or you are going to university where this new government giving you the opportunity to get through with boarding grant and student loan. Is a one-chance in a lifetime, a thing I never dream I could live to see. Arrienne can talk bout youth service because her daddy have money, you hear, and she wrap him round her finger, he will do whatever she want and you left stranded—and so they had both taken the road to Kingston, because Arrienne didn't want him to go alone.

Rachel had put her foot down about his going to Edna Manley Art School for the same reasons. You can go to all the art school you want after you graduate with a degree you can feed yourself on, and when she said this she wasn't looking at him because she felt she was doing something terrible to him.

In the end, they registered for degrees in modern languages, he in English and French, she in English and Spanish, so they would have two foreign languages between them. Rachel was satisfied with Arrienne's argument that he could work in advertising or become a teacher or a translator, though she had no idea how he could be a teacher, the only one of the occupations among the three Arrienne mentioned that she knew anything about. How could he teach when he could not talk? But she felt perhaps he could learn. Teaching she felt was a profession that gave a great deal of space for creativity while providing bread and butter. She had even heard of a blind man who had become a teacher, teaching sighted children, whereas she knew of nobody who had made a living drawing picture or carving image. She thought her son's talent was out of the ordinary yet it wouldn't earn him any bread when she and his father were gone.

"But Mama, look at Leandro," he said. Leandro was her favorite newspaper cartoonist, whose wisdoms she quoted whenever she couldn't put her finger on a verse from Yahweh.

"I sure Leandro have profession apart from the likkle stick drawing-dem wha him do inna *Gleaner*. Yu can go look fi him and ask him when yu reach Kingston. Furthermore, yu don't need fi go a university fi learn fi draw. Yu is mi son but mi nuh shame fi seh yu can draw hundred time better than Leandro aready. So, yu have enough."

But her heart warmed because she knew he was teasing her. She could not have borne it if his response had shown that she had broken his heart.

Arrienne consoled him: "Nuh worry, maybe you can take courses at art school as elective." She had studied her faculty handbooks like someone preparing for a major exam, and already knew all the right words. It was the first time they were knowing the word "elective."

He could not be jealous of her new friends because they were ideological company, people with whom she shared a political outlook and designed political posters and propaganda to contest the student guild elections. Not friends of her heart but of her conviction, and because of that he didn't think they would be permanent. Still, they became in a lesser way his friends too since she roped him in to design and make the guild election posters. The posters he designed were the catchiest in the campaign.

He was not interested in joining any groups, but she said he probably should, maybe they both needed to relate to other people, not be in each other's pockets so much.

Not be in each other's pockets so much.

He looked at her, amazed and speechless.

"Maybe we're too close," she said, as if he hadn't understood what the literal words meant. She looked away from him, a faint blush staining her cheeks under the smooth berry-dark matte of her skin. He always knew when she blushed, a dark ripple under the surface of satin, but she never did so with shyness or shame, only excitement or the explosive rage to which she was prone if anyone she loved (mostly him) was threatened. "Maybe give each other more space," she added, looking worried, when he didn't reply.

"Okay, if that's what you want," he said, speaking to the change in her, the mysterious shadow that he could not read, but he was so closely attuned to her that he knew this was something she needed, in a way that was not clear even to herself, but somehow imperative. It hurt him more than a little, this strange imperative that was so quiet, not urgent, yet pushing without let against the single current in which their lives had run as one up to this moment.

Something seemed to break in her in response to his unprotesting acquiescence. She gripped his hands tight, her great eyes trained with anxiety on his. "We won't lose each other, will we, Mosh? We will only grow up, right?"

"We will only grow up," he agreed, kissing her in reassurance, her eyelids (her lashes drooped shut and she went limp under his kiss, as though her whole body had become liquid, without bones, surrendering to the desire to believe), her cheeks, then butterfly at the corners of her lips, left then right. She moved her head so that their lips met, pressing softly. For a moment her hands tightened fiercely in his. He pulled them away and put them around his middle and held her hard against himself.

In a moment she pulled him to her with all her strength, then pushed away from him, quick and sudden, almost in the same movement jumping to her feet. "I love you, Mosh. Don't stop loving me. Ever. Come on." And she was rushing to the door, her hand in his but pulling him after her. They were late for medieval English class.

The thought of a group, talking to people, was hard for him, but he figured he would try, to please her. In the end he didn't have to try. Word of his gift got around after he'd helped make the UDS campaign posters and he was recruited to help design costumes for the Tallawah carnival. He found he enjoyed doing this. The carnival fascinated him, even if his mother would not have approved. To her, it would have been rampant paganism, abomination to Yahweh. He was captivated by the artistry and the costumes which a person could put on and become someone else, not their true self but a place where they could roll up their true self and tuck it away out of sight while the other, the one in the costume, played.

Though he would never participate except as a designer and spectator, he loved the parade as he loved the plays he and Arrii went to in the theaters. And the designing of something that would be made use of gave him a quiet pleasure that healed a tiny part of his disappointment about art school. So he made his friends there, among the carnival group, not friends of his heart or his conviction, but something in between, which allowed him to use his art in a way that gave him solace, if only for the small time the carnival preparation lasted. Even among them, he remained shy and silent.

He was told that in Trinidad the preparation went on for the entire year, the plans for the next starting immediately after the end of the one before. This that the Trinidadian students did for a few weeks in another country was only a pale approximation of the real. But for him it was real.

He became more famous than he wanted, for the beauty of his costumes. When the band he designed for won for the king and queen costumes and also took the road march prize, the costumes made the local news and the media wanted to interview him. He managed to hide until the excitement died down.

Arrienne left the UDS soon after. "They too rabid for me," she said. "It's all phony. They don't really care about anybody. Only about the words, about being right."

He felt that she might try other groups, and that she would be restless and leave all of them, because at heart, like him, she could not give large pieces of herself to anything, she would give it all in one piece, once, and then an end. And despite her passion for an idea and her tough practicality, she would give herself over only to what seized her heart, not her head.

He did not think that she might want to bring an end to the attention he was giving to the carnival group and their costumes. She was never jealous of his painting, the long hours in his room while she lay on his bed reading. Hnn. (Rachel's words in her mind echoing, Men are mostly blind.)

In the end it didn't happen the way he thought it might. She was exceedingly restless after the break with the UDS, and would not do anything except study or watch him while he painted. She seemed to have lost something of herself that had given her compass, but then dissipated, leaving her wandering. Her presence in his room was brooding, no longer part of the stillness to which he was accustomed when he worked. Now it disturbed him and made it difficult for him to concentrate. She seemed to be pacing up and down the room with long strides, though she sat still in the armchair. One day she said, "I think we should do it."

He went very, very still. Then put down his paintbrush and looked at her.

"I don't care what Mama Rachel thinks. I think we should do it."

He waited, feeling the tension in her seep into his own body. She sat across from him, her hands pressed together in front of her face, obscuring her features except her eyes. Her head slightly bent with its mass of dreadlocked hair made him think of sea grapes heavy on a stem. He absorbed fear and was astonished that she could ever be afraid of him or with him, and his body, startled, reached out to hers in fierce comfort and reassurance. At that she let go of something she had been holding very tight, stranglehold tight; he felt she had been holding it so long that her breath now came out in a long tide of surrender. The sudden hot tide of her giving up was so strong that he cried out as he went under, he drowned, a long drowning, and when he came to, his body shaking as with a fever, she was on her knees beside him, her hair falling over her hands, hugging his legs.

She was trembling as much as he. Dazed, he tried to say something in their silent language and could not. The sounds in his ears were jumbled, as if vocabulary had left him and he would have to start again from the beginning, learning building blocks of syllables. He recalled with shock that they hadn't used that language for a long time, and it gave him a sense of awe, not quite fright, to think that it had left them for good. Then he thought, in confused wonder, that they had never communicated like this, through—what? He did not know. Was this the replacement for their childhood speech? But how would he name it? He had no words for this drowning, and neither did she.

They stayed there silent for a long time. He could hear her breath, and her heart beating against his knee. She could hear his thoughts moving around his mind but not what he was thinking. The sounds in her ears were jumbled, as if she was beginning to go deaf and would have to start over again from the beginning, learning his language.

"We'll go away," he said, his hands moving in her hair.

"Yes."

"We need a place."

"Yes." Ashamed, she wrote on his sketch pad. *There's a hotel.* She wrote the name.

"Okay."

She understood that he was expecting her to make the booking. He was still leaving it to her to arrange their lives, as he had done in the past. This had begun to make her sad.

This episode marked the most profound change in their lives to this point. The end of their living year. She had exposed the part of her that loved him with a woman's love, and in the discovery of it he seemed helpless, acquiescent, and surrendered, like a man who had come to know and accept his fate without the will to claim it.

CHAPTER XIX

A new shadow grew over her in the next days as she watched him, observing every change of his mood and shift in his expression. Yet now she never looked directly at him. And he became uneasy and withdrawn from her, feeling himself judged. This too was a new experience. They felt they were standing on the edge of an abyss they had no sense of how to reconnoiter.

Yet they clung together, as if joined in a pact that had been imposed on them before they were born. (The truth was simpler, far removed from such Sturm und Drang: their lives had come together through an accident of meeting, when he stood hesitating on the steps of the Tumela schoolhouse and she offered him candy and, taking his hand, led him down the steps into the play yard. But their hearts and their experiences were superstitious.)

If he was tempted to feel a sense of betrayal at being pressed into this place where they had never been, he reminded himself that the first betrayals had been his. First his secret visits to Myrtle Kellier, begging the four-eyed woman please to consult her spirit seers again on his behalf, to see if they could tell her more about his biological father. Not telling Arrii because she had been upset by how much the first visit tormented him. Not wanting to cause her more pain, he invented excuses so she wouldn't know he was going. She felt he should let it go, no good could come of it. She did not believe the old woman could tell him more than she already had, or that he could have any way of finding his father. She was worried for Noah, he would be hurt if he ever found out, but he had felt his parents didn't have to find out, and if they did, Noah was too big a man to be offended by his desperate need to know.

That was the first time deception became part of their relationship. The hurt, though he braced himself for it, was bad. Not guilt, but hurt, as if he had cut himself in two. It did not take him long to tell her the truth, or that all the old woman could tell him further was about his mother, who had come to her for the last time in the dark. "She was going to drown me in the cave where she get pregnant with me," he said, his voice lost. "The same cave under the fort where we went on bio trips. She change her mind at the last minute. She give Myrtle a note."

Trembling, her lips gray, Arrienne read the note, his one legacy from his mother except the basket and clothes he'd been wrapped in when he was found. It was written on a torn-off exercise book leaf in a large, childish scrawl, the writing of someone with awkward hands or whose personality was not yet formed. *I changed my mind, Miss Myrtle. But I putting him somewhere where somebody can find him. If he lives, is God forgive.*

They never found her body but the seer-woman knew. "I see it in mi vision. Shi do it in the same place shi did plan to put har son, but last minute har heart couldn't give har fi tek wheh him chance fi live, shi couldn't play the part of Providence wid a life dat not har own. It not easy fi people like wi tek life. Not other people life. Wi always tekking wi own. Di body wash out to sea."

The seer-woman face scrunch up deep, like in anger, but she only remembering and memory cut cruel. "Shi use to visit me all the time. Want mi to help har. But shi never know what shi really want. Shi wouldn't trow wheh di belly. Shi band it down and shi come here to born it."

It was him she was calling "it." She had no thought of dehumanizing him, it was her way. She was telling her memory like prophecy and she was caught up in that, hardly seeing him at all. But it cut him to the heart. "I was going to tek it. I seh to har, 'Give mi di child. Den yu can go back to school and finish yu education.' And maybe shi woulda do it, maybe not. I don't know when shi mek up har mind to do what shi do, one or the other, if is from the beginning when di heart go out of har, or after di child born and shi si what shi si. Shi feel it not fair to leave mi wid a child like dat."

It was the old lady who had shown her how to band down her growing belly so that the round rise did not show and her people did not put her out. She was small enough to get away with it at home, where loose shifts could be worn in the hot heat. But not at school. In her fitted, pleated uniform, the school would eventually have noticed and she would be expelled. But it was summer and school was out when he was born, a less-than-seven-months baby. She had two and a half months of grace.

The four-eyed woman did not tell him how his mother screamed when she saw, not his face, but a devastation where his face should have been. She only told him that when she turned around, so quick it was, his mother and he were not there. "Shi move so fast, I don't know when shi tek yu and fly out di house."

In the smoke-blurred kitchen, the old woman had peered at him through her cataracts. "I see your face now. Not as it was." She closed her eyes in the way he had come to know, and began rocking to and fro as if asleep on her feet. Her toothless gums kneaded themselves behind her lips, which moved in and out like a mollusk pulsing in its shell. "Is Providence business, not mine. Providence know what Him doing. You survive." She was muttering this, turning away, back to her firepit. Her turning away and the switch in her language were his cue that the conversation was finished; she would not tell him any more that time. She shelled out memory and prophecy in small increments and he learned to wait. Later he learned that she would take those back too, deny the thing she had said the last time. He found her utterly untrustworthy. But he trusted the note scrawled on the exercise book leaf. He did not know why. Only his instinct told him that it had indeed been written by his mother, in her own handwriting, and he clutched it like precious metal, not fool's gold.

Arrienne held him tight, her eyes closed as the old woman's had been closed, rocking their bodies to and fro. She never said a word about his lies. She saw where the veins welled up under his skin with the grief of his deceptions, and where just below his diaphragm the skin broke and wept small petals of blood.

And then, Alva. Moshe had lived inside his own head for too long, shut off from everyone except the one person who was his twin, not to consider honestly all possibilities as to why he had wanted to kill Alva. Beyond the sense of violation, of being touched without his consent, might his rage, an emotion so alien to his nature, been the other side of fear? Had he been afraid that he might be like Alva after all? Had his body of its own volition betrayed what his conscious mind had never thought about, much less admitted?

He was willing to consider this. But he also knew that bodies did what they wanted all the time. His body's reaction to Alva's touch might have been no more than a neurological reflex, like a tic or muscle contract, or his penis standing up because it had nerves in it. It used to do that even when he was little. The truth was, all of the possibilities made him feel equally guilty, as if he done something irrecoverable to himself and Arrienne.

Guilt, he came to feel in later years, was not attached to any one act or singular event, but to the sense of one's helplessness in the world. Whether he was gay or straight or a person with acute reflexes had nothing to do with him, his capacity to choose, at all. This helplessness in the bone was what people who were religious, like his mother, called sin.

?◐

She might have arranged the hotel room, in the end, despite her growing doubt and near-regret for what she had allowed to happen. I shouldn't have let him know, she bitterly arraigned herself. Not yet. He wasn't ready.

She felt that in one unguarded moment she had squandered all the effort she had made in keeping so tight a rein on her feelings for so long. She believed he was confused and didn't know what he wanted, either because he was too innocent or because he would never have a clear interest in a woman. Yet a part of her thought that what they were planning would be for the best, that breaking the taboo of brother-and-sister or friend-and-friend would help to clarify for him where his true desire lay.

She could not bear it if he found it was not with her.

Fate took the decision out of her hands.

When the telephone rang he was in his room molding clay, trying through the feel of it in his hands to decide if it was a medium in which he could work. His eyes were closed; he had made an experimental bust and was touching the features through his fingertips, gauging their shape and completeness. Opening his eyes, he saw the dial face on the phone was lit to zero; it was the porter's lodge. One hand clung to the sculpture. The clay was too soft. He preferred the hard resistance of wood. He reached out his other hand and spoke absently into the receiver, his mind still feeling the clay face through the filter of willed blindness in which he worked when he was sculpting or carving.

The porter answered. He sat staring without seeing for so long that the porter spoke again, sharply, Mosh, you there?

Yes, he said, and yes, again. I'm coming down.

It took him a long time, moving in slow motion, to rise from his desk, push his feet into his flip-flops, pick up his keys, open the door, and walk into the corridor and down the stairs, then along the spine, to the hall entrance where Alva stood waiting at the porter's lodge.

He had put on weight since Moshe last saw him. Not fat, muscle. At nineteen he was a big guy, not tall, but with a weightlifter's physique, like somebody who worked out all the time. He was dressed very neatly in a blue plaid shirt tucked into blue jeans above a polished belt. Everything coordinated. The jeans looked like they'd been ironed. He appeared so formal that in spite of himself Moshe thought, smiling, Alva you going to see the headmaster? When he saw Moshe he picked up a heavy-looking BOAC bag that had been sitting at his feet. The bag bulged unevenly. Alva gestured toward it with a quick laugh. "Country provisions."

"How you do, man?" Moshe said. "Wasn't expecting you."

"Of course not." Alva laughed again. His laugh sounded forced, a laugh that said, If you had been expecting me, would you have let me come?

His eyes took in Moshe at a glance, quick, sweeping, and careful not to linger. Moshe at this time was just past seventeen and incredibly arresting. The sunlight tinge that had struggled over the years to become permanent on him had solidified so that his skin looked almost normal (if you thought of him as white, that is). Arrienne had cut his hair in a fashionable style, the sides and tight kinks at the back low, the bangs in front falling only slightly over his eyes. The bangs were bleached in parts; they looked artful, as if the variegation was done on purpose, though it was not, it was only the effect of the sun. He was long and rangy in stonewashed jeans falling low on his hips, his washed-out T-shirt close-fitting, outlining the tight musculature of his chest and back, his face a fine cylinder with sharp bones, pronounced thick lips, and a broad flaring nose.

"Come," Moshe said. He felt no anger or protest, or even shame. Only an acceptance that this was happening, Alva would always turn up without invitation or welcome, and it was up to him to parse how to relate to a man like this who liked to behave like a clown, but in ruthless pursuit of what mattered to him would not take no for an answer.

Arrienne interrupting: *In all the vintage stories of this kind, Grimm or Andersen or Lang or even* The Thousand and One Nights, *there is only one rival to be vanquished, and is usually another woman. But just because this was Moshe and he fool cyaan done, strike two. The princess has her job cut out.*

ί

Up in Moshe's room Alva's eyes took in everything: the two single beds on opposite sides, each flanked by an armchair with books sprawled on the plywood beating boards laid across the armrests, the woman's pink sweater over the back of the chair on Moshe's side of the room, the creeper in a glass bowl on his roommate's side—a gift from his girl—Moshe's drawings and paintings on the walls, the half-molded clay face in the tray on his desk. The face was clearly Arrienne, Alva could not but notice.

"How's Black Beauty?" he said, standing in the middle of the room.

Moshe was irritated by the nickname. He felt it wasn't a compliment but an allusion to a horse. "She went to class," he said, watching Alva's eyes on the sweater across the armchair. "She lives in Taylor Hall. We study together."

Alva shrugged, smiling. His smile said, Of course.

"Sit down." Moshe gestured toward his loaded armchair, blushed, and moved quickly to remove the books and beating board. "Sorry." Some resistance made him not want to remove the sweater, but he did.

Alva sat down in the chair at his desk. "You don't mind?" He gestured toward the unfinished clay model.

"No." Moshe sat down on the bed. You can sit anywhere you like, why ask me? he thought, irritated.

Alva spun the chair sideways, toward Moshe. His broad back blocked half the desk, all of the sculpture, from sight. "I brought stuff. Fry fish, hardough bread, honey, and some of my mother's blue drawers. She's the best. Didn't know if you have place to cook, but just in case I bring some grung food as well."

"Thanks, man. You didn't have to."

"I know." Alva made a movement of his head sideways behind him, toward the sculpture, but he didn't turn around. "You working clay now?"

"Not really. Just experiment."

"Oh. So how university—"

"How your family—"

They had both begun speaking at the same time. "Sorry," they said together. Alva laughed. Moshe laughed too, in that way he had, a brief expulsion of breath with his lips half-open, as if laughter was on ration.

"Nice pad you have here. You fix it up nice."

"I have a pretty cool roommate. Not everybody does."

As if on cue, the door pushed open and Brian and his girlfriend Julie came in.

"Hi," Brian said, barely looking their way.

"Hi. This is Alva. Visiting from country. Alva, Brian, Julie." He found relief in the mundane interruption.

But Brian was only breezing through, as usual. "Nice meeting you, I-dren from country. Going to tek in a fete, Fisher. Just come to change my clothes."

He grabbed pants and shirt from the closet on his side and went out again. He'd be changing in the bathroom down the corridor, not because there was a stranger in the room but because he didn't want to disrespect his girl, changing in front of her in the presence of a stranger. Julie sat down on his bed, leafing through the magazine that had been lying on the coverlet, studiously avoiding interrupting the conversation that Moshe wished she'd interrupt.

Alva talked fast about schoolmates he had seen or kept in touch with since they graduated. Brian came back looking wild in red polyester bell-bottoms and a body-hugging green shirt. Julie teased up his Afro for him with her Afro pic and they went, leaving behind them a curious vacuum, as if someone had sucked energy out of the room. Brian always trailed energy behind him, and took it with him when he left.

"Is a party man that, I-yah," Alva said.

"Yes."

"Strange how he and you live together, and you so quiet."

"He don't bother me."

"No?"

"No."

"Good. Good," Alva said, and again, "good," as if he had something on his mind. He leaned forward in his chair, dangling his hands absently between his knees.

Moshe watched him preoccupied.

CHAPTER XX

A lot of things happened that night. Alva talked a great deal, run-on, monotone, saying a lot of things. He was good at conversation, and he was funny. In the end he said the things Moshe had been dreading but knew were inevitable. What could he expect—it was because of the need to say these things that Alva had come. He was sorry, he wanted to be friends, Alva said, could Moshe forgive him, he hadn't known what he was doing, for a moment he had lost his mind.

Saying this, he began to cry. "Guys like me," he said, "you don't know, we live a strange life in the shadows. You guess and spell who might be like you, and you tek a chance. Sometimes you mek a mistake. I mek a mistake with you. I sorry, man. I sorry."

Moshe was appalled and angry and pitying all at once. He did not want to be witness to Alva's tears, which he felt were humiliating and at the same time manipulative. And he hated himself for feeling this way, for not being kinder, or more understanding, knowing how he himself had always been pushed apart as other and strange. He wanted to feel only these things, but he could not.

At evening they went walking in the chapel gardens. The chapel was a white building made of stone from a demolished great house. The campus had once been a sugar plantation. Alva was fascinated that the gardens, the white church, and the broken aqueducts were so cool and calm to walk in, after all the violence of their past. Moshe showed him the unmarked grave near the northwest aqueduct, which the seniors ragging the freshmen at orientation used to tell them was the grave of a slave who had worked on the plantation. He had no name except a single word carved into the flat concrete slab, *Jaghi*.

"I don't think he was any slave," Moshe said, feeling he was treating Alva like a tourist and himself acting like a tourist guide. "They wouldn't have buried a slave in concrete, just the bare ground." He felt ashamed, fraudulent. (It was only long after, when heritage signs were put up, that we found out Jaghi was a businessman whose people had come indentured from India. So, fraudulent pose aside, his tour-guiding, charting a history of gaps, was more accurate than his doubt.)

"True, true, good perception," Alva nodded, playing his part.

Moshe pointed out other landmarks, the conversation balancing the distance between them.

"Where is this?" Alva asked, pointing to the turnstile that led through to the hospital gate.

"Nowhere. University Hospital. It late." He turned to go back.

There were places he did not tell Alva about. The spot where he and Arrii lay down on the ring road so they could see the night sky, which was low and near in Tumela, weighted with an impossible number of stars, but visible in Kingston only if there was a blackout or you made a deliberate effort to look up. The stone heap by the aqueducts where they sat to watch the sun rise, after an early run to Long Mountain and back. The place near the turnstile where four from the men's hall had beaten a freshman accused of being what Alva was. That was the first time Moshe knew that such an identity could be read in the way a man walked, the flow of his hips and buttocks, or the gentleness of his hands. Or that there was a word for such men.

Arrii had been, as usual, more savvy. "Is the same as what they mean in Tumela when they say 'maama-man,'" she explained. "Is jus that in Tumela nobody don't trouble you."

That was when he understood that Dadoub the mansion builder was not called maama-man because he baked and sold achee and toto, but because he was whispered to be that other kind, a man who liked men. "Batty man," an expression he had never heard before. Dadoub had never been beaten or accused. That was how Moshe came to understand that there were two Jamaicas that spoke two different languages, though very near.

The four had arraigned the freshman in a mock-trial, asking him many questions to force him to declare himself. Moshe had stumbled upon them unawares, on his way to Papine market to buy provisions while Arrienne was at class. The boy was thin and delicate. He half crouched, like an animal, almost on his knees, as if trying to shrink inward into his skin. Moshe had the strange sensation that the boy had already left the part of his skin where his upper body was supposed to be and what he was looking at was not a skin but a sack with a man sunk in its lower parts, halfway down.

For a moment the shocked boy from Tumela country-bush stood frozen. A moment long enough to hear the shameful questions, and then, as if propelled, he went on walking forward, like a man in a dream, not knowing what he would or should do. But the group fell away when they saw him. Walked off in a casual manner in several directions as if nothing had happened at all and they had all been separate passersby. There were to be no witnesses.

Moshe couldn't believe it. It was as if they had melted into the earth, like thin hail used to melt when as a child he tried to grab it in his hands. It slipped away faster than lightning, leaving only its cold burning in his hand.

He helped the boy to his feet. The boy's face was cut and bleeding but he did not want to go to the hospital. Moshe made him go, staying with him until his cuts were dressed. They got a paper to collect ointments for his bruises at the hospital pharmacy, but they left because of the long wait. "You can go back in the morning," Moshe said. The boy did not answer.

In the night he told Arrienne, whose fury could scarcely be restrained. She wanted to report the incident—but, He's afraid, Moshe said. Please, we can't do that.

They couldn't risk putting the boy in a position where he would be attacked again in retaliation. They didn't even know the names, and furthermore, who would do anything about it? The silence around such things was tacit and strong.

His name was Lance Harding. Within a week, he moved to lodgings off campus. Moshe saw him afterward, walking across campus, but when he said hi, Lance turned away. Moshe understood. He knew there was no shame greater than coming face to face with the person who had rescued you from shame. His own shame at having witnessed this humiliation cut like a knife, and made it hard for him to even call out the greeting, which the other youth rejected. He wanted to say, I'm sorry, I'm sorry, I'm sorry, but he knew Lance would never forgive him for such words or such intimacy, or for knowing him at all.

He and Arrii never went to Papine through the turnstile again. And that following summer, as he absorbed Arrienne's grief after the incident with Alva by the river, he felt that her anguish was partly the memory of Lance Harding, their failure to act on his behalf, and partly their new knowledge of what even the posture of a man's body, real or imagined, could bring.

She never told him what somebody, more than one, girls in the dorm, had said to her behind his back, long before Alva came: "You sure your boyfriend not—" and they made the vague unspeaking signs with their hands, not allowing themselves to say the disgraceful word. "How him look so delicate?"

The hurtful thing was that his delicate look was because of his skin, not the desire that both of them feared. Even had his sexuality not been ambiguous to him and her both, he would still have developed a habit of moving his hands with care, from the childhood habit of protecting himself from bruises or falls. She tell di gal-dem two of the badwords to which she resort whenever she fall inarticulate. But her eyes burn.

❧

Alva, it seemed, had made no plans for where he would stay the night, though he knew he could not return to Ora at that time of evening. Moshe phoned Arrienne in her room and gave up his bed to his visitor, himself sleeping on the balcony on the sponge Brian kept for squatters, friends whose money had not come through in time to pay their boarding fees or who had not managed to get a room on campus but needed to kotch for a few nights while they sorted out their situation.

Arrienne, as he expected, did not come over.

Moshe slept fitfully, his mind torn between all the feelings that assailed him in Alva's presence, the pity, the anger, the shame at the memory of violation, the resentment that Alva had turned up once more at the worst possible time, when his relationship with Arrienne was so fragile and turning. The uncertainty between them had yet to resolve itself, in ways he did not even know. She would be upset again. And who could blame her?

Near dawn, he woke to find Alva standing over him, watching him sleep. He cried out in protest as much at the thought that he had been exposed, naked, in his sleep, as at the look of yearning on the other's face. And his voice was cold when he said, "Yu bed tough?"

"No. I just getting ready to go."

Moshe's heart thudded with relief. Brian had woken and was watching from his bed. "Is still night."

"Is awright. Nuh yu tell mi seh mi can call a taxi at di porter's lodge, pick up a bus at Half Way Tree? Time mi reach down there, day almost light."

Moshe saw that Alva was dressed and carrying the emptied BOAC bag and the thin satchel with his overnight things under his arm.

"Wait till morning."

"No. Everything was a mistake. I shouldn't have come." He mouthed rather than said it, so Brian would not hear.

Moshe struggled to stand, unwinding the sheet that had got twisted around his waist.

Alva watched him search for his flip-flops, not saying anything. They went, Moshe in his flip-flops and the tee and sweatpants he slept in.

At the last minute, before the taxi came, Moshe felt an unexpected sadness tinged with shame, the shame that he had been ungracious. Alva had never been to Kingston by bus before, or alone. He had been as far as downtown once or twice, with his father in the family van, when his father came into the city on business. Not many people had a friend who would come so far alone, into such an unfamiliar setting, Moshe thought, to risk and receive rejection.

And it was his tendency to impulse in moments of great emotion, driven by guilt that seemed an indelible part of his makeup, that made him say, out of the blue (later he judged his thoughts in this moment as purely maudlin, and was angry with himself), "Why you come? You love me?" The words left his mouth of their own volition. He could not have explained why he said them, except that he was moved by some vague thought of atonement for failing to understand Alva's predicament even though he himself had lived his life as an outsider. He had no thought that Alva would read the question as an expression of desire.

Alva did not take it as such. He gave a short, startled laugh; Moshe saw genuine amusement in his face. "Goodbye, Fisher," Alva said, and, bending forward where Moshe was sitting on the capstone of the steps while they waited, kissed him swiftly on the side of his face as the lights of the taxicab swam into view, casting long spears that cut the shadows beyond them on the walkway that was called the spine. He could feel that Alva was still smiling, from the stretch of Alva's lips and face against his.

When the rumors broke out, first in murmurs and then open shouts of "White man batty man!" when he passed his hallmates going to his room, he found that his greatest terror was that perhaps he walked in a certain kind of way that he had not known he did, and he became afraid to move his hands.

He wondered if Alva had practiced walking the way he did, arms spread as if he was carrying invisible dumbbells, the movement of his hips a choreograph in neutrality. (You know what was sad about all this? Mosh walked like any other man. In jeans he had the sexiest ass a girl ever saw. Tek it from me, I, Arrienne, interrupting.)

He guessed, but did not know, that they accosted Arrienne on the spineway: "Hey, girl, is wha kinda boyfriend dat yu have? Wha man a-do inna him room?"

Her protectiveness became a terror to him. She was missing classes so he wouldn't go anywhere alone.

When he decided to leave, it was Alva he told, because he knew that Alva would keep in touch. He needed someone who would dare to go and see if Arrii was all right. Someone who would come from far to do it. On the morning when he headed down to Kingston Harbour, he left her a note on his bed and his room key in her mailbox at the porter's lodge.

Apart from minimal clothes, he took with him a Gonzalez she had given him for his seventeenth birthday. The painting was small, but it had cost her all her boarding grant for two terms, and she was living off her father's money.

CHAPTER XXI

The pleasure, glory, and grandeur of England has been advanced more by sugar than any other commodity. —Sir Dalby Thomas, 1745

Bristol

The child's eyes skittered wide open, seeing him standing at the door. "Naw. He baint here."

"Do you mean he's not at home right now?"

"Nope. Don't know 'im."

"Is your name Newland, then?"

"Nope. Vivian. I be Vivian."

In spite of himself, Moshe was amused by the snub-nosed freckled face peering up at him from under its thatch of orange hair, a cartoon urchin's face, its owner clearly bent on giving nothing away.

"Is your dad—"

The carroty head shook emphatically, interrupting, "He be deid."

"What about your mom? Is she—"

"She be Laura." The smile he gave Moshe was angelic, malicious. Legs wide, he spread his small frame as far as it could go across the open doorway, as if barring it from an aggressive attack.

"Laura Newland?"

"Nope. Just Laura. I say, thee bist a pale one, enow? Why bist thou so white?" A flicker of speculation lit the round blue eyes. "Thee be just coming from th' prison, then?"

He himself was very fair of skin, with the pink tinge common to redheads. Ada Pink, Moshe thought irrelevantly. He decided he'd better not take on the question about the relationship between his color and a prison sojourn. "Can you go call your mother, please?"

The eyes narrowed in further speculation.

"Please," he added, coaxing.

"Wot for?" The child was eyeing his pocket in a meaningful kind of way, and in a sudden burst of inspiration Moshe reached for his wallet, for a bribe, but it was too late, or too soon; a woman's light voice was floating toward them from the hallway: "Who is it, Vivvy?"

The boy scowled, as if something in the voice or the words displeased him greatly, probably the pet name Vivvy—who would want to be called Vivvy? Moshe wondered. Especially in the midst of a financial negotiation.

A frowning female face peered at him behind the boy's shoulder. "Go on inside, sweetie. I'll handle this." Her hands moved him out of the way; the boy went, reluctant, glancing behind him at Moshe. The accusing look on his face made plain his displeasure at losing the potential bribe. It was clear that he blamed Moshe for taking too long to get to the point.

She was youngish and dark, with a thin weary face and soiled hands that she wiped down the sides of her pink gingham apron. She seemed to have been kneading dough.

"Yees?" She drew out the word with a hint of impatience, or wariness. "How may I help thee?"

He held out the slip of paper on which the fauve woman had written the name and directions. "Good evening. I'm sorry to trouble you, ma'am." He reached for a standard British form of address and apology. "I am looking for a family, the Newlands. Someone who used to live here, on this street, told me they once lived here. I was hoping—"

How many words he had learned to speak, of necessity! Yet she interrupted him: "We are no Newlands here. Never heard of them, sorry." She made no effort to hide her impatience now; she was already moving to close the door.

He had come too far to abandon the effort so easily. His foot moved, not quite inside the door, but enough that if she shut it she would graze the tip of his shoe. "Ma'am, I'm sorry, but please, I have come a long way. They are my relatives, and I lost touch with them. I was hoping you might know a little bit more, maybe someone else who has lived here a long time and might have known them before they moved away."

"Sorry. This is where we've always lived. Whoever thee's looking for is not here." This time she shut the door. He heard the key click in the lock on the other side.

He had no better luck at the next two houses, one of which was occupied by an old Jamaican man who shouted down from an upstairs window in answer to his knock on the street door, "No, no," gesturing *go away* with his hands.

The police picked him up at the corner of Grosvenor and St. Nicholas. Handcuffed and searched, he thought of the irony of the red-headed child asking if he'd been to prison. He could not have known that less than a year later, another irony would unfold: mere blocks from where they picked him up, new riots would break out, protests against those same SUS laws that had made people who were like him afraid of him, a stranger knocking on their doors, not knowing where he was going, and at the same time made him a target of investigation, a stranger who might have been Irish, or poor, or escaped, or released from prison, but had a West Indian accent and had been seen walking in a particular direction before the neighbors called the cops.

In the end they believed him and let him go, because of his student ID, evidence of the only category in which he was unequivocal.

And how equivocal his journey to Bristol had been! Researched, planned, and plotted, yet without a clear destination or any idea of what he would do or say if by miracle he found the man he was looking for. In the end he did not know whether he was searching on behalf of his mother or on behalf of himself. Which meant he did not know whether his journey was one in search of retribution or reconciliation or simply an end to not knowing. Not that the distinction mattered, until the end. For now, the necessity was all.

Alighting from the train at city center he had purposely taken the route where he knew that, once upon a time, right there in England, sugar had been king. From the waterfront (and he was glad of the sight of the water and the masted boats—it was not home, but the sight revived him), he walked up Guinea Street, named for a place of kidnapping in Africa, a place from where people were captured to become slaves in another part of the world, his world, which was called New. His journey took him past the Ostrich Pub, named for the thought of safari in Africa—stepping inside, he took a picture of the trade card displayed like an heirloom, with the image of the young black slave on it (remembering that when his mother Rachel said, "You look like a image," it was not a compliment, she meant you looked like a buffoon), and he was stared at and noticed, because he walked out after taking his picture, without buying anything or speaking to anyone, then diagonally across the harbor bridge to the Hole in the Wall pub and the custom house, each on either side of the great Queen Square. There was bridge upon bridge, the harbor place was a network of bridges, yet he felt he was crossing not connecting paths but the equivocal zigzag of his life up till now, a journey that had gone in many directions by the acts and will of so many people he had not known and some whom he had known, and perhaps above all, a journey that had gone in directions caused by his accident of skin or lack of skin, but now he thought that this was not wholly true, that if there was a straight line in all of this it was the line of his choices, the decisions he had made, which had governed his life too in their own way; he had never let go of this freedom, circumscribed as it was, and suddenly side by side with his uncertainties, he was glad and calm that he had chosen to come to this Bristol, whatever he might find or might not find.

Somebody was giving a tour of the Redcliffe Caves; he thought he would take the tour but in the end he could not. Because of his mother, and the four-eyed woman's premonition of sharks, and his intuitive fear during biology classes below Fort Charlotte (the fear of waves washing not out to open sea but underground into darkness punctuated by whispers), he could not go under the arch. The tour guide offered him his money back but he said no and turned away. There was a plaque, *Middle Passage*, above the iron grill at the cave mouth—was this irony or acknowledgment or somebody playing insensitive tricks and laughing.

He wanted to know where the slave Pero was buried, but no one at the information center could tell him; perhaps in an unmarked grave near the waterfront, they said; and he thought how strange, and yet how all of a piece, how remarkably it fitted, that Jaghi could have a marked grave in a spot where it was almost certain his body had not been buried, while Pero's grave could not be found in the place where his body most certainly was buried, though Pero, it was said, had been the only one of his kind in that place, and Jaghi, if he had been a slave at all (which as I said, we long after found out he was not), had been one of indistinguishable thousands of his kind who had lived and, without being remarked, died in another place. (But ironies shift, and are fluid, which is why they are ironies, for how could he know that twenty years after, to the day, another bridge would be opened on the harbor front, and they would name it after Pero, in atonement of forgetting, in amelioration of shame that sugar was once king, though if anything changed for Pero's people after twenty years, it may be that as much changed for the worse as for the better.)

He walked past the Old Bank and up Corn Street until he reached Colston Hall and the whole area named for Edward Colston, so much space taken up for and by one man, though his life-size statue took up the smallest space of all, a man who had made so much money from sugar and slavery and from it become a philanthropist, an incongruity so bizarre that the rational mind could hardly contain it, and so from Colston to St. George and then Great George Street, where his eyes opened wide with a sense of déjà vu as could only be experienced by a descendant of superstitions such as he was, staring at the house that Pero's owner, John Pinney (who had never lived in Jamaica, only in Nevis), had built, the facade an exact replica of the schoolhouse across from the cliffs where one mother had abandoned and the other found him and sent him there to be schooled so short a time after he was found, barely nine years, and he had lived one hundred and ninety days out of three hundred and sixty-five each subsequent year of his life for the next seven years, in that school. There was a Great George Street in Savanna-la-Mar, Westmoreland, Jamaica, and a sugar estate called Frome (no river, as there was here, the River Frome, but a Frome estate in Westmoreland that had been the place where a woman had thrown the first stone that broke a white overseer's pate and started the riots toward independence), and there was a picture of St. George slaying the dragon on the English guinea coin (which was worth one shilling more than a pound) that used to be money in his country for more than half of his lifetime. In the circumference of that tight network of streets like a closed-in district, opening through a narrow tongue up into St. Paul's, where the black people lived, side by side with so many Irish, the way they had lived in Ora and Tumela and Frome and a thousand and one other places when sugar was king, he saw unrolled before him the clew of his mother's life, and the way it had been touched by his father's, and the ways both of them had been abysmally intertwined.

Being arrested for vagrancy meant little to him. At some point during the interrogation they tried to figure out if he was the same pale man who had been terrorizing young women walking alone or coming alone off buses, darting in front of them to masturbate and then strangling them with his hands. And though his soul was sick unto death that such an accusation could be leveled at him, that horror too at a certain point left him cold. He felt it all as something happening in a dream, to someone living elsewhere. He had always had this habit when dreadful things happened to him, of feeling like a stranger watching from a distance a play unfolding on a stage, one that had nothing to do with him at all, the only indication of his involvement and deep distress being that he might bleed a little or his skin turn blue. The true event to him was the thought of his birth mother that came to him so vividly in that place, the sensation of chains on his feet, and the uselessness of his quest for a man named Newland, whom he had hoped to find in the wide space between the Atlantic, the Avon, and the Frome, by knocking on doors.

CHAPTER XXII

He was making himself a dinner of mushrooms and herbs when the telephone rang and it was Rachel, her voice grainy through the static on the transatlantic connection. Panic curled in his stomach. It was not her time of the month for calling him. She would have taken the bus all the way to Montego Bay to use the Jamintel pay phones.

"Mama, a wha happen? Yu awright? Wheh Dadda? Him awright?"

"Hush, son, no man, wi awright, wi awright, wi awright," she hastened to reassure him. Her voice sought to make a circle, like a ritual, around him. "Mi jus have this feeling seh yu a-try reach out to wi, so mi call fi find out if yu awright."

"Mama, mi awright. Nutten nuh duu mi. Mi jus waan hear yu voice. Wheh Dadda?"

"Him deh a-sea. Him nah come home till a-mawnin. Mi sorry him cooden come wid mi fi talk to yu. Him mind was runnin on yu whole day yesterday."

"True, Mama?"

"Yes. Whole day him a-sing pon yu name, say him jus feel yu near. Yu sure yu awright, sonny?"

He wanted to say, "Tell Dadda mi love him, Mama," but his family was not a demonstrative family with their words, and such words, especially from him who seldom spoke, would worry his parents. They might think he was on the verge of some dreadful consummation, even death, perhaps. Especially now that they were already worrying.

"Mama, mi awright," he said again. "Mi jus did-a wonder if oonu awright, how oonu deh pon mi mind."

Rachel was silent a moment; he could hear her absorbing this information and making of it what she would. She would translate his words aslant of what the words in themselves said; she would not even think "oonu" meant she and Noah alone or at all.

When she spoke again it was in that split-screen way she had, which he supposed all mothers had, talking about one thing but her thoughts totally layered with another thing, the worry of whether her son was all right, taking not his word for it but her own sense of him beneath the skin. She would be listening to his heartbeat, his kidneys, his liver, his vibes like electrical currents traveling across the airwaves.

"Yu father doing well. With what him earn an what yu send, wi soon finish di addition to di house, and JPS coming dis week to run di light. So when yu come yu go have electric. No more kerosene lamp. Yu wearin flannel on yu chest?"

"Mama, a wha do yu? Mi nuh wear flannel from mi a five," he protested, teasing. "Why yu ask such a question?"

"Yu cold."

"Yu can feel mi cold all di way troo di phone?"

"Yes, yu cold. Yu must tek care-a yuself."

"Yes, Mama. How Maas Sam?"

"Samuel? Him same way. Likkle bit more off him head than when yu si him last, but not too much." Then she was off on another tack: "Is cane crop now. Whole place black-up as usual wid di constant burning, burning. All-a mi curtain-dem mi haffi tek down."

The information hung between them like a thin bubble that would break in a moment, shooting a spray of bright water into the air. Cane crop meant sugar . . . He, Moshe, as a toddler, vomiting every time Rachel gave him his tea, until she learned the sugar was the cause. Noah gathering molasses from the boiling house to put on his thigh. Sugar's by-blow a hex against sugar. Arrii's father groaning on his cushions as the cane burned. Three cushions and hot baking soda bath to keep him from levitating like an orphic balloon through the ceiling.

But not any of this in his mind now, only Arrienne. Three cushions for the king, twenty-one for a princess.

Arrienne waiting with bated breath to see if it would rise in her again too, the swollen corpuscle of blood like a lone leucocyte, rising every August and July to guard Christie bodies from some unknown poison. The body tormented as much by the protective abscess as it might have been by the poison itself.

Arrienne letting out her breath on a sigh of relief when the last truck ambled out of the canepiece, listing on its wheels like a pregnant woman carrying a bloated dulcimina on her head. She knew the end of harvest was her reprieve until the next year. (Who was to tell him that from the day she decide to hate him the thing come back, that as much as he bleed when she refuse to write, her backside fart fire when cane crop come round? And she know it will not stop until she decide to love him again, but she will not budge.)

Arrienne not writing, only cussing and swearing at him in his dreams. Arrienne creating storm and bangarang with her cussing, tears bursting in angry floods from every orifice of her dream-self, her eyeholes, her nose and mouth and nipples and pum-pum and batty and ribs, a hurricane of rapids washing away every raft in sight so he can't cross the water to come back again to the half of himself on the other side.

Static overwhelmed the pause on the telephone. "Mama, yu there?"

"Hold on, son, mek mi put in some more coin."

He heard the *ch ch ch* of the coins falling into the phone box like crushed ice down a chute, then her voice again, the static cleared but she sounding now thin and far away. The transatlantic connection was almost always what Rachel would call "challengin."

"Yu there, son?"

"Yes, Mama."

"So when yu coming home? Graduation nuh gone aready?" His stomach settled. She only wanted him to come home. No calamities to report.

"Not so long now, Mama. Mi jus a-wait till Miss Durham get somebody she like fi look after Maas Percy. Yu soon si mi." He didn't tell her that he planned to go to Spain and then Italy and perhaps Montmartre again before he came home, and that when he came it would only be to say goodbye, because he wouldn't stay. He didn't know anymore how to put down new roots anywhere that he would call home, and he did not know how to explain this to himself or to his parents. But this unknowing both grieved and set him free.

"But si ya sah. Look how mi sen yu go a-school so yu can go turn nursemaid fi old white man," she said, but he knew she was smiling because she was proud of him.

He had looked after the old man for three years, as properly, she felt sure, as she herself would have done. He had graduated top of his class with a first and his work had been solicited for a major exhibition where it had made a stir. Enough to let him know he was becoming famous in a way that scared him, because he was once again forced to hide from would-be invaders of his terror—interviewers, reporters, cameramen—the entire inquisitors' hall of fame.

His own terror frightened him, for he didn't know when his habit of no-show for ceremonies and congratulatory functions would start to work against him and garner the opposite effect to the anonymity and the focus on his work alone that he craved. People were using words like "mysterious," "recluse," and even "prodigy," though at twenty-one years old he was hardly young enough to be called a prodigy. The newspaper clippings with the first two words would make his mother laugh; the last would please her. He himself did not like to read the reports, but he collected them for Rachel and Noah. A mute thank you for his upbringing, and atonement for the lies he had not told but let them believe. His parents would never know how he got to England; they would forever think he had applied for and got a scholarship and on that basis, sailed. Rachel was reconciled to his choosing art school against her wishes, because he had done well. And because he had done it in England, for in spite of herself, the infection of sugar was in her blood and so for her England and praise garnered in England were vindication and prestige.

"Hurry up an come."

He smiled, conciliatory, helpless, forgetting that she couldn't see him.

And she was split-screening again: "Arrienne write yu?"

He went very still.

"Moshe?" Rachel's voice sharpened. "Mosh?"

"Yes, Mama." He was handling his voice with great care. "No, Mama, she don't write."

"She seh she was going write. Mi tell har fi write but har ears hard. Hard-ears gal-pickni."

"What duu Arrienne, Mama?"

"She in good health, son. But mi nuh sure she so rightid in har head. Why she don't write yu? All she a-duu is hurt harself. And when yu come home, wha she go duu? Run wheh?"

He understood that his mother was protecting him. That she was afraid for him—how would he deal with the long rift if reconciliation did not begin before he arrived home?

"Mama, you been nagging her on account-a me? Don't trouble her, Mama. She can't write. She don't know how anymore."

"Cause she lef it too long!" Rachel exploded, grieved. "How oonu cooda get so far apart that that happen? Oonu never use to need words."

"We still don't, Mama. Is awright, trus mi. Nuh fret fi mi."

"Maybe she fraid yu nah go answer, though mi nuh know what cooda mek either a-oonu fraid a-oonu one-anedda. But when yu come, see what yu can do, whether yu hear from har or not. Deep down she don't change toward yu. Is the same Arrienne who was yu playmate."

The phone was crackling again. He called out to her but her response was muffled and he knew she had run out of coins again. This time she wouldn't come back on, because she had used up all the coins she had.

He could discern the feeling of crisis in his mother's heart. He had told her it was all right between him and Arrienne. He had said, "Trus mi," telling himself that some things were unbreakable and when they saw each other again it would all come back together. But he didn't know if this was at all true, or if in his perpetual naïveté he had only imagined that they had still been touching each other by a line thrown across the water.

CHAPTER XXIII

When Gregor Samsa awoke one morning from troubled dreams, he found himself changed into a monstrous cockroach. When a man don't have no mother or father, don't know where he come from, see duppy on him right, duppy on him left, don't see no lifeline, that is how he dead or turn cockroach. He is not hit by a truck, speeding, he doesn't lie down in a hole and pass away, the world doesn't end with a loud noise, neither a whimper, and it doesn't return to its first breath where space-time began. No mourning sheet is wound, and no procession appears. He simply, beyond the outer rim (or the veil), becomes other.

An other.

Anathema.

You may think of this moment in which Moshe is feeling so sorry for himself an aberration, or even ingratitude, for he does have a father and a mother—a mother who, he knows, has nurtured him well on enabling superstitions.

But remember that he has just been arrested for vagrancy and interrogated on suspicion of rape and murder, and, searching, he has failed to find his birth father.

Think it therefore a moment of legitimate grief. A minute of silence will do.

CHAPTER XXIV

He sat in the dark with his eyes closed, all his energy reined in and trained toward the one spot in the room. He had fallen gradually into this habit, convinced beyond reason that if he concentrated hard enough, she would come to him through the shadows. All his life he had been terrified of ghosts, yet believed his mother's spirit would be different.

Mi nuh si how yu have any choice now, he spoke to her in his mind. Yu need fi rest, an yu owe mi.

The darkness was not empty. Behind his eyelids the room, imprinted on his physical memory, appeared as defined as if his eyes were open: the rumpled bed across from the chair in which he was sitting, the makeshift bookshelves, the ghostly sheen of the paintings with which he had covered the egregious wallpaper, the one armchair set diagonally across from the chipped cheval mirror, the desk under the side window that served as workspace, dressing table, and display rack for his carvings. If she came at all, she would walk out from the shadows between the curtains and the wall. Perhaps she would sit in the armchair, or just stand still beside the bed, waiting. Perhaps she would look at him, or perhaps her head would be bowed while she waited.

Please. Talk to me. Don't hide from me anymore. I know about shame.

"Shi was a likkle half-pint thing," the four-eye woman had said, measuring with her hands. "Das why di belly never show; why she cooda hide it so long."

"She look like me?" He asked the question hot and greedy.

The old woman cocked her head, looked up at him sideways, and laughed. "No, yu don't look like nobody I ever si. Yu hair at di back look like fi-har, same pepper grain, bad hair, but shi did pretty-bad. Cool skin black as jet, like yu fren who come wid yu di first time. But shi don't have the hair."

She saw the look of disappointment, even grief, on his face, and said, "Yu tek after har some ways. Shi hardly talk. Yu come to mi fi information an yu don't even find di words fi ask di question-dem wha yu waan ask. Shi same way. Shi use to siddung pon di barbecue"—she gestured toward the terraced concrete area where cocoa seeds were put out to dry before being pounded to make chocolate sticks—"an jus look at mi an look at mi, den shi come out wid one-two likkle word, like, 'Yu tink mi mad?' an lef mi fi fill in di blank."

"Who her people? Where dem come from?"

This was the one question to which her answer never wavered.

"Pon dat mi nuh have no knowledge fi gi yu, sonny." Except that this time she added, "Dem wash dem han of har."

"But you cooda tell mi if yu want. Shi mus tell yu, an even if shi nuh tell, yu can use yu powers find out." He had long ago stopped believing she was his mother's cousin. He did believe his mother had come to her for help.

The old woman laughed, a big dutty kek-keh-keh laugh. The kind you call bad-mind laugh. "If mi couldn' tell yu nutten bout yu puppa excep wha shi tell mi, yu tink mi can discern who yu mumma people be? Yu gi mi powers whole heap-a credit dem don't carry, Maas Young Boy."

But he knew she lied. For some reason private to herself she felt he could not be told who his mother's people were. It was bizarre to think that they must be living very near, perhaps in the same district as the old lady herself, Sandy Bay-on-the-Sea, and unknown to him. For all he knew, he sometimes passed one of them on the road or on the bus on his journeys to see Myrtle Kellier. He and they might even have exchanged words, in the way strangers do, meeting on the road, or as they, strangers, questioned the color of his skin.

But the four-eyed woman had been ruthless, any way you looked at it. According to her, she never told anyone what the distraught girl had done. When his mother did not return that day after leaving the note on the bed, Miss Myrtle Kellier followed her prescient nose straight to the underwater cave beneath the fort and found the rope hanging from the strong stalactite, but no body. Only his mother's left shoe lodged between two rocks beneath the rope. She was going to let people believe the girl had run away. "Any way yu tek it, was better dat way. Fi fi-har sake."

But Ora and Tumela people had always been led by their own mysteries and someone else either knew or had a premonition, for this was how the rumor of suicides in the dark cave where unspeakable things were done to nubile girls from the high school began to creep into the open once again, at about the time Moshe was found.

Moshe was shell-shocked then, as now, to think that she would conceal knowledge that might have led to the discovery of a body, even far out to sea, in order to lay the wandering spirit to rest. Despite the rumors, no one was ever sure. His girl-mother had never been found. They did not know if she had simply run away. So no funeral or wake was made for her. He was left with dreams of a distrait spirit wandering, knocking on doors, asking for burial.

Yet he knew what it meant to want to conceal a shame, even after death, for had all his life not been lived in the shame of his absent skin? A shame that had often become unbearable, and so he bore no grudge against the old woman who had been kind to his child-mother and thought to continue her kindness by keeping quiet.

It did not occur to him to doubt this part of the old woman's story, which changed in metaphorical detail but never in substance. Or at least it did occur to him, for a moment, but he dismissed the doubt. He never thought she might have had anything nefarious to do with his mother's disappearance or death. (You see what I am trying to tell you about Moshe Fisher? What reason is there to choose to believe parts of an unreliable story but not the other parts? Such questions are meaningless unless you are a person driven by superstition, such as the belief in providence or gut feeling. And to tell you the truth, looking back, who am I to say? Such beliefs are without doubt acts of desperation, but so is every act by which we fight against the thought of our cosmic helplessness. Perhaps my own belief in my free will, my absolute right to change the course of my life, is no less a form of superstition. Choose your own poison, someone might say. Hemlock or amatoxin. We are all marching toward death, fiercely believing we were meant to live.)

I could never forgive that old woman because of how it hurt him to think that his mother hanged herself with a rope in a cave because of him. What was the use of this information, which might even have been fiction? But he, he was grateful to her for giving his mother some sort of a face, no matter how distorted in the grimace of death, and then there was the suicide note, in which even I was forced to possibly believe.

He told me that this night now after Bristol he tried with all his strength to summon the spirit, as he had done many times before. Please. Let me see you. I not vex. I don't hold anything against you. Please. The effort pressed moisture through his eyelids and he knew he would find bruises on his chest in the morning. But as before, he was ploughing darkness. Me, he said, he could reach without effort; I had never failed to find him across the transatlantic void, whenever I wanted, if only to cuss him dutty raw. I, five thousand miles away, could feel his heart beat, but his mother, who had carried him under her heart for six and a half months (he had been that premature, the four-eyed woman, like the doctor, said) could not, being too far removed from him in the shadow space between the living and the dead.

He had never tried to contact his father in that way. It did not occur to him that his father might be dead. He had hoped, and then hope became conviction, that as he walked about or rode the bus or the train, one face would detach itself from the scores and hundreds and thousands around him and he would know, this is he. And when it hadn't happened he thought the fauve woman's guidance would be it, but it wasn't.

After the police released him, he walked the Bristol streets one more time until nightfall, searching men's faces and risking being arrested again. His heart told him that Bristol was the place.

But now he had to leave; he would buy his ticket home tomorrow. And knowing this, he felt compelled to do something, to engage in some momentous act that would say, This part of your life has not been without meaning. So at the end of the long hours battling the dark and failing to make it give up its ghost, he pushed himself to his feet and did the only thing that a man of such grave superstitions could think of to do: he held a funeral.

And in writing to me about this (the last letter he wrote), for the first time he told me why he was so afraid of the British Museum and never mentioned it before.

Struggling to reach his mother, he had come upon a different set of ghosts lurking in the shadows. A set that he had "forgotten."

This is how long it took him to bring himself to remember.

The museum had a room, an Egyptian room, that was full of mummies. All standing upright in their coffins. Most of the coffins were raised against the walls in sconces, so that the corpses' upright postures could be seen, but a great many lay scattered flat on the floor, as if there was insufficient room to contain their fecund and proliferating deaths. For Moshe, who had lived all his life in a place where the dead were venerated or feared, this was so frightening a sight that he fainted on his feet and came to only after a long interval, to find that the preternatural wound in his body that skittered to different places as and when it had a mind, had opened in his nose and he was suffering a violent nosebleed.

Other tourists passing by looked with curiosity at him standing there in the corner with his head thrown back against the marble column, his eyelashes stark crescents against the marble of his drained skin, blood making gutters like perpendicular mustaches from his nostrils to his chin. But no one said anything, in the way of English people, so different from the way it would be, twenty-five years later, when he found himself in America and people would rush to ask warm, intrusive questions when he bled like that, though a nosebleed was an everyday thing anywhere in the world, How may I help you, do you have an ID or someone we can call? and then answering their own questions, Don't worry, you'll be okay, here, sit down, it will be all right, don't worry, somebody call 911 please, and he would feel as lonely then and as desperate to be alone as he felt now.

(Though, to be fair to the English people, there in the museum he stood so still, and was so marble-white, that he could have been mistaken for a statue in the permanent part of the exhibition.)

One mummy in particular drew his gaze; it must have been a young man, for the shroud was torn and he could see a little of the face, the dry lips pulled back from the teeth as if in an ironic smile at its own denuding. He could see as well the fingers of a neat and delicate hand, somehow still with the look of youth about it despite the shrunken skin. The body was black, a powdery, ashen black, it seemed all over. He did not know if this was from centuries of preservation or if the young man was really black, in his natural skin, as he had been born. So Egypt was in Africa and people said the Africans were all black, but this he knew was not true, even without taking into account the Arab mixtures in the east and north of the continent or the Semitic heritages from the ancient world. He had met pure-blooded Africans who were the color of burnished bronze and some like dark clay.

Too distrait to read the plaque beside the coffin, he could not tell the name of this young man who must have been a king or a prince or at least a member of a noble house, since he was here in a gorgeous coffin, and in his own bones and skin. This coffin with broken cerements and parts of limbs exposed had replicas all over the museum floor. He wondered, were they new arrivals that would soon be curated and given a neat place in the regulated rows of those lined up against the walls, or perhaps their own glass case in an inner room that was not this waiting room, where their exposure to the elements created the stench that had made him reel and faint on his feet?

Moshe, there is no stench. Only your imagination. Mummies are eviscerated, embalmed corpses. How could they have a stench?

But he kept smelling it for weeks afterward, the mingled odor of rotting flesh and myrrh and frankincense, which his mother Rachel burned to keep away evil spirits that wandered into the house. Refugees from underneath the ceiba cotton tree, they came because they were tired of being ignored despite the enticements of their fragrant foods cooked in pots without fire. They came mainly at crop time, just when the cane was being burned, driving Rachel crazy. "Dutty rotten-navel bitches," she would rage, "what yu want? Yu getting no rum or molasses from me. Kirrout!" and she would drive them out by burning frankincense and myrrh, which made the house stink but accomplished her purpose. She didn't so much mind the incredibly bitter scent that aggravated the torments of crop season (black flakes from the burned cane leaves flying through the windows and making the house a living hell), as long as the duppies fled.

But Moshe, despite her influence, was made of a different cloth. Though the desecrated coffins haunted his dreams and the spirits moaned in his sleep, he felt that to denounce them would have been to compound a serious wrong. So he only pushed them away and tried to forget.

This night, however, as he sat in the dark for the umpteenth time trying to summon his birth mother's spirit from the universe's behindparts, something in him gave out. Pushed over the edge, he decided to make his own conciliations with death. He blessed water and sprinkled it on a cross that he drew on blank binder paper. Then he recited funerals for the dead, first for his mother and then for the Egyptians moved from their burial grounds to unhallowed rooms.

All the time he was doing this hocus-pocus he missed Arrienne so much and was in such physical pain that he was angry with her. The feeling of grievance against her was unfamiliar and he was afraid of it. He pushed it away so it would not break their connection, which he needed at that moment more than anything. She had always been his partner in crazy.

CHAPTER XXV

Yu a mad smaddy, Arrienne thought when she read up his plan. Dem Egyptian-deh did wicked no bitch. Same ting wha ketch dem, a same ting dem used to do to other people. Dem jus get dem comedownance. So why yu want to help dem out?

Two wrong don't make a right, he said.

Arrienne sucked her teeth, cheuups! and turned her back, her body twisted half in anger, half in anguish for him.

So Moshe conducted two funerals before he left London, with himself as congregation, mourner, and officiating priest. His mother's was easy. Funeral services in Jamaica were all more or less the same, give or take a few differences in length or design. (Most went on forever.) So she wasn't likely to be displeased with anything he did, unless it was too short. He conducted her ceremony first, because he wanted to give her his first, best energy, and because he had a crazy notion that, while she had resisted all his other efforts, she might decide to attend her own funeral and come to him at last, and he didn't want a situation where she and the Egyptians might meet and clash in big fight. Then they might hem her in, dozens against one, and she wouldn't be able to leave. Whatever else he was prepared for, it was not a duppy fight or long-term duppy sojourn.

NormalPeople, I am telling you the living truth. This is what Moshe write and tell me he think and do. If it sound crazy to you, I understand, because even I had difficulty putting together why he do a thing like that. It hurt me, for I think about how England have tradition of sending black people mad and Moshe, having no skin, was susceptible.

I wasn't bothered about the funeral for his birth mother. I thought she was owed a funeral long time and it hurt me that he had to do it alone. But the Egyptians? Suppose dem bastards hear his voice and decide to attend the funeral, what would have happen in Moshe room that night? Sweet Yahweh, as Mama Rachel would have said, I don't even want to think about it. Tek di case an gimmi di pillow. In fact, keep di pillow, in case Egyptian duppy decide to tek it fi invitation and come lie down side-a mi.

He had no rum on hand for the wake so he sprinkled water. He played on his turntable a cocktail of Nine-Night songs that no Egyptian could have recognized if they had come to that funeral. So it was a mercy they couldn't come. "Go Down a Manuel Road," "In Jerusalem Schoolroom," "Ribba Come Over," "A Come Mi Dis a-Come," "Death Have a Way," he played religious and secular all together, and kept time on the kette drum he retrieved from the "Jamaica corner" he had made in his room. He imagined himself a whole yardful of people sitting in a circle in the room, drinking coffee, mint tea, and white rum, eating Excelsior tough crackers, and singing along for his mother. That part of the ceremony, he told me later, made him realize how much he missed Tumela Gut, in the way a person misses a place that is home and not home, and maybe if he could have returned just at that moment, through a capsule in time, he would have, and the rest of this story would have turned out differently.

When the wake was done, he lit candles and sprinkled the sanctified water on the paper cross that he had made, cutting the silhouette out with his artist's fastidious care. He placed the cross on his one towel that he spread on the floor so the floor would not get wet. The rest of the paper he saved for writing or drawing, so there'd be no waste.

After that, he simply followed readings he was familiar with from funerals in Tumela and listening to Rachel intone from her Bible.

I am the resurrection and the life. She that believeth in me, though she were dead, yet shall she live. He doctored the pronouns to fit.

He didn't know whether his dead mother had believed any of that, but he understood resurrection. This was what Rachel had done for him when he was dying in the fish pot above the cliffs behind the hospital at Ora-on-Sea, when he could not have heard nor understood such a word as resurrection. But still he had been resurrected. Who was to say it could not be like that for his mother? He thought that at any rate he was giving her something to think about and to say when she got to the pearly gates, if she had a mind to go and knock there.

Rachel would of course have raised her eyebrows in scandalized disapproval at this erratic personal doctrine. "Yu cyaan repent pon nobody behalf, everybody haffi hear an understand an decide fi dem-self. An man cyaan repent inna di grave. Is appointed unto all-a wi to die once an after dat di judgment. A so it seh. Mi son, a-wha kinda hocus-pocus dat yu doin?"

But remember is Moshe wi talking about.

And many years later he said a thing that wrenched my heart and became another reason this story being told ended the way it did. "You can't write somebody else's story on their behalf. Even with permission. You have to stand up and give your own account." But that is for another time. Skip the digress.

He recited for his girl-mother Psalm 90, which always reminded him of the mournful sound of organ music. This psalm Samuel and Rachel used to have big philosophical discussions about, so that by the time he, Moshe, was four years old, he knew the words and the grief-laden cadences by heart:

> Lord, thou hast been our dwelling place in all generations. Before the mountains were brought forth, or ever thou hadst formed the earth and the world, even from everlasting to everlasting, thou art God. Thou turnest man to destruction; and sayest, Return, ye children of men. For a thousand years in thy sight are but as yesterday when it is past, and as a watch in the night.

The words came easier because they were recitation, not words he himself had to make. He only had to give himself over to their rhythm. They gave him comfort, and he wept. *For a thousand years are as a watch in the night.* Words that made a bridge through the past, as if there had been no passage of time between that day or night twenty-one years ago when the desperate girl, his mother, passed beyond unknown portals, and this moment when he stood, offering a gift for her safe going.

Thou carriest them away as with a flood.

Only for her it had been the tide, waves rising in a dark cave then sweeping out on the broad belly of the sea. Could sea waves rise so high and so strong they cut a body down from a rope? Or had she been stolen, then hidden? But it had been the season of hurricanes. And why would anyone steal a dead person?

We spend our years as a tale that is told.

As broken, and as unfinished. Sometimes not heard; or heard, not understood. But all his life he had believed the end of the tale disappeared because hope does not have an end. Hope is Ever After.

> *Return, O Lord, how long? and let it repent thee concerning thy servants. O satisfy us early with thy mercy; that we may rejoice and be glad all our days. Make us glad according to the days wherein thou hast afflicted us, and the years wherein we have seen evil. Let thy work appear unto thy servants, and thy glory unto their children. And let the beauty of the Lord our God be upon us: And let the beauty of the God be upon us, the beauty of God be upon us, Amen.*

After that he recited Psalm 23, his imagination and his artist's hands moving, shaping for her with gestures a quiet mound under shade trees on a secluded hill within sight and sound of good water. But with company. Other mounds besides hers, so when she woke she would not feel alone.

Ashes to ashes, dust to dust, but sleep now. Sleep now, Mama. Sleep.

"I set you free, Mama. Go in peace." The name was strange on his tongue addressed to someone other than Rachel, but it was all right, he felt it was all right, and it gave him a sense of release. He had not called her anything before. Just "you."

Well, he didn't hear any cymbals clash or sound of abundance of rain or ancestors calling greeting or pronouncing blessing, no *me-kyea wo*, I greet you, no *akwaaba*, welcome, no *maadwo, da yie, da yie, yɛbɛhyia bio*, good night, good night, sleep well, or anything like that, and his mother never said a word that he could hear, but that night he cried a great deal, and when it was over he was empty and at peace.

He would have preferred for the Egyptians a ceremony from their *Book of the Dead*, a copy of which he found in the library and pored over for hours, but it was too hermetic to be understood without instruction such as his mother Rachel had had in the mysteries of Yahweh. This inadequacy was the source of his greatest fear. He was acutely conscious of trespassing on unknown territory. But he thought that if he discovered words and symbols neutral enough or universal enough, the Egyptians might not find themselves trans-ported to a place too strange for them to accommodate or even to endure. After all, nothing could be as bad as where they were now.

In the end he compromised by pouring the libations, beating the kette processional, and reciting a mixture of parts of the psalms he had said for his mother, and the part from the *Book of the Dead* that he felt his unknowingness was least likely to bumble, the part that fit best with the understanding of the afterlife that he had cobbled for himself from fragments of Rachel's religion.

Improvising and fearful of getting it wrong, he said the words from the *Book of the Dead* very slowly:

O you who open a path and open up roads for the perfected souls in the House of Osiris, open a path for these, open up roads for the souls of these in company with you. May they come in freely, may they go out in peace from the House of Osiris, without be-ing repelled or turned back. May they go in favored, may they come out loved, may they be vindicated, may they go and speak with you, may they be a spirit with you, may no fault be found in them, for the balance is voided of their misdoings.

Words they had crafted for themselves two thousand years ago, talisman through the gates of Osiris, when they knocked there and the voice of the god said, "Who? Why?"

May they go back to the place where they wanted to be, when they first had ceremonies, before they were brought to this place. May they find peace everlasting in the life to come. This part he added from himself, and because he couldn't help himself, from force of sheer habit he also added, racing the words, "In the name of Yahweh, Messiah, and the Great Shalom. Amen."

The parchment from which he read had been made for the house of Ani. For all he knew, one size did not fit all and the words he recited were no more meaningful to the particular Egyptians in the museum than the psalms had been. He told himself that he addressed this prayer to whoever God was, who had to be merciful or nonexistent, one or the other; if He was not the one, then He must be the other; God who lived could not but act in mercy even if the spirits did not hear him.

The double ceremonies brought a different kind of mental stress, and almost before he had finished his nose was streaming blood again. In the morning he found the makeshift space of the altar ruined, as if a real sacrifice had been done there.

PART IV

lost

CHAPTER XXVI

He said that when he packed up his things after these funerals and set about getting ready to buy his plane ticket, he had every intention of going back home. But a great panic overcame him, and he could not. He knew he'd hurt his parents, but faced with what seemed to him the impossibility of return, he felt he had only one choice.

It was the phone that decided it.

The phone ringing in his room pulled him back from the front door as he was leaving the flat that morning.

"Congratulations, man." Calls from Alva, unlike those from Rachel, who had to travel to find a phone, were frequent, and came at arbitrary times.

"Yu tell me aready. But thanks."

"I don't mean yu graduation. I mean on behalf of yu friend."

Moshe felt the slow crawl of blood cease in his veins. A flash of premonition ran along his bloodstream, which might have been an unconscious leftover from the conversation with his mother days before.

Alva was probing the texture of silence at the other end of the line. "So you mean you don't approve?"

Approve of what, for God's sake? Man, what is it you taking for granted so important that somebody tell me aready? "Approve of what?" Fear and pride made his voice sound cold.

Alva read in it rebuke and distance. "Jeez, man. No gwan so. Mi nuh seh nutten wrong. The woman getting married, mi assume seh yu happy bout it since oonu nuh do nutten dat don't mek each other happy. If mi wrong, mi sorry."

The silence on the other end of the line was like he had stirred up a volcano. Or maybe sheet ice, broken it up and sent it sailing toward himself in avalanches, driven across the phone waves like malevolence.

"Fisher? Fisher? Mosh!"

The line at the other end remained silent, then loud with the buzz of the receiver placed back on the hook. A man can shout badwords in your ear without saying a single word.

He bummed around Europe for a while, moving alone and anonymous through many places, often disreputable: back streets and inner-city lanes that would have made his mother weep with the disgrace of them; red-light districts and drinking dens where he did not fornicate or drink but needed the feeling of energy and loss to get him through the terrible days; obscure villages where he joined armies of fruit pickers, earning cheap money to sustain himself while bruising his body into sleep. During this time he pared his necessities down to the bone and traveled with only a knapsack on his back and a long satchel in which he kept his paint supplies and paintings. He was often ashamed at the cliché and falseness of his life, that he, a poor woman and fisherman's son from a place that colony once upon a time, his ancestry lost in his unlikely confabulation of stains, was here living like a fool born to privilege—reeling from one set-piece abasement to another to another in imitation of storybook rich men's sons on coming-of-age tours. People, places, and ways of living that had nothing to do with him but had been imposed on his mind in storybooks. *And so there was the snow, the snow was falling on the canefields.* Now something cruel had happened in him, and these people, places, and ways became exotic, as though he was living them through the turned-back pages of a book; he did not want to dream of home or think of what was real. And so he came to understand how a person could long to escape to a new world, and if after sailing halfway around the world and stumbling upon a place that was opposite to what he knew he still had not found this paradise of forgetting, he would construct it in the image of his own invention or inventions of which he had heard. He came to understand as well how such feasts of forgetting would peter out in brief Gehennas, searing as the wind's lash on skinless flesh. But for a long time he held his head down against the wind and could not stop within himself this willful conflagration.

He does not tell me how he came out of this funk or how he grew again at last to feel people as people no matter where or when, and during this time I did not sense him; even without my willing it, as I had futilely done in the past, our connection was gone. I understood that I had accomplished this—at the point where I wasn't even trying—to shape betrayal into such a weapon in my hands that it could separate a person from himself.

But he did come out of it. How, is his secret. And for a long time he could not paint, and then he could.

And I know that this sounds unbelievable, but if you look in any history of European art written after 1989, you will see his name there and know that it is true: that Moshe Fisher managed to remain secret and anonymous while his paintings, signed with his long initials *MGRF* (Moshe Gid'on Rachel-Fisher), lived a life of their own, separate and marvelous, appearing in art fairs all over the continent, earning him fame and fortune, while he himself like a scarlet pimpernel in plain sight, a man whose looks drew glances of curiosity or astonishment wherever he went, could not be found for comment or recognition.

The Moshe I knew was incapable of guile or practicality. And I thought I knew him as I knew myself, even when we were separated. Yet I do not know how he managed to persuade his agents to keep his identity secret or even how he thought of doing this, but he did. And in truth, a desperate need can achieve anything. Nobody knows that better than Moshe or I, who through desperate need lost the power of speech and acquired the capacity to speak from deep inside our bodies, secret to ourselves, speech tunneling backward through veins like rechanneled blood or water. I understood how much he needed to be nameless in the places where he went.

He never used any of the money he earned from his paintings. All of it except what he stashed away in savings accounts went home to Rachel and Noah. And in great bitterness of spirit Rachel watched the new house, not board anymore but wall, good concrete and steel, go up bit by bit until it was finished. She told herself she was building it not for herself and Noah but for her son; it was the investment of his money, which she did not want for herself though he sent it for her. She and Noah had always taught him to save, and now she was saving on his behalf.

In this way Rachel held on to the hope that one day a knock would come at the front door, which would still be standing open as doors in Tumela Gut always did, even the doors of secretive houses, and a voice would call out, "Hol' dog!" in the way of Tumela greeting, though there would be no dog, she had never had a dog and had never wanted one, nor could she have had one while Moshe was growing up, for fear that he might catch an infection or allergy and die. And she would come to the front of the house from the new inside kitchen calling in return, "Come, coming, no dog!" and it would be Moshe standing there but she would already have known it was he, for his voice would not have changed, it would be still the same, perhaps a little browner with maturity, but the same barely audible, musical voice, like someone lightly plucking the strings of a guitar. And he would say in his beautiful voice, "Mama, I come home."

Moshe did not write his parents letters. Only postcards, which he made himself and painted with his own drawings. She learned to read the drawings like words, code messages, stories he told her about his life: *Mama, Dadda, I move around too much now. Address don't make sense. By the time your letter reach me I move again.* He addressed his postcards to both Rachel and Noah, and since his postcards had no return address, she could not answer, as she had done with his letters from London, first in her own name and then speaking on behalf of Noah. So the whole seven years she mourned her son's absence and assailed the throne of Yahweh, praying, begging, and browbeating for Moshe's safety. She felt that he did not allow her to write because in his heart he was estranged from her. Why, she did not know, but it cut her to the core.

Yet he was not altogether absent. Sometimes he would send them a phone number, when he would be in a place for a little while, and he would say, *Phone me on such and such days, at such and such a time.* Telephone lines had still not come to Tumela, though it was only five miles from Ora, where people had always had telephones. But there were now public phones in Ora, and Rachel and Noah would go to Ora now to talk to their son on the phone. And his question always was, "Mama, yu awright, Dadda, yu awright?" and his promise, "Mama mi wi come home! Gimmi time!" in answer to Rachel's distraught, "Son, is what happen to yu?"

In the end she stopped asking because she saw that it hurt him and pushed him further away from her. A wise woman, she began to hold her peace. But on the phone he was like a stranger, only wanting to know how she and Noah were, in a fever of worry that she thought of as compensation for his neglect. About himself, his real self, he never said anything, and she was wounded beyond words.

He told her a great deal about the places he went, knowing her love of faraway locales. She found no joy in them.

One day I asked her, unable to stop myself, "Yu tell him about mi?"

Rachel turned bitter eyes on me. It was the first and last time she ever looked at me like that. "I go tell you the truth, Arrienne. You know what he tell me? He tell me, 'Mama, if you want me and you to talk, leave Arrienne out of it. I don't want to know. Not now.'"

"Yu hate mi, don't, Mama Rachel?" I tried to stop myself from knowing, but I couldn't. I wanted to hear her lay my guilt and her blame out in the open, once and for all.

"I don't hate you, child," Rachel said. "I talk to you already, saying please don't do this to him, write him, and when you say yes and don't write, I tell myself there is things I don't know, I don't know what happen between you or how each person bear their grief. All I know is wi have to forgive, and I pray you get to there, but maybe is about more than forgiveness, I don't know, for you don't tell me. And you is big woman so I can't tell you what to do or disrespect your choice. But when my son tell me don't talk about you to him, I have to protect my son."

I cried a great deal then, I couldn't stop, though the pain in my chest from crying was terrible. Rachel held me and rocked me against her knees, and my added guilt was that all the while he was unable to come home I had comfort from his parents. Rachel never uttered a word of reproach or turned me away. But she didn't speak of Moshe to me, or of me to him. It was how she protected her son.

⁊•

Through all of this time Moshe was alone. There was a brief, unsat-isfactory liaison with Ada Pink (he could not call it a relationship, he said; "liaison" seemed to fit the unreality of it all) and once, a fierce encounter with an Italian boy in a cornfield on the banks of the River Po. Ada left him because, she said, she could not find him behind his transparent face. He locked himself away so securely that she felt, in their intimate moments, that she was struggling with a series of dead bolts, each of which led to another and another, like a labyrinth of guarded ruins which had been made on purpose and no trace of a path or pattern could be found. The brief encounter, which was for her a storm and for him the slow flow of ice slipping downriver, left her burned and astonished, him barely sentient.

The boy in the cornfield had been the expression of a sudden, ur-gent desire to know he was still alive, with feelings, but though he bruised himself badly in that desperate coupling, it left him merely con-fused: exhausted, with a feeling of distaste, and relief, as the ghost that had dogged him since Alva on the banks of that other river now left him—he knew with certainty that he was not gay, he was not that way inclined. This does not mean that what he got from the encoun-ter with Ada Pink was the certainty that he was straight. He came away from both with the knowledge that all his sexual relations so far had been acts of self-destruction, and a great fear in case that kind of sex was all he was capable of.

In these encounters he never took his clothes off. No one ever saw the traceries of veins, arteries, and blood that rose on his skin like baroque tattoos. (When Arrienne saw him again naked, she was ter-rified, for the traceries had morphed and come to resemble a form of writing. It reminded her of the writing in the Chinese book in her fa-ther's cabinet that she had tried to read and been driven into speech-lessness by instead.)

It was also during this time that he renamed what was to become the most famous of his paintings, the nude self-portrait which had been simply titled *Nude*. Now he called it *Abarra Vèvè*. Totem of the Abarra, underwater spirit that travel from one continent to another, following after people who cross ocean in chain.

In all, in the seven years, he produced ten known paintings that he sold or exhibited, and a series of three that he did not. One of the three he never finished, though he kept working on it throughout his life, even when he went to America. This was the one he called *Metamorphosis*. It is the only one of his paintings from this period that still hangs in my house, with the inscription at the back that I don't show to anyone, not even you.

As far as his mother was concerned, of course, nothing in any of this escaped translation. Seven years and ten paintings, and then a secret three, all Yahweh's numbers, kabbalahs of completion. And if one painting was unfinished, it was the sign of Yahweh's eternity, and Yahweh's grace, and the arc of human hope "dat never give out no matter how time hard, or how long alligator mout' tek fi grow long." At the end of the seven years, she "knew" her son was coming home.

She was almost right. Moshe came home to me in the spring of '87, six months after he should have arrived, based on Rachel's calculation.

Years later, when I asked him if he had kept on looking for his birth father or being haunted by his birth mother, he said no, and because I asked him this question many times and he answered in the same way with this same certainty, I began to almost let myself think that it was true and he would be all right.

He said that of all the places where he went, it was during three months in Ireland that he felt he had almost found somewhere he could again call home. He saw many people there that were the spitting image of people in our country, except that they were a different color, as if somebody from Tumela had stepped out of his or her black skin and put on another. And for a brief time he kept looking into men's faces again in search of the one he might recognize, but this fancy did not last as he realized that these chance resemblances were the simple product of history, the Irish having lived so long among the slaves as overseers, bedmates, and raptors. *The concupiscence of masters and servants and slaves.*

He was reading and studying at this time a great many West African arts—masquerades, kente cloths, sculptures, fractals, and oriki—and teaching himself the rudiments of Old Irish, burrowing into Irish archives to try to read in the original the mythologies we had devoured in translation in the public library at Ora-on-Sea. *Lebor na hUidre*. *Cath Maige Tuiread*. *Lebor Gabála Érenn*, a history that went back before Noah. *Tuatha Dé Danann*, the book of the people of the goddess Danu. And though in the end the Celtic grammar he had taught himself was hopeless to the task and he had to keep returning to the English translations, the sight of the original words on the page moved him so deeply, almost as deeply as the wondrous illustrations, that he laughed to himself thinking that he must indeed be Rachel Fisher's son, for who else was so persuaded by the magic of original signs?

(And of course it occurred to him how unfitting it was that he was reading African things and things about Africa not in Africa but in the museums and libraries of Europe, and though he thought often of Ghana and Nigeria, he never went, hiding his face from the fear that they would say, "Look, a dopi, a ghost!" in the same way that the man from America had shouted, "Look, a nigger in whiteface!" in the streets of Stratford, and he would have to begin his journey all over again. And so once again and as always, it was the veil of translation—paintings, fictions, Arrii's voices, and the skin of the masquerade—that stood between him and the cutting wind and made his life endurable.)

He found in these totems of far-apart cultures, the West African and the Celtic, an affinity with his imagination and the places where he had been brought up, Tumela Gut and Oracabessa-on-Sea, and his art entered a phase eerily and yet harmoniously marked by all of these, insofar as an art so violent and volatile, so antithetical to rest or peace, could be called harmonious. This shift was to mark his production for the rest of his life, the way Picasso's African epiphany caused Picasso to spin around three times three (when the masquerade seized him, erupting out of the ground in front of his face) and walk backward like douen in another direction that he could not look away from until the day he died.

Moshe tried to paint this epiphany of himself into the canvas that never got finished, and many times before he settled on the name

Metamorphosis he gave it other names, one of which was *Lost in Translation,* which he discarded as too precious, and another, just as maudlin, *My Mother, My Father.*

"I think this was when I stopped looking," he said. "I found I didn't need him after all." Meaning, of course, his father. (And he had already buried his mother, for her peace sake.)

When he told me this he had just come back home, and because in his travels he had been forced to speak or at least understand many languages, at first he had difficulty returning to the common language of Tumela Gut, which was the language of intimacy for most people except him and me. So he answered me in English, which made me wonder if on these journeys he had found that I was one more person he didn't need, after all.

interval

Noah, 1987

Today is Noah's birthday. He's seventy-five. The years have left their mark on him. A short, splay-bodied man, thickly made, and gnarled. His skin the color of burned logwood, textured like old leather, supple, shiny, durable.

There is no fanfare, no celebration. To Noah, this is a day like all other days, to 'turn thanks and get on with the business of living.

He is mending his fish pots, getting ready to return to the sea in the morning.

Sitting low on the cedar stump in his and Rachel's front yard, he works hand over fist, deft movements reweaving the torn fish pot clamped between his thighs. The pot presses against his right thigh because he favors the left, where his perpetual wound is. He is wearing ragged, washed khaki pants and a white merino that has seen better days, his drudging clothes. The black skin of his chest, exposed, is peppered with white hairs, tightly curled, like Moshe's back hair. His head bent over the intricate task is grizzled, his stubble beard yellow-white, the color that gray hair turns when it is discolored by exposure to woodsmoke. Beneath the khaki pants his slippered feet are planted rock solid, digging into the tamped earth of Rachel's immaculate yard. Sitting like this, he reminds me of an old tree, ravaged yet indomitable, and strong as the soil in which it is rooted.

Strange how a man so wedded to the sea can look so planted in soil. Another of Tumela Gut's mysteries, I think to myself. I have learned to accept this place and its contradictions. Though so many of the contradictions are the face of injustice I have come to understand and fight against every day, still so many more are a mystery to

me. How can a place so beleaguered have so much calm in its roots
that this is where I still come back to in order to bush-bath my spirit after every war with government, every pick-up-lick-down fight with
busha-descendant and others like them who sit pon top like peel-
head johncrow, picking out poor people eye? Tumela come in like
the duppies that never leave yet are forever cooking, like Noah who
never hurries but is always working. I never see that man idle or rest.
But he don't look tired. Earth-salt, you call a man like that. And all
salt come from the sea. I have to tell myself there must be after all
something that exist before history, that produce this kind of true
survivor, who, whether he swim or levitate, one thing you know, he
can't drown.

This Noah is a self-contained man, taciturn unless aggrieved, and
then he shouts curses. The way a man drunk with rum gets suddenly loquacious. Rage is Noah's rum. In that, he and Rachel are
alike, though she is not taciturn. He doesn't mind me watching him at
work, and silence, mine or any, doesn't discommode him. How could
it, when he has lived with silence so long? Brought up a son who does
not speak. And then to have lived half his seventy-five years with a
woman like Rachel whom he has learned to meet with silence just to
keep the peace on any given day, for Rachel is exceedingly volatile,
especially now that Mosh is not here, and will cuss Noah out at the
drop of a pin. She used to be quieter, more peaceful in herself and
with Noah, when Mosh was here.

I shift Betina from my right to my left breast and she seizes it
greedily with her gums. The sensation of being grabbed by a suction
clamp is both painful and pleasurable. She is a large, healthy baby, an
enthusiastic eater. She gives no trouble once she gets her food, but
most nights I am exhausted from just feeding or lifting her.

"Di shirt fit, Papa Noah?"

He grunts in his beard. "Mi tenk yu." I had given him a plaid tartan
shirt from Duluth Trading for his birthday. A man's shirt, tough and
unsentimental, in bold blues and reds. Rachel says he wore it with
pride to the 4H meeting yesterday, and received congratulations. He
himself would never tell me that.

I watch him work for a while longer. My daughter drinks her fill and snuffles against the side of my breast. She must be the only person contented here, I think to myself. My mind is still roiled with memory and fear. Noah must be turning over memory in his mind too. Not likely fear, though. Anticipation, surely. His face gives nothing away. But I know that whatever he's feeling, it's not contentment. Some kind of roil too.

"Yu goin back to sea tomorrow."

"Humph." Another grunt.

"How long dis time?"

He doesn't answer for a minute, maneuvering a tricky turn on the basket lid. Then he says, "Two, t'ree day. Depend on how di fish bite."

"If mi never have di baby mi ooda come wid yu."

He looks up from the pot in his hand. His gaze, muddy and frank under the bush of his eyebrows, meets mine across the new verandah where I am sitting near the rail. The house is spacious and new, but he and Rachel haven't yet put up a decent bench outside after the old bamboo one fell apart with age. The wood stump on which he is sitting is the remains of a cedar tree that has been cut down to make room for the bigger house on the half-acre plot. The tree has been sold to a saw mill; it is good wood for furniture and flooring. Tumela uses this wood too for burial caskets.

"So yu goin stay till Moshe come, or yu goin run wheh?"

I feel my face burn hot. "No." I am angry with myself for sounding foolish and then for adding in self-defense, "I don't know what run away have to do with me, Papa Noah. It have nothing to do with me." I don't want to be rude to the old man.

"Humph." The grizzled head bends again to his task. The rhythm of his hands moving in and out, out and in, weaving bamboo wicker, becomes hypnotic to my eyes.

"So yu go show him di baby, then." It is a question phrased as a statement. "An tell him, nuh mek him find out pon di side?"

I love him too, Papa Noah. Is not you one.

If him did want to know mi have baby, him wouldn't did put ban on him mother tongue bout mi. If him did care, him woulda write. So is not a one-way street, Papa Noah. Furthermore, mi sure you and Mama Rachel wi give him any information that I forget.

I change the subject, pushing away the self-defensive lies I am telling myself. What happened between Moshe and me is none of his business. "How old Mosh was when yu first tek him out to sea wid you, Papa?" I am not sure this is the best thing to ask in the circumstances but it is the first thing that comes out of my mouth as I try for a diversion. Too late to take it back.

Betina has fallen asleep. She is heavy. I ease her weight to my other arm. She stirs, smiles in her sleep, but doesn't wake.

"Same age dat yu know."

"Ten."

He doesn't reply.

"Tell me." Am I self-destructive or what?

And surprisingly, he does tell me. It had not occurred to me that this taciturn, weathered man might have been longing to talk to somebody about his son, to give voice to his own feelings of a father that we had taken for granted, Rachel and I, all these years. Women have a way of finding community, as Rachel and I have found with each other. Men, not so much. They have a harder time. After Moshe left, Noah was alone in a woman's world. Moshe was the glue that had held him and Rachel together.

"Yu know, dat likkle runt did tough as shoes leather, yu know, delicate as yu si him look deh. A years him a-bodda mi fi car' him go-a sea. Mi seh no, yu too young, when di time come yu wi know."

"Him did fraid when di time come?"

"Fraid? No sah. Duck to water. Ketch him first fish di berry first day."

I knew all about it. You stole him from me every Friday that summer, old man. One day in the week when he wasn't mine. I was bitterly jealous. At first you stayed out only the one day because Rachel woulda cut out yu liver an chop it up fi dog food if yu kept him out on the raw sea by night. It cramp yu style because fish bite better by night. But you wanted him to learn, and to keep your promise.

"But she learn fi relax an yu start taking him on the boat overnight Thursday and bringing him back Friday morning soon-soon. Before rooster put on him drawers," I say aloud, jumping over the gap between my thoughts and his reply. He will take it in stride.

It is remarkable, I find myself thinking, how the years of our isolation have made us all, not just Moshe and me, capable of speaking without speech, and understanding each other by this wordlessness. We've approached speech sidewise like crabs. What we say is not the sum of what we mean to convey or even what we mean to convey at all. Our proficiency is not speech, but translation. It makes me feel at home but uneasy. There are things I cannot not read. Like how Rachel and Noah feel about the fact that I never wrote to Mosh when he was in England. Do they blame me for his running away when he was supposed to come home? Since the time I asked Rachel if she hated me, they never said anything to me about it, good or bad. They just went on in the same way, as if I was their own. After he didn't come, it felt impossible to leave them. More for my own sake than for theirs, I know. My father was bitter with me because I spent so much of my time with Rachel and Noah instead of with him when I came to Tumela. My mother gave up on me long ago. I don't know why I think being with them is going to do anything to assuage my guilt, and I can never explain how I couldn't write to Mosh, how hard I tried, how more and more impossible it became, though I would have died if he never wrote. But then for seven years he never did and I survived.

The hundred years of our solitude, I say to myself, borrowing Gabriel García Márquez's words again.

"Humph," Noah says. Then, "Yu was a jealous likkle gal. But yu did fraid-a di water."

I feel my face grow hot again. I hadn't known he had known. I don't mean about the water, but the jealousy.

I give a light laugh, dismissing all that; it was only childhood, a long time ago. "Yes. I was jealous. Hated you, in fact. But tell truth, Papa Noah. Wasn't because mi fraid-a water yu never invite me out on the boat too."

"Why then?" His voice challenges me with a hint of a smile in it.

"You wanted those times to be for just you and Mosh together. Father and son."

If that hardened old seaman can blush, I swear that quick darkening that runs upside Noah's cheek and down again is a blush. But he only laughs, slightly in his beard.

The pot is finished. He stands it upright on its base and tests its firmness on the ground. Satisfied, he puts it aside, picks up the other one and surveys it, turning it this way and that to see which section to start on first. Deciding, he pulls more wicker and twine and sets again to work.

"You miss him, Papa?" A lot of compulsive questions today.

The silence carries on for a long time. Not awkward, just ruminative. I sense Noah is grinding words in some underground millworks, making sure they are properly fine, before he answers. We both wait on the process. I get up and carry Betina inside. I put her down in the bed in Moshe's new room, in the center of the white chenille bedspread that is Rachel's best. I bank pillows on either side so she won't roll off. I stand watching her for a while, the soft in-and-out of her breath, her slightly open, puckered baby mouth, and the frown between her eyebrows. She has thick blue-black eyebrows like mine, and a lot of hair that, like me, she was born with. Her skin is hairy like mine too. I've always been glad I could never find any trace of Stephen in her, no matter how hard I looked. At first I hoped I would see marks of Moshe on her, but the imprint of our two bodies on each other hasn't translated to my daughter.

She hasn't inherited the Christie birthmark either. That is always passed on through the father's line. She will be her own person. A different generation, one belonging to a different future, that I tell myself I am determined to fight for as hard as I can. Yet there are many moments when I am afraid for her, wondering if history or family wound can ever be bleached out, either through human work or acts of God over generations. For all I know she might discover late in life an allergy to sugar, or ackee, or saltfish, or even guinep seed, that could make her life miserable at particular seasons.

I go back outside and this time I don't stay on the verandah, I sit down in the yard on the half-buried rock beside the old man. I hand him the glass of lemonade made with crushed ice and molasses that Rachel left in the new refrigerator. They live modestly still, not above their neighbors, but more comfortably, on the money Mosh sends. Rachel will never get used to spending money—she is saving most of it for Mosh, who wants her to use it. But the money for her funeral and Noah's she has long put by, out of their own earnings. It would have been a disgrace had it been otherwise. "Some people seh dem pickni a dem old-age pension," she used to tell me, "but pickni have dem own life fi live, an no pickni shoulda pay fi no parent's finneral. Di least yu can do is bury yu own self. Else what yu time on earth for, if yu cyaan gi yuself dis one dignity?"

"Tenk yu," Noah says gruffly, taking the glass and resting it on the ground at his side. He will drink it suddenly, draining the glass all at once, when he is ready. Strange how that wound won't heal, though he never eats sugar now, only molasses, and though the doctor at the clinic can no longer find a trace of the old sickness in his system. Maybe something has morphed. But they say symptoms often persist long after a sickness is cured. Like the wound left by an amputated limb, which hurts in cold or overly hot weather.

"Sometime a-so i' go." Noah's attitude to the wound's failure to disappear with the drying up of its source is philosophical. "Nutten in life come straight, or clean so. A nuh heaven dis. Yu find seh pickni braught up a certain way, all when him big an live a different life, di old braughtupniss still peep out when him nuh expec. Same ting. A history. I' mark yu. A so i' go."

I pick up the finished fish pot and study the intricate weave of bamboo wicker and twine. And while we're sitting side by side like this, Noah tells me about his son, things I have always known but now realize I have never known, because I've never heard them before from Noah's point of view.

"Luck follow dat bwoy like obeah. Di modda seh is har prayers. Di world balance out though. If yu foot parylize, yu hand get more skill. If yu eye blind, yu ears hear better, till dem si. Until they become eyes. Seem like di universe compensate him fi what him born widout. No skin, an him tougher cause a i'.

"Bwoy tek to sea like him bi mi own. Firs trow him trow him line, him ketch one big grouper. Cooda hardly manage it, fish nearly pitch him offa di boat, but him heng on pon dat line like him hear trumpet. An mi help him pull i' in.

"Mi heart come inna mi mout fa him drop an bleed. Nuh know wha mi a-go tell di modda seh, but di bwoy neva bawl. Him git up.

Plant him foot inna di boat same as how mi show him, wide lakka mahoe stump. Neva let go though mi a-pull di line fi him. Him a-pull wid mi. Same as how mi show him."

I remember that fish. I got half of it to take home. Ugly creature with a bumpy-bumpy head that had a funny shape on top like a crown. It was my first sight of grouper and I hadn't known before that it was a crowned fish. Then when I saw it I thought it was a kingfish, but Rachel corrected me.

"Him bleed nuff dat day.

"Yu tink dat spoil him fi di long haul? No sah. Siddung same way an wait when di fish-dem tek long fi bite. Bwoy cooda wait! Kiss mi neck! Like him si vision an him sure a whole congregation o' fish roun di corner.

"But after dat mi ban' up him hand every time him a-go ketch fish.

"Day after him ketch big fish, him draw picture wid word pon it fi mi read. Das how oonu get fi know seh mi couldn't read. Never get fi go-a school regular fi get di book knowledge. Him hear him modda talk seh mi illiterated, but him neva understand before. Him seh, Dadda, mek bargain. Yu a-teach mi di fishin, mi teach yu di readin.

"Him don't seh nuh tell Mama. Neva seh dat. Every Sat'day morning after him modda gone a grung an nah come back soon, him show mi inna di book. Neva get it so good by di time him lef fi go a university, di head gone bad aready, set like concrete. Nuh easy bruk troo an put book-readin inside. Plus, yu know di talkin hard fi him. Sometime when him talk di mout confuse an bleed. So him draw picture an write word under i' an a-so wi pang-pang gwan-troo till mi learn likkle sinting. Mi learn more when him gone though.

"When him jus go Englan, him write him modda. Him don't write mi. Him write di letta to the two a wi, *Dear Mama and Dadda,* but is him modda address on the hinvilope. So shi read it out loud to di two a wi. Yes, a she read i'. Den jus before him go wheh again—mi mean, lef Englan an tell wi seh him comin home an den him don't come, him go allabout a Japan an China an backa God back deh-so— mi get one letta by myself seh, *Mr. Noah Fisher, Tumela Gut District, Tumela Postal Agency, Jamaica, West Indies.* Das how i' write pon di hinvilope."

A long pause during which he is finishing the second fish pot and I'm getting impatient at last, so I prompt him a little: "And?"

"Mi nuh tink him tink mi cooda read it. Das why a she him sen fi read all-a dem before. A she read dem. But mi practice. Ehn-hn. Mi practice pon di ole Bible she have deh, mi soun out di letta-dem jus as how him show mi. Di word-dem start to sing demself jus like how parson sing dem. *The eternal God is thy refuge and underneath are the everlasting arm. Blessed is the man that walketh . . ."*

I take up the chant with him and we finish it together, *"not in the counsel of the ungodly, nor standeth in the way of sinners, nor sitteth in the seat of the scornful. But his delight is in the law of the Lord, and in His law doth he meditate day and night. And he shall be like a tree planted by the rivers of water, that bringeth forth his fruit in his season, his leaf also shall not wither, and whatsoever he doeth shall prosper."*

The words fall with an odd mournfulness and comfort into a valley of silence between us, their ripples echoing out to sea. It is stuff Mosh and I had to learn by heart when we were children all those years ago at the big school. Bible Knowledge class, the whole school standing up and reciting. The way we recited memory gems. "Boys and girls, remember this I pray, to brush your teeth both morn and eve, and do this every day." That was how they taught us hygiene. And morality. "O what a tangled web we weave, when first we practice to deceive." And respect for elders. "Thou shalt honor the hoary head, and rise up before the face of the old man." That one was from Bible too. And our multiplication tables, "Twice ones two, twice twos four, twice nine are eighteen, twice tens twenty, twice twelves twenty-four!" It seems such a long time ago. Wherever Mosh is at this moment, I think, he is that tree, planted by the rivers of water, bringing forth fruit of creativity every season, never withering, because his heart is good. How could it not, when he was made with such love? Redeemed. That is what Rachel and Noah have done. Redeemed the discarded child. For love covereth a multitude of sins. As it covereth nakedness exposed without skin. Redeemed.

Is like Noah is reading my thoughts, for he says, making me jump, "A Moshe dat. A dat mi pray fi him, ebbery day." Then he goes on, "Mi si di word-dem inna di Book"—he pronounced it with a capital

B, to show reverence for Rachel's Bible—"same so, an mi understand. Never haffi track i' like pickni recitation. Mi get di knowledge of i'."

"So what yu do wid di letta dat him write yu inna yu own name dat one time, Papa Noah? Yu show Mama Rachel?"

Noah smiles. He hands me the second fish pot. "Put dis over dere fi mi."

I take it and, balancing it in my hands, feeling the weight and lightness of it, I sniff its sweet sharp scent of resin and place it beside its twin.

Noah picks up the glass of lemonade, beaded heavily now with moisture, and drinks it whole, throwing his head back so that the sunlight glints on his eyelids and his throat moves as it takes the long swallow. He holds the glass out and I take it in both hands.

"Tenky," he says again.

He gets up and moves to go into the house just as we hear Rachel's voice calling to the chickens as she comes round the side of the house, carrying on her head a grung basket of okra, corn, and gungo from her farm.

"Mi read i'," he says.

Never even knew the old man believed in prayers. Never see him sit down with Rachel and her Yahweh parson at all when they have their arcane palavers on Sundays together. Like me, never darkens a church door except smaddy dead and we attend for the funeral. Just quiet-quiet going about him business, bringing forth fi-him particular fruit in fi-him particular season, no fanfare, no fuss. Tree planted by water. Father and son.

Yu miss him, Papa Noah?

Bwoy tek after mi like him bi mi own. What yu heart claim nuh have nutten fi do wid blood. Yu can bleed out all yu blood an di heart still deh-deh, a-choose what it waan fi choose.

❧

Dear Dadda,

 I am writing this to you from Bristol. I am waiting in the train station to catch the train back to London.

 Dadda, yu well? The fish biting good?

 See you soon. Bringing you a new fishing rod, Champion. They say this kind is the best in the world.

 Tell the sea good morning for me.

Moshe

He didn't write *love* or *your son* but began the letter with a drawing that Noah understood and stood reading for a long, long time.

PART V

the return

CHAPTER XXVII

At last, when she has almost given up believing he had boarded the plane at all, she sees him come through the arrivals door, a nervously skinny young man who draws eyes even in the big crowd. He does not now look unusually strange, but his appearance is still, nevertheless, unusual.

Her eyes sketch him half in relief, half in search and fear of how he might have changed. He is dressed in the careless way of her generation who have thumbed their nose at respectable dress without adopting slogans. No raised fist, no kareba. His olive polo shirt has seen many washings. As have his jeans, once white, now a nondescript gray in the shadowed light inside the waiting area, where the dimness makes a stark contrast to the sun glare hazing the tarmac under the gunmetal sky. Despite the wide leather belt holding them up, the jeans ride low on his hips. They give him a mi-nuh-kya, in-your-face look, the look of a foreigner. The belt is too long, part of it hangs down in front like a protruding tongue or an extra penis, but the possible impression of slackness is annulled by the absent-looking face, as if he does not exist in his own body.

People are looking at him because he is so thin he is vivid, like a drawing, and his face is beautiful but hungry beneath the bone, as if something in him has not been fed for days. His two-toned hair looks like style now, shaved close in the back, the front longer with blunt-cut bangs falling over his eyes. The blond front is bleached the color of silver sand, the color at the back deepened to black-blue. She wonders if he dyes it now, if that is why it appears blacker than it used to be. He was always crazy enough to carry coals to Newcastle, she thinks.

She sees that he moves differently now, not with the old diffidence but the soft gingerly motion of a cat that is wary of heat under its toes. As though he's protecting himself from something he's carrying inside, something he's afraid to jostle in case it breaks and causes his death or an explosion. It is the way a suicide bomber might move. She is oddly disappointed; she does not see the smart choreography he once told her in his letters from London he practices to make his walk look neutral. All she sees is this cat's soft fearfulness.

All of a sudden she finds she is not glad to see him. She is conscious instead of terror mixed with anger, a feeling so strong it makes her nauseous. She moves back into the lee of the rent-a-car office and stays there, struggling to get her bearings and fighting the urge to vomit. She watches him search for her in the crowd at the railing, and her terror prevents her from coming forward to ease his uncertainty. He pushes his thumbs under the straps of the sweat-stained knapsack on his back, hoisting it away from his flesh as if it hurts him. The sack is bulging and seems heavy. His skin is as pale as she remembers; she thinks he still marks easily and she imagines his back a mass of black-blue scars and bruises. He never went red from a cut or bruise, only black and blue.

A red cap porter trails in his wake pushing a baggage trolley loaded with two bulging suitcases. One has a tear and clothes rolled in tight balls are sticking out of the opening. The suitcases are expensive, Samsonite. She thinks he bought them secondhand, for a song.

He reaches the barrier and still hasn't seen her. He turns to say something to the porter and she relents and calls his name, stepping out from the side of the shed.

"Mosh."

His face brightens. He laughs a little and takes his time slinging the knapsack off his shoulders, as if his hands have difficulty maneuvering and he doesn't want this to show. "Hold this fi di I, boss," he says to the porter, dropping it on top of the suitcases. It slips and the porter bends to grab and steady it on the pile.

They hug so close she feels the bristle of his unshaven chin pressing against her scalp through her dreadlocks, the sharpness of his hip bones against hers through the cloth of their jeans. They hug not like friends, holding their lower bodies away from each other as they had been taught adults of opposite sex do for propriety, but like twins, or lovers, the length of their bodies pressed against each other, breasts and groins matched. His body feels so familiar that tears gather in her eyes and her fear drains away like water spilled in sand.

She is full-fleshed but he feels her bones beneath her skin. She is wearing body-hugging jeans and a loose embroidered white smock that skims her waist.

"I thought you weren't coming. You must have been the last person to get off the plane."

He feels her trembling and the wetness against his neck. "It's okay," he says, rubbing the sides of her hair between his two palms. "It's okay now." And then, suddenly smiling, "Is true, I was tempted, it did take me a while to decide to get off. But I couldn't just turn back and mek yu waste yu time begging off work fi come get mi."

He has changed. He was never a teaser, but intense and serious. She used to be the teasing one. But she goes a little cold inside, because she knows he speaks the truth. However he has changed, he will always speak the truth. She has a vision of him sitting in his seat in the plane, stomach clenched, struggling to think whether to stay put until the flight is ready to lift off again (it was a plane on its way to Cuba), or sink the feeling and disembark.

Though her fear-driven anger is forgotten, her nerves are still too raw for levity. "I'll get the car. Wait here."

"Yes." He holds her between his hands, his mismatched eyes looking into hers with a gravity that keeps her still. He wipes the tears from her face with the pad of his thumbs, moving them in a circular motion the way he had done when he eased the knapsack away from his flesh. He hesitates, as if not knowing what to do with the wetness on his hands, then he rubs them on the sides of his jeans.

"I am here now," he says quietly, in the old reassuring way, as if with one glance he has comprehended all her turmoil and is answering the wordless question at the base of her heart. And for a sudden fleeting eon, the time it would take a blind man to feel a one-sided disk in the palm of his hand, it is as if no time or distance has passed and they are standing where they once stood, at the top of a flight of steps leading down into an open play yard, holding each other's hands. Only now it is he comforting her, saying, "Come."

"I'll get the car," she says again, strong and breathless. He smiles, gives her a gentle push forward. But his eyes don't smile. They have not smiled at all, even when he was teasing. They are watchful, like his gait, the gait of a man who would look over his shoulder in daylight.

He watches her walk away. People watch her walk away. People have been staring, from the beginning. She cannot see herself but she knows what the onlookers are seeing. By themselves each is spectacular; together, strange. A striking and odd couple, her blue-black sheen against his uncanny lightness. And because in this country black people don't openly display affection, even at ports of entry and departure, some onlookers disapprove. This public intimacy between two people who are not tourists, or two people one of whom is not a tourist, is unsettling. These two are behaving like foreigners.

But the onlookers know Moshe is not a foreigner. He has the look and aura of a native who has gone away. Returning resident. As for her, it is easy to tell she has never left.

She lopes across the roundabout to the car park, a very tall woman moving with long strides. She gets the car, pays her fee at the security booth, stares blankly when the guard taking her ticket makes a flirtatious comment, drives around to the front where Moshe is standing looking singular among the crowds of laughing, greeting, gathering arrivals and relatives.

They load his things into the trunk and, getting behind the wheel, she drives fast, taking the top airport road instead of the bottom one where traffic is slow with tourists. But she drives through the city center in case he wants to remember old places and see how they have changed. Despite the delays crawling through streets jam-packed with shoppers and made precarious by crazy-hopping, horn-tooting taxi drivers and sidewalk vendors' goods spilling dangerously close to the street, it doesn't take her long to hit the Bogue main road beneath the residential hills and then the long open stretch toward Ora. The sea is now visible on their right, deep blue, turquoise, and green, purple-mauve sometimes, calm and placid except where at intervals it sends spray up above the low retaining wall, filling the air with the smell of jetsam and salt.

They do not speak but she is conscious of him with every cell in her body. Watching her, he has a smile on his face, a smile of diffidence and pleasure and hesitant knowledge; then, suddenly, blankness. In the confines of the car his body is too close, and suffocating. They are just taking the turn at Tryall when he reaches over and touches her thigh, a gesture, very light, that says, Stop. Her flesh jumps and retreats under his hand. She puts on the indicator and swings right, bringing the vehicle to a stop under the pouis lining the roadway. A lone golf cart ridden by a caddy trolls up the hill on the green. The golfer, a large tourist dressed in whites to keep cool, walks behind, unhurried. The sky is exceedingly blue, the sun hazed.

She unsnaps her seat belt and turns, in a dream, to meet his blue-brown gaze, the blank expressionless face with which he also turns to her, and he opens his mouth to ask the question; she knows the question he is going to ask, two questions in one; in fact, three, Why was it you who came for me, and not my parents? Where are Mama and Dadda, why didn't they come with you, or even by themselves? What did I do to deserve your silence? But the scene crumbles in front of her face; the impeccable golfing green and the blue sky, the strolling player and bright orange golf cart with the caddy in it—all fall inward like a house of matches in an invisible wind. Everything falls so silently, so soundlessly, it is like being in a dream, where one watches in slow motion.

She looks at Mosh, Mosh is speaking but she cannot hear his words, and then he too caves like the house of matches. She watches him levitate from his seat like a silhouette of air, hang marionette-suspended for the moment of a breath, then crumble gently downward. Crumbling, he gives off a sensation of clack-clack, like fleshless bones, though there is no hearable sound, as he folds and disappears under the seat.

Then the car too begins to fall, beneath is a giant sinkhole, and she is the one levitating now as everything goes downward into water.

The dream ends as all the dreams end; she wakes, shivering, tears crawling down her face while she sits up in the bed trying to release herself from the tangle of wet sheets that have made a conundrum of her limbs. It takes her long moments to even find the ends of each sheet to unwind.

Childe Rowland to the dark tower came.

She would like to say this is how it all ended: that he came, and all was explained, and understood, and forgiven, and they lived happily ever after, the way the right stories end. Once upon a time, and then they lived happily ever after, no need to tell what happens after the end, because nothing ends ever after, ever after has no end.

He came, and they lived, certainly, but what manner of living it was, she cannot say. She thinks they lived happier than most people ever do, indeed she thinks they were happy, as people are in fairy tales, but she also thinks, What is happy? She does not believe in happiness, the word has such a phony ring to it, as if one should deny the evidence of life itself, the stain that gives living its integrity. She thinks that one may achieve happiness in moments, like sudden dust motes in the air of time; beyond that, the idea is illusion. Always in her sight there is a thin line which sutures the illusion of happiness to life's integrity.

Sometimes she thinks of this line as a ragged perpendicular stain; at others, a vertical or horizontal crease like the scalpel scar from a stitched wound that never goes away, in just the same way the line of the horizon runs where the sea curves, a separation and promise that never go away. Every now and then your heart leaped thinking the horizon was as near as it looked, and then you were happy, or thought you were happy. Every now and then you felt the wound, and your heart leaped with hope, thinking the lost limb was returned. But the line remained perpendicular, the horizon receding, the limb absent.

Perpendicular. Like perplex, it is a word of great weight in Tumela. To say something is perpendicular is to speak of ineluctable conundrums.

A stitched wound. A horizon. Perpendicular.

In just the same way, there was always in her sight Moshe who was with her and Moshe who was now absent like a sailor lost at sea.

The idea that she could have both of him again was as perpendicular as happily-ever-after.

It would have been as easy to say, "For a long time the prince was lost," as it was to say, "And so the prince returned, and they lived. Happily." Except that of course he was no longer a prince but a man, who in his travels had learned the arts of subterfuge, that made of happiness a perpendicular.

So nothing that happened after he came back surprised her.

The day he arrived, despite her sharp vexation with his father for daring her not to run away, she did run, back to her job in Kingston, though her two weeks of vacation still had a week to go. She worked late, paying the nursery extra to keep Betina after closing hours so she would not be at home when the phone rang and Rachel said, He is here, and he's safe. But she went cold with gratitude to hear the message on her voice mail. Arrii, using Moshe's name for her, he come and he well, plane reach Montego Bay on time, Yahweh be praised.

Everything that happened after that was inevitable, everything had always been inevitable, as it is in her second dream when she watches the zygote fuse and cleave and the two cotyledons twist upward into the air.

This embryo consists of two embryonic leaves, the epicotyl and hypocotyl. The embryo will eventually turn into a sporophyte.

Only this one didn't. Consist of two leaves, that is. Impossibly, against nature, the radicle splits, the cotyledons levitate separately, pulling their earth-stained roots with them, each becoming a different plant shaped like a half.

Chunks of text from the tenth-grade biology textbook detach themselves and begin floating before her eyes, breaking up in blocks like Chinese characters and then rearranging themselves in sentences she remembers.

Polyploidy occurs frequently in some organisms. This allows the organism to survive. For example, different kinds of wheat exist because some have two sets of chromosomes, some have four sets, and others have six sets. Through polyploidy, if there are enough changes, we could end up seeing the creation of a new species. The basic cause of polyploidy is fertilization between unreduced gametes. So the new species is formed from a defect that allows the plant to survive, though in a different form. Unreduced gametes are the result of anomalies, or defects, in the ways the plant cells divide, to form new cells.

In this other dream it is always night but also day, and she is working on the half-acre farm with Rachel, in an in-between space like twilight. The air is wet and plants are growing everywhere, so naked and so fast that she can see the entire process from beginning to end. She sees anomalous chromosomes split, divide, and split again; her eyes growing infrared see the tiniest origins of the multiplication of cells; she sees straight through to the origin of species. Her ears grow large as elephants' ears and then larger and larger, until she hears a high thin sound that goes on and on, like the singing of orcas. Then she realizes it is not that. The sound separates itself out into strands and she hears many symphonies, and each separate instrument in each symphony, and she recognizes the music of the plant universe in motion.

She hadn't realized how loquacious the plant world is, their speech never-ending. Did you know, she dreams in astonishment, that plants utter cries of pleasure when they mate, whether with themselves or by the visitation of insects or wind? The sexual pleasure of plants comes with a low sucking sound, a moan that collapses in on itself, followed by a slender joyous spray of laughter, thinner than a steel filament.

A complete lack of sexual reproduction is rare among multicellular organisms. This is especially true for animals.

With her microscopic eyesight comes a new mental focus; among the innumerable oceans of cells her eyes follow the one astonishing anomaly: the split embryo that has not become a set of twins but two halves of itself levitating, flying and yet not flying, turning, each half, like a weather vane or a gyre, in a locked flight that remains inexplicable until she sees that both halves are still joined by a thread of stem that turns in the opposite direction to their flight and is trying to fuse them back together.

Unlike the vast majority of the cells in that green universe, they are silent and dumb, except once, when the split radicle screams as it is pulled from the ground, the way all the cells scream when they copulate.

She always woke at the point where the split embryo flipped in the air and began spiraling downward in a lightning dive and she surged forward and upward, levitating through green water to save them.

From the beginning, the airport dream left her paralyzed; later, the revelation of its accuracy gave her hope. It was only when she faced the reality of what their marriage would be like that she came to interpret the symbolism of the second dream.

She tells herself, This is Moshe and me. An embryo split against itself.

Polyploidy may, in fact, result in the creation of a new species.

A new species born of a defect. Polyploidy that never went in a straight line.

Now irrevocably superstitious, she is convinced that somewhere before history she and Moshe were born as an embryo that split and separated, and happily ever after means working out how nottwins, a split person born in this way, achieves happily ever after. Perpendicular.

CHAPTER XXVIII

Their reunion was not spectacular. When it happened it was very simple, the way important things often are, as if they are already organized from elsewhere.

She was watering her plants when he came. Her apartment had no backyard to speak of, only a tiny patio surrounded by a few square feet of earth. Beyond the earth, a narrow paved pathway that led out to the code-secured front gate. She had filled the square feet with pots of vegetables, flowers, and herbs, and the patio with more, stacked on tall metal shelves reaching up to the ceiling. She had grown up in the age of Joshua when "plant your own kitchen garden, even if you have only a handkerchief of space" was a political slogan aimed at city dwellers. But it was Rachel who had taught her how to become green-fingered. The garden flourished, a luxuriant maze that trapped the sunlight and turned it watery green.

She was standing with her back to the path, aiming the hose upward at the pots on the highest shelves, but she heard his footstep and felt him standing behind her long before he said, "Can I help you with that?" and took the hose out of her hand.

She continued watching the colors of the spectrum that danced in the spray. They formed a shattered arc along the fan of the water. She didn't turn around. She didn't ask, "How did you get in?" She knew how. Rachel had visited her often in the city, especially after Betina was born; Rachel had the gate code. Rachel wasn't leaving anything to chance or her refusal.

He turned off the water and hung up the hose on its metal hook. She watched his hands as he rolled it slowly and carefully in loops like a necklace. His hands were wet from handling the hose, and trembled a little. When he was finished he wiped them down the sides of his jeans. His jeans were low on his hips and white, and he was too thin. He put his hands on her shoulders and she felt their warmth as if she weren't wearing a blouse, and then, as he kept them there, their heat, as if he had peeled off her skin. She turned to face him and saw that he had changed, and he was as he had been in her dream. His android skin looked permanent now; it was a solid color, the color of sun-touched cream. He was so thin he was vivid, his face still perfect but hungry beneath the bone, as if something in him had not been fed for days. She had had days to think about his arrival, days to surrender, and she had given up herself long before she heard his step on the pathway.

But she struggled with her shame and her terror until he pushed his fingers at the sides of her hair and smoothed them over her temples, where the pain was. She turned in to him with a deep sigh, and there is none of the quiet decorous weeping that was in her airport dream but a long, silent shuddering that has built up from waiting over days. She feels the bristle of his unshaven chin pressing against her scalp through her dreadlocks, the sharpness of his hip bones against hers through the cloth of their jeans. They hug not like friends, holding their lower bodies away from each other as they had been taught to do for propriety, but like twins, or lovers, the length of their bodies pressed against each other, breasts and groins matched. His body feels so familiar that the floodgates open and now she does begin to cry.

She is full-fleshed but he feels her bones beneath her skin. She is wearing body-hugging jeans and an embroidered white smock that skims her waist.

She doesn't think he's crying. She thinks the wetness on his face is because it is pressed close to hers. When she presses her hand against the side of his face, he follows the turn and his tongue moves up and down her cheek, drinking her tears.

She tries to laugh, shakily. "I didn't know you drink eyewater."

"Just this once," he says. "In a desert you don't pick and choose."

And that was all.

Or almost all.

"I have to tell you," she said, speaking ragged and fast, wanting to get everything over with, all at once and for all.

"About Betina?"

"How did you know?"

"My mother told me." He was still stroking his fingers down her face, cupping her face between his two hands and smoothing her skin up and away like someone ironing creases.

"She said she would never tell you anything about me again."

"Yes, because I asked her not to. But in the end, she did. She didn't want me to come without warning." He smiled. His smile was different. A little wistful, a little sad. Part of him seemed to depart somewhere. "My mother will always protect me," he said.

She caught her breath. "Did it matter? Her warning?"

"Oh yes. It did."

Reader, I married him.

That simple. Just like Jane Eyre.

But not so simple. At Rachel's insistence, we held the wedding in Tumela. Small and quiet, not befitting the daughter of George Christie or the son of a family who had gone away and made money. In fact, its smallness was something of a disgrace, and many people who were not our friends or close to us in any way were offended that we didn't ask them to come. A few, the ones from the church without music, would not have come because I was divorced. But it was how Moshe and I wanted it, and, thank God, Rachel too. I was never so glad Rachel was a woman who never kept company. Miss Hildreth had died several years before; Samuel was her only other friend, and apart from family he was the only guest invited.

In a way, our wedding was the wedding of the boy and girl who had grown up speechless, and friendless except for each other, and were always on the outside of everything. Rachel and my mother's attempt to make us normal, with a real wedding, only brought home to me how much we would never fit. But we wanted Rachel and my mother and my father to be happy. I don't think Noah cared if we crawled under the house and got married there by night. So long as we were happy with each other. I think Rachel wanted a sign that this time it was real, not a fly-by-night hokey-pokey hole-in-a-corner affair, which was how she thought of my marriage to Stephen. The symbolism of the wedding, all of us dressed up and flowers on the altar, the ceremony intoned, and the rings, and shared wine, made it real for her, like one of Yahweh's signatures.

My father had a long man-to-man talk with Moshe; about what, neither of them ever said. But my father was reconciled to Moshe because he had gone away and come back to me, which meant he was not as fenkeh-fenkeh as he looked; he had gone away and sowed his wild oats but he knew what to value and who a true empress was. My father had taken to calling me his empress because of the way I wore my hair. But I wasn't Rasta; I didn't believe in anything. Except justice and rightness and Moshe. And I had betrayed all three.

But my father thought I was the source of sunlight and he couldn't imagine Moshe being anything but stunned that he should get a girl like me. Though he had no idea what really passed between Stephen and me, or whose fault it was, he never forgave my first husband for not appreciating my worth. "You do a right thing lef him," my father said. "You see when I give you an education? That is your bex-money. I give you your bex-money so any man dissatisfy you, you tell him kiss-mi-ass and leave." This he repeated one day before I married Moshe. It was his way of telling me Mosh was not exempt and if he gave me grief I should leave his backside too. But he smiled as he said this so I knew that this time he was hopeful for me.

And I smiled too remembering how I used to laugh whenever he said this, because it made me imagine myself flouncing off in a scene where a boy tried to do me in his car after a date. I used to imagine myself showing him the handful of vex-dollars in my hand and saying, "I have my taxi fare, yu bloodcloth." Though I never thought of going out with any boy; only word speaking.

My mother didn't try the Talk thing with me this time—what would have been the point? I had been married before (for one night. But she doesn't know that).

It was Rachel who took me aside when we told her we wanted to marry each other.

"Yu sure this is what yu want?" She gave me one of her wi-goin-have-it-out-today looks.

"Of course."

"Look at me, Arrienne. Yu understand what I am saying to yu? Oonu talk bout what to expect? Yu sure is something yu can live with?"

I could feel my eyes flash and she slapped me down before I could say anything. "Don't get up on yu high horse wid me, Miss Ma'am. Yu young an yu have sap in yu body an yu hurt him enough aready. I don't want to hear yu cyaan stay di course an back outa dis marriage."

Her words chilled me. *Yu young an yu have sap in yu body. I don't want to hear yu back out of dis marriage.* I understood what she was insinuating, what she had believed about Mosh all these years. She was putting the ghost of Alva Lawrence between us again, and I lifted my eyes and looked directly into hers. "Moshe and I will have a normal marriage," I told her proudly, and walked out of her house.

I had accepted my mother's plea that no members of the Christie clan that had attended my unveiling as my father's daughter were to be invited. What did it matter to me, I didn't care, I was glad there was to be no crowd and nobody was going to try to stress me out by insisting there should be. But my mother cared, and I think she said don't invite those Christies because she was ashamed of how small and unglamorous the wedding was. She could not show off in front of the family that had wronged her all those years ago, so it was better they didn't come.

But my grandmother, my father's mother, Mama Mai, came, she could not be left out. She arrived in style in a chauffeur-driven Mercedes-Benz and an electric wheelchair. She sat staring at me throughout the brief ceremony, her eyes very black and young and snapping, though she had reached a great age and her eyes were at odds with the rest of her face. She had lost all her teeth but refused dentures, insisting that she was not ashamed of her gums that God gave her. All the time she stared at us, her lips kept working in and out, like a sea creature. I was quite weepy, like any common garden variety of bride, and in my superstitious state wondered if she was about to make some terrible prophecy about Mosh and me. I looked over at Rachel with whom I had almost quarreled over my decision to marry her son. I wondered what she was thinking behind the smooth beauty of her face—was she prophesying too? Or praying? Rachel was more likely to be praying.

My mother said no, Mama Mai was just inspecting me again to make sure she hadn't made a mistake the first time and I was indeed a Christie, my father's true-true daughter. My grandmother brought me a wedding present, a hope chest full of embroidered lace and linen—doilies, tablecloths and curtains, and some translucent cushions. I have never been an embroidery and lace person, or had doilies in my house.

In all there were ten guests (all family except Samuel), but for me that was many. I had married Stephen with two witnesses before a judge. It was something I could have got away with in Kingston but not in Tumela, where family surrounded you like a fence. I was grateful to my mother and stepmother who in recompense for my willingness to be married by a reverend in a church (not Rachel's Yahweh preacher, who, to her disappointment, was not licensed as a marriage officer) did not kick up an almighty fuss about the size of the guest list, despite their mutual desire for carnival-size shenanigans.

Of course, people crowded the churchyard to peer at us through the glass windows, though that was no more than to be expected in Tumela.

Women are supposed to be the ones who cry at weddings, but it was my father who cried on my wedding day. I knew it was in part because he was heartbroken at losing me to yet another man, but I wondered if he was also thinking with sadness of the son he had left behind in Korea, whom he would never know.

I love you, Papa. Trust me, this makes no difference between you and me. Nobody can take your special place.

Betina wore flowers in her hair, and crowed and laughed through the whole ceremony. Afterward she slept on Moshe's shoulder, and cried when Rachel tried to take her away. I noticed my grandmother nodding her head, amazingly, in approval, when she saw how the baby clung to Mosh, and I thought perhaps she had come bringing the last fairy's blessing after all, not the curse of a hundred years.

Lord knew we were needing all the blessing we could get.

Betina stole the show and the best photograph of the wedding was of her clinging to Moshe and refusing to let go.

He was a better father to her than her own father was, and not only then but throughout her life she took to him as if, Rachel said, she were a duck and he were water. Stephen had visiting rights, and the one time he saw Moshe he laughed. I never let him come to our house again after that. I took Betina to him at the library, and picked her up again there when his time was over. Still he could not resist, "A wheh yu get dat-deh dundus man, missis?"

I never answered him—what was there to say to a man who thought like that, what was there to say to anyone at all, about a couple such as we were, two pot covers that did not fit? They had a proverb for this in Tumela Gut: *Two pot cover cyaan shet*; this is how they spoke about the necessity of opposites, and the fact that a thing and itself do not make two.

But what if the two pot covers are not really two at all but one that has been split straight down, like a radicle torn in two, the halves growing separate and incomplete? Then the two pieces if you found them again would fit side by side, so well that unless you looked really close you could not see the perpendicular scar where they were sutured.

In Tumela perpendicular is almost the same as perplex, but not quite; perplex in Tumela has no equivalent in English; it is a word like *suppose*, it is like a phrase such as *what if*, words and phrases that have no end and no accurate translation, they just open out into other words and suppositions, as numerous as the waves of the sea.

Who is to say how people are made, or unmade, or how they should be? Suppose there are as many constellations of people as there are chromosomes of plants, or continents of air, and suppose, every now and then, like one chance in ten quadrillion, or less, or more, one of us tears at the radicle, and has to be put together again?

What if we were to go back to the beginning of time, and observe the moment Derek Walcott said, when the last ape ended and the first human began, and what if, afterward, we could return to now, bringing with us the memory of what we had seen? Could we imagine then that two pot covers could shut, or even that a thing could exist that was itself alone and still be two?

Maybe then we could imagine anything. Maybe we could even imagine the thing that even Tumela says cannot exist, that Borges tried to imagine. A thing that has only one side. But that is not a thing we could imagine with our minds, only with our feeling, a burning sensation, a sudden leap of dark in the light, and then . . . nothing.

But none of these what-ifs really mattered for Moshe and me, because we had made up our minds how we were going to live together, and it didn't concern anyone but the two of us.

In truth, in the beginning, we didn't plan for the way it turned out, we thought it would be different, but when it turned out the way it did, we lived, and we were content. We were whole, and sometimes, like sudden dust motes in the air of time, we were happy.

I was not angry with Alva Lawrence for telling Moshe I had got married in '79. Of course I had not been getting married to anyone, but how could Alva know this, that time I had been a little out of my head and even Mama Rachel was afraid for me, saying, after I started wearing Davon's promise ring, "It better yu talk to Moshe. Yu running yuself into di grung, an yu not being fair to dat young man, yu don't really want him. Don't use people, Arrienne. Don't do to others what yu don't want to boomerang back on yu."

I had not paid Mama Rachel any mind (I was out of my mind then, and she sounded like she wanted to scour me out, the way she had scoured out my mouth the time I cursed in her presence), but when I saw Davon's reaction after I gave him back his ring, I was afraid she was right and something terrible would happen to me for my wickedness.

"Yu si what I tell you?" she said, so righteously that I disliked her a great deal at that moment. "I always knew yu wasn't goin to married him. Das why I don't even waste my time tellin Moshe and puttin di poor boy in unnecessary perplex."

She saw the fire in my eye when she said this, and added, just to provoke me so I would get angry enough to feel guilty, "Though I know that was what yu was hopin I woulda do. But I wasn't playin no pickni game wid yu. An yu wasn't goin to use mi to hurt mi son."

And maybe deep down I was looking for my own punishment, trying to find it before it found me, so that I wouldn't have to be waiting in terror until the sword fell. I don't know how else to explain the fact that I married Stephen almost seven years later (yes, a fairy-tale year and a day before Moshe came home), unless you count the possibility that it was because, like Davon, he was a man willing to wait until marriage to consummate. (What an old-fashioned word, consummate, from the Latin *consummare*, to consume, to eat, to devour, to make perfect by eating or devouring, to abolish a person by devouring them to one's own perfect fulfillment.)

In all my life I have known or known of only two men, Davon and Stephen, who were willing to wait, and of course what are the odds that it had to be a "weirdo" like me who would attract the only two men of this type in a country where men pride themselves on not buying puss inna bag? But Mama Rachel said I was naive. "Who tell yu seh men nuh buy puss inna bag? Dem wi buy it, if dem can boast dat dem was di first. Yes, dem wi buy it, once dem tink dem have reason to believe di bag not empty or have-in someting else."

I don't know about Rachel's reasoning, maybe it was accurate and maybe it was not. Whatever Stephen's reasons for waiting, he was my nemesis, the punishment I had been looking for, except that when it came I wasn't willing to accept it, and our fight that night, the night Betina was conceived, was . . . I'm sorry. I'm sorry. I can't tell you. There is nothing after *was*.

Stephen is a legalist (after all, he is a lawyer), his cutoff point was the wedding night, after that he drew a red line in the sand. What he called my refusal (I begged him for more time) enraged him and took me by surprise. I had no way of explaining to him that I had not planned this. I had every intention of doing what was required of me as a wife. Until I did not.

He did not get off scot-free.

Stephen is a big man; though he is only about my height, he is large and strong.

He still has the scar like a ragged mat across his shoulder and chest where the wine bottle broke, snagged, and went on a rampage.

I don't know why he never prosecuted me. But I think it was the fear of scandal.

And there was one Anna, a prophetess, the daughter of Phanuel,
of the tribe of Aser: she was of a great age, and had lived with a
husband seven years from her virginity; and she was a widow of
about fourscore and four years.

Seven years. I often wondered about this woman in Rachel's Bible, who, despite her being four-eyed, had taken seven years to get rid of a man she didn't want. I didn't have that kind of stamina, and thank God I wasn't bound by society's notions of law and sin the way that poor woman was. I lived with Stephen for one night, only because it was not yet morning. After that I picked up and went back to Tumela Gut and Rachel and Noah and my father. Betina was born there, in '86. But Tumela never became a place of complete healing for me.

The day I married Stephen, even if I had not known I had done anything wrong my body certainly made sure I was advised. It was summertime, during the cane. The Christie birthmark that had gone dormant for so long that I thought I'd escaped it for good started wreaking havoc again. In the bone-racking upheaval that ensued I thought my body was fighting to cast out some vast infection that was lodged in my flesh or spirit. The mark never quite settled down after that, though it was never so bad as it was in the beginning, and it became more bearable after Moshe came home.

CHAPTER XXIX

In the first place, let me treat of the nature of man and what has happened to it. The original human nature was not like the present, but different. The sexes were not two as they are now, but originally three in number; there was man, woman, and the union of the two, of which the name survives but nothing else. Once it was a distinct kind, with a bodily shape and a name of its own, constituted by the union of the male and the female: but now only the word "androgynous" is preserved, and that as a term of reproach.

In the second place, the primeval man was round, his back and sides forming a circle; and he had four hands and the same number of feet, one head with two faces, looking opposite ways, set on a round neck and precisely alike; also four ears, two privy members, and the remainder to correspond. He could walk upright as men now do, backward or forward as he pleased, and he could also roll over and over at a great pace, turning on his four hands and four feet, eight in all, like tumblers going over and over with their legs in the air; this was when he wanted to run fast.

Now the sexes were three, and such as I have described them; because the sun, moon, and earth are three; and the man was originally the child of the sun, the woman of the earth, and the man-woman of the moon, which is made up of sun and earth, and they were all round and moved round and round because they resembled their parents. Terrible was their might and strength, and the thoughts of their hearts were great, and they made an attack upon the gods; of them is told the tale of

Otys and Ephialtes who, as Homer says, attempted to scale heaven, and would have laid hands upon the gods.

Doubt reigned in the celestial councils. Should they kill them and annihilate the race with thunderbolts, as they had done the giants, then there would be an end of the sacrifices and worship which men offered to them; but, on the other hand, the gods could not suffer their insolence to be unrestrained. At last, after a good deal of reflection, Zeus discovered a way.

He said: "Methinks I have a plan which will enfeeble their strength and so extinguish their turbulence; men shall continue to exist, but I will cut them in two and then they will be diminished in strength and increased in numbers; this will have the advantage of making them more profitable to us. They shall walk upright on two legs, and if they continue insolent and will not be quiet, I will split them again and they shall hop about on a single leg."

He spoke and cut men in two, like a sorb-apple which is halved for pickling, or as you might divide an egg with a hair; and as he cut them one after another, he bade Apollo give the face and the half of the neck a turn in order that man might contemplate the section of himself: he would thus learn a lesson of humility. Apollo was also bidden to heal their wounds and compose their forms. So he gave a turn to the face and pulled the skin from the sides all over that which in our language is called the belly, like the purses which draw tight, and he made one mouth at the center, which he fastened in a knot (the same which is called the navel); he also molded the breast and took out most of the wrinkles, much as a shoemaker might smooth leather upon a last; he left a few, however, in the region of the belly and navel, as a memorial of the primeval state.

After the division the two parts of man, each desiring his other half, came together, and throwing their arms about one another, entwined in mutual embraces, longing to grow into one, they began to die from hunger and self-neglect, because they did not like to do anything apart; and when one of the halves died and the other survived, the survivor sought another mate, man *or woman as we call them—being the sections of entire men or women—and clung to that.*

So ancient is the desire of one another which is implanted in us, reuniting our original nature, seeking to make one of two, and to heal the state of man.

Each of us when separated, having one side only, like a flat fish, is but the tally-half of a man, and he is always looking for his other half.

—ARISTOPHANES' DISCOURSE, PLATO'S *SYMPOSIUM*, 385–370 BCE

Well, Maas Plato and Maas Aristophanes, everybody have him version. Rachel Bible have another version too. I will stick with my version. The universe is not three but billions upon billions of constellations within uncountable galaxies and we are neither one or two or three kinds split in two or split because of the jealousy of any god. And we not suppose to be no one-horse comedy either so you can stop your laugh. Long before we start count time we were meant to be this plenitude, a multiplicity of differences so infinite and so vast that none could be replicated, for if I were to think of a God, God not jealous and mean, God is an infinity, and I bend myself to learning this unreplicable singularity that is Moshe and me that arise out of infinity's replications. That is what it mean by ever after. So tek dat, Mr. Comedian Aristophanes.

—ARRIENNE CHRISTIE FISHER, JOURNAL, MARCH 24, 1988

CHAPTER XXX

They say marriage is supposed to be between two people who learn to become one and still remain two. But maybe somewhere in the universe there are other people like Moshe and me, who were meant to be one person from the beginning, but something zigged and then zagged. In the levitation of zygotes, or the transliteration of embryos.

I struggle to understand the twinship between Moshe and me, and why it is that in our splitting apart I was the one who got all the skin and he came naked into the world.

Mosh doesn't let it bother him. Although he used to be the one who was restless with questions—about origins, about where he came from, why he was the way he was. Now, he says, he learned a lot of "negative capability" when he was in England. Negative capability, he said, using the words of the English poet who had been the first poet we both discovered and loved. The capacity to be content with shadows and half answers, without an irritable reaching after the straight line.

"I felt that if I could still feel you even when you were not writing to me," he said now, smiling at me where I sat kotched between his legs, "we couldn't lose each other. Even when all I was hearing from you was pure badword." This was what he called fate. "Everything else is irrelevant."

I thought it was not so much fate, as faith. He had an enormous amount of faith, like Rachel. I wondered how blind you had to make yourself in order to survive by such means. I knew how close we'd come to losing each other.

"But you believed Alva that I was marrying someone else, and because of that you ran away for seven, almost eight years," I objected. I wanted him to see that it wasn't that easy; we had hurt each other a lot, and we had to acknowledge the danger of that happening again if we were going to be all right in the future. "Mosh, you locked me out for seven years. The whole time you were in Europe, I couldn't find you." Even to tell you badword.

"In the end, I married another man, Mosh! I am not blaming you for my decision. I locked you out too. I just want you to understand, we haven't put the hurdles behind us." At this point I didn't want his faith, it made me feel unpardonably guilty; I wanted him to be angry with me, not to be so sure, so forgiving.

"I didn't know how to reconcile who we were and the thought that you were getting married. I never thought the two had anything to do with each other—it wasn't a matter of equivalencies. I couldn't say, We have this connection, therefore we have to marry each other, we cannot marry anyone else. So I didn't think your marrying would break us apart. But it hurt, and I didn't know how to deal with the contradiction. In my head, maybe, if I'd allowed myself to think it through. But not in my heart."

We have always been people who think with our hearts. The two of us.

"But why were you jealous? Couldn't you tell what was going on?"

"You forget that was the first time you really locked me out," he said, his smile dry.

It wasn't. But I did not remind him. That long year when I didn't want him to know my feelings for him had changed, whereas his for me hadn't—that was the first time. I had tried hard not to let him know.

I look back at that time in wonder. It was like a person had been living, just taking her aliveness for granted, and then suddenly became aware that she *is* actually alive. In a moment being alive becomes a rabid question, a summons which you have to answer; you can't go back to the time when you were unaware.

My theory of us having come from one embryo that split without becoming two, but instead two halves, falls apart whenever I get to these thoughts. I don't suppose a person desires himself or herself.

At least not in that way. My physical desire for Moshe has not diminished. I still want him as if he were the satisfaction of the one hunger. Consummate, from the Latin *consummare*. Consume. To devour voraciously, wantonly, recklessly, to take in greedily with the senses or intellect, to open your body and swallow someone whole, to be shattered to perfection, to be filled. Consummately. Consumed.

But maybe along with the skin I took the part of us that could respond or feel in that kind of way.

"Why did you never answer my letters?" It was his turn to ask, and my turn to answer. And because he was Moshe, he didn't ask because he was angry, didn't ask in order to have it out with me; it never became the hot confrontation I needed.

I hadn't known how confused I was until I answered. "I don't know. It was somehow different when we were little. Then, we were so right . . . so . . . seamless. But now I felt I had to protect myself."

He frowned. "Because of Alva?"

"No." And it was true. Though Alva was mixed up in there somewhere. Only not in the way his question imagined. Even now, I couldn't tell him the entire truth, I couldn't say, "Because I was afraid of wanting you too much. I felt I was losing myself, drowning." I was afraid that if I said any of this to him I would push him away, he would think I asked too much of him. A needy woman. Like the girl Miriam in that nasty D.H. Lawrence book. When had we come to this? I asked myself this question in a moment of near despair, then I pushed it away because we were together, here and now, and we were going to be together for as long as we could. It had to be enough.

One thing I had come to know: desire changes everything. Everything.

"Because of what, then?"

"I don't know. I think I was afraid because our relationship was entering . . . uncharted waters, and I was never sure that how I felt was how you felt. For example, I did not think that I would marry anybody else, the way you thought we could. And I felt if you had gone away because of me, because of how much I wanted, it wasn't fair to you, and I should let you go. I thought you wrote to me because you felt guilty. I didn't want that." My words frightened me a little and I reached up and kissed him, to drown out my thoughts and his answer.

His arms tightened around me as he kissed me back. "I wrote to you because I couldn't do without you. You knew that. You could tell. But you were angry with me the whole time."

"I was angry with myself."

"My mother said you kept all my letters. That, more than your breakup with . . . Stephen, made me know for sure. I probably wouldn't have come to see you if she hadn't told me that."

Was I to be grateful to some forgiving hidden power, Rachel's Yahweh maybe, that for once in her life Rachel Fisher had decided to become a blabbermouth? Thank you, Mama Rachel, for saving me.

"Stephen was . . . he wasn't important, Mosh. Not in that way." I gripped his hands, hearing my own urgency. "To think that if I'd waited one more year—"

"And a day. I love you," he said, quiet and deep, and then he kissed me again, and then it was all right again.

CHAPTER XXXI

(But it was all right for so short a time. Try as I would, try as we both did, I could not help seeing that a part of him remained lost to me, some private possession that he withdrew and kept only for himself. And it was like a door that was closed between rooms, ever so gently, so as not to give offense, or a pouch made to protect things in a membranous sac, or, in his luminous moments, a gleam like nacre spread over irritable grains of sand. He was so courtly, and so kind; his kindliness was the faith I saw in him, but the closed door was something he could not help. It was there in spite of himself, and he valued it, he did not wish to open it or abandon the distance it made between the rooms I could enter and the ones I could not.

I could not tell if this reserve was the result of things he had suffered or the natural separation that happens between one person's inner silence and another's, or a distrust deep in his flesh that he could not control, the fear that I had abandoned him once and would do so again.

This pain I was to remember the second time he went away.)

But I had my own closed doors too, doors I had shut from guilt and fear and other things that stood between us like strangers now. Things I had stopped myself from saying in case I woke up and found the dream of return had come to an end. This return was a delicate thing and I was guarding it as I had guarded us when we were little. But then I realized what I was guarding was myself and that wasn't going to work for too long; my father had brought me up to ask for what I wanted and say no to what I didn't; I wasn't used to subterfuge and sooner or later that pea that rubbed my ass under twenty-one cushions was going to erupt and the halcyon days would be shaken.

The hurricane tamped down would fly out of my hair and break the house apart and either we would lose it or build it up together again.

The return is always to a point of entanglement. Édouard Glissant.

How many entanglements around the five words, "It will be all right"?

"I want to tell you about Alva," Moshe said. We were sitting side by side on the new bench in Rachel's yard, and I didn't want to hear.

"We became friends," he said. "When I was in England. He came and looked for me there, once. When he thought I was sad from missing you." There was no accusation in his voice; there never was; he was Moshe. The thought that Alva had gone to see him there hurt so bad I thought I might die of it. "At first I needed him to tell me how you were. Then I was ashamed. You cannot . . . use people like that. As my mother always said." He shifted on the bench and took my hands in his so he could look into my eyes, where I was trying to avoid his gaze.

"I accepted his friendship, Arrii." His gaze was intense, willing me to understand. But of course I didn't. "He was the one who kept me in touch with what was happening to my parents, those seven years. Last month he migrated to the US."

The silence between us was complete. "I want you to understand, Arrii. He was a great friend to me. Truth be told, I got more out of our friendship than he ever did."

The hurricane was brewing. I watched it skirmishing among the banana thickets in the gully that faced Rachel's new house.

"You know, I used to wish people would accept me as I was. I thought if my presence in the world changed people in that way, if everyone stopped staring, everything would be all right," Moshe said.

"Why weren't you happy in Tumela then, where everyone stopped staring?" I had pulled my hands out of his.

"I was happy in Tumela because you were there. And Mama, and Dadda. We both know you don't need the world's heart. Which you can't have anyhow. Only the hearts of one or two who for no particular reason pledge to keep you company. Three if you're extra blessed."

I heard the "Hmn" in my head set the tone for the rest of the conversation.

"Your locks are flying," Moshe said unnecesarily, trying to tamp my hair down with his hands where it was whipping about my face and hitting him in his.

"Hurricane season. A-so di breeze come sudden dis time of year." I pushed his hands away and pulled my hair back with one hand, with the other looping a lock around the rest so it stayed in place a little. "So you were saying about yu friend, Maas Alva."

He watched my hair still trying to fly. The wind stirring it was rampaging in the gully. "Your hair is so beautiful," he said, but his eyes were inward. He laughed that half laugh which wasn't really a laugh but an explosion of breath between his mouth and his nose. As if laughter was rationed. But it was really only the familiar sign that he was thinking something wry. "Without saying anything, he"—his shoulders lifted, dropped in a gesture like surrender. "He helped me understand I wasn't all that different. That the same duty was laid on me that I longed for from everyone else. Just to accept people." His smile now was whimsical. "Even the obnoxious ones. Because there is nobody who is not different. I was extra visible, yes, but my hubris notwithstanding, I wasn't some kind of test that would make a difference. To how the world chose to arrange itself, I mean. Alva was . . . so easy. So effortless. He showed me it was okay to love without being afraid all the time."

He used to visit Noah and Rachel—even though Rachel didn't like him—and he never stopped until he got sick from the sickness that you were not supposed to talk about in those days then. Except in whispers behind doors, in case the name ravage your mouth, but Tumela people call it out loud and rough to face it down dutty rotten navel stinking bitch and call it curse, like how some people call Moshe's skin. Our visits did not often coincide, but when they did I never went by Rachel and Noah but stayed with my mother and my father. Then he went to America. And now it turns out he was the reason Mosh came home. He was no longer there, no longer a lifeline keeping tabs on Rachel and Noah, so Moshe came home. The taste of irony is very bitter.

"In a way he was like you. You give me so much. Without asking anything back." And then he says, "I don't compare you and Alva. In my life, you're two different constellations."

He can still reach for words inside my head.

But now I bex no raas and I not letting him off the hook anymore just because I feel he, or me, or the dream of us, going break. He not any delicate like how his mother say, and I not any more guilty than he.

I start to tell him a story. "Yu know mi fren Ilean Thompson?" Looking at me, he nodded. "You know why she single? She had this man once, the first and the last. One day at the beginning of the romance, when she still have star in her eye, the man sit her down and give her his funeral advance directive. Tell her how him unhappy wid him life, an how him a-go kill himself an she must mek sure dem cremate him so dat nobody can come stare pon him face inna coffin an exclaim how him ugly. When she cry out, yu know wha di man tell her? A fi-him life an fi-him choice fi do wid it what him want, nobody else have the right to say anyting or impose dem feelings on him choice. Like she don't matter at all. She not taken into account."

He was looking at me sideways with a quizzical and disquieted look in his eyes. Wondering where I was going with this. Not wary, just quizzical and wanting to know. Once upon a time he wouldn't have wondered; he would have known, without my words. But I have accepted that that time is long past, and we have to deal now with what we have on the ground, chop bush, clear the debris so we can go forward finding each other again. And this time I am Princess Royal, I want everything.

"Mosh, I am not one among two or three or even four. Not one among your mother or your father or your friend Alva. Or any parallel constellation with other constellation, no matter how nice that sound. You realize I am the only one you take for granted? Your mother teach you this. Alva give you that. And Arrienne? Yu know how yu sound talking to me? Like some sanctimonious white man inna book talking to him kiss-him-ass woman."

At that his eyes flared open and froze and there was no color in his face, if you can imagine such a thing, knowing what Moshe looked like already.

It must be that the eye of the storm arrived more quickly than I had dreamed because I am talking to him now so softly, I can hear my own words inside my head.

"Mosh, yu understand wha mi a-seh? Mi a-seh cut di crap. Yu realize yu never once say yu sorry fi what yu put me troo when yu jus up and lef by yuself, no chance fi seh goodbye, an jus calmly lef letter tell mi seh a-stow yu a-stow wheh inna ship cakka-hole? The whole time we were going down to Kingston Harbour to watch lights you were busy studying ship asshole and how to hide in there and never say a word? Yu know how dat feel?"

I was talking to his back for he was standing by Rachel's wire fence, rigid as a lockbox, and I didn't need to watch the set of his fists to know he was hearing and processing every word.

"Don't get me wrong, Mosh," I said. "I know you are sorry, it was in every word you wrote and every drawing you drew, but you never said it, and I don't know why you were sorry anymore. Alva—you noticed Alva because Alva is a man. Man not supposed to be always there. Don't take me for granted or put me with anybody else. Not even yu modda."

Needy woman or princess, I didn't give a damn, I knew what I wanted from him and it wasn't any less than he had got from me.

A couple of years may have passed, maybe three, before he went from being a statue by the fence and was turned around on the bench beside me, his hands half lifted, asking permission to touch my hair again. There was a lot of wind. (But he always liked the feel of my hair.)

"I didn't not notice because you were a woman. I took your knowledge of me for granted because we grew up side by side, hip by hip, and I didn't know where I ended and you began." He laughed a little, in his teeth without sound, like he had snagged a breath. "In a bizarre kind of way it's like the difference of race in England and Tumela. In England you are fighting it all the time because there was never any sugar plantation there, they never got used to us. Not in any true sense. We were outside. Here in Tumela, everyone eventually becomes 'one o' wi,' and we don't notice that it hurts when somebody says, 'White-Like-Duppy bwoy, come here, tek dis,' or, 'Yu black but yu pretty,' and gives you a gift. Of course I would notice Alva"—his voice made quotation marks around the word "notice"—"he was never a part of my life from before the beginning, the way you were.

He came in from outside. But I don't take you for granted like Ilean boyfriend. I would never give you my funeral directive because I going kill myself." His eyes shuttered but not before I'd seen the wound in them.

His hands had taken their own permission and were cupping the two sides of my face. "Princess Royal, I am sorry, I am sorry, I am sorry, because I love you and I hurt you. I never want what happens between us to be part of any politics."

But it was.

"Don't talk to me about Alva Lawrence again," I said.

"I won't."

Or about the boy on the banks of the River Po. Somehow I don't think I have ever got that story right, and I don't want to know. If the human race is ever to be forgiven, it is because we can't bear too much reality.

In the end, what this man is whom I love escapes even me.

We went inside because I took his hand and the wind was really railing.

CHAPTER XXXII

On the verge of our marriage I finally admitted to myself I had seen all the signs—I knew the signs the moment he told me about the pink-and-red girl who had loved him in London, and the boy on the River Po. (Not Alva Lawrence, because I knew that had been different altogether.) But I told myself we would be all right, because there was no secret of that kind between us now. That when the time came he would stop being afraid and it would be all right. I knew a large part of his fear was the fear that it wouldn't work between us and our relationship would be spoiled by disappointment forever. It was no use telling him that wouldn't happen to us, so I didn't try. How could I say that to him anyway, when he had learned differently over the years of our separation? When we had both learned differently, over those years? I had made a mess of my life because he wasn't there, and he had been pretty much messed up by my not being there for him either. Anything could happen to us, we were not immune from the things that happened to other people. Desire changes everything.

But I thought I had become a little bit wiser about things—about life—and I was willing to wait until we could trust ourselves again. Sure, he'd said we didn't have to be married to each other to be who we were together, but I didn't think anybody else would have us now, we were such a royal mess, and I think it was clear to us both that we needed to protect each other in ways that we couldn't living apart.

Aside from all that, I don't think I could have given up for anything in the world the relief of being able to say, "Yes, I will," when Moshe asked me to marry him. Up to now, I had been the one who asked, or led, and he the one who said, "I will," in almost everything we did together. It felt nice to flip the script, and there would be plenty of opportunity to flip it again and again, either way, for some balance between us, I thought.

We had a June wedding, in the morning, amid lots of rain. The hurricane was threatening, so we decided to stay close to home for our honeymoon. We left Betina with Rachel, who was going to share her with my mother, three days each, and we went to Mammee Bay because it was near enough to Tumela that we could get home quickly if any emergency happened to my daughter.

Dunn's River was in spate and it was fay and wonder to climb the falls and lie down afterward in the great pocket of water that foamed between the rocks just above where the river rolled into the sea. Where the river and the sea met was a long perpendicular line separating the tan water from the blue, and you wouldn't think they had mingled at all if you hadn't known better and instead been fooled by the illusion of the line.

A blur of magic enfolded us that entire day; holding hands, sometimes laughing and talking but more often not talking at all, just feeling each other's closeness, I could almost imagine it was the way we were in the beginning, discovering each other the first time. Our hotel was quiet and very peaceful and in the afternoon we slept there, spooned, on the verandah of the honeymoon suite. They had given us the most secluded of the villas, facing toward the rain forest. The verandah was the villa's front, and, turned toward the sequestered forest, it gave us the feeling that we were completely alone. I dressed up for dinner and my heart thudded in my mouth to see Mosh dressed up in a loose shantung tunic and pale mauve suede jeans. In his wedding clothes he had seemed formal and remote but now he looked like a stranger in a romance and exceedingly beautiful, and though I had never thought of myself as vain or paid much attention to my looks, I was run-of-the-mill female enough to be glad just at that moment that I too was beautiful. Desire changes everything. Everything. Sometimes in the most disastrous ways.

The sky is a bowl turned upside down with its load of stars spilling out, about to fall on the rain forest, the villa, the hotel yard, our hair, any moment now. It has rained all evening into the approach of the night and the stars look deep and wet, the deep blue bowl of the sky is wet—I think of the legend of Rainstorm, stuck aslant heaven with her broom, spilling all her tears.

"At least we know it's not the devil and his wife fighting," Moshe teases me, responding to my flight of fancy. "The sun probably won't come out any time soon with all this rain. Ours is going to be an indoors honeymoon for sure."

"I don't mind," I whisper, reaching up to kiss him in the shell of his ear. "I don't mind that at all."

"No, we've never been afraid of a little rain," he says, laughing, wriggling his ear out of the reach of my tongue and cupping my face in his hands. He has always been super ticklish about his ears.

"No. That's. True." I'm kissing his mouth now, whispering between kisses. I imagine us naked in the rain, walking on the beach, holding hands, picking up shells and laughing, the sea a haze behind the curtain of rain ahead of us, and then falling down on our knees, not laughing anymore, his mouth hot and urgent in mine.

"Let's go inside," Moshe says against the side of my lips.

"Yes." I'm drowning and scared and full and lost, we are standing by the king bed in our room and my hands have a will of their own, I watch his shirt fall away and see with a catch in my breath the hieroglyphs on his chest and his belly, the narrow band of hair, all black, that runs from his navel down into the waistband of his pants is so silky under my fingers, air stings my skin for a moment as my dress slithers down and pools at my feet, his hands have stroked my dress away from my skin and I step out of the pool of silk and my hands are guiding his downward to me, his are guiding mine downward to him, I know this body like my own, I wait for the turgid leap of his flesh into my hands, its spill into my fingers, lying down in the vast expanse of the mattress I see his eyes that are deep and dark as the night sky, you cannot tell their mismatched colors now, and his hair falls over my face. Our thighs are urgent against each other, hard and strong, Moshe cries out my name, and then he presses down and, bracing himself, pushes away from me and I hear his cry of repudiation from a very far distance, the bottom of a deep pool where the current is tugging so strenuously at my drowning that I jackknife down and up in terror, levitating to the air.

The silence between us is awful. Moshe is sitting on the edge of the bed, his back to me, his head in his hands. He is still wearing his jeans. I can hear our breathing, very loud, syncopating.

"I'm sorry, Arrii," Moshe is saying. "I'm sorry. I don't know why, I don't know why."

I sit up in the bed and move over beside him. I put my hand on his shoulder. "My love, it's all right. It's no big deal. This happens all the time. It's just the stress from the wedding—"

His response is violent. He lifts my hand from his shoulder in a motion so full of controlled force that it is single and clean and gentle, and he puts my hand aside, on the bed between us. "No, Arrii. You know that's not true. It has nothing to do with that. It's me."

"What about you, Mosh? What do you mean?" I am really frightened now.

"I don't know," he says, his voice quiet but shouting. And then again, "I don't know." He turns his face to me and it is so wrung I want to cry. "Can't you see? It's me . . . I can't. Don't you understand?"

How could he ask me to understand when he himself didn't? And yet I felt I understood a little bit more than he did.

It strikes me writing this how stale this must all sound, how many penny dreadful and soap opera episodes are made up of this, a honeymoon night that doesn't work because one or other of the partners has some buried deep unconscious problem, not to mention the fact that I was going through this for the second time, only the other way round: the first time the problem had been me and not the man I married . . . how stale and trite, if you think of all the million and one times such soap operas have been written. But perhaps such stories are told only because they happen all the time, really happen all the time, really really happen all the time. Only, none of that has anything to do with me, not the staleness nor the triteness, not the generalizing force of it; this is my one honeymoon, my one love; this terror and confusion and love and hope and despair have never been felt before, because I am feeling them for the first time, they are newly minted under this sky that is so wet tonight, on this bed where my husband is asking my forgiveness because he wants to give me more than he can make himself want to give.

There isn't much more. We had known each other too closely for this to be something we couldn't deal with, we were awfully sensible about it, Mosh said you know it might not change, I said I know, and I want to stay, anyhow it works for us is okay with me. He said, "My darling, I don't want you to have an expectation. I don't want you to be disappointed," and I said no, I won't be, all I want to do is live with you; it'll be enough.

But in my heart of course I hoped, what woman would not hope, and in my heart I wondered if all this was my fault for the years I had abandoned him. Moshe was not an aggressive person like I was, and perhaps deep down the anger and resentment he thought he didn't feel were surfacing at the most anxious moment between us, perhaps he had needed to allow himself to get really really angry and be bitter before he could really forgive me. *Look at you, Arrienne Christie Fisher. Tinpot Freudiana.* And I had to admit that I didn't know anything and all I could do was accept my marriage and my husband for what they were and stay the course of love that Rachel had doubted I had it in me to stay.

But I did. Have it in me to stay. Moshe was the half of me that by itself could not shut. My half radicle lost in the transformation of zygotes. Without him I too could not shut, or be one again.

So, we were very sensible about it. We came back to Kingston, we bought a house in the hills above Irish Town, because it was cool and a bit wild, like Tumela, and Moshe could paint there in peace, and we could rear some animals, which I wanted to do for Betina's sake.

Our country had been through a bloody time while Moshe was away, and we were still living the aftermath of a high murder rate and violence in the city. Joshua's experiment with social justice and national freedom had not gone unpunished; we had drawn the ire of our big neighbor to the north and there had been a lot of economic pressure put on us, and a lot of young men had grown desperate and angry, and violent, and even now the country was still unsettled, and restless. I was fighting all of that but I wanted Betina to experience the innocence Moshe and I had had as children.

We got some Dominique chickens: four calling hens that supplied all our eggs, and a rooster. Betina had a pet goat. We called him Boysie. He wandered about in the house like another child and slept on a mat in Betina's room. We had huge gardens and a handyman, Mr. Gregory, who helped me to keep them in order, though I grew them wild, as unmanicured and natural as possible. It was a lot of work, combined with my three jobs. In addition to my full-time work with UNICEF I was also working part-time as assistant director for the Jamaica chapter of the UN Council for Human Rights, while on the side helping Children's Services set up the Ananda Alert for missing children, and now I became Moshe's local agent and business manager, his buffer between the public art world and his fear of the limelight. For international transactions he still retained his Italian agent. Our local art scene was not large but it was thriving and I stood in for him at art fairs and at exhibitions organized by the National Gallery.

But I was not tired. I had boundless energy, I was whole, and myself again, at last. And though besides everything I had my hands full taking care of my husband and daughter, they were also taking care of me. I don't believe in happiness as the goal of one's life, I think thinking in that way is childish and improper; it flies in the face of whatever gives life its integrity. But in the succeeding years I experienced a lot of those dust-mote moments in the air of time that I call happy.

Rachel and my father came to visit us sometimes, Noah more rarely. More often it was we who went to them. We sent Betina in the summer holidays for as long as possible so she could know what it was like to live in a magical place. For no matter what, Tumela was still the place that had produced and held safe a man like Moshe, and such a place in the broad annals of the world has to be magical. There is no other word for it.

If our parents wondered why there were no other children, they never asked. My father had a good reason for not asking questions. The Christies were not known for their procreativity and I had inherited from the male line the birthmark that said I was a Christie through and through, even if my father was redder than St. Elizabeth earth and I, my husband said, was colored like the sky in Tumela between evening and the first star at night.

Until Betina was ready for elementary school, we homeschooled her between the two of us. She read fluently before she was three, and never tired of stories. Her favorite was the fairy-tale version of "Childe Rowland." She crowed with pleasure hearing how Burd Ellen caught the ball widdershins, opposite to the direction of the sun, and became snatched away mysteriously, and could not be found, and how Childe Rowland went on the quest to find his sister, and how he found her in the end, defeating the king of Elfland at the Dark Tower to take Burd Ellen home. Perhaps because she had no sisters or brothers, she always liked best the stories that were not about princes who would rescue the princesses they would love, but the ones about brothers or sisters who rescued the siblings they already loved.

The other thing she loved was the folk and four-eye women songs of Tumela. Nothing made her scream with laughter and demand, "Again! Again!" more than Mosh and me singing Nine-Night songs for her, swaying on the living room floor to the slow drawl of his kette drum: *"Death have a way, death have a way, to steal us . . . an carry us . . . away! . . . But in Jerusalem schoolroom where I schoooool, I saw Father Abraham stretch forth the palm of his right hand to take me oveeer . . . Jeerrdaaan Riberrrr!"*

Lifting her high above his head and looking down at me, laughing, Moshe said, "She'll be just fine, Arri. I not sure your perpendicular-line theory going stand up with her at all. This little lady go find where the horizon vanish to. And she go understand that is not a one-time ting, is the kind of ting you agree to find over and over again. And lost it sometime too and find it back."

Maybe, maybe not. But if she does find where that horizon goes, it will only be because we are her parents, and we try to show her how you put two and two together and make five, or two halves together and make something single and two and yet completely different.

Is funny, the last thing I forget to tell you. We found an address for the man we thought was Moshe's father.

My friend Ilean Thompson became principal of our old school, and one day, on impulse, I phoned her and said, "Ilean, look if yu si in the records one teacher name Newland, who came there in the fifties," and I explained to her why. Ilean said it was a busy time and the records were really old and tattered and dusty; it would take her several days to go through them. But go through them she did, and bingo! she found an Arthur Newland, a geography teacher, who had come from an address in Bristol in 1955, and left the school in 1958, going where, she could not tell. His letter of resignation did not say.

"Do you want the letter?" Ilean asked. "I can copy it for you."

Moshe said no, it wasn't important anymore. I wasn't sure I agreed with him, but I respected his right not to traverse that painful and perhaps futile terrain anymore. But I did reflect on the irony of how simple it was to find right here under our noses, after a journey halfway around the world, information that might have helped him all those years ago, but which we could not have had then, because we hadn't had the power then, to go up to somebody and say, Look among the school records, we think the source of a scandal is there, and it is Moshe's father. And now we had the power, because we were grown up and our friend was the principal of the school, but it was too late, or not.

"If I was supposed to find him," Moshe said, "I would have. I already got the right name, and went to the right place."

But suppose that journey was only a wrinkle in the road, I thought, suppose you were meant to try again. But I did not say.

PART VI

ever after: the undiscovered country

CHAPTER XXXIII

Everything ends so quiet and so long. The long cracks in the ice as the stone woman finally dies and I step out in the garden like walking out from a chrysalis. Moshe calling my name for the last time, Arrii, Arrii, once, twice, three times just like that, his voice a shiver on the wind before cockcrow, only now instead of "My love, it is not yet time," he smiles and takes my hand through the sheet of ice that falls away like an open door, then even the stone vault crumbles, stone upon stone like a deck of cards falling from a nerveless hand, and the gecko stills to the slow cease of the ululation of the frogs. this recycle and recycle till it confuse and in the morning when I tell the woman in the social worker uniform I didn't expect to see you I thought I died and went to him in the evening, I am so disappointed to see you she answers me same way the way she did yesterday and the day before that and the day before that a myriad of days that I lose count of, it doesn't just happen like that, you know, you have to have patience, you know, she says in her irritated voice the voice in which she speaks to the stone woman who flits in the shadows. you must have patience it is what Moshe said at the beginning, that was yesterday when they buried him for the second time, there are many yesterdays, they bleed so bleed so bleed so into each other and I don't remember which is what or where or when Rachel quarrel with me again, is here in Tumela he belong she says, I say no, the journey too far, too far for what, Rachel's voice is mocking, like a stranger's, after spirit can't get lost, he wi travel to you on any road that is quarried in the clouds. where he gone and you and me going, time have no meaning, he can get to you or you can come to him in the twinkling of an eye whether we church him in Tumela or here. well, in that case I say he staying here and he can visit you in Tumela but he have no wish to leave me alone in this prison-house that become stone to me now, and when I say and furthermore what of our gardens that mourn for him at sunset she call me perverse and selfish but she compromise and say we will have ceremony here and ceremony there and so it end.

In the beginning I said I will terminate this quarrel and make it easy for Rachel two of us in the one grave and then an end but Mosh don't approve, I hear him I witness the slight shake of his head when he say no my love it is not yet time. time, why should we need more time, I have exhausted the revolutions of all clocks, but still when he say not yet not yet is like he speak from a far place of knowledge where I couldn't come where time for him have another meaning just like how the irritating Rachel say, sometimes I don't know which I dislike more Rachel or my daughter or the social worker woman in the white nurse uniform and puss boot that she, Betina, plant on me accusing me of being a danger to myself for she insist I lose my thoughts and mix up my memories even memories of distance and time but this is not news I already know these facts about myself from the minute I passed through the thin stone wall to this waiting room in this stone city waiting for my going or the second coming of my prince from henceforth let no man nor woman neither trouble her for she bears in her body the marks of the twilight kingdom having passed behind the veil.

In just the same way as when he said, "It is not yet time"—with the same separated certainty—as he took his last breath, he said, suddenly smiling as if beatitude had blossomed behind his eyelids, "I see it so clearly now, my love. Don't be afraid or sad. It is no different from flying," and then he died, so simply that he took my breath away. One moment he was there, and then he was not. Levitate. *It is no different from flying.* How I should know? Like She-Who-Is-Always-Right Rachel says, I have never gone where he has gone, though I hunger for it. I have never been enamored of flying, though necessity takes me on many plane journeys to many countries, carrying his handiwork in the delicate satchels. But I will wait as he tells me to, until time come and I hear him calling me one last time through the trees.

She was not at his bedside when he died telling her about this affinity of death and flying. She was only falling into sleep in the corridor where she watched and waited the whole night long because the Sister said you cannot come in even if he is your husband and you've never been apart. (The lie she told the Sister in hopes they would allow her in after visiting hours.) But now she rise up and to them she must have look like an avenging ghost because when she walk past them all, ignoring their consternations, and went to him, she was not hindered. Later, after they know he gone, they let her alone. She hold his hand and sit there till eternity come to an end, she watch his face change and the stirring tree outside the ward, and when the change over she cover his face and walk out on my two feet and then three nights and days to Tumela, walking, like a person demented (they say I have dementia now, so they plant social worker on me) stopping only at night to rest in yards wherever sign post, *Rest Stop*, until I reach Tumela and look in Rachel Fisher face Rachel exclaim you could have meet your death out there, nobody walk anywhere like that anymore, rapist robber and murder-tetess populate the countryside like weed. but I am past the contemplation of hopes that bind by time or danger or earthly shelter of any kind and anything that dispatch me quick is fine. The social worker nurse woman making noise on the phone again I know she complaining to my astrophysicist daughter who I used to like one time a girl with sea-grape hair. though up there in Oregon she's studying where to find dark matter she still don't find how to understand how a sane person can be waiting between now and then or there and here until the missing half of me come back to fetch me through the portal of fire, ice and glass. the social worker woman setting up one cow-bawling Miss Betina she gone off again she think the furniture is guests she is welcoming for English tea you ever see anything so? stupid woman yes I see plenty something so. at the final funeral she was very calm nobody could say they see any storm raging underneath her visible face she don't look inside the casket until the last minute and Rachel don't look neither an old woman of ninety-plus years Rachel don't want to see anything that cause her more pain so she don't look until the she, her son wife, go up to Rachel and say and her voice come out cold and sculpture like she set it on purpose, "You want to see him now?" Rachel look at her without a word, Rachel look undone. Her son wife don't feel no pity pity is like a stillborn child inside of her stone heart and now she add meaning to her words "You are the only other person who will see him as he was." Rachel head jerk up as if somebody stab her unseen in her spine and that is when I know is time, is time. Rachel son wife put out her hand and hold onto Rachel hand and Rachel don't resist when her son wife lead her up to the open coffin I don't flinch when Rachel scream or even when her body begin the slow stylish fall to the ground before Noah catch her and put her on the pew and people come with water. in a dream of stone—the only feeling I have is of myself enameled in a box and vaults of stone and in the beginning I cried out and out again until my ribs cracked wide open and bleed because I could not tell if this feeling of my body was the feeling of his spirit imprisoned in some perverse miscarriage of fate on the other side or because my fear is true and they bury him alive mistaking a coma for his death but then at last he came and told me how it was and made me reconciled to waiting or almost reconciled—in a dream of stone I hear the stranger-woman's voice, far away like someone pronouncing benediction "She will be all right. It is very hard to look upon the face of the dead. But she has always known him better than anyone else." People think she speaking about Rachel but she not. People look at her, this stranger-woman, funny, they think she speaking funny from grief and so as he die and bury rumor resurrect and it reach Tumela and Ora that the face in the coffin was not Moshe Fisher's face but a heap of naked anonymous flesh where his face should be. Rachel son wife is unmoved by this rumor because she know that what everybody see is not different from what they always used to see Moshe Fisher his face-bone flawless like somebody cut-and-carve him but looking asleep his skin now like wax almost transparent without color even the blue edges gone, Betina pronounce that he look just the way he always look Lieutenant-Commander Data except for his black face she don't say nigger anymore because she

American now and in that place language that mark history learn to leach bleach and circumspect.

Whatever Rachel and Rachel son wife see just before the coffin close or what her son wife see in the long vigil in the hospital ward while his face reclaim its mortality, they carry in silence to their grave, even silence each from each

I lose track of all the clocks, in here between stone and stone the twilight is blue I am mixed up between one ceremony and another and between what is real and what is apparition but this I know that Myrtle Kellier come to the funeral in Tumela and she was real she come bent to the ground like a dark spirit issuing out of it the toes of her two feet kissing each other come there and stand like an omen among the great multitude that come from far-and-near to see the last rites of the blue boy from Woie-Woie or Where-It?, Where-it with a question sign, that now pass into legend. this was the first time that the woman locked in stone felt anything like heat in my veins, and it was rage, but it was Rachel who moved, Rachel who got up and went to speak to the four-eye woman where she stood at the church door looking in as though she on a mission to survey and the scarified woman followed behind. and Rachel was in one of her translucent moods, clairvoyant and still. I know you, I know you immediately you are the obeah woman who torment my son. Now it is over. Why you come? Myrtle Kellier look neither surprise nor offend she only become tall like she draw herself up to a straight-straight height though she never move a muscle at last we meet, Rachel Sharma-Fisher I make no quarrel I come to remind you of thing you forget what thing I forget, Myrtle Kellier? I am an old woman now though not old as you but old enough to forget a whole lot of thing. What so special about the one on your mind? and that is how Rachel find out who Myrtle Kellier be, a woman who foster foundlings she foster many and her heart seek out who else have the same heart and who to direct them to and she call them cousin I see you Rachel Sharma-Fisher when you was under the naseberry tree by the red river shedding eyewater because you long for somebody to care and I send the boy to you but you don't believe in me your Yahweh ex me out so you call me Retromesathanas and as she say that Rachel say retromesathanas and though the four-eye woman kiss her teeth and walk out on her own two backaback feet after Rachel chop her hands once twice three times against her rumor have it to say the four-eye woman throw sankofa in Moshe coffin and levitate herself in a ball of black smoke like the smoke that make soot on creng-creng or from canepiece burning, and some say is Rachel throw the ball of smoke exorcize the woman and some say is not a woman is a duppy and I know they say it because Myrtle Kellier looked so old she either dead or well past a hundred the finger of death mark on her myriad facial seam that she bring to Moshe funeral but rumor is nothing for I Arrrienne Christie Fisher see what happen and I know I see it plain and in my right mind.

Sometimes everything is clear as if it is written on stone tablets, and sometimes she thinks it is day when it could be night, then everything passes in a great blur, like time rushing to catch up with itself, and she clutches for compass in this spinning place the things Betina says, the things Betina remembers and says the woman has forgotten. Betina is angry all the time now. Her anger is her compass, and mine, it makes her memory sharper than any two-edged sword, and more cruel. I used to like my daughter. Now, her presence disturbs the house. She accuses me of the upheaval, Mummy what's with you! You've overturned the chairs again! She's sailing through the living room, it's a big room, it takes her a long time to pick up and place the furniture in straight alignments like a prison cell.

I don't know how to tell her or the snake-woman in puss boots she foisted on me that it has nothing to do with me, it is the doing of the woman who comes here, I saw her through the palings. I search for the words to tell her, but the words slip away. I want to explain that there are times I know everything as if past present and future were poured into a crystal jar and at other times everything is a rush of silver coins in my hand and sometimes I feel that I have just been somewhere, just here, but I can't remember where. My head hurts every day now. I wish she would go. But she's staying she says until she's sure I'll be all right. What is sure? How did Moshe and I trying so hard produce such an unpleasant child, and I find I do not want to tell her anything at all, she tells me jokes about the first cosmonauts in space, about Nikita Khrushchev exclaiming after their return to earth why are you still clinging to God, here Gagarin flew into space and didn't see God, she's making fun of Rachel's Yahweh and her stepfather's descent into Christianity near the close of his life, saying, I know, the cross, the cross is the only thing that makes sense of this perpendicular, and though I have lived my life as what Rachel calls an idolater, believing only in Moshe and justice, I have never disrespected their sovereign choice, I know the perpendicularity of being and I have doubted my own ways, I doubt them now, and so I pray, I sue for mercy, without shame, waiting here for the grace of the return of my prince, when she sees I am not laughing she exclaims, "Lighten up, for God's sake, Mummy! I'm not endorsing Nikita Khrushchev. Even a child knows that statement is foolishness."

But is she brought a social worker into the house, a woman in a white uniform and puss boots soft on the floors like a snake who speaks to me in a jockeying voice as if she think mi is her pickni or combolo. I overhear Betina telling the puss boot woman I fire Elise and her sons who worked in the house for twenty years and helped me in the gardens. I hear her telling the puss boot woman I light the gas stove and leave it on for days I'm a danger to myself

The flame comforts me.

I know why you went away. You had better not think I'm a fool.

Why did I go away, Mummy?

Do you ever grieve for your stepfather?

Don't call him my stepfather in that tone, Mummy. He was my parent, just as you are. You know I never thought of him any other way. I hurt too, as much as you!

What has your hurting got to do with me? Impertinent child.

You don't believe anyone except you feels for him, do you? You were always the only one!

The constant noise of their quarreling disturbs me. When the quarrel grows bitter the girl tells the truth to hurt her mother. "I'll tell you why I went away to America, Mummy. It was so I could lose my virginity in peace, without you hovering over me the whole time.

I made up my mind early, I was never going to let love kill me the way it killed you and Uncle Mosh, ever. I wanted to think about sex separate from all that. And I want you to know I haven't been celibate or faithful. To anyone! And I don't plan to be."

Okay, so there.

Then the girl weeps, and the mother, unpitying, too far away to care about things like other people's hurt or weeping—I can see her stone eyes in the dark mirror on the verandah wall, so I know—the mother knows her daughter's tears are tears of remorse and guilt, the girl berates herself for unkindness and impatience toward the woman lost in the labyrinths of memory, its treacherous forgettings and the curious selfishness of a mind losing itself in increments. Almost immediately the girl is angry again now that the other one has fired the social worker. Mummy, you know you forget things. You need somebody. You've even been saying Uncle Mosh went away to America, and you know he didn't, he never did, the only time he stowed away anyplace was when he went to England all those years ago, before I was even born. And after that, love kept him chained to you in chains

The certainty in her voice shakes the other's self-certainty, her eyes in the mirror grow dim with terror, America America no it is not America he went, America was only a dream that haunted, over and over again, until I thought . . . no. *she* went to America, the girl with the long hair like bunches of sea grapes where was it again I knew her? Her voice is light and high like the voice of someone I once knew crying out between bursts of laughter play it again Uncle Moshe play it again a slim sliver of a girl, I have forgotten her name. It is Moshe on the long wind. In the tops of the trees. Under the massed ferns in the gardens we made together. Moshe saying it will be all right my love, it is better here. Soon you will come to me, it will be better here. How can I believe him, this betrayal once again, when he left without me, saying it is time, only just like flying, wait until, and then. Wait until, when? Will you come? Will I go? My feet are bleeding, the glass sides of the mountain are very sharp, as are the stones on the deck of a ship under a mermaid's feet, yesterday someone put a thousand cracks in the mountain, flinging a single stone.

My love, I've walked such a long way to find you, please before the cock crows, not to me again.

But she don't have to go on so. Member I remember now, he did go to America once, tek she same one, this forgetting girl, to college, we went with her together and for a moment I lost him turning the wrong way in a shopping mall and I thought he had left me again stowaway this time in a plane belly what premonitions of stone cells eternities of loss did I have then

They say he died of natural complications from his birth, it was a miracle he lived so long, fifty-plus years, a man with all his organs knotted up inside and his skin unmade. The night before he died a kingdom come in me, in my loins, a conflagration of fire and ice that break up stone never leave me he said his body breaking on the stone of our love but it was he who left again down the long river of time without me, saying wait, please don't force your time to come I cannot be without you even over here and all must be right and in the right way—and shall all be well and all manner of thing be well? I fear I do not know, I do not know.

A rainstorm of tears all day yesterday, I couldn't with her do a thing the social worker is saying, her voice comes to me through a gauze curtain made of filaments of air, I can count each thread so fine it glimmers like the lights on a firefly you should institutionalizing. Consider. Consider institutionalizing her. Betina begins to shout at her through the phone. That's my Bets, my girl, my daughter.

There is a woman sitting in the box chair Moshe made for Betina on the back verandah. A woman whose demeanor is not strange. I feel I have known her a long time ago in another place but I am not sure, her face escapes me. In a moment I shall remember, she has that kind of look, the look of someone whose face in a moment you'll remember. Moshe made the box chair to hang from ropes in the ceiling. It is wide enough to hold two but the woman is taking up all the space. She is a wide woman. She looks like someone who has put on weight in later years or someone who has bent down to the ground and seen in the far distance a great river, and laid her lips to the ground and drunk it whole. The ropes are adjustable. She has adjusted them so the chair is brought low to the floor, out of danger of flying. But she is so heavy with her drunk river or weight of years, there is no danger, it will not fly.

The sun is falling on the green yard with a great tenderness. The yard looks out on itself, not toward the neighbors' houses but toward the wild mountain and the rain forest. I feel that this is a garden the woman has planted. The garden is both overgrown and beautiful, with masses of foliage surrounding pathways made of cobblestones, grass sprouting in the cracks between stones. The garden is overgrown with hostas of many colors, some greenish-gray and blue and pale as angelfishes, and the ferns are giant. Among them weave birds of paradise, anthuriums, ginger lilies, and great fanning palms. She catches wavering flashes of varicolored light where rare orchids bloom on the shadowy trunks of the palms, their quick irruptions like counterpoints in a musical score. In opposite corners of the paradise garden are the shuttered studio and the greenhouse laden with unharvested greens, nobody eats them or is harvesting them now Elise and her sons will come with machetes to harvest in the morning

The woman planted this garden. In another life she was very proud of it. She has vague intimations of unplanned journeys quarrying rare species among far districts where people cooked in smokehouses or roasted saltfish and yams in outdoor firepits, among lost villages where men, women, and children dressed all in white played cricket on a handkerchief of red ground, the faint resonance of names of places she has quarried comes to the woman like the odor of salt from an ancient sea, Holywell Castleton Blue Mountains above Mavis Bank Buff Bay Silver Springs Spur Tree Hill Claverty Cottage Middle Quarters Whitehouse, she hears the sea roar at Whitehouse and suddenly it bursts upon them, a vast open curve almost level with the road, and the little girl cries out in fear and astonishment. They never go north to Mammee Bay where there is always the sound of weeping, she remembers the little girl's eager questions and the man's voice giving answers in the mock-voice of a historian, and the woman whose face she can't remember saying how come you know so much, Mosh, and you never even live here most of your life? And the man says laughing if you was listenin in school when Miss Yvette and Mr. Brown was teaching you your country's geography, you wouldn't so dunce, his laugh a snatch of sound like a person taking a breath between his nose and half-open mouth, not like his astonishing voice which is stringed music, and the fade woman laughs and throws up her hands and cries, "Okay, cree!" I surrender, and the man cries also laughing, "Hey, watch out!" and she laughing puts her palms back, ten to two o'clock, on the steering wheel of the SUV that is full of lurching plants and all three of them are laughing as the big car rocks down the precarious hill.

The woman in the box chair has been trawling the rooms of the silent house all afternoon, listening to its secrets, putting out her hand to touch its ghosts, intruding in drawers full of heirlooms, now she is holding in her hands a box of cedarwood carvings that she is unfolding from tissue that is sacred and soft and furled. A portrait of a young girl with Pinocchio in her face and Medusa hair like tree roots flying. A stick figure of a child dancing, naked heels flying up under her red skort in front of a drum that seems to dance toward her.

All of yesterday she was rearranging my house to fit some seeming logics in her own head, not paying me any mind but moving about as if the house was hers by gift. In one place she tears cushions to shreds like somebody trying to unravel and make over the past. The stuffing is strewn all over the floor of the master bedroom. The living room chairs that she has overturned that Betina and the snake-woman complain about don't look confuse to me the way they say, they form pattern like hieroglyphs because when she turn them over she know that yesterday there were people sitting there and she trying to make herself remember. Sit down, Miss Myra, yes, of course, sit there, the rocking chair's fine. No, not this one so, it will hurt your back. Let me recline it so you will sit safe. Yes, Mrs. Cooper, of course I know just how you take your tea, darjeeling without sugar, Benito, don't quarrel with me, I know you take honey, not Splenda, sit, please sit.

When she do that with the furnishings I laugh but when time she go in the family room and start move like madwoman taking down photographs from their brackets and piling them in everlasting rows on my rosewood table that Mosh give me I get rahtid, and when she take up Mosh self-picture and start kissing kissing and kissing it that is the pale, I box down her hand and Moshe picture fall from her but I catch it and hold it to my chest safe. The right to kiss is still mine.

The woman is weeping, weeping, then suddenly she looks up with an expression of expectancy in her face that is now hushed, she knows, she knows, her tears are arrested as if she had never been weeping at all. To the one watching her the one to whom this house this waiting vault belongs she, the intruder, says, what are you now thinking and the woman the owner of the house says chromosomes in miniscule continents the eye cannot see. The weightlessness of air and the perpendicular oceans. And you? What are you thinking of? The weight, the crushing weight, of love and dying, that we cannot see, except in a glass darkly, and now face to face, the intruder says, and the one whose house this is laughs in silence, as though satisfied with this answer, and then she is not there. First she was there, and then she is not. Disappeared as easily as flying.

My love, my dearest love, you must believe me that I never left. Even when I was in England. You remember, don't you? Come, my love, it is time.

She hears his voice as the ice door and the stone vault crack at the same moment in which her eyes wide open she sees her lonely daughter fly out through the open door her arms lifted beseeching Mummy Mummy and the flying girl stops in her tracks like someone caught in motion at the exact moment when the clock of time has stopped, for she is staring at the tall figure coming to her mother through the window, walking on the air like a road. Her mother's hand is outstretched, her fingers curled as if she has placed them in another's. At her mother's feet are the broken shards of the glass covering of the miniature painting of her stepfather Moshe that has fallen from her mother's hand. The long sigh that she hears on the wind is not one, but two, and in the fleeting moment of my clairvoyance before the one-sided disk slips from my hand, I know she will stay, weeping, to close my, her mother's, rejoicing eyes.

The End

Acknowledgments

My heartfelt thanks are due to many people and to institutions that assisted me in the completion of this book. Thanks especially to Barbra Chin, my graduate assistant at Howard University whose meticulous research helped me with the section set in England and on board the ship (Barbra, I know how to stow away on any kind of vessel now, whether air or seacraft!). To my department chair at Howard University, Dr. Dana Williams, whose unstinting support made possible the sabbatical semester in which I was able to complete the manuscript. To the Department of Literatures in English at the University of the West Indies (DLIE at UWI), Mona, and department head Dr. Michael Bucknor, for so generously affording me the space as writer-in-residence during this time. To my creative writing students at UWI, Nysie, Leslie, Shane, Georgio, Sade Greaves, and Shadicka; and Kenya and Thom at Howard, thank you for your inspiration! You are awesome. Thank you too, Tinho. To the DLIE staff, especially Doniq, Mrs. Gordon-Francis, and graduate assistant Tohru, for your so gracious support. To my ever best and most wonderfully insightful and honest critics, Joan Miller Powell and Nadi Edwards, your advice was always better than my ability to execute, but you kept me reaching for higher ground. All the flaws are my inadequacy. To Julie, Hugo, Phillet, Jane, Carol Bailey, Jarrett, Kezia, Thorell, Anthea Morrison, Lisa and Dorothy Brown, my Bethel and Mountview families, Aunt Cynthia, Aunt Ruth, and the many other friends who through your encouraging words, practical help, and faith in a very difficult time kept me pushing forward. Finally, to Kwame Dawes and my publisher Johnny Temple, for believing in this book.